Twinsation

Tommy Cooper has just turned twenty-one an[d] club scene when he meets Darren Maguire, a [...] ...ot only is Darren about the hottest guy that Tommy has ever seen, but he also has an identical twin brother named Michael who is also a dancer. Things quickly heat up for Tommy and Darren, but Michael doesn't exactly approve. Michael is more serious and wishes his brother Darren would focus more on his education. When Michael meets the man of his dreams, however, he begins to understand the power of romance. Both of the twins become embroiled in relationships, which are sure to affect their future, but in the party environment of a dance club, can any such relationship last? And what of the parade of hot guys that constantly come in and out of their lives? Only time will tell if Tommy has actually met the man of his dreams or if he's simply allowed himself to be swept up by a passing sensation . . . a Twinsation.

Cocktails

Rustin has his Associates Degree and leads a successful life as a retail store manager. He's dissatisfied, though, and wants more. Afforded an opportunity to complete his education while working as a bartender at a trendy gay club in New Orleans, he leaves his Michigan home behind. He's barely off the plane when he encounters Dutch, a Texas cowboy who is visiting the city on business. Will the connection they share that weekend lead to a lasting relationship, or are they destined to go their separate ways to pursue their own destinies?

Business Strip

Chad Curtiss, a thirty-five year old private equity investor, is a ruthless businessman. He believes it's a dog-eat-dog world and doesn't understand people not driven by the desire to acquire their own happiness. Life's about personal responsibility and making the right choices.

Chad travels to New Orleans on occasion for business and while there, he likes to visit the Men's Room. The hottest gay club in the city has the hunkiest dancers, the cutest bartenders and the kind of service a man like Chad knows he deserves. While at the bar, he runs into young Richard Foster, a desk clerk from the hotel where he's staying. He has no intention of becoming involved, but there's something about the kid Chad can't dismiss, and that something just might change his entire outlook on life.

eXtasy Books, Inc.

This work is copyright. Apart from any use as permitted under the Copyright Act 1968, no part may be reproduced, copied, scanned, stored in a retrieval system, recorded or transmitted in any form, or by any means, without the prior written permission by the publisher.

Men's Room Collection
Jeff Erno
ISBN: 978-1-4874-0505-2

Copyright © Jeff Erno 2015

First Edition published 2015
www.extasybooks.com

eXtasy Books Incorporated
P.O. Box 2146
Garibaldi Highlands, B.C. V0N1T0
Canada

Cover Art and Design by Angela Waters

EXTASYBOOKS.COM

Twinsational
Men's Room Book One

By

Jeff Erno

Chapter One

As Tommy stared at his image in the full-length mirror, he wondered why they offered him the job. The last thing he wanted to do was go into that bar looking like a dork. He'd seen the staff, had even met most of them and the one thing they all had in common was that they were gorgeous.

He first visited the Men's Room on his twenty-first birthday. When he showed his ID, the drag queen who manned the door looked at him with skepticism. "Is this really you, sugar?" she asked, raking her nails gently across the top of his shoulder.

Tommy nodded emphatically. "Yeah, it's me. I just had a different color hair then . . . when the picture was taken, I mean."

"Well ain't you just the cutest little thing," she said. "Oh and I see we're celebrating tonight! Another precious little cherub has finally gotten his wings! Twenty-one today?"

Tommy felt his face redden. He rolled his eyes and turned to his friend Lorna.

"Yeah and we're here to par-tay!" she exclaimed.

Lorna had been Tommy's best friend all through college and in many ways, he lived his social life vicariously through her. She possessed all the qualities he seemed to lack—extroversion, communication skills and most importantly, an uncanny wit. She always had a snappy comeback and could dish with the best of them. When Tommy didn't know exactly what to say or how to respond, Lorna was right there, ready to take up for him. Her spiked hair was a shocking pink, which perfectly matched her nail color and at times like these, Tommy felt like her tag-along baby brother. She stood at least four inches taller than him, but when she wore her stilettos, the height difference seemed more exaggerated.

Tommy walked up to the bar and encountered his first Men's Room staff member, Deejay, the bartender. Although Deejay possessed many admirable qualities, dark features, perfect physique not the least among them, the very first thing that captivated Tommy was his smile. Those pearly whites seemed almost to glow in the dank lighting of the bar, the sincerity of his expression melted Tommy's heart. For the first few seconds, he wondered if he already was in love.

However, Deejay was merely one of dozens of hot guys that Tommy would see that evening. When he looked up and saw the nearly naked go-go dancers strutting atop the bar, his eyes bulged as his mouth dropped open. Lorna noticed them just about the same time he did and started hollering. "Fuck yeah!" she said. "We're gonna party tonight!" She pulled a dollar bill from her handbag and waved it in the air, trying to get the dancer's attention."

"What are you doing?" Tommy yelled into her ear.

"I'm gonna get him over here so he can dance for you on your birthday," she said cheerfully.

"No!" Tommy moaned. "Lorna, please!"

She put her arm down, resting her hand on her hip as she looked at him disgustedly. "Come on . . . lighten up and have some fun," she said.

"It's your birthday today?" Deejay said, smiling as sweetly as ever.

"Tommy's twenty-one today," Lorna answered for him. "Tell him to lighten up."

"Happy Birthday! This one's on the house." Deejay slid Tommy his drink, then leaned in next to Tommy's ear. "And she's right. You should relax, enjoy yourself and celebrate your birthday."

"Thank you," Tommy said, again feeling embarrassed.

He'd never been comfortable being the center of attention and really he should have known better than to go out in public with Lorna on his birthday. Nevertheless, Tommy did enjoy himself that night and before it was over, he even had gotten hit on a couple times. Lorna dragged Tommy out on the dance floor a few times, but for the most part, he kept to himself, sliding back into the corner and just watched the crowd. He loved the atmosphere, the people and the music and it was enough for him to relax and simply soak up the energy of the environment.

For the next month, Tommy and Lorna returned to the bar every Saturday night. Tommy started to become aware of all the familiar faces. He started to learn the names of the bartenders, drag queens and even the dancers.

It was when Tommy stopped in one Wednesday evening alone that he found out from Deejay that the Men's Room was in need of employees. Deejay suggested that he apply. If he got the job, he'd be an assistant to the bartenders, their gopher. His job would be to restock the liquor, glasses and supplies, fill the ice and keep everything clean. Basically he'd do anything that needed to be done.

Deejay gave Tommy an application and took him into an office. He filled it out on the spot and gave it back to Deejay, but he didn't seriously think he would get the job. When the bar owner, Ron Wellstone, called him the next day, Tommy was shocked. He went in that afternoon for a brief interview and was hired.

When Tommy again stepped through the door two days later, his hands were shaking. He took a deep breath and tried to calm himself. It wouldn't be good for someone to notice his trembling. Tommy wondered if he really wanted to go through with it. Yes, he needed a job. Lord knows a college kid like himself could always use the cash, but he wasn't sure he'd fit in. He was more of an introvert, on the shy side and it seemed everyone there was really outgoing, not to mention they all were so damned hot looking. Tommy considered himself average at best. He didn't have the muscles or the striking good looks that all the other employees obviously had.

Thankfully, Deejay was the first person he saw.

"Aww, you look good," Deejay said as he motioned to Tommy with outstretched hands. He stepped over and placed his hand on Tommy's shoulder. "Ready for your first night?"

"I think so," Tommy said candidly. "I'm nervous though."

"Don't be nervous!" Deejay's cheerful tone and brilliant smile were quite encouraging. "You'll do just fine. But I have to warn ya, I'm gonna work your ass off."

Tommy nodded, smiled, then turned in a mock attempt to look at his own behind.

"Yeah, I know," Deejay said. "There's not much there to work off, but what you do have is adorable. Cute little bubble butt."

Tommy felt his face redden.

"Baby, you're gonna have to get over that shyness of yours if you're going to work here. I promise you, there are gonna be guys checkin' you out all night, every night."

"You think so?" Tommy asked, surprised.

Deejay put his arm around Tommy's shoulder and spun him around to face their reflection in the large mirror behind the bar. "You see that?"

Tommy nodded. "One super hot guy and one . . . well, kinda dorky guy."

"Dude, don't diss yourself," Deejay said. "You've totally got it goin on. You are one cute little twink. Yeah, you're kinda nerdy, but ya know, a lot of guys go for that."

Tommy sighed. "None that I've met so far."

"*So far,*" Deejay emphasized, "but you will."

Tommy held up his right hand, crossing his middle and index finger.

"Hopefully."

"But anyway, stop stressing. You're here to work, so quit worrying about getting laid. That's gonna just come naturally. So, you ready for me to show you around?"

"Yes!" Tommy said, trying to sound genuinely enthusiastic.

"That a boy," Deejay said. "Let's start here with the bar. I'll show you all the stuff we have to have stocked and where we store everything. We start out the night with everything full, but then after we get busy, shit's gonna run out. It will be up to you to keep your eyes open and re-fill things.

"Most of the customers get their drinks in disposable cups. We'll need about six sleeves of these for each side of the bar. I'll show you where they're kept. We also need to fill the stir sticks, napkins, bar rags, matches, ice bins and all the liquors, wines and bottle beers. Then there are all these containers of garnishes—cherries, olives, lemons, limes, etcetera..." Tommy shook his head, feeling suddenly overwhelmed. "Don't worry. After your first night, it'll be a cakewalk. Come on, let me show you the back rooms and introduce you to everyone, then we'll get started."

Tommy nodded. "Okay."

Deejay led him around the corner and into what appeared to be a storage room. "This here's the ice maker," he said. "And these are all of our supplies."

Tommy looked up onto the shelves and immediately tried to begin memorizing where everything was.

"It's all organized," Deejay explained. "We try to keep things in the same order back here as they are located out at the bar. Over here is the freezer and we also have a big walk-in cooler. Don't be surprised if you walk into the cooler sometime and see one or more of the dancers."

"Seriously?" Tommy asked. "Why would they be in there?"

"They get pretty hot, up there dancing under the lights and they sometimes come back here for a few minutes to cool off."

"Oh man," Tommy said, laughing. "I thought maybe they went into the cooler for something else."

Deejay smiled at him knowingly. "Well, yeah, there's that, too. Speaking of dancers, here comes one now."

Tommy turned around just in time to see what he thought was the hottest looking man he'd every laid eyes upon. Short-cut brown hair and blue eyes and a smile that actually rivaled Deejay's. Tommy's mouth dropped open as he stood there staring.

"Hey," the gorgeous hunk said cheerfully. "I'm Darren Maguire, one of your new dancers."

Deejay stepped over to him. "Yeah, first night. Been expecting you. Colby should be here shortly and he can show you around. I'll show you the dressing room. You can wait there for him."

"Oh cool." He extended his hand to shake with Deejay.

"This is Tommy, it's also his first night."

"Awesome! So we can learn together," Darren said.

Tommy gulped. "I . . . um . . . well, I won't be learning the same stuff as you. I'm not a dancer or anything."

Darren winked at him. "Well, I'm sure you'll be working just as hard as me. I've been in here before and I know how busy this bar gets."

"You got that right," Deejay said. "Come on, the dressing room is right down the hall."

"My brother is supposed to be coming," Darren said. "He starts tonight, too."

Deejay stopped in his tracks and turned around. "Really?" he asked. "You and your brother both . . . huh? You're both dancers?"

Darren nodded. "Yep."

"Does he look like you?" Deejay asked.

Just as he asked the question, another hot guy stepped through the door. Tommy blinked, thinking for a moment he may be seeing double. They were identical.

"Twins," Darren said. "We look *exactly* alike."

"Exactly?" Deejay asked.

"Yeah, exactly . . . right down to the size of our you-know-what."

Tommy covered his mouth and coughed. *Holy shit.*

"Hey guys," the twin said as he quickly stepped down the hall and stood behind his brother. "I'm Michael."

"Darren and Michael . . . twins," Deejay said, shaking his head.

"Double the pleasure!" Darren said.

"Double the fun," Michael chimed in. "Like Juicy Fruit."

Deejay nodded slowly. "Yeah, exactly. But I think that jingle is for Double Mint gum, not Juicy Fruit."

Tommy just stared at them. They smiled at him and Deejay, then in unison, they both winked. Fuck me, Tommy thought, my heart can't take it.

Deejay led them down the hallway and pointed out the dressing room. Tommy peeked inside, surprised at how small it was. "Wow," he observed, "those are kind of close quarters."

"We don't mind," one of the two twins said.

Tommy now wasn't sure which was which because they'd been walking behind him. They were dressed exactly alike and Tommy had yet to identify any distinguishing characteristic on either of them that he could use to tell them apart. He looked down toward the ground and noticed they both were wearing Nikes. One of the two had scuffmarks on the laces.

"Which one of you is Darren and which is Michael?" he asked.

"I'm Darren," said the one with the scuffed laces.

"And I'm Michael."

"I've got to figure out a way to tell you apart," Tommy said.

"Don't worry," Michael said. "We'll let ya know if you get us confused. And we don't mind small dressing rooms. We're used to rubbing up against other guys' bodies."

"I bet," said Deejay and they all laughed. "Well you can either hang out here or go get yourselves a drink from the bar. Whatever you want. Colby should be here shortly."

"We're cool," Darren said. "We'll just hang here for a bit and chill."

"What time does the bar open?" Tommy asked.

"Oh, it's open now, but we really don't start getting customers til around nine. The place will fill up after the dancers start at ten. There's another bartender here. I think you probably already know Paul. He works the other side of the bar, opposite me. I'll make sure I introduce you."

"Yeah, I know who he is," Tommy said. "I don't think I've actually met him yet."

"Okay, well let me finish showing you everything and we'll see you guys around ten." He pointed with both index fingers at each of the twins and winked.

"Good luck on your first night," Darren said to Tommy, squeezing his shoulder affectionately.

"Thanks. You, too."

Chapter Two

"You see the way that kid looked at us?" Darren asked his brother.

Michael, who was examining his chest in the mirror, did not turn to his younger brother when he replied. "Yeah, I saw. He's kind of a nerd though."

Darren shrugged. He leaned back in the chair and propped his feet up on the counter, right next to where Michael was standing. "I dunno. I thought he was kinda cute."

Michael laughed and shoved Darren's ankles off the countertop. "Gimme some space, man."

"You're so ugly," Darren said teasingly.

"Fuck you," Michael responded, still not bothering to turn around and make eye contact. For years it had been their private joke. Darren called his older brother ugly and Michael called Darren handsome, although they were identical.

"He might be a nerd, but I don't care. I wanna tap it."

"Dude, you're sick," Michael said. "He's like twelve or something."

Darren laughed. "He wouldn't be workin here if he were twelve. He's got to be at least eighteen."

"He looks young though, and he's too skinny. Damn! Why do I always get this one single hair here right by my nipple?" He pinched it and jerked quickly. "Ouch!"

"Well, just so you know I've got dibs on him. Keep your hands off," Darren warned.

"Bro, whatever. You can have him and I guarantee you he has no money. He's just a college kid or something. If he's working here as a bartender's assistant, he ain't even gonna make any tip money."

"I don't need his tip money," Darren said. "I'll make plenty all by myself."

"Shit!" Michael said. "You won't make squat without me. We're a team."

"You know what I meant." He propped his feet back onto the counter.

"Move your feet, you fuckin slob!" Michael said, shoving them out of his way again.

Darren laughed.

"And change those laces, too. They're all scuffed."

"You have a big red mark on your ass," Darren said.

Michael twisted his body, immediately trying to examine his behind. He pulled the waistband of his shorts down to get a good look. "Where?" he asked.

Darren stood up and leaned into his brother. "Right here," he said, quickly smacking him hard on the right cheek.

"You fucker!" Michael said. "That hurt!" He pushed his brother away as Darren laughed.

"I didn't bring any shoelaces," he said, "but these are fine."

"Just don't fuck up this job," Michael said seriously. "If you go getting involved with some twink..."

"Who said I wanna get involved with him? I want to fuck him. Besides, he wants me. I can tell."

"Darren, you think everyone wants you," Michael said, crossing his arms over his chest.

"Don't they?"

Chapter Three

Tommy had been a customer enough times at the Men's Room to realize that it was a busy place, but he had no idea exactly how much work was involved when it came to serving all those customers. By eleven in the evening the barroom was packed like a can of sardines, and the square-shaped bar was completely surrounded with customers, at least two-people deep. The bar itself was set up in two sections. Each side was a squared U, and there was a designated bartender assigned to each side. Tommy was their assistant. He was like a runner who got them everything they needed. Throughout the night, he was making trips back and forth to the storage room replenishing cups, napkins, ice, lemons, limes, you name it.

The dancers started performing around ten-thirty, and when they began, Tommy was too busy to even notice. As a customer, it had never seemed warm in the Men's Room, but on his first night as an employee, he was literally sweating his ass off. When he stopped momentarily to wipe his brow and grab a quick sip of water, he happened to glance up. Right before his eyes was one of the twins, standing on top of the bar, gyrating seductively in front of a female customer. Of course, the dancer had his back to Tommy, and the view that Tommy got was that of a pair of very toned and muscular legs and an incredibly smooth bubble butt.

Tommy couldn't believe what he was seeing. The dancer—he didn't know if it was Michael or Darren—had the waistband of his Speedo pulled down below his ass cheeks, and as he bent over, Tommy was amazed at just how smooth and perfectly hairless it was. Tommy felt paralyzed for a few seconds. He couldn't take his eyes off that perfect body with the broad shoulders and narrow hips.

He looked down, trying to compose himself and glanced at the dancer's shoes. The scuffed shoelaces told Tommy whom he was watching. Darren.

"Tommy!" A loud voice behind him brought Tommy back to reality. "Run get me some bloody mary mix," Deejay howled above the noise.

Quickly Tommy nodded and spun around. "Sure..." he said. " Um, sure thing. Be right back."

As Tommy entered the stock room, he took a deep breath and leaned against the wall. "Holy fuck," he whispered. He was sure he couldn't remember seeing anything as beautiful as what he'd just witnessed. "Now I know why Deejay said I might have to step into the walk-in to cool off."

For the remainder of Tommy's shift, he continued to steal glances at the twins. Frequently the two moved close to one another and performed as a team, yet they each directed their individual attentions to specific customers. One in particular was a middle-aged man, somewhat overweight. He wore glasses and sat with his arms pulled tightly against his body. Everything about him—the way he constantly looked down, the manner in which he raised his shoulders up and bowed his head as if cowering—it was obvious that he was self-conscious. Granted, the dude was old enough to be Tommy's father, yet there was something particularly endearing about him, a vulnerability.

It scared Tommy just a bit as he watched the scene. That could be him... in a few years. He could relate to the gentleman, the way he was so shy. It seemed like he wanted more than anything to interact with Darren. Yeah, it was Darren—scuffed laces. But the man was afraid. He was afraid to reach out and touch.

Wasn't that how Tommy himself felt? Wasn't that very same touch the thing Tommy desired more than anything? When Darren knelt down on the bar and gently placed his hand on the middle-aged man's shoulder, Tommy felt his heart warm. He watched how the man responded. Though still too timid to look up and make eye contact, he smiled shyly.

Darren leaned into him, speaking into his ear. Of course, it was too noisy in the bar to know what he said, but Tommy imagined that he knew.

Darren probably said, *It's okay, baby. Don't be shy.* When Darren reached down, still being ever-so gentle and grabbed hold of the man's wrist, Tommy's heart skipped a beat. Slowly he pulled it up toward his chest. "Go ahead," Darren said. "You can touch me."

The man finally forced himself to look up, staring first at Darren's thighs. His gazed traveled up the gorgeous dancer's body, taking in the tight-fitting shorts and the obvious bulge that they held. He stared at the washboard abs. So ripped. So utterly perfect. The man's mouth opened slightly. He truly was in awe of what he was seeing.

When his fingertips finally made contact with Darren's smooth chest, Tommy saw the man exhale. Then at last, he looked up into Darren's smiling face.

"There you go," Darren said, rhythmically gyrating his hips as he knelt there in front of his john. "You like that? You like that chest?"

The customer nodded very slowly.

Tommy wasn't sure, if the man was embarrassed or if his face had reddened simply from being flushed with excitement. He watched as the man carefully slid a bill into the waistband of the dancer's Speedo.

Darren was encouraging. "Thank you," he said sweetly, winking at the man. He then leaned forward and kissed the customer on the side of his face, again whispering into his ear.

Oh God, it was more than Tommy could take. Quickly he spun around. "Uh . . . wow, I think . . . um . . . we need more ice."

Deejay looked at him, confused. They could always use more ice because they went through it quite quickly, but it was hardly an emergency. Tommy rushed to the storage room. He had to get away from the sounds, the lights, the bodies. He had to get away from Darren for he couldn't stop himself from staring. He couldn't stop himself from watching him dance. Watching him thrust his pelvis and shake his ass. Tommy couldn't stop himself from obsessing!

Tommy stopped, leaning against the wall and closed his eyes. He felt his heart beating rapidly in his chest and his cock throbbing in his jeans. He was so aroused, more so than he could remember before. He'd been in this bar many times, had seen many dancers and even tipped them. Why was this one in particular—or these two in particular, they were identical after all—getting him so worked up? He didn't know exactly why, and it didn't matter. All that mattered was how he felt right now in this very moment.

He reached up and ran his fingertips across his chest, allowing himself to imagine it was Darren's touch he was feeling. With his other hand, he groped himself. Very slowly at first and with little pressure, he squeezed his own bulge. He was hard as steel, his erection throbbing against the tight-fitting fabric of his jeans.

"What are you doing?" The voice was sultry, barely a whisper, and he would not have even heard it were Darren's mouth not pressed right against his ear.

Tommy's eyes flew open as he immediately released the grip he had on his own crotch.

"Oh . . . oh my God!" he exclaimed. "You scared me."

He began to slide away, inching his way down the wall away from the stud who was leaning over him. He didn't get far though. He was too nervous, visibly shaking, and he couldn't take his eyes off the gaze of the man of whom he'd just been fantasizing.

"I'm sorry, baby," Darren said. "Don't be scared."

"Why . . . um . . ." Tommy stuttered. "Why are you here? You are supposed to be..."

"I followed you," Darren said, smiling seductively.

Tommy suddenly felt as if he were prey. He felt as if he were trapped, unable to move, but was that really such a bad feeling?

"Why?" Tommy squeaked.

Darren laughed. It was not a mocking laughter. Not in any way mean. It was a sweet and endearing laugh, like a parent chuckling at a small child who'd just said something cute. "I guess cause I like you," Darren said. "And I needed a break." He stepped back and looked down at his shorts. "I've got so much money in this Speedo, it's literally falling out."

Tommy followed Darren's gaze and saw it was true. The shorts were stuffed full of cash.

"And ya know, I could use some help... getting the money out." He winked at Tommy suggestively.

Did he just say that he *liked* Tommy? What did that mean? Tommy may have felt confused by this statement had it not immediately been followed up by an invitation to get in the stud's pants. It was nearly more than Tommy could comprehend, and he wondered momentarily if he were dreaming.

"Well?" Darren said. "Wanna help me?"

Tommy gulped.

Slowly Darren reached up, sliding his index finger along the side of Tommy's face. He traced a line down Tommy's cheek, up his chin and finally stopped at his lips. He held his finger there, as if to shush him. "It's okay, baby. Just nod."

Obediently, Tommy did as he was told, slowly nodding as he continued to stare into Darren's face.

Darren smiled again.

"D-dah-don't you have to go back out there?" Tommy stammered.

"In a bit," Darren said, his voice still soft and soothing, "but I can take a break for a few minutes."

"But Deejay... he'll wonder where I am."

"I'll take care of Deejay," Darren said confidently. "I've been watching you, and you've worked your butt off tonight. You can take a break with me."

"You have?" Tommy said, gasping.

Darren nodded. "Oh yeah, I've definitely been watching you... and you've been watching me."

Tommy stared at him, unable to respond.

"Haven't you?" Darren goaded.

Again Tommy nodded.

"And you liked it," Darren whispered. "You liked watching me so much that you came back here and . . . well, we both know what you were doing."

"I'm sorry," Tommy said, feeling himself blush.

"Don't be sorry," Darren said, chuckling again. "I think it's hot. I like it when guys get turned on from watching me."

"I don't want to get in trouble," Tommy admitted. "I don't want to lose my job."

This time Darren laughed heartily. "Look at where we are, baby," he said. "Do you think anyone's gonna really care?"

Tommy shrugged and bit his lower lip nervously.

"Come on," Darren said, sliding his arm around Tommy's shoulder and guiding him away from the wall. "Let's go in the dressing room, and you can help me like you promised."

Had Tommy made him any promises? It didn't matter, he couldn't stop himself. Before he knew it, he was placing one foot in front of the other, walking with Darren down the hallway toward the office. His heart was beating so fast Tommy thought it might beat right out of his chest. Darren continued to touch, pulling Tommy close against his body as they stepped into the small changing room. Once inside, Darren nonchalantly turned and locked the door.

Chapter Four

The first night on the job had been very profitable, and Michael was riding on a high. Although he'd been around the bar a few times, making his rounds and earning generous tips from numerous patrons, he already had specifically identified a couple who were sure to become his *favorites*.

One customer, a thirty-something professional who appeared to be slightly overdressed for the setting of a strip club, had remained seated at the bar the entire night. Their interaction had started when the attractive young man had slipped a one-dollar bill into the side of Michael's briefs. Michael could tell immediately that this was someone who had potential. His designer shirt and tie along with his obviously meticulous grooming habits told Michael that the guy was no cheapskate. He appeared to have money, and with a little persuasion, Michael was sure that he'd share some of it.

All it took was a warm smile and a gentle touch. Michael started by lightly brushing his fingertips across the man's shoulder. He looked up at Michael, not smiling broadly but rather just smirking. His eyes were big and brown and Michael was sure they were saying to him, *Yeah baby, I want more.*

That is exactly what Michael gave him. A little more. First, it was a little more attention. He smiled at the gentleman when he gyrated his hips. He winked, made frequent eye contact and even bent over to give the man a clear view of his perfectly rounded ass cheeks as he pulled down the back of his briefs.

Soon the man was sliding five-dollar bills into his shorts. With each tip, Michael's incentive increased along with his ego. He loved the attention. He loved to be worshipped. For some of the dancers it was just an act. It was merely a job they were doing, and Michael understood this. Admittedly there were times when he'd felt the same way himself. This wasn't the first bar he'd danced in. He and Darren had been doing this sort of work since they graduated high school, and Michael knew that in order to succeed, he had to be consistent. He had to be just as sweet, friendly and enticing to the repulsive customer as he was to those whom he found genuinely attractive.

It was such a bonus though, when there was a customer who also turned him on. As Michael stared down at the handsome patron, he realized this guy would have no problem hooking up with just about anyone he wanted. He clearly was successful, good-looking and assertive enough to snag a partner—male or female. This made Michael lust for him all the more.

As the evening progressed, Michael returned to the man several times. Eventually it got to the point where he pretty much had Michael's full and undivided attention. Michael learned the customer's name was Brandon and he was an attorney. He also learned that Brandon liked his ass a lot, but he liked his bulge even more.

Some customers loved to smack the ass. It was cool, and he and Darren often had fun with this. Sometimes they'd spank each other. Sometimes they'd bend over and invite the customers to give them a swat. Usually they would egg them on, encouraging them to continue and hit it harder the second or third time... or more.

Brandon swatted him, but very gently. He liked that ass and even said so, but spanking it didn't seem to be what Brandon wanted. He rubbed it and gently caressed it, apparently overwhelmed by its smoothness. Michael spent a lot of time making sure that ass of his was smooth and perfectly shaved. He and Darren knew all the tricks and used all the best products to keep their bottoms soft, smooth, and evenly tanned.

The dance music continued even after the bartenders began announcing *Last Call*. Michael sensed his customer's disappointment. He was obviously aroused and didn't want the experience to end just yet. Michael didn't want it to end either. He wanted to give into his own feelings. He wanted Brandon to take things further—push the envelope—and to go beyond just touching.

Michael was kneeling on the bar directly in front of Brandon whose face was buried between Michael's toned thighs. Michael leaned down, running his hands through Brandon's auburn hair. He leaned in, kissing Brandon on the side of his forehead as he spoke directly into his ear. "Baby, move down to the corner," he suggested, "where it's private. Just you and me."

By this time the crowd was starting to thin out. Still there was lots of activity around them, but Michael didn't think anyone would be paying too close attention to them. He was aroused, and it was obvious. As Brandon reached up one more time and pressed his fingertips against the outline of Michael's now hardening shaft, he allowed himself to throb. He thrust his pelvis forward and moaned, encouraging Brandon to continue. "Take it out," Brandon pleaded, his voice throaty and lustful. "Please."

All night long Michael had strutted up and down that bar wearing nothing but a pair of briefs, and he knew that the tight-fitting shorts were designed to do one thing—entice. They were skimpy and stretchy, and they were specifically chosen one size too small. They made a suggestion to the audience that the package they contained was desirable, and everything Michael did with his body confirmed this assumption.

But now the briefs were an impediment. They were what separated him from the delicate touch of Brandon's fingers. The briefs kept Michael's raging hardon from the soft, luscious lips of this man who stared up at him hungrily. Michael couldn't hold back. He couldn't control himself any longer, and as he slid his fingertips into each side of his briefs, he pushed himself into an upright kneeling position so that his groin was only inches from the face of the man who was about to . . .

Chapter Five

"Suck it," Darren said. "Is that what you wanna do?"

Darren had Tommy backed against the dressing room countertop, his butt pressing against the ledge. He *did* want to suck. He wanted it so badly.

"I want you to suck it," Darren said quietly. "See how hard it is for you?"

Tommy looked down and saw the bulge, afraid to touch it.

"Go ahead," Darren encouraged. "Help me take out the money."

He stepped back a little as Tommy tentatively reached out to him. Tommy's hands were shaking, and his breathing was so shallow he felt lightheaded. He'd been holding his breath, trying to calm himself.

Darren wrapped his hand around Tommy's wrist, slowly pulling it toward his bulge. "It's okay, baby. I know you want it."

He closed his eyes tightly just as his fingers brushed against the fabric of the shorts. The cock was hard, throbbing against the tight-fitting spandex.

"Look at it," Darren said. "Look how turned on I am."

Tommy opened his eyes and stared down. *Oh my God! This cannot be happening.* The experience was surreal, like something out of a movie. Here he was alone in the dressing room with the hottest man he'd ever seen, and the man wanted him. He wanted him so badly that his cock was oozing precum. Tommy felt the dampness through the tight, silky-smooth fabric.

He responded by reflex, finally giving into his lust as he slid smoothly down to his knees. As he did so, he knew it was right. It was so perfect. It was utterly appropriate. This had been what he'd wanted all along. This had been his deepest desire, and it was where he knew he needed to be. It was where he belonged.

He grabbed hold of Darren's outer thighs, steadying himself as his knees made contact with the hard floor beneath him. He barely noticed his own discomfort though. All he could focus upon was the bulge in front of him.

Darren reached in with two fingers and pulled out a single dollar bill from his shorts, holding it up in front of Tommy. "Help me," he pleaded.

Tommy mimicked him, reaching in very carefully, groping around until he found his target. Another bill. He pulled it out, smiling when he saw it was not just dollar.

"Very good," Darren said, smiling down at him approvingly. He held out his hand, allowing Tommy to deposit the twenty in his palm. "See what else you can find," he said.

Over and over Tommy repeated the action, getting a little braver with each of his retrievals. He couldn't believe exactly how much was in there. It was at least twenty times he reached into the briefs before he finally came up empty handed. If that's what you want to call it.

When there was no money left to find, Tommy wrapped his fingers around the only thing left to grab hold of. It was big—*very big*. It was big, hard, and smooth. It felt so hot against his fingers. Darren moaned appreciatively as Tommy began to stroke his fingertips across the shaft.

Darren stood there a few moments, allowing Tommy to kneel and worship. Tommy felt Darren place his hands on his shoulders. They moved along his neck, ever-so slowly and eventually were cupping the sides of Tommy's face. Finally, he looked up.

"Suck it," Darren said again. "Take it out and suck it."

Tommy grabbed hold of the sides of Darren's waistband and quickly tugged them downward. They slid down his thighs and Darren's rock-hard cock popped out, bobbing twice in front of his face. Quickly Tommy grabbed it by the base with one hand, cupping the ball sac with his other, and before he could talk himself out of it, he opened his mouth and swallowed it whole.

It felt so smooth against his tongue. It was a perfect combination of hard and softness simultaneously. He pressed his tongue against it, sucking as he forced his head downward. He wanted it all. He wanted every centimeter!

The sound of Darren's moan above him encouraged Tommy to continue. He inhaled deeply through his nose, taking in the musky scent of the dancer's sweaty crotch. He was now himself throbbing, horny as hell.

Tommy didn't want to start choking. He wasn't that experienced, but he'd learned that if he could relax and remain determined, he could suppress his gag reflex. He kept the cock buried balls-deep and sucked ferociously. The taste of Darren's salty skin made his mouth water all the more, and the grip of Darren's fingers in his hair told Tommy he was pleased.

That really was what it was all about. Tommy knew this. He'd known this all along, from the second he laid eyes on the twins. Tommy was born to please men like Darren and Michael. To him, they were larger than life. They were like gods.

Slowly Tommy backed off, sliding all the way up the hard shaft. With it still in his mouth, he looked up to see Darren towering over him.

"Good boy," Darren said. "You're a good little cocksucker."

With those words of encouragement, Tommy kicked into overdrive and began sliding on the rigid pole. He started bobbing up and down, taking each thrust as deeply as he could, keeping his tongue pressed firmly against the underside of the sensitive shaft. With one hand, he continued to grip the base, palming it and sliding upwards with each upstroke of his head bob. It was a continuous flow of stimulation, and Tommy allowed his saliva to drip down, providing a slippery lube for both his sucking and stroking.

"Oh God!" Darren moaned as he began to gyrate his hips. "Feels so damn good!"

Tommy moaned and continued, not even completely aware that he was himself aroused almost to the point of orgasm.

Darren's grip on Tommy's head tightened, and he began to assert himself, thrusting his pelvis harder with each stroke. Tommy released Darren's cock, placing his hands firmly against Darren's thighs. He slid them around Darren's legs, grabbing hold of his ass cheeks, making every effort to convey that he welcomed Darren's assertiveness.

Tommy's welcoming gesture was all the encouragement Darren needed, and he widened his stance slightly. Still holding firmly onto Tommy's head, he began to fuck. Tommy opened his jaw as wide as he could and allowed Darren to stab his cock deeply into him, impaling his throat.

"Fuck yeah!" Darren shouted as his cockhead popped into the tight channel of Tommy's throat. Keeping it buried, he then began to hump.

Had Tommy been able to moan—or even breathe—he would have made it abundantly clear to Darren how much he desired his dominance. He would have been begging for more. He would have been pleading to the man who towered above him, to fuck his throat like he owned it.

He didn't need to say anything though. Darren seemed to know. He repeatedly and forcefully rammed his cock in, rhythmically thrusting, knowing exactly how to maximize his own pleasure.

Tommy felt his own cock throbbing, now finally aware that he was about to lose it. He released his grip on Darren's ass and groped himself. Just one squeeze was all it took. He erupted in his own pants!

At that very second, Darren moaned and thrust deeply into his throat, remaining buried balls-deep. Tommy felt the cock pulse against his tongue.

"Fuck!" Darren cried. "Oh fuckin Christ! I'm gonna nut!" He uttered an animalistic moan as he gripped Tommy's head tightly, digging his fingers into Tommy's scalp. Then he erupted.

The flood of cum was like a geyser, blasting off directly into Tommy's stretched throat. Eagerly he gulped, concentrating on taking every drop. Jet after jet of the creamy, salty juice fired into the back of Tommy's mouth.

Both of them were trembling as Darren drained himself.

Chapter Six

As soon as Michael began to pull his briefs down, Brandon took over. The handsome, young attorney reached up and grabbed hold of the waistband, sliding it down Michael's thighs. Michael looked down, watching eagerly as his hard cock popped out.

Michael grinned as he stared down at his customer. "Go on," he urged him.

The feel of that warm and silky mouth around his raging hardon was like heaven. It felt so slick and hot. Within seconds, Michael was aware that Brandon was no novice cocksucker. He thrust his groin forward, abandoning all thoughts of the possibility that someone could be watching. Squaring his shoulders, Michael tossed his head back and moaned as Brandon took his manhood deeply into his hungry mouth.

The music that surrounded them provided the perfect beat. The bass was heavy, and the tempo was upbeat. Brandon bobbed on his now-throbbing cock, sliding rapidly up and down the shaft. His expert tongue pressed against the most sensitive area, just under the crown, and as Michael looked down, he sensed the man was not just sucking him. He was worshipping.

Michael gently slid his hands around Brandon's shoulders, but he had no desire to dominate. He knew the admirer was there to shower him with affection and adoration, and Michael loved every second of it.

They didn't have much time. If one of the staff saw, they'd surely be interrupted—or worse. Michael gave into the feeling that passed over him, allowing himself to become swept away. He willed himself to move quickly toward that delicious moment, that wonderful point when there was no turning back, and it happened perfectly.

"I'm gonna shoot," he said, his voice raspy. He was trying not to cry out. "Oh yeah. Yeah baby, suck me dry. Worship me. Take me. Take all of me!"

Michael felt the snap of his release and thrust his pelvis forward, suddenly convulsing as the wave of orgasm engulfed him. A white-hot flame shot through his groin as he erupted, blasting at last into the hungry mouth of his patron.

"Oh God! Oh fuck!" he said. His voice was like a whimper. He grabbed hold of Brandon's shoulders to steady himself as he allowed every drop of his seed to fire into the man's mouth.

Brandon kept his mouth around Michael's cock, until he was completely spent. "Oh, baby, thank you," Brandon said, leaning in to kiss his forehead. "Oh that was so good."

The customer then leaned back and smiled, licking his lips. He reached up and pulled Michael's shorts back up, snapping the waistband in place. He then dug into his pocket and pulled out a crisp one-hundred dollar bill and slide into Michael's briefs.

"No," he said. "Thank *you*."

Chapter Seven

"You know what's so crazy about it?" Tommy said to Lorna. "He was so sweet and loving with me. I'd even say he was like... um, gentle, but only at first."

"Yeah, but you got him turned on, then he wanted to fuck you like an animal." Lorna wasn't even looking up at him. She was concentrating on painting her toenails and chewing a big wad of bubble gum.

Tommy sat down on the bed beside her, sighing. "But we didn't fuck. I just sucked him, and that was it."

"The way you described it, babe, sounds to me like he fucked you. He fucked your mouth, and ya know, to those kinda guys, a hole's a hole."

Tommy lightly swatted her arm. "He's not like that!"

"Hey, watch it," she warned. "You better not make me mess up my nails."

"You're doing a good job of that on your own... without my help." She returned the swat, only harder.

"You're such a bitch sometimes," he said, scowling as he rubbed his arm where she'd just hit him.

"I know. But, baby, I'm not sayin it's bad. It's all good. You loved it, right?"

Tommy thought for a minute, smiling to himself as he remembered the scene from the night before. "Oh yeah," he confessed, "I loved every second of it."

"So when are ya gonna do the other one?" she asked.

"The other one?"

"You said they're twins, right?" She looked up at him, staring him in the face. It was as if she were implying she'd stated something very obvious that he was not bright enough to comprehend.

"What's that got to do with it?"

"You've never had a fantasy about doing it with twins?" she guffawed. "Think about it!"

Tommy's grin broadened as he stared off at the wall, not focusing on anything in particular. "Yeah, cause they are *exactly* alike. It'd be like having..."

"Double the pleasure," she finished for him.

"Double the cock!"

"That's what I'm sayin! Hey, are these guys totally gay, do ya know?"

Tommy turned to her and gave her a dirty look. "Yes! Totally."

Chapter Eight

Truth was Tommy didn't know if Darren and Michael were totally gay. It sure seemed like Darren was, though, the way he'd come on to Tommy. Then again, Tommy had watched all that night as Darren flirted with the customers and employees at the club, both male and female.

He understood that it was the job of the dancers to be flirtatious. They were supposed to be enticing and welcoming, and the better they made people feel, the more likely it'd be that they'd stay longer, buy more drinks and return for future visits.

What Tommy did not know was whether Darren felt even a fraction of the desire that Tommy felt of him. It was unnerving, the way Tommy couldn't get the dancer out of his head, and Tommy feared that his obsession might be not only unrealistic, but also unhealthy.

Darren was hot. Everyone knew this. Both he and Michael were, and people of all ages, shapes and sizes who came into that bar noticed them. What Lorna had said about the twin fantasy was something that extended far beyond Tommy and Lorna. It certainly was a common fantasy. People were fascinated with the very concept of two people who looked exactly alike. Tommy's assumption that one physical encounter with a guy like Darren meant anything significant was beyond presumptuous.

In spite of what Tommy knew in his head, he couldn't change how he felt in his heart. He couldn't stop himself from dreaming, from hoping, from imagining. A guy like Darren was just too good to be true, yet Tommy found himself asking all those what if questions. *What if he asks me out? What if he wants to do it again? What if he becomes my boyfriend?*

The other factor that Tommy could not help but analyze was that all of this had happened on his first night at a new job. Regardless of what the future held with Darren—and even his brother Michael—Tommy was going to have to figure out a way to work with them. He really liked the job and wanted to keep it, and he also liked the other guys who worked there. If his encounter with Darren was nothing more than a one-time-only blowjob, Tommy would have to be able to let go over his obsession and act as if nothing had happened.

But he wanted more. He wasn't satisfied with giving a quick blowjob in the dressing room. Question was how did Darren feel?

Chapter Nine

"So where did you take off to?" Michael asked.

"Bro, when are you talking about?" Darren replied. They were at the breakfast table having toast and coffee.

"Last night, at the bar right before closing."

Darren shook his head as he spooned some strawberry preserves on his toasted bread. "I was right there, dude. What do you mean?"

"You took off," Michael said insistently. "Deejay even asked about you. And that kid . . . he was missing, too, about the same time."

"I took a break for a minute. Jeez, it's no big deal. My shorts were stuffed and I had to stash the money. Just chill . . ."

"You were doing that boy, weren't you?"

"Michael—"

"I knew it!" Michael said, pointing his finger. "Dude, you are so gonna get us fired."

"I'm not gonna get us fired, and I don't know what boy you're even talking about."

"That Tommy, the skinny kid you said was cute. You were fucking him, weren't you?"

Darren shook his head emphatically. "No," he said truthfully. "I was *not* fucking him."

Why the hell did Michael have to be this way? Yes, he was the older brother, but only by twelve minutes. All Darren's life, Michael had been trying to tell him what to do. He was the leader, the decision maker and the responsible one. Usually Darren was fine with this, because frankly it was easier to just go along with it. It was easier to just yield to Michael's judgment. In this case though, Michael was going too far.

"You know, it's really none of your business," Darren said.

"The fuck it's not! Bro, we're a team. If you fuck up and lose this job, we both do!"

"Come on! Think about it," Darren protested. "We work in a strip club, for fuck's sake. We strut around that bar all night long selling sex. Now you're gonna bitch at me for a fucking blowjob?"

"So you *did* do him!"

"He blew me, all right? Get the fuck over it!" Darren had pushed his chair back and stood up. "And you know what? I liked it! I *loved* it, in fact. I loved it so much I might just let him blow me again tonight!"

Michael sighed exasperatedly. "Please, Darren, don't get involved with the help. It's just gonna be messy. That kid is too young, and you're gonna break his heart."

"Why can't you have *any* faith in me? I'm not gonna break his heart. He'll probably break my heart, if anything. I just think he's cute. I like him. Is that so hard to believe?"

Michael rolled his eyes, then leaned forward, placing his elbows on the table as he stared up at his brother. "Our job is to make everyone think we're in love with them. Our job is to get our customers to want to worship us. Well, when it is middle-aged guys—or women—who understand this and who know they are just there for a night of entertainment, well . . . no harm, no foul.

"But this is just a boy. He's probably never even been laid before. The sad thing is that he's probably head over heels in love with you."

At this point Darren turned away and paced across the dining room floor. He turned and stepped back toward the table. "You're right. He is young, and I know he's probably really green, but I don't think he's all that inexperienced. He sure seemed to know what he was doing. "I'm not gonna hurt him."

"And we aren't gonna even be there that long," Michael pointed out. "Three or four months top. Then what?"

"I have no fuckin idea! Ask me in three or four months! Look, I'm not doing anything wrong. Whoopty fuckin do, I got head in my own dressing room. It wasn't like I did it out on the bar or something."

As Darren glared at his older brother, it suddenly dawned on him. Michael was guilty of something. His face was reddening, a telltale sign of guilt. "Oh my God," Darren said, "who did you do?"

"I have no idea *what* you're talking about!"

"Hey, big guy," Deejay greeted Tommy as he walked through the door. "You're back!"

Tommy smiled at him.

"You made it through your first night, all in one piece."

Tommy laughed. "Yeah and I think I'm gonna really like this job."

"Well, you're early, so pop a squat. I'll get you a soda." He stepped over to the bar and filled a cup with ice. "What'll it be?" he asked.

"Coke's fine."

That smile of Deejay's was about the brightest and toothiest Tommy had ever seen. The contrast of the pearly whites against Deejay's dark skin tones and jet black hair was striking, and Deejay also had very dark brown, sexy eyes. Tommy had noticed Deejay the very first time he'd come into the Men's Room as a customer, and he was always the same. His demeanor was consistently welcoming and congenial, and Tommy thought he was certainly a perfect fit for the job he held. That wife beater t-shirt he was wearing was also a nice fit—very snug, accenting his buff upper body and displaying the entirety of Deejay's rippling biceps.

"How come you're not a dancer?" Tommy asked.

Deejay laughed uproariously. "Oh hell no!" he objected. "That's really not my style, strutting around nearly naked. Plus, I'm not that good of a dancer. These go-go dancers we have working here are fantastic, and they do a great job, but you have to be a certain sort of person to display yourself like that."

Tommy nodded in agreement. He took a sip of the Coke that Deejay had just set in front of him. "Exhibitionists," he said.

"Right. Exactly. Oh and what do ya think of our new guys, the twins?"

Tommy stared at him wide-eyed for a moment and then looked down at his soda. He shrugged. "I like em," he said in a very quiet tone.

Deejay laughed again. "Yeah, I could tell. I saw you checkin em out more than once last night. They're hot."

"Do you think those guys are gay?" Tommy asked.

Deejay raised his eyebrows and cocked his head. "Um, yeah," he said. "I'm sure they're gay."

"Oh . . . I just wondered. Well, cause I saw them dancing for both men and women."

"Honey, you're in a gay bar, and where there are gay men, there's going to also be women. A big percentage of our customers are female, and most of them are straight. Just like gay guys, straight women like to check out hot male bodies."

That made sense. The women were customers too, and the job of the dancers was to provide entertainment to all the club's patrons. Still on some level it seemed strange to Tommy that Darren would be thrusting his crotch into the face of some middle-aged woman one minute then getting it on with a guy in the dressing room just a few moments later.

"I really like them—especially Darren."

"I don't know how you can tell the difference," Deejay said. "I kept getting confused over which was which."

"Well last night Darren was wearing a Speedo, and Michael had on a pair of briefs."

"Hmm, that's pretty observant of you," Deejay commented.

"And Darren's shoelaces were dirty. They had scuffs on them."

Deejay laughed. "Dude, I think you might be a little obsessed over these twins or something."

Tommy felt a hand on his shoulder. He quickly turned to see one of the twins standing beside him. "Who's obsessed with the twins?" he asked, sliding his arm around Tommy's back and holding him.

"Uh . . . no one," Tommy said. He wasn't sure how much of the conversation had been overheard.

"Well, I'll tell ya a secret," the twin said. He held out his hand in front of Tommy. "See my middle finger there—that tiny white scar on the knuckle?"

Tommy nodded.

"That happened when I was fourteen. Accidently fell into the sliding glass window on our back porch. I was on my skateboard trying to do a jump. The whole fuckin window shattered, and lucky for me, all I cut was my hand."

Tommy looked down at the ground to see if the twin was wearing the same Nikes as the night before. Sure enough and they were scuffed. "And you're Darren," Tommy said.

He leaned in and placed his lips right next to Tommy's ear. "Are you gonna meet me in my dressing room again tonight?" he whispered.

Tommy blushed and nodded.

"Okay then," Deejay said loudly, "and where's your other half?"

Darren shrugged. "Dunno, he's around here somewhere. He must've gone straight down the hall to the dressing room. We rode together." He then turned his attention back to Tommy. "So are you in school?" he asked. Darren was still standing with his arm around Tommy's back, and his voice was still sultry and sexy.

"Yeah," Tommy said meekly. "I go to the university. I'm a computer science major."

"No shit?" said Darren. "I am, too, but I'm taking my liberal arts classes at the community college. I'll probably be at the university next semester. Do you live on campus?"

Tommy had turned slightly in his chair in order to make eye contact. "Nah.

I share an apartment with three other students—all girls."

Darren laughed. "Figures. You're probably the envy of every straight guy on campus."

"And I couldn't care less," Tommy said, laughing. "No wait . . . I mean I love my roommates, but not that way."

"Yeah, I knew what ya meant."

Darren was wearing jeans and a dark brown leather jacket. Tommy inhaled, taking in the scent of Darren's cologne and the smell of the leather. That whiff alone was enough to get him hard. By this time, Deejay had stepped away and was busying himself on the other side of the bar.

Darren whispered in Tommy's ear again. "Baby, I got to go start getting ready."

"I know," Tommy said, smiling. "I have to get to work, too."

"Promise you won't leave tonight without coming back to see me."

"I promise," Tommy said. His heart was already racing.

Chapter Ten

Michael couldn't believe he'd let himself get sucked off on the bar the night before. But God was it ever hot. He knew it wasn't smart, especially not when it was his first night on the job, but those lips and that tongue had felt so good, and that guy was so gorgeous. Michael wondered if he'd be back again tonight.

He and Brandon had been at the far end of the bar in the corner, and chances were that no one had seen what was going on. Unless they stepped around and got a full frontal view of Michael, they wouldn't have realized Brandon was actually blowing him. Lots of times the dancers knelt on the bar in front of customers, and it wasn't even unusual for the customers to stick their face right up in the dancer's crotch.

The way that bartender Deejay had looked at him, as he climbed down off the bar, made Michael a little nervous. He wondered if perhaps Deejay had seen the action. He didn't say anything though. He just sort of raised his eyebrows and smiled slyly.

Darren knew though. All of their lives the twins had been able to sense when the other was trying to keep a secret. As Michael had bitched at Darren earlier about getting frisky with the bar boy, he knew that he'd done something equally as dangerous himself—if not more. At least Darren had had enough sense to take it to the backroom.

Well, Michael decided he was going to play it cool tonight. He wasn't going to let things go that far, no matter how hot the customer happened to be or how much he himself got turned on. He'd just chalk the experience up to one of things that had happened. A crazy moment. The fulfillment of a public sex fantasy.

After stripping down and checking himself in the mirror, Michael decided to peek out into the bar and see if they were starting to get busy yet. He stepped out into the hallway and headed down past the office and the walk-in cooler. He stopped in the archway that led out to the bar and glanced around. His brother was at the bar standing next to that skinny kid. He had his arm around the kid's shoulder.

Yeah, he guessed Darren was right. The kid was pretty cute. He could imagine himself tapping that. He smiled to himself as he thought of it. The bartender Deejay was in the corner at the other end of the bar, right about the same place where Michael had gotten his cock sucked the night before.

Now that was a hot one, Michael thought. He could envision some action on that front as well. Deejay had such big strong arms and a superb chest, and he looked killer in that tight black wife beater.

Just as Michael was beginning to allow his mind to wander, he caught someone from the corner of his eye stepping up to the bar on the other side. It was him. Brandon was back, and he apparently had come early enough to ensure he'd snag a front row seat.

Michael's heart beat rapidly in his chest. It was going to be one hell of an interesting night.

Chapter Eleven

Lorna and her roommate Carrie showed up at the bar around eleven-thirty. Tommy was extremely busy at the time, but he did have a chance to offer a quick greeting. "Here," he said, thrusting two drink tickets into her hand. "I get these for free."

"Thank you, honey," she said, smiling at him sweetly and leaning across the bar to kiss him on the cheek. "Oh my God, I see what you mean about those twins!" With a movement of her head she gestured toward Darren who was on the bar a few feet to her left.

"That's Darren," Tommy said. "His brother Michael's on the other side."

"Holy crap, I think I need a closer view." She whipped out a dollar bill from her clutch and began waving it in the air toward Darren, trying to get his attention.

Tommy laughed. "I'll try to get back over if I ever get a break."

"You go ahead, honey, we're fine all by ourselves." She wasn't even looking at him, being too engrossed in what she was seeing strutting down the bar. Darren came over and danced for her, squatting down to allow her to insert the tip into his shorts.

That's how it went the whole night. Darren seemed to move back and forth along the bar interacting with numerous customers. He didn't spend too much time with any given one of them. His brother Michael, on the other hand, seemed to be focused upon one man in particular. It was the same guy that Tommy had noticed the night before, the one who'd been wearing the nice suit.

Tonight he was dressed more casually, but still very sharp. On one occasion when Tommy was down at that side of the bar, he had to do a double-take. Did he just see the man slipping a fifty into Michael's briefs? Wow, most of the customers tipped with dollar bills. Apparently, this dude was a high roller, or he just *really* liked Michael.

Friday night had seemed busy, but it paled in comparison to Saturday. Tommy wondered if any more people could possibly squeeze into the limited space offered by the club. Even the dance floor was packed as well as the upstairs bar.

Deejay had explained to him that on Saturdays they opened the upstairs simply because it got so crowded. They had a bar and a couple dancers up there, and according to Deejay, things sometimes got pretty raunchy. This meant that the twins pretty much had the downstairs bar to themselves. Colby was the lead go-go boy, and he went back and forth, spending some time upstairs and some down.

At one point Deejay had sent Tommy upstairs to see if they had an extra bottle of Crown Royal. While there, he was shocked to see that one of the dancers was atop the bar completely naked. A female customer was holding his skimpy briefs in her hand and waving them above her head like a flag, cheering fanatically. The dancer stood there, his beefy cock hanging down, semi-hard, smiling and gyrating his hips.

Fuck, Tommy thought. Deejay wasn't kidding when he said things got pretty raunchy.

Tommy was excited, and he couldn't stop smiling throughout his shift. He kept thinking about what might happen in the dressing room later, and although he was extremely busy, it seemed the night dragged on. The anticipation was killing him, and as he would look up to steal glances at Darren, his idol, he'd feel a tightness in his own shorts and a quickening of his breath.

Tommy made a point to stick around at the bar for last call because he didn't want to piss Deejay off. If he made a habit of disappearing around closing time, he was sure Deejay would not be pleased.

The overhead lights came on, and Tommy was somewhat overcome by their brightness. The crowd already was dwindling, and Tommy was busy toting items from the bar back to the walk-in cooler. Deejay had taught him how to use the three-basin sink to wash, rinse, and sanitize the non-disposable glasses, and he had them all done. He then went around gathering and emptying ashtrays and wiping down tables.

It was almost three o'clock when Deejay finally came over and put his hand on Tommy's shoulder.

"Dude, I'm so impressed with you," he said.

"Thanks, Deejay," he said, somewhat startled. "Um, I'm sorry about last night, the way I disappeared at the end."

Deejay shrugged and gave him another of his award-winning smiles. "I get it," Deejay said. "When opportunity knocks . . . "

"I gotta tell ya something though," Tommy confessed. "I don't understand it. I don't get what Darren sees in me."

"You're joking, right?" Deejay said.

Tommy shook his head.

"Guy, you are one hot little number, like I told you on the first night. You need to quit putting yourself down. Darren likes you because you're adorable. You're cute, polite, smart, hardworking, and you have an ass that . . . well . . ."

Tommy felt himself blushing but continued to stare Deejay in the face. "I've never had anyone say such nice things about me," he said. "Thank you."

"All true," Deejay said, then leaned in to kiss Tommy gently on the lips. "Go on now . . . have fun."

Chapter Twelve

Michael wasn't sure he liked what was happening to him. Wasn't it supposed to be the customer who became obsessed with the entertainer? Many times previously, he'd had specific customers who'd become fans. They returned with the express intention of seeing him, tipping him, and getting a few moments of his attention. That was just how it worked. That was how he made his money.

This situation with Brandon was very different though. Michael could genuinely sense that Brandon was attracted to him and possibly even a bit obsessed, but he was unable to turn off his own feelings toward Brandon. After their shared experience the night before, Michael was starting to become obsessed himself.

And God, Brandon looked hot as fuck tonight. He looked like a million bucks and he smelled like two million. His broad shoulders and dark eyes drove Michael crazy, and even though he knew he should be out working the bar, he just kept coming back to Brandon. It really didn't cost him anything monetarily, at least not in the short term. Brandon was tipping him and tipping him well, but Michael also knew that it was his job to provide entertainment to as many of the customers as possible.

Just before closing, Brandon pulled Michael down to whisper into his ear. "Come with me," he said. "Come home with me, just for one night . . . please."

Michael didn't know how to respond. He just leaned back on his haunches and stared down at his gorgeous customer. "Baby, you're tempting me," he said, then quickly stood up and started to dance again.

A few minutes later, around last call, Michael finally climbed down off the bar and walked around to where Brandon was sitting. Now standing next to him, it seemed to change the dynamic entirely. It wasn't Michael who was towering over Brandon, but vice-versa.

"About that invitation," he said as he sidled up next to his lawyer man.

"It still stands," Brandon said, burying his head in Michael's neck. He kissed it and darted his tongue out, successfully targeting Michael's erogenous zone.

Michael felt a shiver travel up his spine as he tossed his head back. "Oh

God . . . why am I so fucking crazy about you?"

"You just are," Brandon said, now holding Michael's head in both hands. "Go get your clothes and meet me out front." He leaned in and pressed his lips to Michael's.

Michael responded by literally melting into him. He wrapped his arms around Brandon's neck and pressed his body closely against the other man. Their mouths connected, tongues dueling in an attempt to find their way deeply into the other's mouth. Brandon tasted of whiskey and cigarettes, and the feel of his five-o'clock shadow tickled Michael's chin.

"Oh man," Michael said, sighing, as he pulled away. "Give me five," he said. "I'll meet you out front."

Michael quickly changed and threw his money and clothes in his duffel bag, then headed back down the hallway. He passed his brother along the way. "I won't need a ride," he said flippantly.

"What? Where the fuck you goin?" Darren asked.

"I'll see you in the morning," Michael said and then dashed down the hall and out the front door.

Chapter Thirteen

Standing outside the dressing room door, Tommy took a deep breath before knocking. It was only about three seconds later that the door flew open, and there he was, Darren in all his glory. Still wearing only his Speedo and sneakers, his body glistened with sweat. He didn't say a word, but smiled at Tommy sweetly. Then he took Tommy by the hand and pulled him inside.

Within seconds, Tommy was sitting atop the dressing room table and Darren was standing between his legs. Darren leaned in and kissed him, passionately driving his tongue into Tommy's mouth. Tommy responded to the kiss, wrapped his legs around Darren's waist and grabbed hold of the bigger man's shoulders.

"Did you think about me today?" Darren asked, whispering in his ear.

"Yes," Tommy responded breathily. "You were *all* I thought about."

"I have some good news for you," Darren said. "At least I hope you think it is. My brother's not coming home with me tonight, so I have the place all to myself."

Tommy stared at him, unsure of what Darren was suggesting. "Do you mean you want me . . ."

"To come home with me . . . if you want."

"I . . . um . . ."

"Unless you wanna just let me fuck you right here on this table," Darren said, smiling.

"You wanna fuck me?" Tommy asked, his voice high-pitched.

"You want that, don't you?" Darren asked. "I think you want it real bad."

"I want . . . um . . . I want it like last night, too," Tommy said.

"Oh you wanna suck me, too? I want to suck *you*," Darren whispered.

"You do?"

"I do," he answered, "then fuck you."

"Oh God!" Tommy said. He was now throbbing.

"You wanna do it here, or wait til we're back to my place? If we start now, I'm not gonna be able to stop."

"Oh . . . oh yeah. We can wait." Tommy grabbed hold of Darren's head and again kissed him passionately.

When they pulled apart, Darren was grinning. "Not so shy now, are you? I knew you were a little tiger. Let me get dressed. You got all your things?"

Tommy nodded. "I don't have any things," he said. "It's just me."

"It's okay. I'll share my toothbrush with you."

Chapter Fourteen

As Michael slid into the leather passenger seat of his companion's BMW, Brandon reached out and took hold of his hand. "You were wonderful tonight," Brandon said. "Thank you." They pulled away from the curb and headed down the street.

The interior of the car was dark, and Michael couldn't clearly see the expression on the young attorney's face, but he squeezed his hand in reply to his compliment.

"I have a question for you," Michael said.

"Sure, babe. What is it?""

"Brandon, do you think I'm a prostitute?"

They had only traveled a couple blocks, and upon hearing these words, Brandon immediately slowed the car and pulled into an empty parking space. He shifted into park, turning in his seat to face Michael. "Oh God . . . Michael, no I don't think that. Do *you* think that?"

Brandon was again holding Michael's hand as he looked over to stare into Brandon's dark brown eyes. "I suppose if you have enough money, you can buy anything," Michael said. "And I have to be honest with you, it was your money that first got my attention.

"This job, I know it looks like a lot of fun, but sometimes it's not so easy. Every person that steps up to the bar and looks up at me, every person—no matter how old they are, how fat or ugly, or dirty—they're all just dollar signs. My job is to please them all. I'm their entertainment. The hot, young piece of flesh they dream of using—of owning."

"Michael, you're not the only entertainer to use sex appeal to promote themselves. Christ, it's a benchmark of the entire entertainment industry. Musicians, actors, even television commercials—they all use sex, and they're not hookers."

"But you paid me a hundred bucks after—"

"I'm sorry Michael. I didn't mean to cheapen it. I paid the money because . . . well, because that's what I do. That's how I express myself. It's how I show my appreciation."

"I know," Michael said softly, suddenly overcome with emotion. God damn it if he wasn't going to start crying.

"Baby, no. You're not a prostitute to me."

"And will you say the same thing tomorrow morning?"

"And the day after that . . . and the day after that. God, who knows what will happen. I know nothing about you at this point. I know you're a hell of a dancer and you're just . . . well, hot as fuck. And I know you have an identical twin." Brandon reached up and wiped the tear that was streaming down Michael's cheek. "But I can tell you I want to know so much more, and I don't just want this to be sex for money. We don't even have to have sex . . . it's up to you."

"I'm a college student. Pre-law," Michael smiled at him through his tears.

"No shit?" Brandon said.

Michael nodded. "One more semester, then law school."

"Where? Have you been accepted anywhere."

"Columbia," he answered.

"Michael, that's my school."

"I should have known. What kind of law do you practice?" Michael asked.

"Oh, nothing glamorous. Tax law mainly."

"I want to be a criminal lawyer," Michael said.

"Yeah, everyone does," Brandon said, laughing. "But you know you'll probably be a damn good defense attorney. If you're as passionate about defending your clients as you are about your customers . . ."

"I'm not that passionate about *all* my customers," Michael interrupted him. "Only the hot looking guys who give really good head."

Brandon reached down and placed his palm against Michael's crotch, squeezing it playfully. "I'll blow you right here, baby," he whispered seductively.

"Then we'll be arrested and we'll both need a criminal defense attorney," Michael said, laughing.

Brandon grabbed hold of Michael's zipper and slid it down as he leaned across the seat and buried his head in Michael's lap.

Chapter Fifteen

"So it's just you and Michael who live here?" Tommy asked.

"Yup. We both go to college, and our tip money pays for this apartment. Michael's a law student, and like I said earlier, I'm at community college."

"Why don't you both go to the university?" Tommy asked.

"Money," Darren said. "To be honest, Michael's the smart one. Well, maybe I should say he's the disciplined one. He applied himself more in high school, earned the scholarships. He's always been that way. Technically he's my older brother."

"But you're twins," Tommy said, laughing. They were sitting together on the sofa in the twins' studio apartment.

"Try telling him that," Darren said, rolling his eyes. "He's twelve minutes older and has never let me forget it."

"So he bugs you sometimes."

Darren nodded. "It's no different than any other family. That's how brothers are. What about you? Do you have any brothers or sisters?"

"A little sister. She's fourteen," Tommy said. "Her name's Teresa."

"Tommy and Teresa," Darren said. "Cute."

"It's crazy how you two look exactly alike," Tommy said. "I mean, I know it's no big deal. You're twins, so why wouldn't you look alike? Right? But it's just kind of fascinating to me. I wonder if *everything* about you is alike."

Darren laughed. "You would not believe how many people ask that, and well, yeah, pretty much everything is alike, other than this." He held up his middle finger to show his scar. "All our lives, we've gained weight, put on muscle, gotten sick—literally everything, exactly on the same schedule. When we go out, we like to dress alike. We just are genetic replicas, I guess."

"Which means your . . ." Tommy looked down at Darren's crotch.

"Yeah, our Mr. Happys are exactly alike, too."

Tommy felt himself blush. "What a perfect name for it," he said. "It sure made me happy last night."

"Oh don't get me started . . . not just yet." Darren leaned in and kissed Tommy lightly on the lips. "You're such a doll baby," he said sweetly.

"I can't believe you think that."

"It's true. I swear. I've always been attracted to guys like you. I think it's why I got into computer programing and gaming and shit. That's where all the nerds were..."

Tommy suddenly felt crestfallen, and it was apparently obvious by the expression on his face.

"No, wait," Darren said. "I'm such an idiot. I don't mean you're a nerd. Not a dorky kind of nerd... but you, well, you just have that look. You're slender and you look smart and kind of a little geeky, and I just totally am crazy about little guys like you."

"I guess it's the whole jock-nerd kinda thing."

"Yeah maybe," Darren admitted. "And last night..." He ran his fingers gently up Tommy's forearm. "Last night the way you worshipped me. It was fuckin unreal. That sort of thing just really gives me a major rush."

"Which might be why you're a dancer. You have a whole audience worshipping you," Tommy said.

"Sometimes," he said. "No dancer is gonna be able to do it for everyone. Some people don't go for my type. And some people I'd just as soon not be attracted to me."

"I can't imagine who you'd be talking about," Tommy quipped. "The people not attracted to you must be the blind customers."

Darren laughed. "See that's what's so charming about you. You say the cutest things, and you do it totally deadpan. Like you're completely serious."

"I am serious," Tommy insisted. "You are so gorgeous and muscular and... God... sexy—anyone who can't see that must be blind."

"I think you should shut up and kiss me," Darren said.

"Yes, sir." Tommy slid over into the big jock's waiting arms.

Chapter Sixteen

"Oh God! Oh fuck!" Michael cried out, biting the back of his hand in an attempt to stifle his scream. "I'm cumming!" His hips bucked upward involuntarily as he released the load. Brandon continued to hold the suction of his lips tightly around the base of Michael's cock as he drained himself.

As the orgasm washed over him, he was overcome with a powerful shiver, and his body began trembling. "Oh, Brandon! Oh my God!" He was gasping for breath, trying to compose himself.

Brandon slid upward, kissing first Michael's neck and traveling up to his quivering lips. "How was that, baby? Still think I give good head?"

"Oh God," Michael gasped, "on a scale of one to ten, that's a fucking fifteen!"

For the entire drive to Brandon's house, Michael had a smile on his face. "I can't believe you blew me right there on the main street of town."

Brandon glanced over at him, smiling evilly. "The night is still young," he said. "More to come."

Christ, it was already approaching four in the morning. In another two hours it'd be daylight, but Michael wasn't about to argue. He was hoping the night would never end. He wanted nothing more than to spend as much time as possible with this gorgeous, sexy attorney.

The house was spectacular. Brandon described it as neo-colonial, but Michael just called it awesome. It was a two-story home with a wooden porch supported by classical columns. Brandon parked the car in the garage where Michael noticed two other vehicles. When they entered the house, Michael was astonished by the spaciousness of the rooms and the multi-paned windows.

After setting the alarm, Brandon extinguished the downstairs lights and took Michael by the hand, leading him up the spiral staircase.

"Your house is beautiful," Michael said.

"Thank you," Brandon replied. "I'm very fortunate. I had it kind of easy. Most of the money I have was inherited."

"I just thought it was because you're such a brilliant attorney," Michael said, smiling.

"That, too," Brandon said as he gave Michael a wink. He opened a door to one of the rooms, apparently his bedroom. "Do you need a shower?" he offered.

"I don't know. Do I?" Michael asked.

"Not as far as I'm concerned. I'll take you just as you are." He stepped into Michael's personal space and nuzzled his chin against Michael's neck. "I don't know if I can wait that long."

"Why don't you join me?" Michael suggested.

"Why don't I?" He then directed Michael to the adjacent master bathroom. As could be expected, it was huge. Brandon pulled Michael against his chest once again and leaned in to kiss him.

Michael closed his eyes and allowed himself to be swept away by the passion of the kiss. Pressing his hands against his lover's chest, he rubbed them back and forth, as he felt Brandon cupping his ass cheeks.

Michael reached around his partner's back and gently tugged on his shirttail, slowly working his way around front, then began unbuttoning, starting from the bottom. All the while, his fingers fumbled with the buttons, he continued kissing passionately.

Brandon's hands were also busy, sliding around to unzip Michael's pants. By the time Michael had the shirt completely unbuttoned, Brandon had Michael's pants pulled halfway down his thighs. Michael's fingers quickly found Brandon's hard chest. His fingertips gently caressed the hardening nipples, and Michael sighed as he felt the soft chest hairs beneath his touch.

They finally had to pull away from each other in order to discard their clothing. As they did so, Brandon looked down to check out the bulge in his lover's pants. Twice Brandon had seen him, but this was his first look at the man he was about to make love to.

Brandon was quick at undressing, carelessly tossing first his shirt, then pants to the floor. When he pulled off his briefs and socks and stood there completely naked, Michael was truly in awe. "And you paid *me* to touch my body?" he asked.

"A mere fraction of what you're worth," Brandon said.

"Flattery will get you everywhere." Michael stepped forward, reaching down to slide his fingers under Brandon's ball sac. "I want you so bad," he whispered.

"You have me," Brandon said. "Take all you want."

Without hesitation, Michael slid to his knees and swallowed the already-hard shaft. He inhaled deeply as he took the entirety in his mouth in a single, smooth movement. He heard Brandon moan above him. The musky scent was appealing, and Michael held the shaft in his mouth, slowly savoring the taste.

He slowly caressed Brandon's balls with the fingers of both hands as he began to suck.

"Baby, don't make me cum," Brandon said. "Not yet."

Michael eased off, slowly sliding up the shaft. "Why not?" he said playfully. "You already made me cum once."

"At your age I bet you have no problem cumming three or four times a night," Brandon said. "Not so sure I'm up to all that myself."

"Turn around then," Michael said.

Brandon grinned down at him momentarily and then did as he was instructed, turning and placing his hands flat on the countertop. His stance was wide so that Michael was able to slide between his legs as he raised himself into an upright kneeling position. Using both hands, he spread Brandon's ass cheeks apart and slowly began licking the tender flesh that lined his hole.

"Oh fuck!" Brandon said, moaning, as Michael buried his face in the ass. *I may be young,* Michael thought, *but I sure know how to toss a salad.* Brandon's ass was clean yet the pungency still stung Michael's tongue as it vigorously darted in and out of Brandon's hole. Expertly Michael found Brandon's pucker and drilled his tongue into it, causing Brandon to wriggle his ass responsively to the tickling sensation.

"Oh, baby, feels so good," Brandon said, but he didn't allow it to continue for very long. He slowly pulled away, sighing as he did so, then turned to pull Michael up to his feet.

When they got in the shower, it was like a car wash, jets streaming from all directions. They each lathered the other generously. Michael played some more with Brandon's nipples as Brandon leaned back to rinse his hair, and Brandon stroked Michael's cock in return.

Their hair was still wet, and each was wrapped in a blanket-sized towel when they headed back to the bedroom. "Will you make love to me?" Michael whispered as he kissed his lover once again.

Brandon steered him toward the bed and gently eased him back onto the mattress, sliding his own body atop the naked dancer. "You're absolutely beautiful," Brandon said. "Every fuckin inch of you." Brandon undid his towel and tossed it behind him on the floor. He then reached down and pulled Michael's towel away.

"I want you inside me," Michael said. "I want you so bad."

Brandon stepped back as Michael repositioned himself on the bed. Opening a drawer in the bedside stand, Brandon removed a packet of condoms and a tube of lubricant.

"You were prepared," Michael said sweetly.

"Always." He removed a condom and tore it free from the wrapper. His cock was already hard. Michael leaned over and helped him slide it on, then spun around so that he was on all fours facing away from Brandon. He felt the heat of Brandon's chest against his back as he leaned forward and kissed Michael's neck. Brandon slid his hands under Michael's body, finding his nipples and tweaking them gently.

Michael moaned. "Please, I need you."

Brandon removed his hands from Michael's chest, and soon Michael felt them probing his ass. Brandon was now upright, and his index finger was coated with lubricating gel. Slowly it entered his hole, and Michael squirmed in anticipation. The finger alone was enough to make Michael throb.

Brandon started slowly, working his finger into the hole using a circular motion. Gently at first, he increased the degree of pressure and speed, then graduated to two fingers, thrusting more deeply, and when they finally hit Michael's sweet spot, his head flew back and his back arched reflexively. "Ah fuck!" he cried.

The evacuation of Brandon's fingers left Michael feeling momentarily empty, but it was a short-lived sensation. Michael then felt the heat of Brandon's groin against the cheeks of his ass as Brandon pressed his sheathed cockhead against the loosened pucker. The careful entry was excruciating, and Michael wanted him just to thrust it in. He wanted it so badly. Wanted Brandon to fill him, to fuck him ferociously.

Michael thrust his ass backward, willfully impaling himself on Brandon's cock. Brandon responded by grabbing hold of Michael's hips and grunting loudly as his cock slid deep into the tight hole.

"Fuck me!" Michael cried. "Fuck me hard!"

Brandon needed no further encouragement and began to thrust in and out. Holding tightly to Michael's waist he repeatedly slammed into him, his groin slapping hard against Michaels ass cheeks. The size and force of Brandon's rigid pole stabbed repeatedly against Michael's prostate, causing him to buck and throw his head back wildly. "Oh God! You're gonna make me cum! Please fuck me! Don't stop! Fuck the cum right out of me! Oh God!"

As Michael quickly escalated to the point of no return, he felt Brandon thrust violently into him, practically lifting him right up off his knees. Brandon stopped thrusting, burying himself to the hilt and leaned forward to press his chest against Michael's now-sweaty back.

"Oh fuck!" Brandon cried. "Aaaaahhh!"

At that exact moment, as Brandon fired his load into Michael's ass, Michael himself went over the edge and groaned as his own cock began to fire copious spurts of cum. It sprayed all over his chest and the mattress below. They both were sweating and moaning and ultimately crashed onto the mattress entangled in each other's arms.

Michael turned and kissed Brandon one more time. "Oh God, that was so hot."

Brandon was shaking his head and laughing. "You have no idea," he said, sighing. "You have no fucking idea how much I've wanted to do that these past two days."

"I think maybe I do," Michael said, smiling.

Chapter Seventeen

As Darren took Tommy into his arms, Tommy clung to him, swept away by the overpowering strength of the massive biceps, chiseled chest, and immensely broad shoulders of the man who held him. Tommy felt so small and helpless and realized that this very man who was showering him with kisses of affection had the strength and ability to utterly crush him were he to be so inclined. Instead, Tommy knew—or at least he believed in that moment—that Darren would never hurt him.

It was an amazing feeling of security, surrounded by such power and strength, to feel so protected. Tommy had been around a lot of buff, muscular guys, especially since he started going to the Men's Room. While being mesmerized by their beauty and most certainly appreciative of their stunning physiques, he had not been drawn to any the way he was to Darren. It was because of Darren's assertiveness—the way he'd pinned him against the wall the previous night in the hallway, the way he'd so aggressively directed Tommy to do exactly what he wanted—that Tommy was particularly attracted to him.

Tommy's desire to feel dominated in this way was something he did not even understand. He was just beginning to recognize what it was and to connect the dots, but he couldn't quite explain it. Certainly, it wasn't that Darren was a muscle god or bodybuilder. It wasn't that Darren was controlling or mean either. It was about contrast. Tommy was short and slender whereas Darren was taller and athletic. Tommy had softer mannerisms, a quiet voice, and was by-and-large introverted, but Darren was outgoing, masculine, and boisterous. Did this mean that Tommy wanted to assume a feminine role with Darren? Did it mean he was forever assigned to a position of subservience and inferiority?

No, this wasn't how Darren made him feel. If anything, it was the opposite. Although, Darren took charge and was quick to make the first move . . . then the second and third . . . Tommy didn't feel weak or emasculated. Instead, he felt elevated. Darren had very directly stated that he loved to be worshipped, and yet it was Tommy who felt that Darren was worshipping him.

This was precisely what Tommy felt as Darren grabbed the tail of his shirt and pulled it up over his head. He placed the palm of his hand flat against

Tommy's hairless chest and gently pushed him back on the sofa, and Tommy couldn't help but moan softly as he felt that palm pressing against him and those fingers gently caressing his upper body. As Darren continued to touch him so intimately, he leaned into him and pressed his lips against Tommy's. The combination of the kiss and the ongoing touching of his bare chest created a powerful sensation, as if an electric charge were surging through his body, running straight down from his neck to his groin and pulsating in his throbbing cock.

Instead of responding by reaching up to grab hold of Darren, Tommy simply allowed himself to relax. He sat there with his arms at his side and his eyes closed as Darren ran his hands all over Tommy's sensitive skin. Goose pimples erupted on his arms as Darren's fingers lightly traveled up and down. His abdomen reflexively tightened as Darren probed his navel. His nipples hardened as Darren tweaked them.

Tommy simply gave into him, surrendering to Darren's control, and soon Tommy was sitting there completely naked. Darren had removed his pants and underwear and was now kneeling between Tommy's outstretched legs. The fingers which moments before had been caressing his upper body now were exploring the inside of Tommy's thighs.

Tommy knew he was not as well-endowed as Darren, but somehow it just didn't matter. He felt such an overwhelming sense of trust that it didn't occur to him to be self-conscious. And as had once been pointed out to him, size was always relative. His six inch cock appeared just as impressive on his small body as did an eight-incher on a man who was much bigger and taller. In any event, Darren didn't seem a bit disappointed, and when Tommy felt the moisture of Darren's lips against his hard shaft, he opened his mouth just a little and moaned.

The reality of what was happening was surreal. Tommy felt almost as if he was in a dream, and when the heat of Darren's mouth surrounded him, it was all he could do to keep from crying out. Darren's tongue pressed against the underside of Tommy's rigid shaft as his soft lips surrounded the pole, forming a suction that felt silky and warm. As Darren slid down Tommy's cock Tommy felt like he was soaring to heaven, and he spread his legs wide, moaning with sheer pleasure.

One night before, it had been Tommy on his knees servicing Darren, and now their roles were reversed, yet the experience was entirely different. There had been no question the previous night as to who was in control. Darren had fucked Tommy's face with abandon. Now, however, although it was Tommy being serviced, it still seemed that Darren was in complete control. Tommy did not reach down to grab hold of Darren's head. He did not thrust deeply into his throat. Instead, he allowed Darren to do with him as he wished.

It certainly did not appear that Darren was lacking in experience. He swallowed Tommy whole, and there was not a single second in which Tommy's cock and balls were not being stimulated, either by Darren's lips, tongue, or fingers.

Tommy tossed his head back against the headrest on the sofa and moaned quietly. He was edging so close to orgasm but didn't want the experience to end. It was such delicious torture as Darren brought him right to the edge then eased off enough to keep Tommy from reaching climax. Tommy frantically grasped at the sofa cushions beneath him as he hips involuntarily bucked. He didn't thrust, though, and continued to allow Darren to take the lead.

The feel of Darren's palm cupping his balls as his mouth slid up and down Tommy's throbbing shaft was inexplicably satisfying—far more than when Tommy had jacked himself off. Although he'd given a few blowjobs himself, this was only the second time in his life that someone else had sucked him, and his first experience paled in comparison.

"Darren," he cried, his voice a whimper, "you're gonna make me cum!"

Darren looked up, Tommy's cock still in his mouth, and continued to suck with an even greater intensity. Tommy felt it building, knew it was right there, but couldn't quite get to that anticipated point of release. "Oh God! Oh fuck!" he cried just before he blasted off. He grunted and squeezed the sofa cushions tightly in his fists as at last the volcano erupted.

The heat of Darren's mouth continued to surround him as a volley of cum bursts fired rapidly from Tommy's throbbing cock. The pulsing continued as Darren's suction drained him, triggering blast after blast of powerful bursts. Each one fired up the shaft with a violent pumping action of his pulsating shaft. Tommy had never before cum into another person's mouth, and the feeling was indescribably heavenly.

"Oh, oh my God," he said, trembling uncontrollably. His entire body began to shake as he finally reached out to grab hold of Darren's shoulders. He did this more to steady himself, but Darren took it as a sign to back off.

Darren looked up at him smiling, then immediately climbed atop him, smothering his face with sticky kisses. Tommy melted into him, wrapped his arms tightly around Darren's torso and pulled him close. A blissful post-coital euphoria swept over him as his trembling started to subside, but his cock continued to throb.

"Oh, baby," Tommy whispered, "thank you so much."

"I want to make love to you," Darren said, just before drilling his tongue deeply into Tommy's gaping mouth. They flailed around, both panting and clawing at one another.

Finally, Tommy pushed back, coming up momentarily for air. Gasping, he pleaded, "Please . . . I need you inside me."

Without hesitation, Darren slid one arm beneath Tommy's knees and cradled Tommy's shoulders in his other, smoothly lifting his naked body from the couch. He carried Tommy effortlessly into the bedroom and placed him gently on the mattress of his double bed. Tommy watched as Darren rapidly stripped off his clothing and tossed each article carelessly behind him. He then stepped over to a bureau, which was against the wall and pulled open a drawer, taking out a packet of condoms.

Tommy's heart beat rapidly in anticipation, and he couldn't help but stroke his own cock. Though he'd just cum, he remained hard and was easily up for at least one more round. It took Darren no more than five seconds to sheath his cock with the tight latex sleeve, and then he stepped over to the bedside stand where he frantically pulled out some lubricant. Smearing some first on the outside of the condom then more on his fingers, he tossed the tube of gel onto the mattress beside Tommy and slid onto the bed himself in a kneeling position.

Tommy looked up, staring at the man who was now between his legs. As Darren reached down to grab hold of Tommy's ankles, Tommy cooperated, allowing Darren to push his legs back. Tommy held his knees tightly against his chest. He was now completely exposed, his hole wide open. Darren leaned down, sliding backward a bit on the bed and drove his face into Tommy's ass cheeks, drilling his tongue in as deeply as possible.

The sensation was unbelievable and Tommy squirmed involuntarily. Darren continued to rim him as Tommy moaned and stroked his own cock. Darren pulled back and immediately replaced his probing tongue with a probing index finger. Tommy felt a tiny bit of irritation as the digit pierced his pucker.

"Darren," he said quietly, "I . . . uh . . . "

Darren looked up at him expectantly before continuing. "What is it baby? Is this your first time."

Meekly, Tommy nodded.

"Oh, babe," Darren said. "Are you okay? Do you want . . ."

"Don't stop," Tommy pleaded.

"I'll be gentle," he promised. With his free hand, Darren reached up and grabbed a pillow from the other side of the bed. "Lift your bum," he instructed Tommy, then slid the pillow beneath him. "Now tell me how this feels. Tell me if it hurts, okay?"

Slowly Darren pushed his finger in further, starting to rotate it.

"It feels good," Tommy said honestly. "Oh God, it feels so good." Tommy closed his eyes and enjoyed the sensation.

"Try to completely relax," Darren said. "If you're tense, your sphincter will tighten, and it'll hurt more."

"Will it hurt bad?" he asked.

"Maybe, but only for a little while," Darren said.

In spite of his trepidation, Tommy remained hard. So far, there was no pain, and as Darren continued to probe him, Tommy kept his eyes closed and tried to relax completely. Once Darren had entered him with the entirety of his finger, he began to thrust, but slowly.

"Oh . . ." Tommy gasped. As Darren's finger plunged deeply into him, his own cock throbbed. "Oh man . . . feels so good."

Darren worked a second finger in and began to thrust with both. Tommy barely noticed the difference and continued to moan.

"Do you want more?" Darren asked. "Are you ready?"

"Yes!" Tommy exclaimed, practically pleading. "I need you inside me."

Darren assumed a kneeling position between Tommy's legs, pulling his fingers completely out. He grabbed hold of each of Tommy's ankles and pushed his legs all the way back. "Baby, rest your ankles on my shoulders," he instructed. Tommy complied.

"I'm going in part way at first," Darren warned him. "It will probably hurt, and that's okay. Just bear down, like you're going to the bathroom, and it will make the pain stop."

"Okay," Tommy said as he stared into Darren's eyes.

"Keep looking at me," Darren said. "Look right into my face."

Tommy nodded, not daring to take his eyes off his lover. As Darren had predicted, the pain was intense as Darren eased into him. It was far worse than he'd imagined it would be. He grimaced. "Oh fuck! It hurts!"

"Bear down!" Darren reminded him as he stopped pushing. He remained inside but did not attempt to go any further.

Tommy grunted and pushed, just as Darren had told him to do. The wave of pain began to subside, and Tommy gasped.

"You okay?" Darren asked.

Tommy nodded.

Darren pushed in further and Tommy again grimaced.

"All right, I'm backing out," Darren said, and immediately he pulled back. The second wave of pain was excruciating, and Tommy grasped frantically at the bed coverings, trying to ride it out.

"Now relax," Darren said, gently rubbing his fingers along the inside of Tommy's thigh. "Just relax, baby."

Tommy tried to do as instructed, but it was difficult. The pain in his rectum seemed to radiate throughout his entire body, and by impulse, he wanted to tighten his muscles rather than relax. He concentrated though, lowering his legs slightly so that his feet were flat on the mattress and allowed the wave of pain to wash over him.

Tommy continued to stare up into Darren's eyes.

"I'm sorry, baby... I don't mean to hurt you." Darren reached down and slowly stroked Tommy's softening cock. As the pain subsided, he began to stiffen again in Darren's hand.

"Try again," he said.

"Are you sure?" Darren asked. "Are you ready... we can stop."

"No, I want it. I swear."

Darren again grabbed hold of Tommy's ankles and raised them to their former position. He slid back between Tommy's legs and used one hand to steer his cock into the crevice of Tommy's cheeks, inching in so his cockhead pressed against Tommy's pucker. Slowly he eased forward.

This time there was virtually no pain, and Tommy smiled as he stared up into the face of his handsome jock.

"Are you okay?" Darren asked.

Tommy quickly nodded.

"Babe, you're so tight. You feel so good." Tommy's cock throbbed against his belly, simply from knowing his lover was pleased.

Darren slid all the way in, burying himself balls-deep. "Ahhh," he moaned.

"Fuck me," Tommy said. "Please."

Darren withdrew partway then immediately slid back in. His cockhead stabbed into Tommy, piercing him in the same manner as did his finger earlier, and Tommy cried out. "Oh yeah!" He reached up to run his fingers across Darren's chest.

"You like that?" Darren asked, and Tommy smiled and nodded. Darren withdrew again, this time further, then quickly thrust back in. Over and over, he repeated the thrusting, penetrating Tommy deeply each time. His pace began to quicken, as did Tommy's breathing.

"God... it feels so good!" Tommy cried. He reached down and began stroking himself. "How the fuck can it hurt so bad then feel so damn good?"

Darren laughed, apparently encouraged, and began to thrust harder. He leaned back, grabbing hold of Tommy's ankles and held them out like he was holding a wishbone then began to fuck fiercely. As he continued, he also began to moan, occasionally closing his eyes then reopening to stare into the face of his lover.

Tommy reached up for him, and Darren bent down. Grinding hard, Darren leaned all the way forward, bringing his lips close to Tommy's face. He reached up and wrapped his arms around Darren's neck while encircling Darren's waist with his legs. His ankles were locked together behind Darren's back. As they kissed passionately, Darren continued to hump him.

The friction of Darren's abdomen sliding across Tommy's throbbing cock added to his stimulation, and Tommy realized that he wouldn't be able to hold off much longer. He pulled back. "Oh God! You're gonna make me shoot."

"Shoot it, baby!" Darren commanded. "Let me fuck the cum right out of you!"

"Ahhh, ahhh!" Tommy cried out, then felt himself again passing that point of no return.

His entire body convulsed as he shot the load across his belly. It splashed up against Darren's chest, who had not hesitated to continue with his assault on Tommy's virgin ass. Finally, Darren groaned and thrust deeply into his boy, burying his cock and holding it. His face crinkled and he moaned loudly as he released his load.

It seemed as if every muscle in Darren's body tightened. He grabbed hold of Tommy and pulled him into himself, again kissing him while remaining deep inside his hole. Tommy's heart was racing so rapidly he thought it would beat right out of his chest. He continued to tremble, visibly shaking while Darren held him close.

"Oh God, Darren. That was so hot! Oh God... oh fuck!"

They lay together for the next several minutes until finally, Darren's erection subsided and he pulled off the condom. He kissed Tommy before getting up to use the restroom. A few seconds later, he returned with a warm cloth and towel and cleaned Tommy.

"You were amazing," Darren said. "Thank you for letting me be your first."

"Thank you, Darren," Tommy echoed the sentiment. "I think I love you."

Chapter Eighteen

Sunday did not start until noon for Michael, and it began with breakfast in bed. Brandon had allowed him to sleep in and gently woke him with a tender kiss.

"Wake up, sleepy head," Brandon said cheerfully, and slowly Michael began to stir.

Opening his eyes, barely squinting, he peered into Brandon's smiling face. "Hey," he responded groggily, trying to force a smile in return. "You look ... fucking amazing this morning."

Brandon laughed. "You thought you could wear this old man out," he said, "but I beat you out of bed this morning and even made you breakfast."

"Oh God," Michael said, rubbing his eyes sleepily, then yawned. "You didn't have to do that."

"I know, but I wanted to."

"What time is it?"

"Noon," Brandon said casually.

"Oh fuck, I better call Darren," Michael said. "I don't want him to worry."

"Why don't you send him a text instead?" Brandon suggested. "So we can have breakfast together." He winked suggestively.

"Oh yeah ... good idea." Michael grabbed hold of him and pulled him back down for another kiss.

When they pulled apart, Brandon got up and retrieved the breakfast tray he had placed on the dresser. "We have scrambled eggs. We have toast. We have bacon. We have coffee and orange juice ... *and* fresh fruit."

"Holy crap," Michael said. "You know how to cook?"

Brandon laughed. "Of course I know how to cook. Do you know how to eat?"

"I could eat you right up," Michael said. Brandon held out a strawberry and fed it to his lover. "Crawl back in bed with me. We can eat breakfast together, then I'll eat you."

"Deal," Brandon said, "first eat your bacon, then I'll feed you a big fat sausage."

"Mmm, you're making my mouth water."

Chapter Nineteen

Tommy woke before Darren and lay there for a few moments unsure if he should quietly make an exit or wait for Darren to wake up. He looked over at his sleeping lover, still finding it hard to believe what had happened. The idea of a guy like Darren actually being attracted to him was something that was going to take a while to get used to.

What had happened just a few hours prior, though, did a lot to convince Tommy. Maybe his friend Lorna had been right all along. Maybe he needed to just have a little more faith in himself and start accepting the fact that he was worthy.

He looked at Darren's sleeping face. He was so beautiful, even as he lay there snoring softly. As Tommy watched him, he remembered how Darren had kissed him so many times the night before. He remembered how they'd made love. He was starting to get some morning wood as he thought about it.

If he were more confident, he might just make a move about now. He might just be brave enough to wake Darren up and make love to him again. But Tommy wasn't confident at all. He always doubted himself. He always worried about offending someone or doing the wrong thing, and he feared that if he stuck his neck out and did something he shouldn't that there would be repercussions later.

But there he was with the most gorgeous man on the planet, lying twelve inches from him. And here Tommy was, sporting a raging hardon. What would it hurt to just touch him? If Darren rejected him or snapped at him and told him to go back to sleep or to leave, that wouldn't be the worst thing in the world. Would it?

Yeah... it really would. These past few days, all Tommy could think about was Darren. He didn't want to do anything to jeopardize what they had. Maybe he should just write Darren a note and sneak out. He could jack off after he got home... like he usually did.

Just as Tommy was about to drag himself out of bed, Darren stirred. He sighed then took a deep breath and finally rolled over onto his back. He still was sleeping soundly though. Tommy looked down at the sheet that loosely covered Darren's body and smiled when he saw the bulge. Tommy wasn't the only one with morning wood.

All thoughts of leaving quickly vanished, and Tommy quietly slid his body down the mattress, carefully pulling back the sheet. Tentatively, he placed his hand against Darren's thigh and rubbed gently. He looked up to see if Darren would stir. Still nothing.

He now was staring directly at Darren's fat hardon. It was so beautiful that it nearly made Tommy's mouth water. He sat up a little bit and climbed over Darren's leg and positioned himself between Darren's thighs. Very slowly he pressed his face right up next to the hot flesh of Darren's hard cock and ever-so gently kissed it. He then looked up once more to see Darren still in a state of blissful slumber.

When finally he wrapped his palm around the shaft and pulled it up to his mouth, he knew there was no turning back. He opened wide and pressed his tongue against the underside of the pole, then wrapped his lips tightly around its circumference and... down he went. Slowly and worshipfully he sucked, savoring Darren's musky scent. At first there was no noticeable response, but after about ten successive head bobs, he felt Darren's hands on his shoulders.

Tommy glanced up, Darren's cock still in his mouth, and saw a smiling yet sleepy face staring down at him.

"Good *morning*, sunshine," Darren said.

Tommy smiled around Darren's cock then continued sucking. He felt Darren stretch his legs out a bit and glanced up to see him stuffing another pillow behind his head, propping himself up a bit. Tommy was glad Darren made no effort to discourage Tommy from continuing.

"This is my *favorite* way to wake up," Darren said. "We're gonna have to have slumber parties like this more often."

Darren's cock, which had been hard to begin with, was now throbbing. This only encouraged Tommy to continue. Remembering what Darren had done to him earlier, how he'd nearly made him cum when he shoved his finger up Tommy's ass, Tommy decided to try something. He backed off Darren's boner and continued to stroke it with one hand. With the other hand, he slid his middle finger into his mouth, lubing it liberally with his tongue.

Tommy again wrapped his lips around the shaft and slid down while simultaneously wriggling his slick finger into Darren's pucker. Darren's response was to spread his legs a little wider in order to allow him better access. When Tommy got it all the way in, he jabbed deeply, using staccato movements to thrust in and out. He tried to mimic what Darren had done to him hours before.

Darren's moans of pleasure were accompanied by a throbbing of his cock in Tommy's mouth. Tommy felt Darren's firm grip again on his shoulders. "Oh God, babe you're getting good at this!"

Tommy continued to suck, rhythmically timing the thrusting of his finger to coincide with the bobbing of his head. When Darren began writhing around, digging his heels into the mattress and twitching his legs spasmodically, Tommy took that as a sign he was doing something right. He doubled his effort, sliding up and down the pole more quickly while simultaneously finger fucking Darren's ass.

"I'm gonna cum," Darren growled. "I'm gonna *cum!*"

Tommy dove all the way down the shaft, until the cockhead drilled into the back of his throat and continued to suck ferociously. He felt the pulsing against his tongue as the cumload first fired into the shaft. Darren then grunted loudly and released, and Tommy's mouth filled instantly with hot semen. Hungrily he gulped as Darren continued to drain himself, firing multiple globs of sticky, salty jizz directly into Tommy's mouth and throat.

When Tommy finally pulled back, Darren was visibly shaking. "Oh fuck," he said, laughing and smiling.

"Good morning," Tommy said sheepishly.

Chapter Twenty

"So what's going to happen when I go away to New York in a few months?" Michael asked. He was sitting in Brandon's car out front of the twins' apartment.

"I'll fly up to visit you, or I'll fly you home," Brandon said, matter of factly.

"Really?" He knew he'd only known Brandon two days and had only spent one full night with him, but already he felt as if he couldn't imagine ever being without him.

"Really," Brandon said. His tone was very certain, and it made Michael feel secure, even if he questioned whether it was merely a false sense of security.

"My brother is going with me," he said. "We've never been apart."

"He's going to law school too?" Brandon asked.

"He'll be going to NYU as a computer science major."

"How do you think he'll feel about us?"

"What do you mean?" Michael said, turning in his seat to look directly at Brandon.

"I mean since you're so close, does he ever get jealous?"

Michael laughed. "Actually I'm more the possessive type myself. I'm the one who always watches out for him and warns him about getting serious with other guys. I just want to make sure nothing fucks up our goal. I want us both to get a good education."

"Well that's commendable," Brandon said, "but you didn't really answer the question."

"There's not going to be any problem with Darren. He'll be happy for me. If anything he'll be jealous of me more than he's jealous of you."

Brandon laughed. "Well you know, I've always had a fantasy about doing twins."

Michael looked at him slyly.

"I'm sorry, I shouldn't have said that."

"I think it's normal," Michael said. "I think most people have that fantasy, and a lot of times we capitalize on that when we dance together."

"Have you ever done it . . . I mean have you ever fulfilled someone's fantasy like that?"

Michael felt a bit embarrassed. "I have to answer that, don't I?"

"No. No you don't have to answer anything you don't want to answer." Brandon took his hand.

"Well yeah. Sure, we've done stuff together. Christ it used to be sort of like we were one person in two different bodies. We have this indescribable connection where we share a lot of the same thoughts and we can tell what each other is thinking or feeling. And we always know when the other's lying."

"So it was just natural for you two to be attracted to the same type of guys? You're both gay, right?"

"We're both gay but we are definitely not attracted to the same sort of guys. It's so weird." Michael smiled as he looked directly into Brandon's dark brown eyes. "In our day-to-day life, I'm more of the decision maker. I'm the responsible one and the leader. Darren's the goof off who constantly needs a foot up his ass to get him motivated. That's why he's in community college now and I go to university. I kept my grades up and got a scholarship.

"Don't get me wrong. I'm not complaining. Darren works hard, and we pool all our money together. We've spent far more of it on my own education than his. Even with scholarships, I ended up paying a lot more. With community college, the financial aid pretty much covers everything. But in spite of the fact that I'm more dominant in that way, he is totally a top, and I'm almost totally a bottom. Weird, isn't it?"

Brandon ran his palm along the side of Michael's face and shook his own head. "No, it's not weird at all. I think it makes sense that Darren would be more of a top. He's the sort of guy who is carefree, who likes to fuck around."

"Yeah, maybe. But anyway, as we were growing up, we used to jack off with each other. It didn't seem incestuous or anything though. It was more like jacking off in front of a mirror."

Brandon laughed right out loud. "That's fucking hot," he admitted.

"We didn't think so at the time. It just was natural. Then we'd do things together with other guys. It wasn't like we were doing each other. It seemed more like when were in those situations we each were an extension of the other. Watching Darren fuck or get sucked is like watching a video of myself."

"That's amazing."

Michael looked at him suspiciously. "I think I know what you're thinking right now."

It was Brandon's turn to be embarrassed.

"I'll ask him, okay? But if we do something together, you've got to promise me . . . don't go getting him confused with me. Don't start having feelings . . ."

"I guarantee that'll never happen."

"And no kissing him!"

Brandon made a gesture of crossing his heart. "But wait. How will I tell you apart?"

"Oh I'll make sure of it."

Brandon leaned in to kiss him.

"I better get going," Michael said. "Thanks for everything."

"Stop it. Stop thanking me . . . I'm the one who's grateful to you. I haven't felt this wonderful in . . . God, years."

"Well we never even talked that much about you," Michael said. "So next time, you owe me."

"Deal," Brandon said.

They kissed once more and Michael got out, waving goodbye before turning to head upstairs to his apartment.

Chapter Twenty-One

"Sweetie, how long have you known this guy?" Lorna had met Tommy at Starbucks after he texted her while leaving Darren's apartment. It was now three in the afternoon, or Sunday morning in club-life time.

"Why does it matter?" Tommy said. "I know how I feel."

"You know how you feel right now, but honey you've only known him for two *days*... Not two months or even two weeks—two fucking *days*. I'm not saying this isn't going to work and it isn't going to last forever. I'm just saying it might be too early to tell."

"I thought best friends were supposed to be supportive and excited for each other when they found the love of their lives. This coffee is shit, by the way. Needs more sugar." He got up, stormed over to the condiment bar where he picked up the canister of sugar, and liberally poured the equivalence of four heaping tablespoons of sugar into his already-sweet coffee.

"You know I love you," Lorna said when Tommy returned and was stirring his sludgy, syrup-like mixture. "I just don't want you to get hurt. I think you should just have fun for now. Enjoy your time with Darren, and don't worry about whether or not it'll last forever. If it's meant to be, then it's meant to be, and you two will be together for years and years. If not... then you had a great time."

Tommy made a sour face. "Lorna, nobody's *ever* made me feel like this. He makes me feel special, ya know. I just never in my wildest dreams thought a guy like him would be interested in someone like me."

She smiled at him sweetly. "That shit's nasty, by the way." She pointed to his coffee cup. "It's like why don't you have a little coffee with your sugar."

"Starbucks coffee is like battery acid," Tommy protested. "It *needs* a lot of sugar."

She shook her head and rolled her eyes. "Baby, you're so wrong about yourself. I just wish you could see what a cute, smart, funny, and charming guy you are. I'm not at all surprised a guy like Darren would find you attractive. I'm not surprised that any guy would consider you a real catch."

It was Tommy's turn to roll his eyes.

"Think about it, okay? Darren is a dancer. He has guys and girls falling in love with him every night of the week. You said yourself, his thing is that he loves to be worshipped. And seriously, romance in a gay club environment usually lasts like ten minutes. I see guys falling head over heels in love at the drop of a hat, then they're over it as soon as the next hottie walks by."

"I'm not like that, Lorna, and you know it."

"I know you're not like that, baby. But what if Darren is?"

"He's not. I know he's not."

"Well then good. I have never before wanted so badly to be wrong about something. I honestly hope you're one hundred percent right. You know me, I'm a natural-born skeptic. You follow your heart and do what makes you happy, and I'll be your friend no matter what. Of course I support you." She smiled sweetly at him and reached over to place her hand atop his.

"Thanks, Lorna," he said.

"But remember, if anything bad does happen, I'm here for you."

"Oh brother," he said. "For a second there you had me convinced that you really did support me."

She scowled at him, puckered her lips, then finally laughed. "I love you, Tommy."

He shook his head and rolled his eyes again. "I love you, too," he conceded.

Chapter Twenty-two

Darren was stretched out on the sofa with his feet hanging over the edge, watching football, when Michael walked in. Michael tossed his duffel bag on the floor and shoved Darren's feet off the armrest to make a place for himself to sit. "Move over," he said.

Darren complied, without complaint, but remained fixated on the television.

"What'd you do last night? Just come home?" Michael asked.

"Yeah," Darren said. "How was your . . . um, date?"

Michael snatched the remote from the coffee table and clicked off the TV.

"Hey, I'm watching that!" Darren protested.

"Darren, I'm so fucking crazy about this guy," Michael gushed, ignoring Darren's protest.

"Who? That lawyer dude?" he asked. "Come on, you just met him."

"I know. It's so crazy. I'm starting to act like you."

Darren laughed. "Well, I brought that Tommy kid home last night," he said.

Michael scowled. "You better be careful. He's so young."

"He's almost our age! What're you talking about, and he's a total doll."

Michael sighed as he turned in his seat and placed his arm over the sofa's headrest. "I'm just saying, I bet he's not too experienced, and you're gonna end up hurting him. I bet he's like madly in love with you already."

"So what if he is? I'm fine with madly in love." He repositioned himself on the couch, scooting backward and plopped his feet in Michael's lap, who immediately shoved them away.

"I know *you're* fine with it, but you're gonna break his heart. You know we're leaving in a couple months. Have you even told him?"

"You're leaving in a couple months," Darren corrected him. "I haven't decided yet."

"And what's that supposed to mean? You're gonna stay here and live in the dorms?" Michael asked disbelievingly.

"Maybe. I don't know yet."

"Christ, you're already enrolled at NYU. Why you got to always do shit like this? You can't go changing your mind at the last minute. Plus we're a team and I can't afford an apartment in fucking New York by myself."

"So get a roommate," Darren suggested. "Or a rich lawyer friend to sponsor you." He smiled and winked at his brother.

"Darren!" Michael was frustrated. Darren could be such an irresponsible ass sometimes. "Look, just tell the kid. Tell him you like him and want to have a little fun, but don't get too serious."

"Fine. I'll tell him if you tell your lawyer the same thing."

"I already told Brandon about Columbia. It's no big deal. If he wants to see me, he's got the money to fly up there whenever he wants."

"You know, that is such bullshit," Darren said. "It's totally a double standard."

"A double standard? You can't be serious." Michael laughed incredulously. "We're talking apples and oranges here. Brandon is a thirty-three-year-old professional who owns his own home and three cars, a swimming pool, has a law practice for God's sake. Your kid is a college student!"

"What's that got to do with anything," Darren said, scowling at his brother. "You can be such a snob sometimes. Tommy's going to be a computer engineer and will probably end up making ten times the bucks as your lawyer dude. But really, who gives a fuck? It's not even about that. I like him, and that just pisses you off cause you're worried it might fuck up your plan." Darren sat up and turned away, picking the remote back up from the coffee table.

"It's *our* plan," Michael said. "Look, I'm sorry. I never would have thought..."

"You know, that's your problem. You *don't* think sometimes, or you think too much. Whatever. I don't even know yet what I'm going to do. I've only known this kid like three days or something, and we had fun. He's got a great ass and gives really good head." Darren looked over at Michael and smiled.

"I knew this was gonna happen when we started at this bar. We should've stayed at the other one."

"No, that place was bone dry. I couldn't make shit there anymore. Bunch of stingy old queens."

Michael sighed again. "Will you just try to at least play it cool and take things slow with that kid? Be honest with him. Do you really want to get involved with someone at this point anyway?"

Darren shrugged. "Maybe not, but I do like him."

"I'm sure you do. I'd probably like him, too. He seems really nice, but you don't have to marry every guy you think is nice. You don't even have to marry every guy you fuck."

"Well who said anything about marriage? It's not like you're about to marry your lawyer either."

Michael looked at him and raised his eyebrows.

Chapter Twenty-three

Tommy wasn't scheduled to work that evening. Sundays were usually a little slower, and they did not have as many dancers. He decided to go to the club after all because the twins were going to be working. It might be fun seeing Darren from the perspective of a customer rather than as a coworker. Bottom line was that he was truly obsessing over the guy and didn't want to wait any longer to see him. Tommy had class in the morning, though, so he wouldn't be able to stay until closing tonight.

He had to park his car about two blocks down due to the limited parking spaces on the street. There was a designated lot for employees, and he knew it would be okay to use it as long as there were ample spaces for those actually working. With only a few employees scheduled that evening, it was all good. Tommy pulled into one of the empty slots and quickly checked his appearance in the mirror before turning off the interior dome light and exiting his car.

It was about a quarter to eleven, and he knew the dancers would have just started. Had he not been so intent upon seeing Darren again, he may have been a bit more aware of his surroundings. He may have noticed the group of guys on the other side of the street and not crossed over until he was down at the corner under the light. He may have been more aware of how he was conducting himself and at least attempted to avoid appearing so bouncy and light on his feet. In other words, he might have tried to butch it up a bit so as not to look like a fag.

But Tommy didn't notice anything. He didn't think it through because he was focused upon one thing only—getting to Darren. And when he suddenly found himself surrounded, there was only one thing that he could feel—panic.

"Where ya goin, faggot?"

Tommy turned, attempting to distance himself from the voice, only to spin around and come face-to-face with one even more menacing.

"We're talkin to you, bitch!"

"Please... I don't have any money," Tommy squeaked. Laughter peeled through the night air. Someone shoved him. Another gruff voice.

Jeff Erno

"I said, where the fuck you goin? To the faggot bar? You goin to the faggot bar to find you some faggot dick to suck, bitch?"

This sort of thing didn't happen in real life. It happened in movies and books, or you saw it on the news. To Tommy it didn't seem real, and yet a wave of fear washed over him and he felt a surge of adrenaline course through him, but within a split second, he was trapped. Each of his arms were restrained by two of the street thugs, and his body was hurled against the building beside him. They held him there, pinning his arms and legs so he could not move, and all he could do was plead for mercy.

"Please, you can have my money. I don't have much!"

"Shut up, faggot!"

Pain shot through his abdomen as a fist suddenly connected. He gasped and tried to double over, but his assailants held him in place.

Suddenly all Tommy could see was a bright light. His arms were released, and he crumpled to the ground.

"Freeze! Hold it right there!"

Tommy heard loud voices and shouting and the sound of feet running, trampling quickly across the pavement. Then there was a hand on his shoulder. The light went away, and he squinted to focus.

"Are you okay?" Tommy looked up to see the face of a young officer, blonde and slender.

Tommy started to cry, tears streaming silently down his cheeks. He nodded as he realized he was shaking.

"Are you hurt anywhere? Bleeding? An ambulance is on the way." The officer's voice was soothing and very reassuring to Tommy.

"I'm okay," Tommy said. "Not bleeding."

"Darren," Tommy said. "I need Darren."

The officer was squatting down beside him. "Little guy, who's Darren? Is he your friend? Your boyfriend?"

"He works at the club . . . a dancer."

"And what is your name?"

"Tommy," he said. He felt as if he were going to throw up, and he couldn't stop shaking. "I don't need an ambulance. I need Darren."

"Okay, listen . . . you're safe now, and I'm not going to leave you, but we have to make sure you're okay. We have to have the paramedics look at you. I'll get Darren for you after the ambulance is here."

Tommy nodded, the tears still streaming down his face.

"My name's Kyle, and I'm going to help you. We'll wait for the ambulance together."

"Okay," Tommy whimpered. He stared into Kyle's blue eyes. The officer had a warm, friendly smile, but he seemed a little nerdy. That's okay. After all, Tommy himself was a bit of a geek. Tommy tried to smile at him.

Being that they were only a block from the club, the lights and siren attracted some attention from the bar patrons. Soon a crowd began to gather.

"Everyone back off," Kyle ordered. "There's nothing here to see." By this time, there were other officers and two paramedics.

Kyle had stepped away as the paramedics examined Tommy. They checked to make sure he was not in pain and was not bleeding before leading him over to the ambulance.

"I don't want to go to the hospital," he protested.

"It's just a precaution," the female paramedic told him. "Just to check you out and make sure you're not hurt."

Kyle stepped back over and again squatted down beside Tommy. "I have good news," he said. "We caught the guys, all three of them. I'm going to go see if I can find your friend now, okay? Are you going to be all right?"

"Sir, I don't wanna go to the hospital. I'm not hurt." All Tommy wanted to do was leave and find Darren.

"What is Darren's last name?" Kyle asked. "If I can find him, I'll bring him to the hospital."

"Maguire," Tommy said. "He's one of the dancers, and he has a twin brother."

"Got it," Kyle said. "Don't worry, it'll be okay. We'll meet you at the hospital."

"Thank you," Tommy said.

Chapter Twenty-four

As Michael strutted across the bar, gyrating his hips and posing sexily for one of his female customers, he couldn't help but notice a police officer at the door—a gangly, blonde guy, quite young, with a very serious look on his face. Somebody must've done something, Michael thought. He dismissed it and smiled sweetly at his customer. When he looked up, he realized the bouncer and the officer had approached the bar and were motioning for him to come down.

A bit startled, Michael sidestepped his customer and jumped down to the ground. "Something wrong?" he shouted. He had to speak loudly for his voice to carry over the music.

"Are you Darren Maguire?" the officer said.

Michael shook his head. "No, I'm Michael. Darren's my brother." What the fuck did Darren do, Michael wondered. "Is something wrong? Is my brother in trouble?"

The officer shook his head. "No, but I need to speak with him right away."

Michael turned and pointed to the other side of the bar. "He's over there."

"Please, don't call my mother," Tommy said to the nurse. "She'll go crazy."

"Are you sure, sweetie?" the heavyset lady said as she stood by his bedside.

"Yeah, my friend should be coming."

"You were very lucky," she said, "that the police officer happened to be there."

"I know," Tommy said, nodding. "He saved me." Just as Tommy said this, he looked up and saw the same officer walking into the room, and he had Darren with him. "Darren!" Tommy shouted.

Darren quickly stepped over to his bedside. "Oh God, are you all right?" he asked.

Tommy couldn't help it, he started to cry again. "Yes," he said, reaching up to throw his arms around Darren's neck. "Thank you for coming."

"Are you hurt?" Darren said, framing Tommy's face with the palms of his hands and gently kissing his forehead.

"No, they just punched me in the gut and scraped up the back of my arms a little. They would've done worse, but Kyle saved me." Tommy looked over at the officer.

"Officer Mason?" Darren said.

"Yeah, you can call me Kyle," he said, smiling broadly. "It's just luck that I happened to be there at that exact moment. Normally I don't walk down those side-streets when I'm on patrol."

"Well, we're sure glad you did tonight," Darren said.

"Darren, I'm sorry," Tommy said. "I . . . um, I shouldn't have asked for you. You're gonna lose your tip money tonight."

Darren waved his hand dismissively. "Nah, don't be silly. You're more important, and besides, it was a slow night tonight."

"I'll leave you guys alone for a bit," the nurse said. "I've got to get some paperwork together then I'll be back to release you." She reached down and squeezed Tommy's hand.

"Thanks, Brenda," Tommy said. "Thank you for being so nice."

"How could anyone not be nice to a cute little guy like you?" she asked.

"Exactly," Darren said, rubbing his hand affectionately across the top of Tommy's head. He sat down on the edge of the mattress as Brenda exited the room. Kyle stepped over to stand beside them.

"So you got to ride in a police car?" Tommy asked, grinning.

"Nope," Darren said.

"I'm on street patrol tonight," Kyle explained, "so I don't have a car. We drove over here in my own car."

"Those cheapskates don't even give you a car to use?" Tommy objected. "Geesh."

"Well, I could've called for a car, but I wanted to come myself to see if you were okay. Remember I promised I'd see you at the hospital." As he smiled warmly at Tommy, he reached up and pushed his glasses back on his nose. Tommy thought to himself that Kyle really didn't look much like a cop. He looked more like a kid dressed up in a police officer uniform for Halloween.

"Who were these guys who attacked him?" Darren asked. "Do we know?"

"A gang," Kyle said. "Racists. It's part of their initiation to jump a minority—either a gay person or someone who's not white. They especially like to pick on Blacks and Latinos."

"So they were like just hanging around near the bar waiting for someone?"

Kyle nodded. "More than likely. You should talk to the bar owner and tell him that your parking arrangement is not safe. Or at the very least, you shouldn't ever come alone."

"We usually come together," Darren said, winking.

Kyle blushed, and Tommy started to laugh.

"No, seriously, I know what you mean, and usually when I get there I'm with my brother."

"I heard about you and your brother," Kyle said. "I can't believe I actually got to meet you."

"You heard about us?" Darren said, sounding surprised. "You mean we have a reputation?"

"Well, I have a friend who goes to that bar. He told me there was a pair of twin go-go boys that just started. I was sort of curious, ya know—that whole 'twin fascination' thing."

"Ahh," Darren said as he nodded knowingly. "So is that why you were hanging around the bar?"

Quickly Kyle shook his head. His face was still beet read. "Oh no, not at all. I ... um, well I normally am assigned to street patrol anyway. If I got the chance I was going to peek in, if I could come up with a good excuse."

"And what a coincidence," Darren said, "that you ended up having to come inside and ask specifically for me."

"Yeah, right?" Kyle said. "Funny how things work out sometimes."

There was a bit of awkwardness for a moment, until Tommy finally decided to speak. "Well I'm so glad your friend told you about Darren and Michael. If not, you might not've been there and I might be dead right now."

Kyle nodded vigorously. "True, very true." He really did look kind of nerdy, but when he smiled he was kind of cute, Tommy thought.

Darren stood up and turned toward Kyle. "So let me ask you something, officer." He'd lowered his voice to almost a whisper. "Are you ..." Darren raised his eyebrows without finishing his sentence.

"Gay?" Kyle finished for him. He smiled. "Yeah."

"I thought so," Darren said, placing his hand on Kyle's shoulder. "You look pretty good in that uniform, if I may say so."

Kyle's face really did redden at that point. "Thanks," he said. "But ya know, I'm on duty."

"Oh ... sorry. What time are you off?"

Tommy felt a pang of jealousy in that instant, but he knew Darren was just being Darren. Flirting as usual.

"Well honestly I'm almost done with my shift." He looked at his watch. "Oh, it was supposed to be over at midnight—twenty minutes ago. After I take you two back, I'll have to return to the precinct to fill out a report, then I'll be done."

"Why don't you let us wait for you, and we'll take you out for a bite to eat or a drink or something? You know, just as a way to express our appreciation," Darren suggested.

Kyle looked first at Darren then over to Tommy. "Hmm, well I guess..."

"We insist," Darren said. "It's the least we can do."

Chapter Twenty-five

Tommy was sitting in the back seat of the car while Darren rode shotgun in the front passenger seat. When they got to the police station, Tommy and Darren waited in the car. Darren called the bar and first spoke to Deejay, letting him know the status of Tommy. He then asked to talk to Michael.

Tommy decided not to call Lorna or his mom. There was no point in worrying them when everything was okay. He'd tell them both about the incident in the morning. He was extremely grateful that Kyle had happened to be there at the exact minute he needed help, and he wished there was something he could do to repay him. On the other hand, he couldn't help but feel a bit jealous of the way that Darren kept flirting with Kyle.

Kyle wasn't all that attractive to Tommy, although he had to admit he was kind of cute in a nerdy sort of way. It made sense that Darren would like him. He'd already said numerous times that he was attracted to that type of guy. Tommy really just wished the whole incident had never happened. He didn't know how to compete with a guy like Kyle who was a little older and more confident. To be honest, he didn't want to even try competing. It just wasn't in his nature to be competitive.

Darren seemed very relaxed though, and he actually was quite flirtatious with both Tommy and Kyle. That was just Darren. Probably what bugged Tommy more than anything was the manner in which Kyle kept checking Darren out. Well it really was kind of hard to be around a guy like Darren without noticing those rippling muscles and those tight, rock-hard abs, not to mention Darren's perfect set of pearly whites. When he smiled he just made Tommy's heart melt a little more each time.

When Kyle hopped back in the car he was wearing his street clothes—jeans and polo pullover. He looked casual and he smelled really good. Obviously he'd taken a quick shower while inside because his hair was still damp.

"Hope I didn't take too long," Kyle said.

"Nah. I called my bro and told him Tommy was all right. You scared the hell out of him when you walked in and called him down from the bar."

Kyle laughed. "Sorry. Did he think I'd come to arrest him?"

"I don't know, but the first thing I noticed when I saw you was that big club of yours. Then the handcuffs."

Kyle kept smiling. "I bet you have a pretty big club of your own." Tommy cleared his throat and coughed. Kyle glanced back at him. "Oh, sorry. I take it by your reaction that you agree."

"Yeah," Tommy said. "It's pretty big."

Darren was obviously loving the attention. "Big enough," he said. "There's plenty to go around."

Tommy didn't know exactly how to respond to this. He'd only been seeing Darren for a couple of days. It wasn't like they were officially a couple or anything, but he really wanted to be Darren's boyfriend. It was starting to seem that Darren might not have the same degree of interest.

When they got to the all-night diner, Tommy and Darren sat together on one side of the booth across from Kyle. Tommy was relieved when Darren draped his arm around the back of the seat and occasionally hugged him. Tommy rested his hand on Darren's thigh. They were in a district that was pretty gay-friendly, and Darren was not a bit shy about showing affection. A couple of times he even leaned over and kissed Tommy on the lips.

These mixed signals were confusing to Tommy. It seemed that Darren was oblivious to how it was making him feel. Darren was very carefree and continued to make suggestive remarks toward Kyle, yet at the same time, he remained affectionate and rather protective of Tommy.

"Why'd you become a police officer?" Darren asked.

Kyle's manner was very self-effacing, and he smiled sweetly. It was obvious he was not entirely comfortable talking about himself. "I just always knew," he said. "I was interested in law enforcement back in high school, and I started researching different fields I could go into. I could be a probation officer, a federal marshal, a game warden, or even a prison guard. There are so many different areas of criminal justice I could have gone into, but bottom line is this is what I really wanted. It's what I love—being a beat cop."

"So you have a degree?" Darren asked.

"Yeah, I have a degree in criminal justice, and I went to police academy."

"Wow, you don't seem old enough." Darren said.

"Twenty-six. Well, it's just an Associates Degree. I've been a police officer for six years."

"And you're gay. That's so cool. I wish we had more gay cops," Tommy said.

Kyle looked directly at Tommy and smiled. "You know, that's what I thought, too, and that was really why I decided that this was what I wanted to do. Back in school, I used to get bullied a lot, and there were other kids who had it a lot worse than me.

"I didn't really know how to deal with it. There wasn't much I could do. My escape was comics, and I had zillions of them. Lately—these past few years—they've come out with all these super hero movies. Well, I know all of em. Spiderman, Superman, Green Lantern, Captain America—you name it.

"I guess being a cop is the closest thing to a super hero that I can think of."

"Well, you're our super hero," Darren said. "It was really cool that even after you saved Tommy from getting beat up, you stayed with him then came to get me, took me to the hospital. All of it—it's just really awesome what you did."

His face reddened a bit. He was a strawberry blonde, very fair, and it was obvious when he was blushing.

"Don't you have a boyfriend?" Darren asked.

"Can you believe a hot guy like me is single?" he said sarcastically, holding his arms out to his side. "Where's the justice in that?"

Darren shook his head, laughing. "No kidding. I bet guys are lining up to date you."

Kyle busted up laughing. His laugh was hearty, and Tommy thought it rather sweet, the way his whole body seemed to shake a bit and his shoulders jiggled. It was rather infectious, and the three of them were soon laughing together.

"How long have you two been together?" he asked.

Darren looked at Tommy. "What's it been? Three or four days? We just met last week."

"And it was love at first sight?" Kyle asked, somewhat jokingly.

"Tommy took one look at me and fell head over heels," Darren said. He wasn't being serious, but Tommy knew it was true. "Nah, actually we both started working at the club on the same night. We hit it off right away. "

"Wow, it just seemed you'd been together a long time."

Darren hugged Tommy, squeezing his shoulder. "Really we're still getting to know each other, and now we're getting to know you."

Kyle raised his eyebrows, not responding. He took a drink of his water and set it down in front of him. "I can't believe I ordered pancakes."

After they finished eating, they sat in the diner for about an hour talking, and finally Darren suggested that they take Tommy back to get his car. "If you don't mind, we can follow Tommy home. Make sure he gets in all right."

Tommy was a little disappointed. He'd hoped Darren would ask him to spend the night again, but he also knew he had class the next day and it was already two in the morning. When he pulled into his driveway, Darren got out of Kyle's car and walked over to him. He escorted Tommy to the door.

"Are you gonna be all right?" he asked.

"Sure," Tommy said. He wanted to ask Darren the same thing. He wanted to ask if *they* were going to be all right, and if anything was going to happen with Kyle. He didn't have the courage to say it though. It killed him to think that Darren was going to get back in the car with Kyle and leave, and Tommy would have no control over what he did. "I'm not really even tired," was all Tommy could manage to say.

"Well, you look beat," Darren said. "You should get some sleep. What you went through tonight would wear anyone out."

Tommy grabbed hold of him, feeling himself again being overcome with emotion. He didn't want Darren to go. He didn't want Darren to leave him, but to say it out loud would sound so damned needy. "Can I call you tomorrow?" Tommy asked.

"Sure, sure you can. I don't work the next two days. Maybe we can do something."

"Really?" Tommy asked.

"Yeah ... of course." Darren pushed Tommy back, holding him by the shoulders in order to look him in the eye. "Are you sure you're okay?"

Tommy nodded and looked up at him. "I'm fine. Thank you so much ... for coming to the hospital and everything."

Darren leaned in and kissed him. "Go sleep, okay? Call me in the morning ... no wait. Make it the afternoon." Darren laughed. "I'm really not a morning person."

"I know," Tommy said, smiling. "Good night."

They shared one last kiss, and then Darren left. Tommy quietly made his way up to his room without looking for Lorna or his other roommates. They were probably asleep already. He fell asleep thinking of Darren and wondering what would become of the situation with Kyle.

Chapter Twenty-Six

"Okay, dinner tonight," Michael said into the phone. "I already miss you. Can you believe it?

"Good bye, now . . . yes . . . okay . . . sleep well . . . night."

He smiled to himself as he set his phone down on the coffee table. Brandon hadn't come to the club tonight because he was working Monday morning, yet here it was at almost three in the morning and they were on the phone together. Michael had been surprised when Brandon had called at two-thirty. He said he couldn't sleep and had been thinking of Michael. They were going to do dinner Monday night.

When he heard the door, he turned to greet his brother. He was a bit surprised to see that Darren was not alone.

"Hey," Michael said, standing up, "how is he?"

"Tommy? He's fine. Scraped up his arms and legs a little. Other than that, he was just really scared."

"How terrible . . . I mean, for that to happen right there, so close to the club."

"You met Kyle, right?"

Michael stepped over to shake Kyle's hand. "Well, we didn't officially meet. Not on a first name basis, anyway.

"Hi, I'm Michael." He extended his hand.

"It's nice to meet you," Kyle said.

"Can I get ya a beer or something?" Michael offered.

"Um, yah sure. Why not. Thanks. Hey, can I use your restroom?"

"Right through there," Darren said, pointing down the hall.

"Thanks," Kyle said. "Be right back."

As Michael stepped into the kitchen to grab a beer from the refrigerator, he motioned to Darren with a nod of his head, signaling him to the kitchen. "What the hell are you doing?" he asked in a hushed tone.

"What do you mean?" Darren asked innocently.

"Come on! Why are you bringing a guy home?"

"I'm not allowed to bring someone home now?" Darren replied.
"Bro, just yesterday you were like all crazy over that kid."
"So. Can't I be crazy over two guys at once?"

He always answered every question with a question, and it was infuriating to Michael. "I told you yesterday, you're gonna end up breaking that kid's heart. This isn't cool."

"Michael, I just met Tommy like four days ago, so chill. I'm not breaking anyone's heart, and besides, Kyle just saved Tommy's life. I want to repay him . . . or at least express my gratitude."

"Oh come on!" Michael guffawed. "You're kidding, right?"

"He's totally my type, Michael. Look at him! He's adorable."

"Well, try to keep it down," Michael said. "I'm going to bed." He handed Darren the beer and stepped toward the living room, on his way to his bedroom.

"Wait! Dude, I was hoping . . ."

"What?" Michael asked, frustrated.

"I was hoping you could help me."

Michael stared at him, squinting. "No way," he said, matter of factly. "No fucking way."

"Come on! He has a fascination with twins . . . it's his fantasy."

"Every man on the fucking planet has a fascination with twins. Big deal. *Brandon* has a fascination with twins . . ." Michael suddenly remembered his conversation with Brandon and how he'd promised him to talk to his brother.

"Okay then!" Darren said, stepping over and placing his hand on his brother's shoulder. "You help me out, and I'll help you out. You scratch my back, and I'll scratch yours."

Michael couldn't believe what he was hearing. "So . . . you're asking me to do a three-way with this guy you just met a couple hours ago, and in exchange you'll fool around with me and Brandon?"

"Exactly," Darren said, smiling.

"And what about the kid?"

"Tommy? What about him? I'm doing this for Tommy."

"Come again?" Michael couldn't believe some of the stupid shit Darren came up with sometimes. *This ought to be real good.*

"Kyle saved Tommy, and I just want to say thank you."

"You just want to get your rocks off. Who do you think you're kidding?"

"Well that, too," Darren admitted, grinning evilly. "So do we have a deal?"

Michael rolled his eyes and sighed. "All right, but I'm not getting fucked."

"He's a bottom, Michael."

"How do you know?" Michael asked.

"Trust me. I fucking *know*. You take the front, and I'll take the back."

"You're so crude sometimes," Michael said.

"I know," Darren said, laughing.

Chapter Twenty-seven

Tommy's ringtone awakened him. At first confused, he glanced over at the digital clock on the nightstand. It was 3:02 AM. Quickly he picked up his phone and smiled when he saw who was calling.

"Hi, Deejay," he answered.

"Were you asleep already?"

"No, I just got home," he lied. "I'm lying here but not asleep yet."

"Oh man, I'm sorry. I'll just call you in the . . ."

"No wait, you're fine," Tommy said. "I'm glad you called."

"I just wanted to check on you. I was still kind of busy when Darren called earlier. He's not still with you?"

"Nah, we went and grabbed a bite to eat, then he followed me home. Kyle was taking him back home."

"Kyle?"

"The cop," Tommy said.

"Oh yeah, that skinny one that came in here," Deejay said knowingly.

"He's the one who saved me," Tommy explained. "He was on patrol and saw those . . . um . . . whatever they were, thugs or gang members or whatever—he saw them and rescued me."

"Thank God. Fuck, I was so worried about you. I should have just called Ron and told him I had an emergency."

"Oh no! No, you didn't need to do anything like that. I was okay. I wasn't even hurt, other than a few scratches." Tommy couldn't believe Deejay would say something so sweet. "To be honest, I'm kind of embarrassed about going to the hospital and all when I wasn't even injured."

"You shouldn't be embarrassed, man. It's a good thing they took you to the ER and checked you out. Sometimes when you're in those sorts of situations, you get hurt pretty bad and don't even realize it. Your adrenaline is pumping and you don't even feel anything."

"You're right. It didn't even seem real to me. It was like some sort of bad dream or something, like it was happening to someone else and I was just watching." Tommy thought he might start to get emotional again.

"Hey, are you sure you're gonna be all right?"

A tear began to stream down his cheeks. He reached up angrily and wiped it away. "Yeah, I'm fine."

"You don't sound fine," Deejay said. "You want me to come over?"

"Well . . . no, I have class in the morning."

"Can't you miss one class? Look what happened to you." He was silent for a moment, waiting for Tommy to respond. "Look, I'm right outside. I'm at your house right now. Please let me come in just so I know you're okay."

"Deejay, how'd you even know where . . . "

"Your application. I got your address from your application, and I don't live far from here. I couldn't go home til I knew you were all right, and dude, you don't sound all right . . . not at all. Please at least let me see you."

"I'll be right down. Wait at the door."

Chapter Twenty-eight

"Why don't you have a seat on the sofa," Michael said, motioning for Kyle to sit down. Once Kyle was seated, he slipped around him and sat down himself. "So I heard about what you did. That was really brave the way you saved that kid." Michael placed his hand on Kyle's lower thigh, just above his knee.

Darren stepped up behind them, reaching around Kyle and handing him his beer. "Yeah, that was really impressive," he said.

Kyle's face looked flushed. "I was really just doing my job," he said.

Darren placed his hand on Kyle's shoulder. "You're a hero," he said. "And I like heroes. I think they're sexy, and they turn me on." Darren was smiling broadly.

Kyle laughed nervously.

Darren leaned in and kissed Kyle on the cheek, nuzzling his nose into Kyle's neck. "And you looked so hot in that uniform," he whispered.

That was Michael's cue, and he slid his hand smoothly up Kyle's thigh until he finally stopped at his crotch, squeezing gently. With his other hand, he took the beer bottle from Kyle and placed it on the coffee table.

At first Kyle stiffened, but soothing words of encouragement and four hands on his body soon helped him to relax. Darren began massaging his shoulders, and Michael slid off the couch, kneeling down between Kyle's legs. As Michael looked up, he saw Darren's lips connecting with Kyle's.

Briefly, Kyle pulled back. "But what about . . . your boyfriend?"

"Kyle, I don't have a boyfriend," Darren said sweetly. "If you mean Tommy, we just met. He's very cute, but we aren't really a couple, and . . . well . . . Tommy's just a boy."

"I just, um, don't wanna split anyone up."

"Shh, don't worry babe. You're not splitting anyone up. We're just having a little fun." He leaned in again and kissed Kyle once more, this time passionately.

As they were kissing, Michael began unbuttoning Kyle's jeans. Once he had the fly open, he reached down and tugged off Kyle's sneakers, one at a time, tossing them aside. Grabbing hold of the waistband of Kyle's jeans and undershorts he said quietly, "Lift up for me, guy." Kyle thrust his hips forward slightly, raising his bum enough for Michael to slide of his pants.

Simultaneously, Darren pulled Kyle's polo over his head.

"Nice!" Michael said with genuine enthusiasm as he took in the sight of Kyle's eight-inch hardon. "Bro, this officer's got one hell of a Billy club," he said, chuckling.

Darren slid his hand across his chest, inching his way down to Kyle's abs. "Oh fuck yeah," he whispered, "and look how rock hard he is. Michael, I think Officer Kyle is really glad to see you." Darren grabbed hold of the shaft while Michael gently cupped his ball sac.

"Aw fuck, you guys," Kyle responded, sighing dramatically.

"Looks pretty tasty," Darren said. "Why don't you go ahead and try it, Bro." Still holding Kyle's cock in his hand, he pushed it outward, away from Kyle's body and toward Michael's face. Eagerly Michael responded by grabbing hold of the baton that was passed to him and sliding his mouth around the bulbous head.

As Michael sucked him, Darren hopped over the back of the sofa, so that he was seated beside Kyle. He began playing with Kyle's nipples and again kissing him passionately. Kyle didn't seem to know what to do with his hands. He had one hand on Michael's shoulder and with the other was caressing Darren's cheek.

"You guys, take your clothes off . . . please."

"You didn't get enough of us earlier . . . when you saw us dancing at the club?" Darren teased.

"I don't think I can ever get enough of you," Kyle said, gasping. He drilled his tongue into Darren's mouth

As they continued, the twins began to disrobe, carelessly throwing each article of clothing aside. After Michael was completely naked, he renewed his focus on Kyle's cock, now sucking with even more intensity. Kyle grabbed hold of Darren's cock, who was now kneeling on the sofa beside him. Kyle started to stroke it while Darren continued to play with Kyle's nipples and kiss his face and neck.

Michael could sense that Kyle was getting excited and possibly approaching orgasm. He slowed and backed off a bit, not wanting to get Kyle off too soon.

"You wanna come in the bedroom with us?" Darren suggested. "I have a big king-sized bed."

Kyle nodded eagerly. Michael stood and took Kyle by the hand, helping him up off the couch. Darren took hold of Kyle's other hand, and the three made their way down the hall to Darren's bedroom. Michael slid onto the mattress, on his back as Kyle did the same, lying right beside him. Kyle began caressing Michael's chest, kissing his skin, and running his tongue across the hardening nubs of Michael's nipples.

Darren was behind them, retrieving a condom and lube from his bureau. By the time he'd slipped the condom on and lubed up his fingers, Kyle had already found Michael's hard cock. Michael lay back, enjoying the sensation of the warm mouth that surrounded him.

Michael stared up at his brother as he placed his hands on Kyle's narrow hips. Gently he pulled his ass checks apart then bent down, burying his face in the upturned mounds. Kyle moaned as he continued to suck Michael, hungrily devouring the entirety of his shaft. Michael began to thrust upward with his pelvis, driving his cock deeply into Kyle's tight throat, while Darren continued his tongue bath of Kyle's manhole.

Darren pulled his face from Kyle's ass and quickly replaced it with his fingers, apparently drilling at least one up the slender officer's chute. Michael stared down at Kyle's face, watching his expression of sheer ecstasy as Darren found his sweet spot.

Michael pulled out of Kyle's mouth and slid from beneath him. He placed an arm around Kyle's shoulder and pulled him into an upright position so he was kneeling, though bent slightly forward. He reached around to the front of Kyle, grabbed hold of his throbbing cock, and began to stroke it.

Darren slid his cock into Kyle's tight hole right about the time Michael slid down on his belly and again began sucking his cock. Darren buried himself deeply in Kyle's ass while Kyle drilled his cock into Michael's throat. Darren grabbed hold of Kyle's shoulders and began to fuck—hard.

As Darren drilled the slender, strawberry-blonde police officer, Michael sucked his cock ferociously. Kyle was holding onto Michael's shoulders, trying to steady himself and Darren was holding onto Kyle. Michael felt Kyle's cock throbbing in his mouth. Kyle began to moan loudly. "Fuck! I'm gonna cum! I'm gonna . . . ungghhh!"

Michael pulled off of Kyle's cock just as it erupted, spraying a jet of jizz right across his lips and face. Michael had hold of the base of the firing love pistol, and he pumped it, milking out the copious load. Burst after burst erupted, spraying across Michael's neck and shoulders.

Darren was sweaty as he continued to drill deeply into Kyle's tight hole. His face twisted in agony as he approached orgasm. Finally, he thrust in deeply, burying himself, and moaned pleasurably. Michael knew he was cumming.

He'd seen it many times before.

Michael rolled over onto his back and jacked his own cock, quickly bringing himself to the point of no return. He blasted a huge load over his own abdomen and chest, and the three collapsed together onto the mattress, exhausted.

Chapter Twenty-nine

Tommy and Deejay lay together on Tommy's single bed. Deejay was fully clothed and Tommy was in his boxers and tee shirt—his pajamas. The bed was small which made it cozy, and Tommy loved the feel of Deejay's strong protective arms around him. He rolled over to face Deejay, laying his head into the crook of the bigger man's arm.

"What if he doesn't love me the way I love him?" Tommy asked.

"Then you find someone better, someone who appreciates you. You deserve someone who truly loves you."

"I think they're together," Tommy said. "I think he took Kyle home with him."

"And now we're together," Deejay said, "and everything's gonna be okay."

"It just hurts so bad," Tommy said, the tears streaming down his cheeks.

"I know," Deejay said, "and I'm sorry. I wish I could make it stop hurting for you. Would it help if I told you I thought you were really cute? Downright sexy, in fact."

"No!" Tommy protested, then suddenly stopped, his body stiffening. "Well . . . yes."

"Good," Deejay said soothingly, "because it's true."

They lay there together until Tommy fell back asleep. When he woke a few hours later, he was sad to see that Deejay had left, but he smiled to himself when he found the note Deejay had left on his dresser. He was right, everything was going to be all right.

Chapter Thirty

Michael climbed into the passenger seat of the BMW, leaning over to kiss Brandon hello. "Did ya miss me?" he asked.

"Very much," Brandon replied.

"I need to talk to you," Michael said seriously.

Worried, Brandon looked at him. "What's wrong?"

Michael shook his head reassuringly. "Oh nothing. Nothing's wrong... really. It's about our conversation the other day, when you asked about Darren and me..."

"Never mind that. I've been thinking," Brandon said. "You're enough. I don't need some lame fantasy of doing it with twins. What I need is you and only you."

"Really?" Michael said, smiling.

"Yes, absolutely." He leaned in and kissed Michael again on the lips, this time more passionately.

"Well that was what I was going to talk to you about. I don't think I can do it, but I have to tell you something."

"What is it, baby?" Brandon said.

"Darren brought a guy home last night."

"That young guy from the bar?"

"No, a different guy this time—a cop actually. He talked me into doing something with them, and in exchange he was going to do a three-way with you and me."

Brandon's expression was serious. "And what happened?"

"Well, we did it, and... um, well it was fine I guess. The cop liked it anyway. So did Darren, and to be honest, I got my rocks off... but then on the other hand, I guess I didn't really like it after all. I mean I've done it before, and it was kind of hot, but I can't imagine you and me doing that."

"I can't either," Brandon said.

"I told Darren this morning that was it, I won't be playing with him that way anymore."

Brandon smiled. "Good."

"I only wanna play with you," Michael said sexily.

"Mmm, can we go play now?"

"I thought you'd never ask."

They kissed again before Brandon put the car in gear and pulled away from the curb.

Chapter Thirty-One

"Tommy, someone's at the door for you," one of his roommates hollered up the staircase

"Be right there!" He quickly jumped up from his desk chair and headed out the door and down the hall. As he made it to the foyer, he was a bit startled to see who it was.

"Hey, Darren," he said.

"Sorry I didn't call you this week," he said.

"It's okay," Tommy said. "We both work tonight anyway, and you could have talked to me there."

"Actually, that's why I'm here. I won't be there tonight. In fact, I don't work there anymore."

"Oh? And Michael?"

"We both decided to do something else." Tommy looked into his eyes and thought they looked so sad.

"Wow, that's a surprise," Tommy said. "You two were a big hit."

"Well I should have told you this from the beginning, but we were only planning to be there a short time anyway. We're moving to New York."

"You did tell me that . . . or you said your brother was."

"Well, I am too. I'm going to NYU."

"Okay," Tommy said. "How'd everything go with Kyle?"

"It went fine," Darren replied. "Look . . . I'm sorry. That's why I'm here. I never meant to hurt you. I was really attracted to you, though. You've got to know that. I was crazy about you."

"For three glorious days," Tommy said, laughing softly.

"I'm sorry . . . really."

Tommy stepped over and placed his hand against Darren's bicep. "No, don't be sorry. I'm serious, it was three of the most glorious days of my life. Oh my God, I had passionate sex with a hot go-go dancer, and he kissed me like a million times."

"You're a sweetheart," Darren said, "and you deserve a good guy. To be honest, that's why I need to end this now. I really don't want to hurt you. I don't want to lead you on and let you think that there's a possibility that I'm gonna be ready for something serious right now."

"I appreciate that," Tommy said honestly. "Plus, you really have the hots for Kyle."

Darren shrugged. "That too," he admitted.

"Sunday night when you dropped me off, I was devastated," Tommy said frankly. "I couldn't believe you would leave me and go off with some other guy, not after what had happened."

"Like I said, you deserve someone—"

Tommy shook his head. "No, it's not about what I deserve. That's not what I'm saying. I'm saying that it really made me think. It was totally crazy that I thought I was in love after knowing you for like two days. Silly actually." He laughed quietly to himself. "But that's what happens. It seems like the guys at the club do it all the time. They fall in love in like ten minutes. They're ready to get married and live happily ever after . . . until the next hottie comes along.

"I want more than that. I want a guy who is totally hot for me, who thinks I'm the greatest thing since sliced bread, but one who is going to think that same thing tomorrow and the next day and the day after that. And I don't want to have to worry about him hopping in bed with the next hot guy that walks—or dances—by."

"I understand," Darren said.

"And do you understand that I hope you eventually find someone like that, too?"

Darren smiled. "Yeah, I truly believe you mean that."

"I do," Tommy said. "But for now, go on. Have fun . . . Kyle's probably waiting for you somewhere."

It actually looked as if Darren were blushing.

"It's okay, really it is," Tommy assured him. He reached down and grabbed hold of Darren's hand. He looked at it as he patted it gently with his other hand. He stared for a moment, noticing there was no scar on his middle finger.

He looked back into Michael's eyes. "Thank you for coming. It means a lot to me."

"You're welcome."

Michael leaned down and kissed him sweetly on the lips. Tommy let him out and watched him as he crossed the street and climbed into the passenger seat of the BMW.

Chapter Thirty-two

"Tommy, I need a couple more sleeves of cups!" Deejay shouted.

"What?" Tommy hollered. He was in the storage room, and Deejay was out at the bar. "I couldn't hear you. I was coming out of the cooler."

"Baby, can you bring me more cups?"

Tommy stood in the doorway and stared out at the bar. God that man was sexy, with his rippling muscles and gorgeous smile. "Sure," he said, "I'll grab em and be right there."

He turned and dashed back down the hall, reaching up to grab two sleeves of cups from the rack. As he turned around, Deejay's arms surrounded him. "Hey," Tommy said. "How'd you get back here so fast? I just saw you at the bar . . . Um, you don't have a twin or something, do you?"

Deejay laughed. "Hell no. I just saw you standing there looking so sexy and ran back here."

"Good, cause I only need one of you. That's more than enough."

As Deejay pulled Tommy into his chest, Tommy forgot all about the cups and dropped them on the floor. He wrapped his arms tightly around Deejay's neck and kissed him passionately.

"I love you," Tommy said.

"Not as much as I love you," Deejay replied.

"Hey, it's only eight-thirty," Tommy said.

"And?"

"And that gives you time to help me in the walk-in cooler."

"To help you?"

"I need some help, yeah. I need to unwrap my pepperoni."

"But we don't sell pizza here," Deejay said with mock seriousness.

"I know," Tommy smiled as he pulled his lover in for another passionate kiss."

Cocktails
Men's Room Book Two

By

Jeff Erno

Cocktails

"Sir, are you all right?"

The flight attendant was leaning over him, her hand resting on the back of his seat. Dutch gulped and nodded, fiercely gripping the armrests of his chair. "I'm fine, ma'am," he said, trying to sound convincing. "I guess I'm a little nervous about flying."

"Oh, now don't you worry. It'll be over before you know it. Do you need something for motion sickness? Glass of water or anything?"

Dutch shook his head. "Really, I'm fine." *Really,* Dutch was not fine. He had a terrible fear of flying. Once in the air, he'd be all right, but he suffered overwhelming anxiety prior to takeoffs and during landings. He tried to avoid flying at all costs, but sometimes there was no way around it.

He had to be in New Orleans that afternoon to meet with the executor of his late aunt's estate. Normally, he'd have either driven his pickup from Dallas or rented a car. It was only about an eight-hour road-trip. He simply didn't have time.

"Whiskey," he blurted out. "Ya'll have Crown Royal?"

She smiled sweetly. "Why, yes. I'll get that for you right away. On the rocks?"

"Straight up," he answered.

Dutch wasn't much of a drinker either. He liked to have a cold beer occasionally but wasn't one to go out and get smashed. If ever there were a better time to get drunk, he couldn't say when that would be. Then again, he needed to be at least somewhat clear-headed for his afternoon meeting with the attorney.

Delta always had been Dutch's favorite relative. She'd had no children of her own, and in a way Dutch thought she considered him to be her son. During his youth, he'd spent part of every summer at her home. He had loved those Louisiana vacations. Those three weeks were the only time during the summer that he wasn't working his tail off. Now Aunt Delta was gone. It didn't seem possible.

Dutch tossed back the drink quickly, then placed the glass on the tray in front of him. He closed his eyes and inhaled, trying to calm himself. He was thankful he'd paid the extra money for a first-class ticket. Dutch could just hear what his daddy would say about wasting money like that for such a short flight. "Damn foolishness!"

He didn't care. It was his money and Daddy wasn't around anymore to bitch at him. Besides, Delta would have insisted he fly first class. Everything she did was stylish and sophisticated. She had smoked those long, 120 mm cigarettes and drank imported wine from crystal champagne glasses. She was outspoken and sassy, and she'd never given a rip what anyone had to say about her.

Aunt Delta was the only person in Dutch's family that he'd come out to. In fact, he didn't really even remember a dramatic moment in which he'd made an earth-shattering revelation to her. She seemed to have always known. Come to think of it, she was the one who wove it into the conversation. They were at one of the clothing emporiums, and Delta was sifting through the racks of young men's shirts. She pulled one off the rack and held it up for his inspection.

"Why Dutch, wouldn't you be just dashing in this?"

He smiled and nodded eagerly.

"You'd surely catch the eye of a handsome young suitor wearing a blouse such as this."

He felt his face redden and responded, "Aunt Delta, we don't call them blouses. I'm a boy, so it's a shirt."

"Oh tsk," she said. "You're still going to be dashing," and she bought it for him.

She had just sensed the truth about Dutch. She knew it instinctively, and seemed to take it with a grain of salt. They never had late night conversations where he'd cried and confessed to her how he'd agonized over his sexuality. They never discussed the morality or immorality of being homosexual. Dutch just was himself when he was around Aunt Delta, and that was the beauty of their relationship.

During the winter months, Dutch would write to her. He told her of his first crush, which resulted in his first kiss. He told her how he and his classmate Clancy had to sneak around and keep everything secret. His letters described their personal hiding space where they had their rendezvous, a loft in the barn. And when Delta replied to his written correspondence, she was careful to always remain discreet. Never once did she betray any of his confidences.

A tear streamed down Dutch's face as he recalled the memories of his dear aunt. Her death had been so sudden and so unexpected. Well, not entirely. Dutch had known she was getting up there in years. He knew she wouldn't be around forever. Perhaps it was a blessing that she went quickly. A long, protracted illness would not have been befitting.

He held his glass up as the flight attendant approached. "One more," he said.

"We'll be landing in about fifteen minutes, sir," she said, reaching out to take the glass from him.

"Perfect," he said, "then make that one a double."

"Michigan sucks," the young man said, nodding his head as he stared at the girl sitting beside him. "It's too dang cold."

"Yeah, like it seems they always have like ten feet of snow." She was chewing a big wad of gum, which she had insisted was most helpful in preventing her ears from "popping" due to the change in cabin pressure.

Every time he flew, Rustin seemed to get stuck sitting next to someone like this. When he first sat down, he'd pulled out a book and placed it on his lap. He'd even opened it and begun reading, but of course that didn't matter. People who were talkers didn't notice details like that. They thought what they had to say was all that mattered. After four or five attempts to get into the story, he finally gave up and tucked the book back into his laptop case.

"Well, I'll be glad to leave the cold weather behind," he said and smiled at the girl sweetly.

"You know, you have the most beautiful smile," she said. "You should be a model or something. Or no wait—a bartender. You know how the really good bartenders are? Always smiling. Always making every single customer feel like they are most important person in the world. That's how you are with that sweet smile of yours."

"Thank you," he said as he struggled to maintain eye contact and accept her compliment gracefully.

"I could never be a bartender myself," she said. "I just can't stand when complete strangers feel the need to like share their whole life story. I'm like, 'Who do I look like? Dear Abby?' Well, plus I don't like stay in any one place long enough to keep a steady job like that. That's why this job I have now is just perfect for me."

Rustin took a deep breath and continued to smile at her as sweetly as he could.

"I never thought I could make a living off selling cleaning products, but ya know, this stuff sells itself. Oh here, let me get you a catalog." She reached into her carry-on and pulled out what appeared to be a pamphlet. "And the best thing about our line of products is that they are 100% guaranteed. Sure, they like cost a little bit more, but they are made with all natural ingredients, and if you're not completely satisfied, the company will pay you double your money back."

"Wow," he said, taking the tri-fold brochure from her hand and staring at it momentarily. "I ... uh, don't really do that much cleaning." He laughed. "Up til now I've lived with my folks."

"Well then you just give that catalog there to your Mama," she said. "Ask her if she wants to have a party. We're running a special right now, and every hostess who has a party this month will receive an extra fifty dollars in free merchandise, and that's like a lot of furniture polish."

Rustin nodded slowly. "I'll tell her that," he said. He didn't bother reminding her that his mother was back in Michigan. By the time the plane landed, he was ready for a stiff drink.

The other annoying thing about flying coach—besides getting seated next to lunatics—was the long wait when de-boarding. By the time he made it into the gate and started heading down the corridor of the terminal, the thought of a cold beer really did sound appealing. Impulsively, he slipped into one of the small airport bars and ordered a Budweiser.

Well, this was it. This was the start of Rustin's new life. It didn't seem real, that he'd actually taken the plunge. When he first began talking to his friend Deejay about the possibility of moving to Louisiana, Rustin never really thought it would happen. Things were comfortable for him in northern Michigan. He had a steady job, not the best in the world, but nothing to be ashamed of. Rustin had been a grocery manager at his hometown supermarket. He'd taken classes at the community college and earned an associate's degree in business management.

Living at home with his parents, Rustin had been able to save quite a bit of money. He had a sizeable nest egg for a guy his age. He also had a decent car that was completely paid off. The next logical step for him was to take a leap of faith and move out on his own. Although his parents had never pressured him, he knew they expected he'd either get his own apartment or possibly even buy a home. They were waiting for him to meet the right girl and to perhaps get married and settle down.

Rustin had no interest in marriage though. He had no interest in meeting girls either. Every Saturday night for the past three years, he drove his Mustang fifty-six miles to Traverse City, which had the only gay bar in northern Michigan. He had friends there, and he felt accepted and popular. He usually didn't get home until late Sunday afternoon because after last call he almost always was invited to an afterglow party. After the afterglow he usually was invited somewhere else.

He had fun. Wasn't that what was to be expected of a twenty-four year old guy like Rustin? He was in shape, rather good-looking. He had a confident, extroverted personality. He dressed nicely and was a fairly good dancer. Rustin was the type of customer that every gay bar welcomed. He was the red meat. He was the eye candy.

To be honest, Rustin liked it. It made him feel like a celebrity, the way everyone at that bar knew him and always seemed thrilled to see him when he walked through the door. Hardly ever did he have to buy his own drinks.

It was at that bar, Sidetraxx, that Rustin had met Deejay one weekend. Deejay and his boyfriend Tommy were in town on vacation, and Rustin was instantly captivated by Deejay's smile. He had one of those faces that always seemed cheerful. He was always grinning.

That first encounter with Deejay had been almost a year ago. They stayed in touch by email and by phone, and Rustin began confiding in Deejay. He told his friend about how frustrating it was to live as a gay man in small-town northern Michigan. He confessed that he dreamed of escaping, starting his life over. That was when Deejay planted the seed.

"You should move here," he suggested casually. "You could work at the bar."

Deejay was the bar manager for one of New Orleans' hottest gay clubs. He described it in detail to Rustin. They had go-go dancers almost every night of the week, drag shows every weekend, the best dee jays and hottest young crowd. The tips were fantastic, he'd said.

"I don't know shit about bartending, though," Rustin said, "and I sure as hell am not gonna be a dancer."

Deejay laughed. "It's cool. You don't have to be a rocket scientist to serve drinks. We can teach ya. You've already got all you need to be a great bartender—a friendly personality and a killer smile."

When Rustin finally decided to do it, he knew it wasn't going to be easy to tell his parents he was leaving. How could he explain to them that he'd decided to give up a job making forty grand a year in order to go tend bar at some club in Louisiana?

"I'm gay," he said. That was his opening line. "And I'm moving to New Orleans."

Rustin figured that if he was going to drop a bomb on them, he might as well come clean. He might as well tell them everything and step completely out of the closet. His father didn't say much. He just sat there stone-faced as if contemplating what Rustin had said. His mom, though, was quite hysterical.

"How can you know that? Have you even been with a woman?"

"Mom, I'm twenty-four," Rustin said. "Believe me, I know."

"And now . . . what? You're just going to head off to some big city, give up your job and your family? Oh my God, Rustin . . . please!"

"If I stay here, twenty years from now I'll be in the exact same place I am today. I'll be stuck in retail my whole life."

"And working as a bartender is a better alternative?" his father said.

"I want to enjoy my life now while I'm still young. I want to be around people who understand me. People who are *like* me," he said. "If I stay here, I'll always regret that I didn't try. Plus I'll be able to go to school when I'm there. I'll get my bachelor's."

"Why don't you do that first?" his mother suggested. "You can go to school here. If you don't like your job at the store, you can just get a part time job somewhere and go back to school. Please think about it."

Rustin's mind was made up. He'd already thought about everything, and he wasn't about to be dissuaded. Now, here he was, four days later, sitting in an airport bar in New Orleans, Louisiana. He pulled his phone out of his pocket and sent a text message go Deejay.

At the airport. See you in a few.

He'd have a drink and then take a cab over to Deejay's apartment. He was going to be staying there for the first few weeks until after he started his job and found himself his own place.

As he took a swig of his beer, he glanced up and noticed a young blond guy walk through the door and take a seat on the opposite side of the bar. He looked like a cowboy, wearing tight jeans and a western shirt, and Rustin had to quickly look away before the stranger caught him staring.

A few moments later, when Rustin again allowed himself to glance across the bar, he noticed the cowboy suddenly avert his eyes. Rustin smiled to himself, realizing that the guy had been checking him out. He considered his options, contemplating whether he should buy the man a drink, go introduce himself, or just let it pass.

Finally they both looked up at the same time, and as they made eye contact, the cowboy smiled wryly and nodded his head. Rustin's heart rate quickened, but before he could do anything, the sexy stranger stood up and tossed a couple bucks on the bar, then turned and left.

Rustin stared at the man's scrumptious behind as he swaggered confidently out the door. He took one last chug of beer and then picked up his carry-on luggage that was on the floor beside him, and headed out. He hadn't yet seen much of his new hometown, but so far he liked what he saw.

As he left the airport and hailed a cab, Dutch's thoughts returned to the meeting that was looming that afternoon. He wasn't looking forward to facing the reality that Aunt Delta was gone. On any other day, Dutch would have pursued the hottie who'd been checking him out at the airport bar. It was obvious that the kid was interested, but Dutch had business to attend to.

After two drinks on the plane and a third at the airport bar, Dutch was feeling somewhat tipsy. He was thankful for the numbness. He popped a breath mint in his mouth and checked his reflection in the cab's review mirror. He felt his cell phone vibrate in his pocket and reluctantly retrieved it, looking first to see who was calling.

"Hello, Mama," he said. "Yeah, I just landed." He listened for a moment while running a hand through his hair. "At least a couple days, but if I can get everything wrapped up, I'll try to be home by the first part of next week . . . Yes, well I'm sorry. Maybe Kirsten can help."

His mother was not happy about his departure. He knew she'd never much cared for her sister-in-law Delta, and after Daddy passed on two years prior, she no longer made any pretense. Dutch was now pretty much running the ranch himself. He realized he'd become his mother's rock, her stability. She needed him, perhaps a little too much, and she didn't take too kindly to the idea of him being gone for more than a day or two.

"I'm on my way over to the law firm right now. I'll call you when I'm done, and I should know more by that time about how long I'll have to be here. I don't know yet how we're going to . . . um . . . dispose of her personal effects. Her clothes and jewelry and—"

He shook his head as his mother cut him off, going on about a purchase order she didn't know how to handle.

"It'll be fine. Trust me. I'll take care of all that when I get home. Listen, I do have to go, though. I'll call you in a little bit. I love you."

The cab pulled up in front of Dutch's hotel. "Okay, I'm going to go check in real quick, and I'll be right back," he said to the driver. "You'll wait?"

Thankfully there was no line at the front desk. He picked up his room key and requested that the bell hop take his bags up to his room. After tipping the attendant, he quickly headed back to the cab. "Okay," he said, as he climbed in, "thanks for waiting."

"It is not a problem, sir," the driver said with a thick accent. "And now to the address . . ."

"Yeah, the Dingham Law Firm. The address I gave you."

"Very well, sir. It is not a problem." The driver turned and smiled at him, making eye contact.

Dutch smiled back at him, picking up a vibe that the young man was being a bit flirtatious. "Hey, I got a question for ya," he said.

"Yes sir?" the driver said.

"Do you know of any good bars around here?"

"Oh sir," he said, nodding seriously, "there are plenty of night clubs here in the French Quarter." He spoke precisely, clearly enunciating each consonant. "Which type of club do you seek?"

"Ah, well, ya know," Dutch said with a wink, "maybe a . . . well, do you know where the *gay* clubs are?"

The driver smiled. "Oh of course, sir. You are in luck. Only two blocks, walking distance from your hotel, is the Men's Room. It is the city's biggest and most popular gay club."

"Really?" he said. "Well that's good to know."

"Just follow this street here, and it is on the right," he said, pointing. "I can take you there now so that you see."

Dutch shook his head. "Oh no, thanks. I'm sure I can find it easy enough. Thanks for your help."

"Oh, you are most welcome, sir," he said, returning the wink.

Rustin depressed the buzzer, inhaling deeply, as he waited on the front porch. The cab had already left, and he worried for a moment that he might have gotten the address wrong.

"Hello?" an unfamiliar voice came through the speaker.

"Uh . . . hi there. It's Rustin . . . from Michigan."

"Oh, hi Rustin! I'll buzz you in . . . no wait. Let me come down and help with your bags."

Rustin was about to reply that he really didn't need any help, but the speaker was already dead. Seconds later he heard the sound of footsteps approaching the door. As the door flew open, a smiling face greeted him from inside.

"Rustin!" the cheerful kid exclaimed as he grabbed hold of Rustin and hugged him.

Cocktails

Rustin smiled. "Tommy, it's so good to see you again. I didn't recognize your voice through the speaker."

Tommy laughed. "Everyone says I sound formal on the phone . . . maybe over the P.A. too."

Rustin shrugged. "Well it's been awhile since I talked to you. You look great."

"Thanks," Tommy beamed. "You too. Is that it? Just two bags? Here, let me take one."

"Oh, well thanks."

Tommy scooped up the bigger of the two bags and led Rustin inside. "Deejay's down at the club. He called and told me you were on your way here."

"Oh, he goes into work this early?"

"Not usually," Tommy continued to talk as he trudged up the stairs. "He doesn't officially work today, but he's doing paperwork and writing orders and stuff like that. We can go down there in a little bit, and I'll show you around."

"Sure," Rustin nodded. "That'd be cool."

"So, how was the flight?"

"Oh my God. I got stuck next to this girl. She wouldn't shut up. Chattered the whole time, nonstop."

Tommy giggled. "I bet you get a lot of girls wanting to chat with you."

Rustin rolled his eyes. "Yeah, unfortunately."

"Well hey, you better get used to it. You'll have boys and girls both checkin' you out constantly at the bar, especially the way you look."

Rustin felt his face redden a bit. "Think so?"

"I *know* so," Tommy said. They'd reached the top of the stairs and Tommy nodded toward the appropriate door. "There are two apartments up here. Ours is the one on the left. Another guy from the club lives in this one." He pointed to the door on the right. "His name is Carlos but everyone calls him Kay Why."

"Kay Why? As in KY Jelly?"

Tommy laughed. "Yup. He's a drag queen."

Rustin smiled and shook his head. "Cool."

"He's a sweetheart . . . you'll love him."

Tommy set the bag down and inserted his key. "Sorry, the door locks automatically. I've locked myself out a couple times. Sucks. Deejay's getting a key made for you."

"Wow, this is nice," Rustin said as he followed Tommy into the apartment. "It's big—really spacious."

"And of course you'll have your own room. It's two bedrooms, and me and

DJ just need one."

"You two are such a cute couple," Rustin said. He spotted their photo on a shelf in the living room. Deejay had his arms around Tommy and they were both smiling.

"I love that picture," Tommy admitted. "Deejay has the most gorgeous smile."

Rustin stared at the picture for a moment, nodding. He sighed. "Yeah, he sure does."

"Come on, I'll show you your room," Tommy said. "We want you to feel at home. We've got to share the only bathroom, but I already cleared out one side of the vanity for you. Help yourself to anything in the fridge. Do you smoke?"

Rustin shook his head. "Nah, not usually."

"Well, if you do, we have a balcony. We don't smoke inside."

"Sure," Rustin said. "Cool that you have a balcony."

"You're in New Orleans now," Tommy said, smiling. "Almost everyone has a balcony."

"I'm in New Orleans now," Rustin repeated. "I can hardly believe it."

"Well, believe it," Tommy said. He was beaming ear to ear. "And now we're roomies."

Rustin sighed. "It's a whole new life for me," he said, his voice barely a whisper. "It doesn't even seem real."

"It's real," Tommy said, stepping over and wrapping his arm around Rustin's waist. "It's real, and you're gonna have so much fun. I just know you'll love it here." He walked Rustin down the hall to his room. "Ta da." He used his hand to make a sweeping gesture like Vanna White on Wheel of Fortune.

Rustin smiled. "My gay bedroom."

"Oh so you noticed the frilly bed skirt," Tommy teased. "What's gonna make it really gay, though, is that string of hot hunks you bring home from the bar every weekend."

"Don't worry, I'll share," Rustin assured him.

"Promises, promises," Tommy shook his head. "I appreciate the offer, but I've already got more man than I can handle."

"And you two are . . . ya know . . . exclusive?"

"I'll put it this way," Tommy said. "I totally trust Deejay, and I know he trusts me. And it's really nice to be with a guy like that—to not have to worry about him cheating."

Rustin didn't doubt Tommy's statement. Deejay and Tommy both seemed very loyal, and Rustin sort of envied their ability to be monogamous.

"You got yourself a keeper there," Rustin said. "I don't think Deejay would ever cheat on you."

"I know he won't," Tommy agreed, "although with his looks and his job at the bar, I'm sure he's tempted sometimes."

"Nah," Rustin said. "When you've got something as special as what you two have, there's no temptation."

"I hope so," Tommy said, "but that place is like a candy store with all kinds of tasty treats just begging to be sampled."

"Sweet," Deejay said, smiling and nodding in approval. "They're gonna eat you up."

Colby was on the bar, strutting back and forth as he demonstrated his newest dance moves. Wearing only his tight-fitting jockeys and a pair of sneakers, Colby was one hot number. He jumped down from the bar and landed smoothly beside Deejay.

"Aw, thanks," he said, placing his hand on Deejay's hard chest. "I'm glad you liked it."

Deejay continued to smile at him. "You're a flirt, you know that?"

"Me?" Colby said demurely.

"Don't be coy," Deejay said as he leaned in and kissed the dancer on the cheek. "I love your moves, Colby, but I'm already taken. And I don't cheat."

"Who said anything about cheating?" Colby used his index finger to trace a line down the center of Deejay's chest, stopping just above his navel. "Tommy's a little a cutie. Bring him over sometime and the three of us can—"

The front door opened before Colby could finish his sentence, and in walked a tall blond cowboy. Colby spun around, his train of thought interrupted. "Howdy," he said enthusiastically.

"Are ya'll open?" the newcomer said as he approached the bar.

Deejay smiled at him warmly, stepping away from Colby. "Sure," he said. "Can't you tell?" At two o'clock in the afternoon, the bar was completely empty. "Have a seat," Deejay said with a wink. "I'm just messin with ya. This is the slowest part of the day. What can I get you?"

"Coors Light," the young man said.

"Not a problem. Actually, Colby here is supposed to be tending bar, but since we had no customers he was showing me his new dance moves. He's one of our go-go dancers."

"Hi," Colby said, squaring his shoulders and straightening his posture.

"Nice to meet you. I'm Dutch."

"I'll let you two get acquainted," Deejay said, excusing himself. He pulled out his cell phone to check his messages as he stepped into the storage room. Tommy had texted him to let him know that Rustin had arrived. He punched the call back button and waited for Tommy to answer.

"He made it," Deejay said. "What're you guys doing?"

Tommy chatted with him for a moment, telling Deejay he and Rustin were just hanging out together getting the suitcases unpacked while Rustin settled in.

"You guys wanna come down? I'm about done here for now. We can grab a bite." Tommy said they'd be down in a few. "Okay babe, love ya. See ya when you get here."

Deejay headed down the hall and entered his office, which doubled for a dressing room. The dancers used it every night to change. He smiled to himself as he looked down at the desk, cluttered with unopened mail and junk. He remembered clearing off the desk one night rather hurriedly in order to use it for personal business. That was the night he'd fucked Tommy for the first time.

The music had been loud in the bar, yet still Deejay had to hold his hand over Tommy's mouth. He was screaming so loudly, and his shrieks were anything but cries of pain. Deejay reached down and rubbed his crotch as he recalled the way Tommy had begged him to fuck harder.

It was just one of those things that Deejay could not explain. He knew from the moment he laid eyes on Tommy that he was the one. Part of it was that Tommy was his "type". Deejay liked slender guys—especially if they were cute—and Tommy had the most adorable face. He was a bit nerdy, but in a very endearing manner. And Tommy had that sweet little bubble butt and that narrow, twenty-eight-inch waist. Deejay loved wrapping his palms around the side of Tommy's hips and drilling that tight ass of his.

He'd better clear his head before they got to the bar. Already he was sporting a hardon. He toyed with the idea of rubbing one out real quick before they arrived but decided to hold off. It'd be all the hotter later on when he finally got Tommy alone. Instead he focused on tidying up the office a bit.

Deejay and Tommy had vacationed in Michigan a few earlier ago, where they'd met Rustin. The three of them hit it off, and Deejay thought at the time how great Rustin would be at the Men's Room. He had an outgoing personality and seemed to always be happy. His cheerful smile was welcoming, and this sort of demeanor was not a characteristic that was easy to find. It was going to be a pleasure to work beside Rustin and train him to tend bar.

Not only did Rustin have a great smile, but he also had a great body. He was

Cocktails

going to look fantastic on those nights when the bar got crowded and sticky hot, when most of the staff stripped down and worked shirtless. If Rustin were so inclined, he could easily become one of the go-go dancers. The possibilities were endless, but Deejay that Rustin's real desire was to simply start life anew. Moving away from his small hometown was a big step for him. He'd be able to embrace his identity and be who he truly was.

Deejay knew exactly how important it was for Rustin to find his own way. In the past, he had helped other guys like Rustin. Coming out as a gay man wasn't easy for anyone, but the situation was always worse when there was no family support. Deejay was committed to providing this kind of unconditional acceptance to guys like Rustin.

Rustin paused briefly as he stepped through the door of the Men's Room for the first time, taking in the delicious sight of the shirtless bartender who was leaning across the bar to interact with a customer. When Rustin realized that the customer who was seated there was none other than the cowboy he'd encountered earlier at the airport, he smiled to himself. *A small world, indeed.*

"Deejay's probably in his office," Tommy said, tugging on Rustin's elbow. He didn't seem to notice the hot guys Rustin couldn't take his eyes off. "Oh," Tommy said with a dawning realization, "that's Colby. He's one of the dancers, but he covers the bar sometimes in the afternoon."

Rustin stood there motionless, shaking his head slightly. "No . . . um . . . the other one."

"Ohh," Tommy said with a giggle. "Wow, I've never seen *him* before."

"I did. I saw him earlier today at the airport."

"Really? Did you talk to him?"

Rustin shook his head.

"Well, it looks like maybe you should have," Tommy said. "Should we go find Deejay or do you wanna just stand here a while longer with your tongue hanging out?"

"Sorry," Rustin said, snapping out of his trance. "He looks *damn* good," he whispered.

Tommy laughed and headed down the hallway. "Come on. You'll have plenty of chances to hook up with hot looking cowboys. Right now we're starving and need to eat."

"Gotta keep my strength up if I'm going to be riding a cowboy."

"I hear that," Tommy said cheerfully.

When they entered the office, Deejay jumped up and wrapped his arms around Rustin, embracing him tightly. As usual, they both were all smiles. "Well this is it," Deejay said. "You've made it to New Orleans, and this is the Men's Room."

"Complete with hot strippers and gorgeous cowboys," Rustin said, grinning broadly.

"Oh, so you met Colby?"

"I saw him as we walked in. We didn't meet."

"Yeah, he's a hottie. I'll introduce you to everyone later. Are you anxious to get started?"

Rustin shrugged. "Sooner the better," he said.

"No, we're eating first," Tommy announced.

Deejay looked over at Rustin while thumbing his fist toward Tommy. "Weighs like ninety-eight pounds and can eat me under the table. The kid's always hungry."

Rustin laughed. "Yeah, well I'm a little hungry myself."

"There are all kinds of restaurants around here," Deejay said. "What do you like? Cajun?"

Rustin wrinkled his face. "Uh . . . not really."

Deejay shook his head in mock disgust. "You move to New Orleans and don't like Cajun food?"

"Pizza," Tommy said decidedly. "I'm totally in the mood for pizza."

Rustin agreed. "Sounds good to me."

"You know, it's good that the two of you are so agreeable since you're going to be working with each other," Deejay said.

"Really? Cool, but I thought I'd be working with you," Rustin said.

"Tommy is my bar back. He's like a gopher. Fills all the supplies, restocks the liquor. He's like an assistant. You have to learn that job before you can become a bartender. Plus, it's sort of like on-the-job training. I'll start teaching you how to make drinks while you're working with Tommy."

"Well, that's a relief actually," Rustin admitted. "I kinda don't know anything."

Both Tommy and Deejay laughed. "Kind of?" Tommy said. "How can you *kind of* not know anything?"

"I mean I've never worked in a bar."

"You'll be fine," Deejay promised. "As long as you can stay focused on your job and not the dancers."

"Or the cowboys," Tommy interjected.

"Yeah, I saw that new guy when he came in," Deejay said. "He's not a regular, but whoa . . . you like?" He looked at Rustin.

"He's all right," Rustin said casually.

"I had to scoop Rustin's jaw up off the floor when we walked in. He was drooling all over the place," Tommy said, laughing.

"Let's go eat," Rustin said, changing the subject.

"So is it true what they say about things in Texas?" Colby asked as he slowly raked his index finger down the center of Dutch's chest.

"What's that?" Dutch said, a smirk on his face.

"About them being bigger."

"Ahh, well yeah. I guess that *is* true. Lots of things from Texas are pretty darn big."

Colby was now on the outside of the bar, standing beside Dutch's stool. He placed his other hand on Dutch's thigh. "What kind of things?" He slid his fingers toward the crotch bulge.

"Maybe you'd like to see for yourself. What's big to one person might not be to someone else."

"Well, what do *you* think?" Colby whispered.

"I don't think I have anything to worry about," Dutch said as he took a swig from his beer.

Colby chuckled. "Confident. I like that."

"Those people who say that size don't matter—they're the ones with pin dicks."

"I see," Colby said. His hand was now pressing against the denim surrounding Dutch's package. "How long you in town?"

"At least a couple more days," Dutch said. "I'm staying at the Bourbon. Room 312." He slid out of his seat, turning to face Colby. He reached in his pocket and pulled out a twenty, tossing it on the bar. "Come see me when you get off."

"Six o'clock," Colby said.

"Don't keep me waiting," Dutch said as he placed his hand on Colby's bare shoulder.

"Oh, I won't, big boy." Colby smiled at him.

That Colby was quite the looker. Broad shoulders, narrow waist, smooth and well-defined chest. He also had a smile that just wouldn't quit. He might be just what Dutch needed. The whole situation with his aunt's estate was weighing heavy on his mind, and he needed a distraction.

Dutch hadn't expected the news he'd received that afternoon. When the attorney informed Dutch that his Aunt Delta had left him the entire estate, he was flabbergasted and more so when he discovered the value of his newly inherited assets. The cash alone would easily be enough to ease all of his financial burdens and to leave him set for the rest of his life. He should be overjoyed, yet he couldn't shake his melancholy. He'd rather not have the money but have Aunt Delta instead, and he couldn't quite believe she was actually gone. The hardest part would be going into that house without her being there. It wasn't something he looked forward to.

"Mother, I'm afraid I may need to be here a little longer than I'd planned." Dutch was on his phone in the hotel room, lying back on the sofa with his feet propped on the coffee table. "Well, I own this house now, and I have to decide what to do."

"I'll call Lawrence right away and have him list the property. I'm sure he has associates in Louisiana." Lawrence was a family friend and real estate agent.

"No, I haven't decided."

"You haven't decided?" His mother's voice was shrill. "What is there to decide? You already have plenty of property here. This is your home and your business, and what are you going to do with that big ole house in New Orleans, of all places?"

"It's Aunt Delta's home, and I don't think I want to sell it." He picked up the remote control and began surfing through channels on the television although the sound was barely audible.

"Have you forgotten your fiancé?" his mother asked. "You're going to be getting married in three months. There is so much to do with the wedding, not to mention the ranch."

Dutch sighed. "Well actually you did just mention it, and no I haven't forgotten Kirsten. I don't see how keeping Aunt Delta's house is going to affect the wedding. If anything, this will make matters much easier. Not only did I inherit the house but also all of her savings."

"Oh?" His mother finally sounded interested.

"Anyway, give Kirsten my love. I'm exhausted after this whole ordeal, and I'm going to take a nap. I probably won't go over to the house until tomorrow. I'll also go to the bank."

"Dear, please just don't get so wrapped up in this nonsense that you forget about your obligations back home. We need you here."

"I know, Mother. I'll be home in a few days. Stop worrying."

"You're not thinking of moving there permanently..."

"I hardly think Kirsten would agreeable to an idea like that."

"Exactly. This is your home—and your daddy's ranch."

"I know, Mother. I really do have to go. I'll call you tomorrow."

After ending the call, he dragged himself up off the couch and plodded over to the bathroom. He turned on the shower and began stripping off his clothes while waiting for the hot water. He wondered if Colby would show up. His pulse quickened as he contemplated it. Dutch hadn't been with another man since... God, it'd been months. Miles was one of the ranch hands, a temporary employee.

Dutch thought about how he and Miles had often met secretly. They used the same hiding place in the loft that Dutch had shared with his boyhood crush Clancy. But Miles was no boy. He was every bit a man, and he could suck cock even better than Clancy. Miles had that same sexy build and the same tight, rock-hard abs as Colby. Dutch really hoped the guy showed up. He was sporting a raging hardon by the time he stepped into the shower.

Resisting the urge to pleasure himself, Dutch stood in the shower and allowed the hot water to beat against his back. He tilted his head back so the stream pelted his scalp and moaned at the pleasurable feeling. If only the water could wash away the anxiety within his heart. He had only known of his aunt's passing a few days, and his chest was still tight with grief. Dealing with this loss was practically unbearable, yet he had no one to turn to. He couldn't talk about it with his mother, and certainly not with Kirsten.

He wanted Miles. He needed strong arms to hold him. He wished there was a shoulder to cry upon and a hand to hold, someone he could confide in and share just how much Delta had meant to him. She was the only person in his life who'd really known him, and now she was gone.

How had he gotten to this point where he was living a lie? His life was the polar opposite of all Aunt Delta had taught him to be. It was just that things were different back home. It was so much harder. There were expectations, and as the only son of their county's biggest rancher, Dutch knew that the responsibility of running the ranch had fallen on his shoulders. Filling his father's shoes was something he'd been groomed to do from the time he was young. Being gay did not fit into this equation. There were no gay Texas ranchers, at least not that Dutch knew of.

Dutch had stopped messing around with Clancy around the time that he and Kirsten started dating in the tenth grade. By the time they graduated, everyone pretty much knew they would be together. Kirsten's family was respected by Dutch's parents, and he felt good about the fact that he'd gained his daddy's approval. When his father passed, Dutch felt even more pressure.

He didn't love her though, at least not the way a man should love his bride-to-be. Kirsten was very sweet. The two of them shared a lot of the same interests and viewpoints. Spending time with her was easy, and when they allowed themselves to relax, it was a fantastic relationship. It was an extremely close friendship. He'd heard people say that the basis of a strong marriage was a grounded and enduring friendship, so why did he feel so lousy about everything? Why couldn't he love Kirsten the way he wanted to?

Kirsten did not excite Dutch the way Miles did. When Dutch saw Miles in those tight jeans strutting across the yard, it was all he could do to keep from jumping him. And he smelled so damned good. He had dark hair and eyes, and a gorgeous muscular chest that was covered with the thinnest layer of hair. Dutch liked to nuzzle his face against that soft hair. He liked to rest his head in the crook of Miles's shoulder and listen to him breathe after they'd made love.

And now Miles was gone. There was no more Miles and no more Clancy, and Aunt Delta had passed away. Everything real in Dutch's life had disappeared, and all that remained was pretense. He cared about Kirsten but did not love her. He was good at his job running the ranch, but it was not his passion. He did it because he was supposed to. Because Mother expected it and because it was what he'd been groomed to do.

Wrapping a towel around himself, he stepped out of the shower and stood in front of the full-length mirror. The reflection was a person Dutch did not even know. He didn't seem real because his entire life was merely a façade.

He thought about Colby, and his heart skipped a beat. He thought about those fingers that had traced a line down the center of his smooth chest. He thought about those pouty lips that had uttered such suggestive and dirty little remarks. He thought about Colby's smooth skin and tight, rock-hard abs. Dutch wanted him. He wanted Colby to show up and hoped the guy had not just been playing him.

Dutch turned to the sink and picked up his toothbrush. He was rinsing when he heard the knock on the door. He felt his cock throb with excitement against the towel that was cinched around his waist. He turned off the faucet and wiped his mouth with a hand towel, then turned around and stepped out of the bathroom. The look of pleasure on Colby's face as Dutch opened the door completely overshadowed the self-doubt Dutch had felt just moments before.

"Well come on in," Dutch said. "Sorry I didn't have time to dress."

"Hmm, well I was gonna say you're a tad *over*dressed," Colby said, raising his eyebrows. "Lose the towel," he whispered.

He lay on the bed, stretched out and relaxed, as the warm wet mouth slid all the way down his throbbing cock. Deejay moaned. "Fuck yeah," he said in a throaty whisper, "I love how you do that, baby."

Tommy was a natural-born cocksucker, and there was nothing Deejay enjoyed more than a nice, slow, deep-throated blowjob. They were back at the apartment. As Rustin was setting up his room and getting settled in, Tommy pulled Deejay into the bedroom for some quality alone time. Three seconds after the bedroom door was locked, Deejay was sprawled out on the bed naked with his legs spread wide, and Tommy was lying on his belly slurping on Deejays raging hardon.

"Babe, I've been thinking 'bout your hot mouth on my cock all fuckin' day," Deejay said.

He felt Tommy's tongue press against the smooth and sensitive underside of his rigid pole as Tommy slid up and down. Deejay resisted the urge to squirm when Tommy gently cupped his balls. The way Tommy expertly massaged his nut sac while deep throating him was almost enough to send him over the edge.

"Nice and slow, baby, or you're gonna make me cum."

Tommy moaned in response and slowly slid back down the shaft. On the next upstroke, Tommy looked up and made eye contact with Deejay. Those big brown eyes told Deejay that his boy was hungry for him. He was eager to please. He wanted Deejay in the worst way, and nothing got Deejay's motor running more than seeing that kind of desire. Tommy's craving and eagerness to please made Deejay want to fuck his boy's face hard. He wanted to grab hold of Tommy's head and drill his boner deep into that tight throat.

Instead he said, "Show me how much you love that cock," and Tommy began to bob. Rather than grabbing hold of Tommy's head, Deejay grasped the bed spread. His legs stiffened as he balled his fists and tossed his head back reflexively. He savored the feeling of Tommy's warm mouth and its powerful suction surrounding his cock.

For the next five minutes he lay there, willing himself not to get too excited. He liked it when Tommy brought him to the edge a few times and then started over. He loved that gradual build up, knowing all the while there would be an amazing climax, but not allowing himself to get there quite yet.

And Tommy was like the Ever-ready Bunny. He never seemed to tire when it came to sucking dick. Deejay loved the fact that his boy could suck him for hours if he'd let him, but it was Deejay who couldn't seem to let himself go for more than twenty minutes or so until he just had to nut.

Deejay felt himself getting close again. He wanted to edge one more time, but he knew he couldn't hold back. He couldn't help himself and reached down to grab hold of Tommy's head, gripping it firmly with both hands. "Fuck!" he shouted as he forced Tommy all the way down. As the head of Deejay's cock popped into Tommy's tight throat, Tommy continued to press his slippery wet tongue against the rigid pole and Deejay felt that amazing tingling he'd been working toward achieving. It was his point of no return.

"AAAHHH!" he moaned as he thrust his pelvis upward, holding Tommy in place on his cock. His eruption was like a volcanic blast, and his boy continued to suck as Deejay released jet after steamy jet of hot jizz into his hungry mouth.

Deejay was trembling by the time he finished draining himself. "Oh God, you're one fuckin' hot cocksucker, baby," he said. As he began to relax, he released his grip on Tommy's head, but the boy didn't move. He continued to suck and slurp as if he couldn't get enough. Deejay had to reach down and pull him off, this time very gently gripping his head. They again made eye contact.

"I love you," Tommy said.

"Oh baby, I love you too," Deejay said. He smiled and laughed. "You're so damned good at that."

Tommy moved up Deejay's body, kissing his abs and then finding Deejays hard nipples, sucking them with his hot little cum-coated lips. Deejay grabbed hold of the boy's head and leaned in, kissing him passionately. He tasted his own sticky saltiness as he drove his tongue into his lover's mouth.

Deejay wrapped his arms around him and rolled him over so that Tommy was beneath him. They continued to kiss as Deejay groped the boy, running his hands all over Tommy's smooth chest and abs. When he found Tommy's groin he realized there was already a wet spot.

"Babe, did you cum already?"

Tommy laughed and looked him in the eye. "Sorry," he whispered. "I guess I got a little excited."

He'd cum in his pants! "Fuck, that is so hot," Deejay said. "I love it when you cum without touching yourself."

Rustin was sitting on his bed shirtless with his laptop open when he heard the moaning. At first he was alarmed until he realized it was Deejay's voice that he was hearing. They were going at it already. Rustin smiled as he reached down and squeezed his crotch. Just imagining it was enough to make him hard, but actually hearing them in the next room was better than watching porn.

Since he had the laptop out, he opened the folder containing his favorite videos and pulled up a hot blowjob scene. Muting the volume, he lay back with a pillow propped behind him and unzipped his pants. He leaned over and retrieved a tube of jack-off lube he'd stored in the drawer of his bedside stand just moments before.

It had been over twenty-four hours since Rustin had last busted a nut. He had been too keyed up in anticipation of his trip when he took his morning shower. Typically he jacked off at least a couple times per day, and after seeing the way Deejay and Tommy were so affectionate with each other, he was all the hornier. Seeing the hot dancer and cowboy back at the bar had also heightened his libido.

After removing his shorts and underwear and tossing them to the floor beside him, he squirted a small dab of the gel in his right palm. It felt chilly, but he liked the sensation of the cool gel against his fiery hot prick. He wrapped his fist around his hardon and spread his legs wide. He moaned as he began to stroke, all the while staring intently at the cocksucker on the screen next to him.

As he stroked, he could hear Deejay through the wall. Rustin knew Tommy must be blowing him just like the cocksucker in the video was doing to the muscular jock he was servicing. Rustin wondered if Deejay was hung like the porn star and if Tommy was as skilled at sucking dick as the kid on his knees in the video.

He felt himself getting excited too quickly. He didn't want to cum before the video was over. He liked to edge a bit and tried to time his climax to coincide with the money shot. He could tell just from Deejay's moaning that he too was getting close. He continued to stare at the computer screen, knowing his favorite part was coming up. He loved it when the top grabbed hold of the cocksucker's head and started to pump it. He loved the way that guy took control, and he wondered if Deejay was the type of top to be aggressive like that.

Just as the porn star began to drill the throat of his cocksucker, Rustin heard Deejay begin to groan. His voice was deep and raspy, and it sounded as if he was growling. It coincidentally provided a perfect audio for the video Rustin was watching. He began to pump his dick faster, squeezing another liberal glob of gel onto his engorged cockhead.

He was so close. He couldn't hold back much longer. He had to do it. He had to let go. Oh God, it was such delicious torture. The buildup ... edging closer and closer, but not quite there. *Oh fuck! Here it goes!* "AHHHH!" His abs had been clenched tight up until that magnificent moment when he erupted. He released his tightened muscles at the exact moment that the pumping started, and a volley of cum fired from the head of his cock. It blasted out of him rapidly and copiously, spraying his chest and abs. Some even landed on his shoulder, and a sizeable glob nailed him right on the side of his cheek.

He sighed as he leaned back against the pillow. He was now drenched by his own cum. He was going to really like living here, he decided. New Orleans was going to be just great.

Colby was one hot fuck. Dutch was standing over him, holding each of Colby's ankles and spreading his legs like a wishbone. The dancer lay naked on the queen sized bed, staring up into Dutch's eyes. "Do it," he pleaded, "please fuck me hard!"

His hard cock was already sheathed with a condom and Colby's tight, shaved boy pussy was lubed and ready to be stuffed. Dutch released one of Colby's ankles and grabbed hold of the base of his shaft. He pointed it toward the hole and leaned in, thrusting his pelvis. In a smooth forceful movement, he impaled the bottom boy, savoring the heat and tightness of his twitching hole.

"Ah fuck," Dutch moaned.

He grabbed hold of both ankles as he drilled his cock deep inside his boy. Colby whimpered. "Oh God. Fuck me!"

Dutch continued to stare directly into Colby's beautiful face as he began to pump his cock in and out. He loved seeing his bottom's expressions—a delightful mixture of ecstasy and agony. The pleasure-pain combo. Dutch was big, and it pleased him that Colby could handle the entirety of his girth. The kid was obviously a pro.

"Harder!" Colby begged, and Dutch began to pick up the pace. He slammed his cock in hard, drilling as deeply as possible, then backed out and repeated. With each thrust, he got faster and more forceful. His thighs slapped against the back of Colby's legs as he pounded him. The more he fucked, the louder Colby moaned.

Dutch knew the dancer was loving every second, and not just by the sound of his verbalization. Colby's cock was rock hard. Dutch reached down and grabbed hold of it, wrapping his palm around the boy's shaft. He started to pump it, coordinating his strokes with the thrusting of his own cock into

Colby's tight ass. Colby slid his ankles onto Dutch's shoulders and Dutch leaned in to tower over him. He had the boy pinned beneath him, and he released Colby's cock so he could place both palms flat against the mattress on either side of Colby's head.

Dutch's abdomen now rubbed against Colby's hardon as he continued to thrust. "Oh fuck! Dude, you're gonna... Oh God! You're gonna make me cum!"

Dutch was like a wild animal, humping his boy with abandon. Both were sweating and moaning, and the bed was squeaking beneath them. "I'm gonna fire my load up your tight ass, boy. You want it?" Dutch said.

"Oh God, yes! I'm cumming! Oh fuck!"

They erupted simultaneously as Dutch felt his body convulse. He blasted his load into the condom, six consecutive jets of steamy cum firing out of him like a rocket. Colby's load erupted at the exact same time, splashing against Dutch's tight abs and rock-hard chest.

Both were sighing and gasping for breath when Dutch leaned in to gently kiss the dancer on the lips. "You were great," he said. "Thank you... let's get cleaned up."

Dutch loved the architecture in New Orleans and especially that of his Aunt Delta's house. The Creole Greek Revival home had a covered balcony with both a lower deck and an upper gallery. This double gallery made the house look stately due to the ornate columns that supported it. Aunt Delta had been emphatic about maintaining the integrity of the architecture. Often Louisiana homes such as this were supported by wooden columns that had to be replaced when they became weather-worn and began to rot. Delta spared no expense in this regard, insisting on authentic materials and careful attention to the details of the design.

There was so much history in the home, and Aunt Delta had been proud of the fact that it was constructed in the mid-1800s. It had been her father's home and his father's before him. By rights the home should have been passed down to Dutch's father, but he had left Louisiana in his youth to begin a new life in Texas. With Delta being single, she stayed and continued to live in the home of her ancestry.

The idea of placing the house on the market about turned Dutch's stomach. He couldn't bear the thought of strangers owning something that was a part of his family's heritage. He had thought his mother would understand this. Daddy grew up here. Why would she want to just get rid of it? Dutch had memories of his own associated with the property. His summers with Aunt Delta had been the highlight of his childhood.

As he stepped onto the portico, Dutch inhaled deeply. There was a certain scent, something in the air that he noticed whenever he was in New Orleans. Perhaps it was the mixture of the Cajun spices and the smell of the Gulf. Maybe it was just his imagination. He really felt at home here, more so than in the state of his birth. Though raised in Texas, most of the time he felt like a transplant or trespasser. It was a feeling he'd first noticed when returning home at the end of summer the year he was twelve.

As he stepped through the door and took in the sight of the home he knew so well, he felt like he was twelve again. He expected Aunt Delta to be there, eager to embrace him. Instead he was met with silence. The empty home was exactly as he'd remembered. Spotless. Fully furnished and ornate. No, he was not going to sell it. He'd never sell this house, no matter what his mother said.

"These big buckets here are what we use for the ice," Tommy explained. "They are the *only* thing we use for ice, and we don't use them for anything *but* ice."

"Got it," Rustin said, nodding. "Big buckets. Ice. Nothing else."

Tommy laughed. "Sorry. I'm used to training morons. I learned that I've got to talk to the newbie's like they're third graders until they prove otherwise."

"Oh, I understand. I've done training myself. There's a lot to learn, and sometimes it's easy to forget things. You have to assume that your trainee knows nothing."

"Which is what you said," Tommy reminded him. "You said, 'I know nothing'."

"That I did," Rustin agreed.

Tommy had actually proven to be a terrific trainer. He made Rustin feel very comfortable. Throughout his first evening, Tommy repeatedly stopped him and offered to give him a break, which Rustin politely refused. He'd never been one to take breaks on his previous job. Whenever he tried, he just sat around for the duration mentally itemizing what all he should be doing.

"Actually, it's good you started during the middle of the week. The bar isn't too busy. In fact, I don't normally work on Tuesdays and Wednesdays."

"But you are this week just to train me?"

Tommy nodded. "If we try to start a new bar-back on Friday or Saturday, it's just too crazy. Even though I started on a Saturday myself."

"And there are no dancers tonight."

Cocktails

"Which is why we aren't that busy," Tommy said.

So far Rustin had learned about all the bar supplies, the mixers, the bag-in-the box syrups for the drinks on tap, the kegs, the cups, glasses and pour spouts. He learned where everything was stored and the replenishment guidelines so that he would be able to keep everything stocked appropriately. Tommy had explained that it would be much different on the weekend. He'd be running his butt off, probably unsure of what to do and when to do it.

"I'll just follow your lead," Rustin said.

"Exactly. Shadow me, and don't be offended if I boss you. Sometimes I forget to say please and thank you."

Rustin doubted this was true. So far Tommy had been extremely polite—almost too polite to be a boss. "Don't worry. I don't offend that easily. I know what it means to be a boss."

"Deejay's the boss," Tommy clarified. "He just put me in charge of training you."

"Right," Rustin nodded. Tommy was really cute sometimes.

"Did you see who's back?" Tommy asked.

Rustin shook his head. "Nuh uh."

"Your cowboy." Tommy smiled and winked.

"The one who was here yesterday talking to that stripper?"

"To Colby, right. I saw the cowboy dude coming in as we were headed back here to the ice machine. Why don't you take a break and go talk to him?"

Rustin stared at Tommy in disbelief. "Um . . . I don't think so. What would I say?"

"*Want a blowjob?*" Tommy suggested.

Rustin cracked up. "Nah, I don't think so."

"Seriously, just go talk to him. Ask him where he's from. What's the worst that can happen?"

Rustin shrugged. He knew the worst that could happen. Rejection. Embarrassment. Humiliation.

"You should have a little more self-confidence. I bet guys like that cowboy want dudes who are not wimps. If you act like you're afraid, he's gonna think you're a pansy."

It seemed weird to hear this advice coming from the mouth of a tiny guy like Tommy. "Well, what makes you think I'm even interested in that guy?" Rustin asked. He was surprised at how defensive he was feeling.

"Oh I don't know, other than the way you were drooling all over yourself yesterday."

"Okay fine. I'll go talk to him!"

"Good," Tommy said, grinning. "Go get 'em."

Rustin knew Tommy was right. It was high time he stopped being so passive. After all, he'd moved halfway across the country to start his life over. If he didn't have the balls to put himself out there and take the bull by the horns—or the cowboy by the balls—then he deserved to be alone and lonely. Plus he'd never had a problem picking up guys back home in Michigan—why should he start doubting himself now?

"Hi," he said as he slid onto the barstool next to the cowboy.

The handsome stranger looked up, eyeing him for a moment. "Oh hey. You were at the airport yesterday, weren't you?"

Rustin nodded and smiled. "And you remembered. I'm impressed."

"Uh . . . well you're kind of hard to forget."

Rustin paused, unsure how to respond. "I guess I should take that as a compliment?"

"Definitely," the cowboy said. "Name's Dutch."

"Rustin," he said, extending his hand.

"And what brings you to The Big Easy?" Dutch asked.

"Well, I just moved here, and this is my first night at work."

Dutch stared at him confused.

"Here," Rustin said, using his index finger to point at the ground. "I work here at the Men's Room."

"Oh wow. Well, that didn't take long. I mean, for you to find a job."

"I'm going to be going to school here, and one of my friends is the bar manager. He offered me a job before I moved."

"Let me guess. You're a dancer."

Rustin laughed. "Uh . . . no, not quite. I'm learning the bar right now, but I got sent on break. And what brings you here?"

"Well, I guess it's the hot looking employees," Dutch said with a wink.

"You know what flattery will get you . . ."

"Laid?"

Rustin cracked up this time. "You know you're making me think *very* dirty thoughts."

"I hope so."

He felt his cheeks getting hot and tried repeating his question. "I meant, what are you doing here in New Orleans?"

"Family business," Dutch said. "I had a relative that passed away."

"Oh man, I'm sorry," Rustin said, gently placing his hand on Dutch's arm.

Cocktails

"Thanks. But ya know what? It's gonna be all right. I'm sure this relative wouldn't want me wallowing in depression or crying in my beer. Speaking of beer, you want one?"

"Thanks but I better not," Rustin said. "I don't think I'm supposed to drink on the job."

Dutch spun slightly on his barstool in order to face Rustin. "Seems like I've seen bartenders drinking before, but it's cool."

"How bout I get *you* a drink," Rustin offered. "Ready for another beer?"

Dutch shrugged. "Sure," he said.

Rustin slid off his stool and quickly made his way around the corner and behind the bar. Deejay was standing in the opposite corner finishing up with a customer.

"I'm gonna grab a beer for this customer," Rustin said, gesturing toward Dutch.

Deejay turned around to see who Rustin was talking about. He smiled and winked. "Go for it," he said. "Can you handle the register yet?"

"I'll manage," Rustin said.

"Hey," Deejay said, grabbing hold of his elbow to stop him, "you think you got a pretty good feel of everything here? The back room and all the supplies?"

"I think so," Rustin said. "Tommy's a pretty thorough teacher."

"You probably don't need to stay any longer . . . I mean, if something comes up and you wanna take off."

"Really?" Rustin said. "Are you sure? I don't wanna bail early on my first night."

Deejay shook his head. "This isn't even really your first night. That'll be Friday. We'll just consider this a preview—your training."

"Cool," Rustin said. "Thanks, man."

Deejay slapped him affectionately on the shoulder.

Rustin placed the beer bottle down in front of Dutch and leaned in. "Guess what?" he asked. Dutch looked up to stare him in the eye without answering. "I got the rest of the night off."

"Cool," Dutch said, smiling. "And what're you gonna do?"

"I don't know. Maybe I'll look for someone to hang out with."

Dutch looked first to his right and then his left, then turned back around to reestablish eye contact. "Pretty dead in here. Good luck."

Rustin laughed. "You hungry?"

"You know, I actually *am* getting a little hungry, but I don't have anyone to eat with."

"Him," Rustin said, cupping his chin in his palm and trying to look pensive. "I don't have anyone to hang out with and you don't have anyone to eat with. Maybe we could . . . I don't know . . . go out together to eat?"

"Why didn't I think of that?" Dutch said. He tossed a ten-dollar bill on the bar for his beer. "But I guess I better finish this beer first," he said.

"Take your time," Rustin said. He picked up the ten and stepped over to the register. He rang up the transaction smoothly and made change.

"Wow, you really did pick up on the register quickly." Deejay had stepped behind him.

"I've been running registers for years. It's not that different."

"You're gonna do great at this job," Deejay said. "I'll start teaching you how to make drinks next week, after the weekend."

"Can't wait," he said. Rustin turned around to give Dutch his change. "Deejay, have you met Dutch yet?"

"Yeah, we *did* meet briefly." He smiled at the cowboy.

"Not officially," Dutch said.

"We met yesterday when Colby was here."

"Ah yes, Colby. He's not working at all today?"

"He'll be back Thursday," Deejay said. "He'll be dancing."

"I'll have to stop in," Dutch said.

Rustin felt a twinge of jealousy as he saw Dutch's eyes light up. There was no question that Colby was a good-looking dude, but the fact that Dutch had acknowledged this made Rustin feel a tad insecure.

"Where should we go?" Dutch asked. Rustin looked at him, the question not immediately registering. "To eat," Dutch clarified. "Is there someplace in particular you want to go?"

"Oh . . . uh . . . your choice. Anything's fine by me."

"So you said you're going to school here," Dutch said. They were seated in a restaurant booth waiting for their order.

"Well, not yet. I just got here yesterday, remember?"

"So what are you planning to go into?"

"I have an associate's degree in business administration now. I'll probably just complete my bachelor's."

"I never went to college," Dutch said. "But I do have a business. Well, it was my daddy's, but now he's gone."

Dutch looked down at the table in front of him. He always felt uncomfortable talking about himself that way, but there was something about this kid that made him want to open up.

"I can't imagine what it'd be like to lose a parent," Rustin said.

Dutch looked up and smiled, sensing the genuineness of his friend's empathy.

"If you don't mind me asking, who was the relative you mentioned earlier?" Rustin said.

"My aunt. She lived here in New Orleans all her life and recently passed away. That's why I'm here, to take care of her estate."

"And you were close to her?"

Dutch smiled and nodded. "I think I was closer to Aunt Delta than even my folks. I don't know. She was just one of those people who really understood me. Maybe the *only* one."

"I'm so sorry," Rustin said, reaching across the table to place his hand on Dutch's arm.

"And now I have her house. My mother wants me to sell it, but I'm not going to."

"Was Delta your mother's sister?"

"My Dad's," Dutch said.

"Oh wow. Do you think that's why she wants you to just sell the house? Maybe she doesn't like that you were so close to her sister-in-law."

Dutch nodded. "Yeah, that's part of it. But Mamma really took it hard when daddy died. I think it is more about the fact that she's afraid of losing me. Afraid maybe that I will leave Texas and move here."

"What do you want?" Rustin asked. "Do you want to leave?"

"I can't leave. Don't matter what I *want.*"

"Dutch, that's the *only* thing that matters," Rustin said. He leaned forward in his seat. "Why do you think I'm here? My parents didn't want me to leave either. No parent wants to see their kids grow up and leave the nest, but you have to do what's right for you."

He shook his head. "No, it's more complicated than that."

The waitress arrived with their food. When Dutch looked down at the heaping pile of fried shrimp on his plate, he remembered how hungry he was.

"Well, if you can't move here right away, that doesn't necessarily mean you have to sell your aunt's house. You could rent it out or even just keep it for a vacation home."

"I don't know. I wish I'd had a chance to see Aunt Delta before she died. She was the one person who seemed to always know what to do, and she was probably the only one who ever really knew me."

"She knew you were gay?"

Dutch nodded. "Well, I'm not sure. I guess I don't put a label on it."

Rustin laughed. "You do realize we met in a gay bar, right?"

Dutch smiled at him. "Yeah, I know, but being 'gay' is not really an option for me right now, least not with my family."

"Then maybe that's just one more reason why you need to keep your aunt's house. You can come here and be who you really are. It will give you an outlet—a place to get away."

"I've thought of that," Dutch said, "and you're probably right. I just am tired of living this lie, though."

"Do you date women back home? Have a girlfriend?"

Dutch looked away, fumbling for the bottle of ketchup. "Let's talk about you," he said. "So you're a business major?"

"We talked about that already, and you are avoiding my question."

"There was a guy I was seeing back home, but he left," Dutch said. "He worked on the ranch."

"So you're going through some shit," Rustin said. "I don't mean to keep repeating this, but I'm really sorry. If there's anything I can do to help . . ."

"You're helping," Dutch said. "Honestly, you're the first person I've ever talked to about any of this."

"Good," Rustin said. "You can talk to me any time."

"Thanks," Dutch said. They stared at each other for a moment without saying anything.

"This guy—this obviously *stupid* guy who left you—if you really care about him, why don't you go after him?"

"Because it's not like that," Dutch said. "We have a lot of employees who are temporary. They come and go, and I wouldn't even know where to find Miles if I wanted to."

"His name is Miles," Rustin said, nodding.

"Yeah. And now he's miles away."

Rustin shook his head at the lame pun. "So forget about Miles. He's history, but maybe you learned something from knowing him. He certainly helped show you who you really are."

"Did he?" Dutch said. He took a drink of his soda.

"I saw you with that dancer yesterday," Rustin said. "Looked like you were pretty sure of what you liked."

"Ah, Colby again." Dutch shrugged. "Why's his name keep coming up?"

"I'm just saying, you didn't seem too confused when he was rubbing up against you. Actually, you didn't seem confused earlier when you were flirting with me. Dutch, you already know in here what you really want." He pointed to his chest. "Don't you?"

"What I want and what's expected of me are two different things."

"And only you have the power to change those expectations. If your family doesn't know who you are, how can they have the right expectations for you?"

Dutch laughed. "Are you sure you want to go into business? I think you'd do better as a motivational speaker."

"Or a psychologist?"

"Yeah, there ya go."

"I'm just trying to be your friend. You got a little ketchup on the side of your mouth." Rustin pointed to his own face to indicate the location. "No, over more. Here . . ." He reached across the table and wiped the tiny red smudge from the corner of Dutch's mouth. Dutch grinned at him.

"Thanks, Mom," he said. They laughed. "I do think we're gonna be really good friends."

"Am I going to have to get out the paddle?" He stood there with his hands on his hips staring down at the boy who was kneeling before him. "I said, 'Kiss my fucking feet, boy! Do it NOW!'"

Tommy knelt there looking up at his Master. "Yes, Sir," he said and then made haste to lower himself as ordered. He placed his hands flat on the ground in front of him and pressed his lips firmly on the top of Deejay's left foot. Without looking up, he then repeated the action with the right foot.

"Good boy," Deejay said. "Now go get the paddle."

Tommy's heart pounded in his chest as he scurried to retrieve the paddle. He knew what was about to happen, and his cock throbbed in anticipation. He raced into the hall closet and flung it open. He had to stand on his tip toes and stretch to reach the top shelf, but within a couple seconds he had his fingers wrapped around the handle of the sturdy fraternity paddle.

He slammed the door and took two steps down the hall back toward the living room. Suddenly he stopped as it dawned on him that Deejay had not instructed him *which* paddle he wanted. Tommy turned back toward the closet.

"Hurry the fuck up, boy! You know I don't like waiting."

"Coming, Sir!" he cried.

Seconds later Tommy was back in the living room sliding again on his knees before his Master. In one hand he held the fraternity paddle and in the other a smaller one that resembled a ping pong paddle. When Deejay stepped over to the chair beside him and sat down, Tommy was pretty sure which instrument of discipline would be used.

Without getting up, he inched his way toward the chair, crawling on his knees. He bowed his head, awaiting his Master's instructions.

"Boy, what do you have to say for yourself?" Deejay demanded.

"I'm sorry, Sir," Tommy squeaked.

"What? Speak the fuck up!"

"I said I'm sorry, Sir." Tommy's voice was a little louder.

"And what are you sorry for, boy?"

Tommy gulped. "Sir, I'm sorry for being bad. I'm sorry for . . ."

"What?" Deejay shouted.

"For looking at the dirty pictures on the computer, Sir."

Deejay stared down at him, maintaining as stern a look as possible. Tommy feared one of them might start giggling at any moment and ruin the scene. He bit his lip to keep from laughing. Deejay took a deep a breath and cleared his throat. "Do you think that's funny, bitch?"

"No, Sir!" Tommy responded.

"Then you better wipe that smartass smirk off your face, boy."

"Yes, Sir." Tommy continued to look down at the ground.

"Take off your clothes," Deejay said calmly. Tommy dropped the paddles and pulled his t-shirt over his head, peeling it off and tossing it beside him. He stood and unzipped his jeans, allowing them to fall. Then he slid down his underwear and stepped out of them.

Deejay pointed to the ping pong paddle. "Assume the position," he instructed.

Tommy stepped closer to the chair and slid down, stretching himself across Deejay's lap. His hard cock pressed against Deejay's thigh as Deejay used his left arm to press down on Tommy's shoulders. He stared at the ground below as he felt Deejay place the paddle in the middle of his back.

"You have such a smooth little bubble butt," Deejay said. He rubbed his palm across Tommy's ass cheeks. "So soft. So perfectly round. But you're such a bad, bad boy." Without warning he smacked the ass hard.

Tommy squirmed a bit on Deejay's lap, and as he did so, his cock throbbed against Deejay's leg.

"Looking at those nasty pictures. All those hot guys fucking and sucking each other, shoving shit up each other's ass." He leaned over and allowed a stream of his drool to drip into Tommy's ass crack then shoved his index finger deep inside.

"Ohhh," Tommy moaned, startled by the unexpected intrusion.

"You know you have to be punished, don't you boy?"

"Yes, Sir!" Tommy cried. "Please punish me, Sir."

"I'm gonna paddle this smooth little ass of yours, and then you know what I'm going to do?"

"No . . . uh . . . no, Sir," Tommy replied.

"Then I'm gonna fuck it!"

Tommy's cock again throbbed as his excitement heightened.

Deejay pulled out his finger and slapped Tommy's ass again, this time harder. Deejay laughed as the boy wiggled on his lap. "Already getting red," he said. "Imagine how it'll be when I use the paddle."

"Please sir, I need my punishment," Tommy pleaded.

"I decide when to give the punishment!" Deejay said authoritatively.

"Yes, Sir," Tommy replied.

Tommy felt the ping pong paddle being lifted from his back, and he knew the paddling was about to commence. He grimaced in anticipation as he heard Deejay lifting his arm to swing. Two seconds later the paddle came down and cracked against his sensitive ass.

"Ahh!" Tommy cried. The swat stung, and it was all he could do to keep from reaching back to rub his own ass. Deejay held him down so he couldn't move and immediately delivered another blow.

Tommy bit down on his lip as he felt the fiery bite of the paddle against his soft bottom. Over and over, Deejay swatted him, at least five or six times.

"What do you have to say now, boy?" Deejay asked.

"I'm sorry, Sir. I will never be naughty again."

"Never? Hm, well I think you need another five swats then. For lying to me!" He then delivered five more quick blows.

Tommy's bottom was on fire by the time Deejay finished, but his cock was about to erupt. He wanted more than anything to shoot his load, but concentrated on calming himself.

"Get over to the sofa," Deejay said as he lifted his arm and allowed Tommy to stand.

Tommy scurried across the room and assumed the position he knew he was required to take. He grabbed hold of the back of the couch and leaned over. He heard Deejay behind him as he stripped off his clothes and threw them to the floor. He heard the tearing of the foil around the condom, the squirting of the lube onto Deejay's palm. He felt Deejay's left hand as it grabbed hold of his hip.

All the while Tommy continued to look down at the sofa cushions beneath him. All the while his cock continued to throb. And all the while he knew he was about to get his ass reamed hard.

Deejay inserted his finger into Tommy's hole once more, this time working it around in a circle, loosening him a bit. He pulled out and Tommy then felt the head of Deejay's enormous cock as it pressed against him. Tommy stood there, not moving a muscle. He was bent at the waist and his legs were spread. He placed his hands flat against the sofa cushions.

In one smooth movement, Deejay impaled him. "Ahh fuck!" Tommy cried as he felt himself being stabbed. Deejay's cock was deep inside him, ramming his sweet spot. *How the fuck did he know how to find it so fast?*

Deejay grabbed both of Tommy's hips and began to thrust. Quick to increase the speed, he was soon pounding him with abandon. Tommy heard Deejay moan as his piston pumped rapidly in and out of Tommy's tight hole.

"Oh God! Oh fuck!" Deejay hollered.

"Fuck me hard, Sir! Fuck me, hard!"

Deejay smacked the side of Tommy's ass as he continued to drill him.

"I'm gonna cum!" Tommy cried. "Oh God!"

"Fuck yeah! Shoot your load!"

They both cried out as they reached their point of no return, and Deejay slumped down against Tommy's back, wrapping his arms tightly around the smaller man. "Oh Tommy, I love you," he growled into his ear just as Tommy heard the door behind them open.

Tommy and Deejay craned their necks to see what they'd heard, and there stood Rustin and Dutch.

"Hi guys," Rustin said cheerfully. "Hope we're not interrupting anything."

"I'm sorry bout that," Rustin said as they descended the staircase. "I didn't think they'd be home from work yet."

Dutch laughed as he draped his arm around Rustin's shoulder. "I guess we could have stayed and watched."

"We can go back if you want—"

Dutch stopped walking and held Rustin in place. They turned to look into each other's eyes. "It's getting late, and I should get going."

"I can walk you back to your hotel room," Rustin suggested.

He shook his head. "I'll be fine. Thank you for tonight. Thanks for listening."

Rustin leaned into him, their lips moving closer together. "Thank *you* for a wonderful evening . . . and for dinner."

"I know I should invite you back to my room," Dutch said.

"Why don't you?" Rustin whispered, their lips now barely touching.

"I don't know," Dutch said, and then kissed him.

Rustin wrapped his arms around Dutch's torso, grasping his shoulders, as Dutch framed Rustin's face in the palm of his hands. They remained together, tasting each other for the first time. Rustin's heart was pounding in his chest as he felt the passion rising. He drove his tongue into Dutch's mouth while he felt his body being guided backward until his back was pressed firmly against the wall of the stairwell.

Rustin was fully aroused, his cock throbbing against the denim fabric of his tight-fitting jeans. He allowed his hands to explore Dutch's back, trailing his fingers up and down his spine, grasping the twin mounds of Dutch's sexy ass and pulling his pelvis into him. They moaned simultaneously.

"I could take you right here—right here on this staircase," Dutch threatened.

"Please," Rustin pleaded.

Dutch pulled his mouth away from Rustin but continued to pin him against the wall with the weight of his body. He placed his hands flat against the wall on either side of Rustin. "I don't want it to be like this," Dutch said.

"What . . . what do you mean?"

"It's just complicated." Dutch lowered his arms and stood upright. He stepped backward and grabbed hold of the railing. "I have to go. I'm sorry."

"Wait," Rustin said. Dutch descended the stairs two at a time.

"I'm sorry," he repeated as he reached for the door knob.

"Call me!" Rustin said. Dutch was already gone.

Rustin climbed to the top of the staircase and sat down, shaking his head. What had gone wrong? He was sure that Dutch and he had shared a connection. He felt in Dutch's kiss that the attraction was mutual. Dutch was the one who'd pinned him against the wall. He had made the first move, but then he suddenly backed off. Something was going on. There was something Dutch wasn't telling him.

Rustin thought about their conversations earlier that evening. He remembered how Dutch had asked about the dancer. Then again at the restaurant, he was a bit defensive when Colby's name came up again. And now he was telling Rustin that things were complicated. That had to be what it was. Dutch had already become involved with Colby. Why couldn't guys just be honest? Why hadn't he just explained the situation in the beginning instead of leading Rustin on?

He rested his elbows against his knees and cupped his chin in his palms, sighing. This wasn't such a good start to his new life. The fear of rejection he'd experienced earlier had not been baseless after all. He closed his eyes and thought about their kiss. The way Dutch had asserted himself didn't feel much like rejection, but his reaction afterward was a crushing blow. It was pointless to torture himself. Dutch obviously had issues that he had to work out.

As Rustin opened his eyes, resigning himself to the fact that he'd be spending the rest of the evening alone, the door at the base of the stairwell opened. Hoping it was Dutch returning, he raised his head to see who was ascending the staircase. A slightly-built Latino guy about his age stopped a few steps below him. "Well, hi there," the young man said, a broad smile gracing his face.

"Hi," Rustin said, returning his smile, though unenthusiastically.

"Someone doesn't look too happy," the dark-haired stranger observed. He had long, full eyelashes that were rather noticeable as he batted them at Rustin. He was wearing tight-fitting skinny jeans and carrying a leather handbag. Placing one hand on his hips, he stood there maintaining eye contact.

"I think we must be neighbors," Rustin said. "I'm staying with Deejay and Tommy."

"Ah, Deejay and Tommy." He held up one hand and pointed toward their apartment door. When he did so, he bent his wrist in an exaggeratedly feminine flourish. "Cute couple," he said. "I'm Carlos, from next door."

"AKA Kay Why?"

Carlos grinned. "My reputation precedes me."

Rustin smiled. "Tommy says you're a sweetheart."

"Oh, well that sounds like something he'd say," Carlos nodded as he looked down, feigning modesty, but only momentarily. "Guilty!" he said, pointing to himself.

Rustin laughed.

"And what on earth is a gorgeous specimen like you doing sitting here all alone in the middle of the night? And do you have a name?"

Rustin shrugged. "Rustin, and I got dumped," he said. "*That's* why I'm sitting here all alone."

Carlos gasped and placed a hand over his mouth in mock astonishment. He took another couple steps up the staircase and seated himself beside Rustin, sliding his arm around Rustin shoulder. "That just doesn't even seem possible," Carlos said.

Rustin cocked his head to the side slightly and nodded. "What can I say?"

"Why don't you come inside with me?" Carlos suggested. "Let Carlos help you forget all about that mean, mean, and *stupid* man who dissed you."

Rustin looked over at Carlos's cherubic face. He took in his bright red, full lips and deep chocolate colored eyes. "Okay," he agreed.

Carlos reached down and grabbed hold of Rustin's hand. "Come on!" He stood and pulled Rustin up, leading him into his apartment.

Dutch knew by the chimes of the grandfather clock that it was exactly three a.m. when he entered his new Louisiana home. Yes, it was now his, for Aunt Delta was gone. Fond memories flooded his mind as he turned on the desk lamp and allowed his gaze to fall on the bureau where the lamplight cast its illumination. In his mind's eye, he could still see her seated there, and it was in that very desk chair she'd seated herself while penning him dozens of letters.

He needed one of those letters now. He needed her advice, but it was too late for that. He wondered how she had taken the news of his engagement to Kirsten. Certainly it must have come as a shock to Delta to discover that Dutch was engaged to a woman. He had no doubt she would have supported him in any decision that he made for himself, yet it saddened him to think that he might have in any way disappointed her.

It all went back to the issue of authenticity—being his true self and embracing who he was. But that would require courage, and Dutch didn't feel very courageous. The young man he'd spent the evening with was a true example of courage. He'd come out to his family, left behind all he had known and been comfortable with, in order to live an authentic life. Dutch was not brave enough to do this, and that was why he had to leave. That was why he could not allow himself to become emotionally attached to a guy like Rustin. More importantly, he could not allow Rustin to become attached to him.

No matter what Dutch said or did over the weekend, come Monday morning it all would be over and he'd be on a plane back to Texas. Even keeping Aunt Delta's house would not be enough to change the course of events that were mapped out for his life. There would be a wedding. He would continue to run his daddy's ranch and look after his mother. He'd become a good husband, possibly even a father. These were the expectations, and he was not big enough to rise above them. Colby had been wrong in that regard. Not all things from Texas were so big.

The bureau at which he sat had been his aunt's domain. In all of the visits Dutch had paid to her home, never once had he invaded her privacy, but now it belonged to him. All that had been Delta's was now his property. Realizing this, he reached out and pulled open the desk drawer. As he might have expected, the drawer was very organized. It would have been out of character for Delta to have a "junk drawer" of any kind. Ink pens, paper clips, scissors, and post it notes all had their designated compartments. The only thing that seemed out of place was a single envelope in the center of the drawer.

When Dutch picked up the envelope he realized it did not contain a letter. It was unsealed with the flap merely tucked under, and when he pulled it open he discovered a pair of gold rings. He removed them, holding each under the lamplight to examine them for inscriptions. There was nothing. The rings were very plain, containing no stones or markings of any kind. The envelope was unmarked.

Dutch placed the rings back in the envelope and re-tucked the flap into a closed position. He slid it into his shirt pocket and pulled the drawer all the way out to see if there was anything he might have missed. He tried to remember if he'd ever noticed Aunt Delta wearing one of the rings. As far as he knew, she had never been engaged or married. Of course he hadn't known her when she was young. By the time Dutch began his regular summer visits, Delta was already in her fifties.

Perhaps she had been married before Dutch was born and these were her wedding rings. It seemed odd to Dutch that no one in the family had ever mentioned it, though. In all likelihood Delta herself would have spoken of a serious relationship such as this. He knew Delta had inherited the house from her father, and all her money had come from Dutch's grandfather. Certainly his mother would know the story, but he wasn't about to call her at three in the morning.

Dutch took a deep breath and contemplated what to do. He probably should head back to the hotel and get a few hours sleep. Staying in the big empty house alone was too depressing, but it felt appropriate to be surrounded by the essence of his late aunt. He could almost feel her presence, as if she wasn't really even gone. He supposed these sorts of feelings were normal. He didn't want her to be gone, and the material possessions she'd left behind were stark reminders of who she had been.

He pushed the chair back and stood up. "I'm sorry, Aunt Delta," he whispered. "I wish I were strong like you. I wish I had the courage to be who I really am."

He extinguished the light and walked down the dark hallway to the front door. Everything would seem different in the daylight. After the weekend, when he was back home in Texas, things would be back to normal. He knew what he had to do. He'd call the real estate agent in the morning and have the house listed. He had to just put this all behind him and get on with his life.

"Fuckin holy hell!" Rustin declared. "Where the *fuck* did you learn to suck cock like that?"

Carlos looked up at him, grinning. He was on his knees in front of the sofa, between Rustin's outstretched legs. "You like?"

"Do I *like?*" Rustin repeated incredulously. "You just gave me the best head of my fuckin life, and you ask if I *like?* Holy fuck! Dude, do you even have a gag reflex?"

Carlos shrugged. "Honey, she knows how to dress, and she knows how to suck. What mores' a girl got to know?"

"Well, get up here, baby, and let me take care of *you* now."

"I'm all set, handsome," he said with a wink. "Pleasing you pleases me, if you know what I mean."

"At least gimme a little smooch . . . please."

Carlos climbed up on Rustin's lap and kissed him squarely on the lips.

"I think I'm going to love having you for a neighbor," Rustin said. He ran his hand down Carlos's smooth back and cupped one of his ass cheeks. "And what about this?" he asked.

"How bout we save that for next time?" Carlos whispered.

"Good morning, sleepy head." Tommy's greeting was a tad too cheerful, and it was all Rustin could do to force a smile. "Not much of a morning person, are we?" Tommy said.

The unintelligible groan that escaped Rustin's throat was all the answer Tommy needed.

"Well, good news then. It's *not* morning! It's already 11:30."

"Close enough," Rustin mumbled.

"I hope we didn't embarrass you last night," Tommy said as he poured Rustin a cup of coffee. "Cream and sugar?"

Rustin nodded. "You didn't. Look, sorry for the interruption. I had no idea you guys would be home so early."

"Weeknights are slow at the club. We're out of there by 1:30 or two usually." He opened the refrigerator to snag a carton of half-and-half, which he placed on the countertop next to Rustin's cup.

Rustin picked up the sugar decanter and poured a liberal amount in his cup, not bothering to measure. "It was a strange night all the way around," Rustin conceded.

"Hm, I don't know," Tommy said. "You really think the spanking is all that strange? I hardly even consider it kinky."

Rustin stared at him for a moment, perplexed. "No, not that. It was strange because of that Dutch guy. He just like took off on me all of a sudden."

"After you left here?" Tommy asked. "You hungry? I'll make you an omelet."

"I think I just want toast or something," Rustin replied. "Yeah, we were out in the hallway after . . . well, ya know . . . after we barged in on you. Then he kissed me and just suddenly bolted."

"Aw, that's kind of romantic," Tommy said, smiling. He grabbed a loaf of bread from the top of the refrigerator. "We only have seven grain bread. Is that okay?"

"Sure," Rustin said, "I can get that."

"Sit down and drink your coffee," Tommy said. "You need to wake up still. But tell me all about this kiss. What was it like?"

Rustin stared blankly ahead, focusing on a fridge magnet in the shape of a banana. It was positioned adjacent a photo-shopped image of a shirtless Bill Clinton with his arm around an equally hunky and buff Al Gore.

"It was wonderful," Rustin said. "You know, like two minutes of heaven. Then all of a sudden he said it was too complicated and left me standing there."

"Ohh . . . well that doesn't exactly sound good," Tommy said. "Wonder if he has a boyfriend already."

"Colby," Rustin said flatly.

Tommy started to laugh. "Um no. Be serious. Colby is too much of a slut to be anyone's boyfriend."

"Maybe so, but Dutch probably doesn't realize this. He's not really even out all that much. He's only had one boyfriend—some ranch hand that worked on their family's farm."

"I bet when he says 'complicated' he's talking about his situation back home. If he's still in the closet, it probably scared him a little. I mean, in all honesty, I could see how he'd fall hard for you."

"I don't know, but I don't want to play those games. Whatever."

Tommy shook his head reprovingly. "That's crazy, dude. He kissed you, so what're you bitching about? I can't believe how quickly you've adapted to gay time. In the real world, things don't always happen overnight. There are a lot of guys who like taking things slower, and you guys really just met yesterday."

"He's leaving in a few days and going back to Texas."

"Texas. Big deal. It's not like he's headed for Siberia."

"I guess I just don't do rejection too well."

"So you had to jack off last night. You'll get over it. I think you should call him sometime today and ask for a second date."

Rustin laughed. "Well, I didn't exactly have to jack off."

"What do you mean?" Tommy stood with his hands on his hips.

"Well, I met the neighbor."

"Carlos?"

Rustin nodded. "And let me tell you, if you've ever wondered where the expression, 'he can suck a golf ball through a garden hose' came from, look no further."

"Oh my God, and I thought Colby was a slut!"

"Shut *up!*" Rustin exclaimed. "What was I supposed to do? Dutch got me all horny and then just fuckin' left."

Tommy sighed and shook his head. "Shame, shame. Well, just so you know, Carlos is not the boyfriend type either. I don't see him settling down any time soon."

"Nah, I know. Actually I think it just pissed me off that Dutch took off. I figured he was probably gonna hook up with Colby, so . . ."

"Now you're rationalizing," Tommy said. "Why don't you just admit you wanted a blowjob and Carlos was there, eager and ready."

"That too," Rustin agreed.

"Call Dutch today," Tommy said in a rather stern voice. The toast popped up, and he grabbed it and threw it on a plate. He stepped back over to the fridge to locate a tub of margarine.

"I'll think about it," Rustin said.

"Do you want jelly?" Tommy asked.

"I had her last night," Rustin replied, "*Kay Why* Jelly."

"Very funny." Tommy rolled his eyes as he slammed the refrigerator door.

The hotel room was so dark when he awoke that Dutch thought it was still the middle of the night, but the digital alarm clock read 12:06. Had he slept all day? He'd crashed as soon as he got back to the room, without even bothering to get undressed, and he hated the grubby, unclean feeling of sleeping in his clothes. When he pulled back the curtain of the bedroom window, blinding light flooded the room, and he realized it must be approaching mid-day.

He stumbled to the bathroom and relieved himself, then popped a couple aspirin in his mouth and took a swig of the four-dollar bottled water that had been left on the vanity by housekeeping. Nothing was free any more, not even water. What he really needed was coffee, but he didn't want to mess around with the rinky-dink, in-room coffee maker, so he trudged out to the living room area of his suite and used the hotel phone to order room service.

If he didn't keep moving, he knew he'd become complacent and waste the day. There was too much to do. He had to call the real estate agent, begin sorting through his aunt's belongings to see if there was anything he wanted to keep, and of course force himself to make an overdue call to Kirsten, the woman he was going to be marrying in three months.

Dutch knew what to expect when he returned home. It would surely be a whirlwind of activity, not just with the ranch, but also with the wedding. Between his mother and his fiancé, they would have a litany of activities scheduled. Fittings, rehearsals, caterers, cake decorator, florists. Most of the details had been decided, but Kirsten was very emphatic about maintaining a pretense that Dutch's opinion actually mattered. She wanted him to be "involved."

He was going to have to stay focused. His first couple days in New Orleans had been filled with distraction. He never should have gone to that club. Hooking up with the dancer was a huge mistake, and even worse was the date he'd had last night with the bartender. Dutch had said too much. He'd opened up to the kid and told him things he'd never put into words before, and that was never a good a thing. There was no way Dutch would ever be able to make Rustin understand his situation. He didn't really even understand it all himself. How'd he ever got himself into this mess?

Everything would be fine as soon as he got back home. Things would return to normal, and he'd be able to forget about New Orleans. He'd be able to put behind him the memory of Aunt Delta and focus on his real life. Most importantly, he'd be able to forget about Rustin and the way they'd kissed. He'd be able to bury the memory of Rustin's lips pressed against his own, Rustin's hands wrapped around his shoulders, and his powerful, masculine scent. He'd be able to forget how hard his cock had throbbed when the boy drove his tongue deep into Dutch's mouth.

He was aroused now, just thinking of it, so he dragged himself out of his chair and charged into the bathroom. He started the shower—cold—and stripped off his clothes, tossing them into a pile on the bathroom floor. For ten minutes he stood under the frigid stream, trying to wash away his feelings—his homosexuality.

When Dutch stepped out of the bathroom, he felt better. His head was clearer, and he knew he'd be able to face the day. He just had to get into the right frame of mind. Work mode. Do the things he had to do in New Orleans and then get back home. He opened the dresser drawer and pulled out some comfortable clothes—Jeans and a t-shirt. He'd be doing physical labor, rummaging through the contents of his aunt's house, boxing things up and carrying packages. He wasn't going to dress up.

He was almost dressed when he heard the knock on the door. It must be his coffee. He grabbed his wallet off the dresser and headed over to the door, barefoot. As he flung the door open, there stood Rustin, holding a tray of coffee.

"Fresh coffee!" Rustin said, smiling.

Dutch was flabbergasted and didn't immediately know what to say.

"Can I come in?" Rustin said, laughing.

"Oh, yeah." Dutch stepped aside and allowed his guest to enter. "I must've been in the shower when room service got here."

"They were outside. I tipped the dude and told him I'd deliver your java."

"Oh, well thanks. Here, how much do I—"

"Don't worry about it." He walked over to the coffee table and set the tray down. "I hope it's okay that I just showed up like this."

"Actually . . ."

"You left so suddenly last night. Why'd you take off like that?"

Dutch closed the door, not looking Rustin in the eye. He stood there for a moment, running his fingers through his damp hair. "Rustin . . ."

"I thought we had a good time last night. Meaningful conversation, a nice walk after dinner . . . a passionate kiss on the stairwell . . ."

"About that . . ."

"*What* about that? Was it as good for you as it was for me? It sure seemed like it."

Dutch sighed and stepped closer to his unexpected guest. "Rustin, I tried to tell you last night, things are complicated for me."

"Yeah, and what does that mean?"

"It means they're complicated. You know I'm here on business. I'm here to take care of my aunt's estate, and then I'm gonna be leaving. Going back home to Texas, and we probably will never see each other again. Do you really want to get involved?"

"It's just that if that's what you're really worried about, why didn't you just fuck me? I'm not so fragile that I can't handle a one-night stand."

Dutch laughed. "No, you hardly seem fragile, but maybe I am."

"Dutch, Texas is not the other side of the world. It's a few hours from here."

"You have no idea. It might not be all that far from here geographically, but believe me, it's a world away."

"I think there's a bigger issue than just you and me. I moved here in order to begin my life and embrace who I really am. I couldn't continue hiding out in a closet."

"Rustin, I think that's great. You came out, and that's very brave of you. But my situation is different. *I* am different. I don't know if I'll ever be ready to be that open. It's just not possible."

Rustin stepped closer to him. "Why? Can you at least tell me what it is that's preventing you from allowing yourself to be happy?"

When Rustin placed his hand on Dutch's arm, Dutch softened. He didn't immediately pull away, but stared directly into Rustin's eyes. "You said you don't think it was a coincidence that we met. Well, nothing about my life is coincidental. It's all been planned—mapped out for me from the time I was very young. I've always had to do the things that I'm *supposed* to do."

"What if you're supposed to do the things that are *not* expected of you?" Rustin asked.

"Rustin . . ." Dutch's voice trailed off. He couldn't think of anything else to say. He had no counterargument because he knew the internal war that waged within him was a battle between his heart and his mind. With Rustin standing right in front of him, touching him and staring him in the face, Dutch felt his heart starting to win.

He moved closer to Rustin, reaching up to touch his face with the very tips of his fingers. "You're so beautiful," he whispered.

"Dutch, please give me a chance."

Dutch grabbed hold of him, pulling Rustin into himself as they pressed their lips together. Suddenly Rustin's arms were around him. Hard pecs pressed against Dutch's muscular torso. Dutch grabbed hold of the young man's head, running his fingers through the short hair. Their tongues met, and they tasted one another. Their embrace lingered, and for whatever reason, Dutch didn't pull away this time. He couldn't pull back. He couldn't let go.

The passion escalated as they clung to one another, and Dutch knew he had never wanted anyone the way he wanted this man who was now in his arms. The urgency within him bubbled up and was translated into sensuality. It was so much more than lust. It transcended sexual desire. It was as much about Dutch and who he was as it was about Rustin and his attractiveness.

Finally another who understood Dutch's turmoil. At last a man who'd been through the same struggle. Dutch had never felt secure enough to embrace his identity and be his authentic self, but Rustin had. And now Rustin conveyed to him how very much he believed in Dutch. He had a confidence that Dutch admired and envied. Might it be possible that Dutch could find this same strength within himself?

And Rustin was hot. He was drop dead gorgeous with his dark eyes and caramel hair. Just seeing him made Dutch's pulse quicken and his cock twitch. The man was sex on legs, and Dutch wanted all of him he could get. He could not get close enough. Couldn't drive his tongue in deeply enough. Couldn't hold him tightly enough.

"Why do you make me feel this way?" Dutch gasped. "I've never . . . never wanted anyone so bad."

"I feel the same," Rustin said. "Oh God, I want you."

Dutch steered him backward, leading him toward the sofa. Not taking his eyes off of Dutch, the young man trusted him, and as they eased themselves onto the cushions, their mouths remained pressed together. Dutch slid his hand under the tail of Rustin's shirt, running his fingers across the grooves of Rustin's rippled abs. As he explored the body of his sexy companion with his fingers, he used his mouth to kiss him all the more passionately.

Rustin responded in kind, grasping Dutch's bicep with one hand while holding the back of Dutch's head with the other. The tight grip of Rustin's fingers on the back of his skull told Dutch how desperately Rustin wanted him. They gasped, intermittently coming up for air every few seconds, as they continued to ravage one another.

Soon Rustin was fumbling with the button on Dutch's jeans, trying to release it with one hand. Dutch responded by sliding his hand further up Rustin's body, past his navel, till he found one of the nipples on Rustin's hairless chest. He used his thumb and forefinger to tweak it as Rustin continued his fervent assault on Dutch's mouth, ardently probing with his tongue. They moved their heads from side to side—kissing, tasting, and devouring one another.

It was Dutch who pulled his face away first, but only in order to explore more of the young man in his arms. He burrowed his face into the hollow of Rustin's neck, lapping the most sensitive area with his tongue. Rustin's response was to writhe and moan, indicating to Dutch that he'd found an erogenous zone. With his mouth pressed firmly against the delightful region of Rustin's neck—the soft spot between his chin and collar bone—Dutch shifted his weight, leaning into Rustin's body. He continued to tweak Rustin's nipple with one hand, and with the other he pressed his palm against the massive bulge in Rustin's crotch.

Rustin threw his head back and bucked his hips while spreading his legs wide apart. His body language sent Dutch a clear message to continue and he began to lick, tweak, and massage with abandon. As Rustin tugged at his t-shirt, pulling it rapidly over his head in one smooth movement, Dutch pulled back for three seconds that seemed an eternity. Rustin tossed the shirt aside and settled back against the sofa while Dutch wrapped his moist lips around Rustin's nipple, flicking it repeatedly with the tip of his tongue. While using his mouth to suck the right nipple, he pinched and gently twisted the left. Rustin was now moaning and clutching Dutch's shoulders.

Dutch continued his descent downward, tracing the line that separated the rippling muscles of Rustin's abdomen. You didn't get an eight pack like this without spending some serious time in the gym, and Dutch knew a man's abdominals were his core. If Rustin's abs were this toned, then Dutch couldn't wait to see the rest of him. Dutch slid off the sofa and onto his knees between Rustin's legs. He glanced up to take in the sight of Rustin's smooth chest. He was muscular and perfectly proportioned, though not bulky. His pectorals and biceps were not as beefed up as were Dutch's, but they were *fine.*

He wasted no time in unbuttoning the fly, and with Rustin's cooperation, he slid the jeans and boxer briefs all the way down to Rustin's ankles. Rustin toed off his sneakers, allowing Dutch to tug off the pants and toss them aside. Rustin spread his legs wide as Dutch positioned himself between them. He used both hands to caress Rustin's inner thighs, taking in their beauty as he did so. Long and graceful, yet sinewy and masculine, his powerful legs conveyed strength and confidence. Rustin sat there like a king on his throne, and Dutch was on his knees ready to worship.

He cupped Rustin's ball sac with the palm of his left hand, gently massaging it, and with his right grabbed hold of the base of Rustin's rigid shaft. It was bone-hard, the head engorged and oozing precum, and its searing heat was like fire in Dutch's hand. He bowed his head, leaning in to press his lips against the bulbous head, at first kissing it. Lapping up the precum with the flick of his tongue, he inhaled the musky aroma of Rustin's manly scent. Unable to hold back any longer, he lunged forward, mouth agape, and devoured the entirety of Rustin's massive prong.

Dutch pressed his tongue firmly against the underside of the shaft and clamped his lips around the girth of the pole, forming a moist, slippery suction. His intention was not to waste time with foreplay, but to make a lasting impression on the first intake. In one smooth motion, he slid all the way down, opening his throat to welcome the entirety of Rustin's full eight inches. Dutch's nose burrowed into Rustin's neatly trimmed patch of pubic hair as Rustin moaned above him. Dutch felt the hands of his lover suddenly grip his shoulders as he began to suck Rustin's cock in earnest.

Dutch knew all the tricks. He knew the hot spots—where to focus his attention—and he used his tongue expertly to massage the sensitive, spongy area just below the crown. With his saliva, he lathed Rustin's cock, creating a slick coating around the shaft. Holding the base firmly in his hand, he began to bob up and down, massaging with his tongue on the down-strokes and sucking his way back up the shaft. Never once did he take his mouth off Rustin's cock.

"Aw fuck!" Rustin cried. "Un-fucking-believable."

As he pleasured Rustin's shaft with his mouth, he stroked his balls with his free hand, rolling them with his thumb and gently brushing with his fingertips. Rustin responded by spreading his legs further apart and running his fingers through Dutch's hair. Dutch glanced up to meet Rustin's gaze. The way he looked down at him said to Dutch that he was both content and incredibly turned on. It only spurred Dutch on, and he redoubled his effort by sucking with all the more vigor.

"Babe, you got me so close. I'm so damn close!"

Dutch impaled himself, thrusting his head downward all the way so that Rustin's cockhead was completely surrounded by the tight walls of his throat. He felt the pulsing of the shaft against his tongue, which coincided perfectly with Rustin's elevated moans of pleasure.

"Ahh," he cried, grabbing hold of the sides of Dutch's head. He fired his load, erupting with multiple and successive jets of copious semen that filled Dutch's gulping throat. He eagerly swallowed, but the flood was so torrential that it quickly backed up onto his tongue. Dutch savored the somewhat bitter and salty flavor, sliding off the shaft just a bit in order to gulp down every drop.

"Oh my God!" Rustin exclaimed. "*How?* What the fuck is it about this city? Is it the blowjob capital of the world or what?"

Dutch smiled and looked up. He was still holding the base of the shaft and licking the head like an ice cream cone. "What do you mean?"

Rustin was panting. "I got blown already . . . yesterday . . . and I thought it was the best fucking head of my life. Until now."

Dutch grinned at him. "You slut," he teased.

"You don't know the half of it," Rustin said, "but I have a feeling that from this point forward I won't be needing anyone else's services."

Dutch slid back onto the sofa, leaning into Rustin for a kiss.

"I need you inside me," Rustin whispered. "I need you so bad."

By three o'clock that afternoon, Dutch had still not called his real estate agent. He and Rustin were lying in bed together, naked. Dutch lay on his back, and Rustin was curled beside him, his head resting in the crook of Dutch's shoulder.

"Do you really think you're up to a fourth round?" Rustin asked as he ran his fingers through the patch of short hair on Dutch's chest.

Dutch laughed, staring up at the ceiling light. "I thought I would get a lot done today," he said.

"You *did*," Rustin assured him. "Well, you got one thing done several times."

"One *person*," Dutch corrected.

Rustin snuggled closer to him. "Yes, you did me. You did me damn good."

"Rustin, why don't you rent my aunt's house from me?" Dutch suggested. "You could move in and take care of it, and when I came here to visit, I'd know just where to find you."

Rustin shifted, using his elbow to prop himself up so he could look Dutch in the face. "Dutch, I'd love that, but I can't."

"Why not?" he asked. "It's too soon . . . I know."

"No, it's not that. I'm a college student, and I work as a bartender. I could never afford . . ."

Dutch shook his head and placed his finger over Rustin's lips to shush him. "No, I don't mean rent. You wouldn't have to pay anything."

Rustin stared at him, a shocked look on his face. "I don't know what to say."

"Say yes," Dutch said. "I mean, after you've seen the place. We can go look at it today. Right now, if you want."

"But Dutch, isn't it too soon?"

Dutch shrugged. "I've been racking my brain, trying to come up with a solution. I don't want to sell the house, but I can't move here. If you lived in the house, I could at least visit, and it'd give me time to figure things out."

"And what if you don't figure them out? What if you don't ever get to a point—"

"A little bit ago you told me that I had to embrace who I am and start coming out of the closet. Maybe I'm not ready to do that entirely, but at least this is a start."

"So you're saying that if I move into your aunt's house, eventually you may move in with me? You may leave Texas and move here?"

"I don't know," Dutch said. "I told you, things are complicated. But this would buy me some time, and it would give *us* time too."

"I'm not sure I want a landlord like you, though," Rustin said in mock seriousness.

"Oh really. Why?"

"I think you'd be riding my ass constantly."

"You know I would," Dutch said, laughing. He wrapped his arm around Rustin and pulled him onto his chest. "Just say yes."

"Yes," Rustin whispered, and then they kissed.

An hour later, after showering together, they headed out. They'd decided to take a carriage ride over to look at the house. Dutch stopped at the front desk and asked if housekeeping could pick up a bag of laundry from his room.

As they exited the hotel, they noticed a middle-aged man standing near the door smoking. Rustin asked if he could bum a cigarette.

"You smoke?" Dutch asked incredulously.

"Only after sex," he said, reaching down to cup one of Dutch's ass cheeks.

Dutch turned to the middle-aged man standing next to them, who was holding out a Marlboro Light and smiling broadly. "Can I just buy that whole pack off you?" Dutch asked.

"I'd suggest you just go across the street and buy yourself an entire carton," the man said with a wink.

Yeah, New Orleans was certainly a world away from Texas.

"So, did Rustin say anything to you about last night?" Deejay asked as he poured olives from the decanter into the square container that was kept behind the bar.

"He was embarrassed a little," Tommy laughed.

"I told him he didn't have to officially start until tomorrow, but if he wants to work tonight, he can."

"He's with his cowboy," Tommy said with raised eyebrows. "I think you should just let him have the night off."

"No problem." Deejay picked up a bar rag and wiped up the olive juice that had splashed onto the countertop. "Just be prepared to run your cute little ass all over tonight then, cause it's just you and me."

"What cowboy are you talking about?" Tommy turned around to see Colby rounding the corner. "You don't mean *my* cowboy, do you? *Dutch?*"

Deejay gave Tommy a surreptitious look but didn't speak. "Colby, he's not *yours*, and you know it," Tommy said.

"Well I had him first," the dancer stated confidently. Tommy didn't like the arrogance of his tone.

"Colby, you're adorable and all, but we all know you're not interested in anything more than a one-night stand. Be glad you got *that*, and let Rustin work on something that may actually prove to be long term—or at least meaningful—with Dutch."

"Rustin can have his straight boy," Colby said flippantly. "I got better things to do than chase after closet cases."

"What are you talking about?" Tommy said, stepping closer.

"The guy's engaged to be married. His girlfriend—or fiancé or whatever—called him when I was in the hotel room."

"You're making this up," Tommy said, shaking his head.

"Swear to God," Colby said, raising his right hand.

Tommy stood there with his mouth open. "No wonder he told Rustin it was complicated. Oh my God, poor Rustin."

"Poor *Rustin?*" Another voice was heard from, as Carlos stepped up behind Colby. He was making tsking sounds with his tongue. "There ain't no reason you should *ever* feel sorry for that boy. Let me tell you, he is *blessed*, and when I say 'blessed', I'm talkin at least nine inches."

Colby guffawed. "Well forget the cowboy! I'll take the horse."

"Stop it, both of you!" Tommy scolded. "Obviously the two of them have some issues to work out, and they don't need interference from either of you."

Deejay placed his hand on Tommy's shoulder. "Baby, you can't be everyone's mother."

"That's right, Sugar," Carlos said, placing a hand on his hips. "Sometimes you just got to let boys be boys."

"And the cowboy's not gonna be around that long," Colby added. "He's going back to Texas after this weekend, and I'm pretty sure our new employee is going to be just heartbroken."

"And in need of some tender loving care," Carlos said.

"Which I will be happy to provide," countered Colby.

"You slut."

"Bitch!"

"Wait, why can't we share?"

Deejay turned to Tommy and laughed. "I think I'm staying out of this one."

Cocktails

"Maybe I should, too," Tommy said. "What a mess."

"What a mess is right," Dutch said as he surmised the condition of the attic. "It's going to take me forever to sort through all this stuff."

Rustin was standing behind him. "Why bother?" he asked. "I mean why bother right now? You have the rest of your life to go through all this. If I were you, I'd just do it a box or two at a time. As long as you're keeping the house, why does it matter if this stuff is up here in the attic?"

Dutch nodded. "Good point. And you know there are probably generations' worth of memories here. Delta inherited this house from my Granddaddy."

"Yeah, you're making the right decision by not selling. If you got rid of this house, I guarantee you that down the road you'd really regret it."

Dutch stepped over to one of the boxes and opened the lid. "Pictures," he said. "Weird. My aunt was so persnickety. It's not like her to just throw photos in a box like this."

"I dunno. My family has some boxes of old pictures too. I think probably every family does," Rustin said. "You always think one day you'll get around to putting them in an album or something, but you never do."

Dutch knelt down beside the box and pulled out one of the photos. It was a 5x7 black and white picture of two young women, probably in their twenties. "This is a cool picture," he said. "Look at the dresses they were wearing."

"Who is it? Do you know?"

Dutch shook his head and turned the photo around, looking for an inscription on the back. "It's my Aunt Delta, and the other girl is someone named Bonnie."

"Her sister?"

"No, she was the only girl."

"But they're holding hands," Rustin said.

Dutch shrugged. "It must be someone Aunt Delta knew when she was younger. I never heard her talk about anyone named Bonnie."

"Look, there are more pictures of her."

Dutch picked up one of the photos that Rustin had pointed out. "Here's another one of them together." It was a larger print, and a more close-up shot. The female couple was sitting together, Delta with her hand atop Bonnie's. Dutch noticed she was wearing a ring.

"Are you sure your aunt wasn't a lesbian?" Rustin asked.

Immediately Dutch shook his head. "No, of course not. I would have known."

He started rifling through the box, pulling out several other photos. He found some of Bonnie alone. She was wearing a ring identical to the one Delta had worn in the previous picture. "These rings," Dutch said as realization suddenly dawned, "I know them. I found them last night in the desk drawer."

"Wedding rings," Rustin said. "They were married."

"Do you think..."

Rustin nodded. "I think your aunt had a lover named Bonnie, and they were married. Not legally, but still married."

"Holy shit!" Dutch said, smiling. "No wonder my mother hated her."

"Your mother hated her because she was gay?"

"My mom's old school. Very traditional, and she... well, she doesn't understand."

Rustin placed a hand on Dutch's shoulder. "What about when she finds out about her son?"

"I don't even want to think about it," Dutch said, "and so I'm not going to."

Walking beside his lover down Charles Street, Dutch wanted to take hold of his hand. He resisted, unable to free himself of the self-consciousness ingrained by his conservative Texas upbringing. He wasn't in Texas, though, and since arriving in New Orleans he'd observed several same-sex couples in the open, carelessly displaying their affection. The atmosphere was different here. Though steeped in southern tradition, the immutably pastoral city surged with a progressive energy. It was a city that never slept, where all were welcome. The architecture and moderate climate were constant, yet the historical city seemed to absorb the waves of change that flooded its crowded cobblestone streets. The traditional backdrop was a glaring contradiction of the surging and vibrant carefree atmosphere that thrived within the heart of the French Quarter.

He sidled up next to Rustin, allowing his shoulder rub against his lover's. How had so much changed in twenty-four hours? Earlier that morning, Dutch had resigned himself to his fate of returning home and leaving behind the temptations of this deliciously decadent city. He'd decided to do what was expected of him, to go back to the life that had been laid out for him by his family. There seemed to be no other choice.

Now, a few hours of love-making later, he felt as if he were on an entirely different path. It was cowardly, he realized. It was only a compromise. He was kicking the can down the road so that he could avoid making a painful decision.

He knew that the dark secret he kept from Rustin would lead to a catastrophic confrontation, but he was not ready to bare his soul. If he told Rustin the truth about his engagement to Kirsten, all would be ruined.

So he parsed his words. He was very careful not to make promises. Instead he offered solutions. Wasn't that what his daddy had taught him? You can't please everyone, but you sure as hell can make them think you can. Keeping Delta's home afforded him a means to provide for Rustin and assured that he'd be available to Dutch when he needed an escape from the pretentious life he was doomed to live. It was something he could easily explain to his mother. Presently the market was not good, and it would be foolish to sell at a time that property values were so low. Rustin was just his tenant, and nothing more.

Rustin leaned into him, pressing his hand against the lower part of Dutch's back. "I love the house," he said. "It's unbelievable. Thank you for . . . well, for everything. It's going to be just perfect."

Dutch smiled at Rustin without speaking. He looked down at the pavement beneath his feet.

"You have a decision to make." A stranger's voice interrupted them.

"You have a decision to make," Colby repeated to the customer. "Do you want to slide that bill down the front of my shorts . . . or the back?" He was kneeling on the bar, leaning over to speak directly into the ear of the middle-aged man who'd been tipping him.

The gentleman smiled, revealing a row of tar-stained incisors. "Where do you want it, baby?"

Colby leaned back on his haunches and then slowly thrust his pelvis forward, right into the customer's perspiring face. Beads of sweat rolled down the man's chubby cheeks as he fumbled with the dollar bill, snatching the elastic waistband of the shorts with one hand and using the other to cram the bill deep down into Colby's privates.

The portly customer giggled, bouncing on his barstool as he stared up at the nearly naked dancer. Colby continued to smile at him sweetly. "Thank you, baby," Colby said, again leaning down to whisper into the man's ear. "I love it when you touch me that way."

The customer wiggled in his seat as he plunged his hand into his own pocket, pulling out a fresh wad of bills. Without any further encouragement, he peeled off a twenty, and slid it into the dancer's waistband.

"Oh yeah," Colby said. "Feels so good."

Tommy stood less than three feet away, taking in the scene. He shook his head as he turned to his partner. "Colby's got himself a live one tonight."

Deejay nodded. "He's definitely a payer. Some sort of newspaper editor or something. He'll drop two or three hundred tonight easy."

"I don't get it," Tommy said. "Why doesn't he just hire himself an escort? I mean, it'd be a lot cheaper."

Deejay shrugged and grinned. "Babe, it's the whole atmosphere. The music, the public setting. Look around. That man thinks that out of all these people in this bar, Colby has chosen to shower *him* with affection."

"But that's because he's paying."

"Part of the illusion," Deejay laughed. "The fantasy."

"Well, I guess I can't fault the guy. I know how easy it is to be swept away by a fantasy, especially when it involves a go-go dancer." He was remembering his own experience when he'd first started working at the Men's Room. Tommy had dated one of the dancers briefly before he started seeing Deejay.

"It obviously makes the man happy. I don't think anyone here can look at him and say he's not having a great time."

Tommy laughed. "Well, that's easy for you to say. You're not the one who's going to be scrubbing down that bar stool at the end of the night."

Deejay snapped his towel, nailing Tommy on the cheek of his butt.

"Ouch!" Tommy protested. He balled up his fist and slugged his boyfriend on the upper part of his bicep.

Deejay stuck out his lip as if pouting then reached up to rub his arm. "I can't believe you just hit me!"

"Poor baby," Tommy said in a tone dripping with sarcasm. "I'll be back. We need more ice."

"Let the Oracle guide you," the old woman said. She had her bony fingers wrapped securely around Dutch's elbow. The light from the streetlamp reflected in the black beads that hung around her neck. "You've come to the right place for answers, young man . . . you simply must believe."

Startled and unsure what to do, Dutch pulled back. "Um . . . no, I'm sorry. Ma'am, you've got the wrong . . ."

"Wait," Rustin said, smiling. "Dutch, let's do it. Let's have her read your fortune."

Dutch shook his head, staring wide-eyed into his boyfriend's face.

Rustin started laughing. "Dutch, you can't *seriously* be afraid?"

"I . . . um . . . we don't believe in this sort of thing."

"There's nothing to fear, child," the elderly woman said to him. She spoke in a hushed tone though her voice was raspy.

"It's the occult," Dutch insisted, "and it's of the Devil."

Both the fortune teller and Rustin laughed together. "No it's not!" Rustin said. "It's just for fun. They use cards and make predictions about your future. Give you advice. There's nothing Satanic about it. Am I right?" He looked to the old woman.

She nodded and once again reached out to Dutch. "You are correct, son," she said. "The legend of the Tarot is as old as time itself, and the insight it provides is far greater than the problem with which you now struggle."

How could this woman know anything about Dutch's inner turmoil? How could she possibly know he was facing a big decision?

"How . . . how do you know about me?"

"I can sense when a soul is questioning, and this is why I'm here. I've been sent to help those who are in need of guidance."

"For a small fee," Rustin added, winking at Dutch.

"A mere twenty dollars," she said. "Even those who are called to a spiritual profession must eat. Don't you agree?"

"Come on, Dutch," Rustin said. "I'll pay the fee. Let's do it . . . it'll be fun."

They didn't have this sort of thing where Dutch came from. Anything paranormal or spiritual was deemed un-Christian. It was of the occult, which meant that it was from Satan. Dutch had been warned from the time he was young to avoid such witchcraft at all costs. He shook his head defiantly.

"The rings have brought you here," she whispered. "The very rings that will determine your fate."

The rings? She couldn't possibly mean the rings that had belonged to his Aunt Delta. "How do you know about the rings?" he asked. He felt a shiver travel up the back of his spine.

She took hold of his hand and began to lead him across the sidewalk to a small card table she had set up. The table was situated beneath a makeshift awning—a tarp held up by four wooden posts.

"Sit, child," she instructed him. At this point, Dutch was unsure what to do, but he was too spooked to even say anything.

Rustin followed them over to the table, pulled out his wallet, and handed the seer a twenty.

"Another twenty will ensure a full and comprehensive reading," she coaxed. "The twelve-card layout is forty."

Rustin shrugged. "What the hell," he said and handed over another bill. No sooner could Dutch blink than the money disappeared, tucked away somewhere in the billowing fabric of the old lady's gown.

She moved to the other side of the table and took a seat while Rustin pulled up a chair beside Dutch. "Welcome, my young friends," she said. "You have entered the realm of the impossible, where the arcane is revealed and where the future is laid before us."

Dutch cleared his throat.

"Dutch, is it?" she asked.

"And I'm Rustin," Rustin said with enthusiasm.

"Ah, very good. My name is Roslyn. You're an attractive couple . . . and you have been lovers for how long?"

Dutch felt the heat rise in his cheeks.

"Oh my dear, there is naught for which to be ashamed," she said. Roslyn reached across the table and placed her hand atop Rustin's. Dutch remained seated with his arms folded across his chest. "The ability to love another of the same gender is a great gift of the gods—something for which you should be proud."

"We just met a couple days ago, actually," Rustin said. "But you're right. It *is* like a gift." He smiled and glanced over to meet Dutch's gaze.

"First, my love, you must relax," she said. "Dutch, place your hands on the edge of the table, palms up, and take a few deep breaths. Close your eyes and inhale deeply through your nose, exhaling from your mouth."

Seriously?

He looked at Rustin, who gave him an encouraging nod, and then turned back to the seer. Forcing a smile, he sat up straighter in his chair and squared his shoulders, then placed his hands on the table as instructed. As he closed his eyes and inhaled, he became aware of the enchanting aroma of the incense that was burning nearby.

"Very slowly," she said in a most soothing voice. "Just relax and allow your mind to completely clear."

How did one allow their mind to clear? If you were thinking about clearing your mind, then your mind wasn't really clear, was it?

Dutch tried to do as she said, willing himself to relax. With his deliberate intake of crisp night air, he allowed the wafting aroma—a heady mixture of jasmine and sandalwood—to soothe him. He released the breath equally as slow and repeated. The husky voice of his soothsayer was melodic, lulling him into a state of calmness.

"Just relax, my boy," she said, "and open your mind to the past, present, and future."

The contrast of her soft fingertips to his calloused palms was stark as Roslyn placed her hands within his. Her gentle touch aided his relaxation.

"There is a strong presence that surrounds you," she whispered. "A woman."

Dutch's eyes shot open, and as he stared directly into her face, he felt the grip of her hands tighten. The flickering candlelight illuminated her wrinkled brow, and with her sapphire eyes aglow, Roslyn met his gaze. He felt as if she were looking directly into his soul.

"A lost loved one. Someone for whom you cared deeply."

Mouth agape, Dutch simply nodded.

"Delia?" she said. "No, Delilah? It's not clear . . . *Delta*," she finally stated with confidence.

A single, plump tear welled in Dutch's eye and trickled down the side of his cheek. "My aunt."

He heard Rustin gasp.

"Your aunt is with you now." No longer grasping for the right words, but rather channeling those of another, she spoke with a voice of authority. "I love you, Dutchy," she said.

Delta was the only person he'd ever allowed to get away with the nickname.

"Why?" he whispered. "Why did you leave me like this?" The tears that streamed from his eyes scalded his cheeks, but he dared not pull away from his medium. He continued to grip her hands with fierce intensity.

"I have not yet left you, love," she said.

"I need you now." The whimpering sound of his childlike plea made him feel so small. So helpless and vulnerable.

"Dutchy, I won't leave until you're ready, but soon you must let go."

He didn't know what she was saying. Was he to sell the house and move on with his life? Was his aunt telling him that he had to let go of her memory?

Roslyn spoke again. "Let go of your fear, and follow your heart."

"It's so hard," he confessed. The words escaped his throat in a sob.

"The rings will guide you . . . a perfect fit."

Suddenly she released his hands, pulling her arms back into herself. Her entire body trembled as if a chill had come over her.

Dutch and Rustin both stared at her, not daring to move a muscle.

For a moment she seemed unsure of herself, and then reached for the cards. "Shall we begin your reading, young one?"

He shook his head, rising from his seat. "No, no . . . I've heard enough," he said.

"But we've yet to begin," Roslyn said.

"Thank you," he said, wiping the tears from his face with his fingertips. "Thank you for everything. He reached in his pocket and pulled out his billfold. He tossed a hundred-dollar bill on the table. "Thank you," he said again, and extended his hand to Rustin.

"But wait," she protested, "We haven't even started the reading."

"It's okay," Rustin said, turning to her as they walked away hand in hand, "he got what he needed."

The young blonde stepped up to the counter, clearing her throat. It had been a long day, and she wanted to get checked into the hotel, take a hot bath, and spend a relaxing evening with her fiancé.

"Excuse me," she said, forcing a smile as the desk clerk looked up to meet her gaze.

"Checking in, ma'am?" the spiky-haired teen asked.

"Yes, I believe my fiancé is already here. I'll be staying with him. I just need a key."

He nodded and stepped over to his computer monitor. "Name?"

"Dutch Southworth," she said.

He scowled as he focused his attention on the screen. "I have an Elwood Southworth."

"Yes, that's him. Dutch is his nickname."

"I'm sorry, ma'am, but he does not have you listed on the room."

She rolled her eyes, annoyed. "Look, I'm his fiancé. How would I even know he is here otherwise? Just give me the key ... please." She offered another pretentious smile, this time batting her eyes.

The clerk was unaffected. "I'm sorry, but I will have to call Mr. Southworth for confirmation."

She sighed. "Very well, call him ... but I wanted this to be a surprise. Haven't you ever had anyone special in your life that you've wanted to surprise?"

He glanced up at her, and when she saw the glint in his eyes, she knew she'd made a connection. "Is he the cowboy?" the kid asked.

"Why yes, I believe that would be the one. Tight jeans, broad shoulders and blond hair."

"Yeah, I *definitely* know who you mean. He's your fiancé?"

She gave him the sweetest, toothiest smile of her life, holding up her left hand to display her diamond engagement ring.

"Lucky girl," the desk clerk muttered. She wasn't sure if he was referring to her fiancé or her ring.

"Yes, I certainly am. Won't you help me out, Richard?" She looked down at his name tag. "I promise I won't tell anyone."

Richard sighed and reached under the counter. "You're sure he's okay with this? He's not one of those types who hates surprises is he?"

"Dutch *loves* surprises," she assured him.

The kid looked around, glancing first to his left and then right. "Okay. I hope I don't get in trouble for this," he whispered.

"Thank you so much, Richard. You're a doll."

"That's what my boyfriend used to say . . . til he dumped me."

"Mr. Southworth?" the desk clerk sounded startled as he looked up.

Dutch let go of Rustin's hand. Well, perhaps everyone in New Orleans was not open-minded after all.

"Can ya'll check my messages?" he asked.

"Of course, sir," the young man said. He first looked on his computer screen and then turned to the wall behind him. Reaching into one of the compartments, he retrieved an envelope. "The housekeeping department found this in the pocket of one of your shirts when they were sorting your laundry."

"Oh my God!" Dutch exclaimed. "It's the rings."

"Your aunt's?" Rustin asked.

"Yeah, I must've forgotten to take them out of my pocket."

He pulled open the flap of the envelope and looked inside. Relieved to see both rings, he let out an audible sigh. "Oh thank you. Thank you so much." He glanced at the clerk's name tag. "Richard."

"You're welcome, sir."

"I would have been so upset if I'd lost these."

The kid smiled. "Then it's a very pleasant surprise."

Dutch laughed, nodding his head. "Yeah, this time it is, but I've gotta tell ya, I usually *hate* surprises."

"You do?" the slender, spiked-haired kid asked, gulping.

"Well don't you worry. It was my own fault. My mind was on other things this morning, and I forgot to take the rings out of my pocket."

"Yeah . . . all kinds of *other* things," Rustin said. He sidled up next to Dutch and grabbed hold of one ass cheek. Dutch jumped, surprised. In spite of himself, he laughed.

"Let's wait til we get back up to the room," he whispered.

"Don't know if I can wait that long," Rustin teased.

"Mr. Southworth," the clerk interrupted, "have you yet dined in our in-house restaurant? It's a five-star establishment."

Continuing to stare into Rustin's eyes, he shook his head. "Nah, we've already eaten, and now I'm ready for dessert."

"But sir," the boy said in a rather insistent tone, "I don't think you want to go up to your room just yet."

Dutch looked at him, noticing the kid was wringing his hands together. He looked nervous.

"Why not?" Dutch asked.

"Um . . . housekeeping is cleaning the room now."

Dutch cocked his head slightly, puzzled. He glanced down at his watch. "It's almost eleven o'clock at night," he said.

"It was a busy day, and . . . um, they fell behind schedule. My apologies, sir. If you'd like to wait in the dining room, your dessert is on me."

"I can hardly believe the restaurant is even open this late," Rustin said.

"How about the bar then?" the kid suggested.

"You know, the room really wasn't that messed up anyway," Dutch said.

"And we're probably just gonna trash it again," Rustin added.

Dutch laughed. "Don't worry, kid. I'm sure housekeeping won't mind if we send them on their way. I'll give 'em a nice tip."

"Oh crap," the clerk said. "Or I mean . . ."

"Really, it's okay," Rustin said, stepping up to the counter. "We don't care about the room being clean."

"Here," Dutch said, pulling out his wallet. "Richard, why don't you let me give you a reward. A finder's fee for the rings."

"Oh no," Richard said, shaking his head. "That won't be necessary."

"I insist," Dutch said, handing him a twenty. "Boy, you need to relax. Everything's fine."

Dutch turned and grabbed hold of Rustin's hand. "Come on," he said, "I'm *really* craving dessert now."

"Hello," she said as she picked up the receiver of the in-room hotel phone.

"Look, there's been a mistake, and you've got to leave the room. Now."

"I beg your pardon?" Kirsten said. She was already showered and wearing her sexiest negligee. She was not about to leave the room for any reason.

"Ma'am, you told me Mr. Southworth was your fiancé," he said.

"Yes, because he *is.*"

"And you said he loved surprises," Richard said.

"Well, I might have made that part up, but I can assure you, he'll be very happy to see me."

"I just . . . um . . . I don't want to lose my job. I *need* this job."

"What's going on here?" she asked. "Is something wrong?"

She heard Richard sigh into the receiver. "Your boyfriend . . . or, um, *fiancé* . . . he's on his way up to the room now."

"Oh. Okay good," she said, smiling as she glanced into the mirror to check her hair.

"Ma'am, he's not alone."

"What?" she said. *Another woman?*

"Mr. Southworth is on his way to the room now, and he has no idea you're there. But he's not alone."

She felt her cheeks getting hot. *Unbelievable. No wonder he wasn't returning my phone calls. He's cheating on me, three months before our wedding!*

She removed the receiver from her ear and eased it back into its cradle, ignoring the pleas of the desk clerk who was begging her not to get him fired. She turned and stepped toward the door. That son of a bitch, she thought. How dare he do this to her? And here all this time she'd felt sorry for him. Worried to death about him because she'd known how badly he was grieving the loss of his grandmother—or aunt, or whoever the fuck it was.

Come to find out he was here in Louisiana probably fucking every whore this side of the Mississippi. Well, she wasn't about to turn tail and run. She wasn't going to *leave* as the little faggot at the front desk had suggested. She was going to face him head on, and the slut he had with him. She'd meet his ass at the elevator.

With brisk steps, she stomped over to the door, grasping the handle as she took a deep breath. She flung the door open but then stepped back, astounded by the sight before her eyes. There stood Dutch, locked in a passionate kiss with another man!

"Holy fuck!"

Tommy's eyes rolled back in his head as Deejay swallowed him whole. They were in the office, and Tommy was stretched out across the desk, his legs spread wide. Deejay had cornered him in the storage room when he came back for ice.

He then dragged Tommy into the office and stripped him, ordering him up on the desk.

Tommy always knew when he needed to submit to the instructions of his superior. After all, Deejay *was* his boss.

"Oh God! Deejay, that feels so good."

The firm grip of Deejay's palm around his nut sac and the sensation of the tight throat that sheathed his throbbing cock, were nearly enough to make Tommy shoot his load right away. He willed himself to hold back, enjoying the warmth of Deejay's hungry mouth.

Deejay looked into his eyes as he slid back up the length of Tommy's hardon.

"You're so good at that," Tommy said, moaning.

Deejay began to slide up and down, bobbing on his cock. Tommy leaned back, using his elbows to prop himself upright on the desk. There was no question about it, Deejay knew how to suck dick. Tommy felt the silky smoothness of Deejay's tongue as it glided across his shaft. It was the most heavenly feeling he'd ever experienced. Not wanting to cum too soon, he closed his eyes and relaxed.

As Deejay continued his ministrations, Tommy allowed himself to edge closer and closer toward orgasm. His pulse quickened, and he began to buck upwards into Deejay's mouth, forcing his cock into the depths of his throat. Deejay offered no resistance, but swallowed his entirety with ease. Tommy thrust his pelvis into Deejay's face and moaned, realizing he'd reached his point of no return.

"I'm gonna fuckin shoot!" he cried out. Deejay went all the way down on his cock, taking him in balls-deep. Tommy whimpered as his body trembled. The volcano erupted, blasting a powerful stream of cum deep into his lover. "Ahhh!" he screamed.

When Deejay slid off his cock, Tommy was still trembling and gasping for air. Deejay leaned into him, offering a chaste kiss.

"Better get back to work," he whispered. "Or I'll have to dock your pay."

"Yes, sir," Tommy said with a sigh. He grinned at his boss as Deejay turned to leave the room, picking up the bucket of half-melted ice on his way out.

"What do you think she meant about the rings?" Dutch asked.

They were in the elevator, on their way up to Dutch's room.

Rustin thought a moment, careful to offer the right response. "I think it might be one of those things you will understand when the time is right," he said.

Dutch nodded. "A perfect fit," he said, repeating the words of the psychic. He reached into the envelope and took out one of the rings, sliding it onto his finger. "Look," he said, "it really *is* a perfect fit."

"Wow," Rustin said, "well I guess we know who one of the rings belongs to."

Dutch pulled out the second ring, holding it up. He couldn't be suggesting what Rustin was thinking. "Me?" Rustin asked, his voice a whisper.

"Try it," Dutch said.

His left hand was shaking as he held it out. Dutch wrapped one hand around his wrist, and with the other he held up the ring. Very carefully he slid it on. With ease, it slid into place, snugly resting at the base of Rustin's ring finger.

Rustin gasped, covering his mouth with his free hand. "Oh my God," he said.

The elevator door opened. They were on their floor. Dutch took Rustin's hand into his own and led him down the hall. Before inserting his key into the door, he turned to Rustin and looked him in the eye.

"Rustin, does this mean what I think it means?" There were tears in his eyes.

"I don't know," Rustin said, "but I know how I feel about you. I've never felt this way before. I've never been with anyone who made me feel so *right*."

Dutch shook his head. "Remember how I told you that things are complicated for me?"

Rustin nodded.

"Well, it's worse than complicated. There's something I haven't told you."

"Dutch, we can take it slow. You can tell me whatever you need to tell me when you know the time is right."

"I want to tell you everything. Now."

Rustin smiled. "Okay."

"When we get inside," Dutch said.

"Okay," Rustin stared at him, waiting for him to insert the key.

Dutch grabbed hold of him, turning away from the door. "Rustin, I . . . I think I love you."

"Dutch . . ." Rustin was overcome with emotion. He wrapped his arms around his cowboy, leaning in as he felt the crush of Dutch's lips on his own. Their tongues met, and their bodies pressed together. Closing his eyes, Rustin allowed himself to be swept away.

Until the door opened.

"What the *fuck?*"

Shocked, Rustin pulled away from Dutch, staring open-mouthed at the woman in the doorway. She was young and blonde, and very scantily dressed.

"Who . . ." Rustin began.

"Who the *fuck* are you?" she shrieked. "Dutch! Oh my God, Dutch!" She turned away and headed back into the room, leaving the door wide open.

"Dutch, what's going on?" Rustin asked, very confused.

"Shit!" he exclaimed, burying his face in his hands. "Fuck, Rustin I'm so sorry."

"This can't be what I think it is?" Rustin asked. A sense of dread enveloped him. He knew what Dutch was about to say.

"I was trying to tell you," Dutch said.

Rustin shook his head and turned away. "She's your girlfriend?" He said the words as an accusation more so than a statement.

"My fiancé," Dutch confessed.

All he could see was red. He felt the fury rise within him. The embarrassment. The realization that he'd been played. Lied to. Used.

"How could you not tell me?" Rustin asked.

"I'm sorry. I . . ."

Rustin backed away, reaching down to slip the ring off his hand. He held it out. When Dutch did not respond, he leaned forward and slid it into Dutch's shirt pocket. "Don't forget to take it out this time before they pick up the laundry."

He then turned and dashed down the hall toward the stairwell.

"Dude, did you lose your key?" Tommy asked.

Rustin was sitting at the top of the stairs, just outside the apartment door. He shook his head and offered a wan smile. "Nah, I was just sitting here. Thinking."

"Everything all right?" He and Deejay looked down at Rustin. They apparently were just getting home from work.

"What do you do when the man of your dreams turns out to be a schmuck?" Rustin asked.

Tommy placed his hand on Rustin's shoulder. After a moment, he plopped down beside Rustin on the step. "You find another man of your dreams," he whispered and looked up at Deejay who was standing a couple steps below them.

"I can't believe how quickly I fell for this guy. I should have known. I should have realized it was all moving too fast."

"Oh baby, I know. Believe me, I *know*."

"Earlier today he asked me to move into his house. Then tonight he put a ring on my finger."

"*What?*" Tommy said. Rustin realized how incredulous it must sound.

"I guess you had to be there," he said, forcing a laugh.

"But what happened? Did you end up having a fight already?"

"His girlfriend is what happened. She showed up, wearing her diamond engagement ring and a burgundy teddy."

"Oh *fuck!*" Tommy gasped.

"Dude, I'm sorry," Deejay said. "That really sucks."

"Rustin, wait," Tommy said. The lilt in his voice was a bit too cheerful. "Maybe it's a good thing you found out so soon. I mean, you've only known him a couple days."

"True," Rustin agreed, "but it would have been even better if I'd known before we ever went on a date. Or before he fucked me three times."

"Aww, baby," Tommy said, grabbing hold of his hand. "You know what? Fuck him! You deserve better than that shit. And honestly, he's the loser here."

"Then why do I feel so horrible?"

"*You* feel horrible?" Kirsten repeated back to him. They were outside, standing on the balcony, and she was still wearing only her teddy. She took a long drag off her cigarette as she leaned against the railing. "Dutch, that's real nice and all. It helps a lot to know how *horrible* you feel."

Her sarcasm was cutting, but he realized how much he deserved it. He deserved much worse, actually. There had been so many times he wanted to tell her. The last thing in the world he wanted to happen was this.

"I'm sorry. I wanted to tell you . . ."

"And when was it you were planning to drop the bomb?" she asked, her voice even. "Our wedding night? After the honeymoon?"

"I know. I know," he said. "I should have told you months ago . . . years even."

"So this is something you've known all along? It's not just some crazy experimental thing?"

"It's not experimental," he answered. "And yes, I've always known."

She turned around to face him. Even in the dim light, he saw the tear streaks on her cheeks. "What's your mamma going to say?"

He sighed and shook his head. "God, I don't know. She'll disown me, I'm sure."

Kirsten smiled through her tears. "She won't disown you. Dutch, you're a goddamn fool."

"I know," he said, hanging his head.

"I guess I always knew," she admitted. "Or I suspected. I knew something was going on with you and Miles."

"You did? You knew?"

"I saw how you looked at him. How you'd get all nervous when he was around."

"I was kind of obvious, huh?"

She nodded. "Well, in hindsight—yeah."

"If it's any consolation," Dutch said, "this wasn't planned. And I was going to have this conversation with you when I got back home. I'd finally decided I couldn't continue living a lie."

"I see," she said.

"Can I have one of those?" he gestured toward her cigarette.

"You don't smoke," she said, her voice still calm. "Believe it or not, Dutch, I do understand. I know it must have been hard for you. Knowing your parents and all the expectations they've always had of you. But you know what? That's not an excuse. You're not the victim here, no matter how badly you're hurting."

"I know," he hung his head.

"You lost your daddy and now your aunt. I know you're still mourning. But honest to God, how do you think I feel right now?"

"Like throwing me over this railing," he said.

"Exactly," she said. "And then jumping myself."

"Kirsten..."

"Do you remember my cousin Billy Ray?"

Dutch nodded. "I think so."

"The skinny red head. Anyway, he's gay."

"Yeah." Dutch wasn't surprised. He'd suspected as much.

"He's my favorite relative," she admitted. "Very sweet, and always knows exactly the right thing to say."

"I guess that's not a trait that always goes along with being gay. I *wish* I knew what to say right now."

"*It's not you, it's me,*" she suggested. "Or *I love you, but just not that way.*"

"It *is* me," he said, "and I *do* love you . . . just not that way."

She laughed.

"And you look very beautiful," he added. "Especially in your... what is that you're wearing?"

"Negligee," she said.

"Yeah. It's sexy."

"Who was that guy?" she asked. "The one who had his tongue down your throat?"

Dutch coughed and gripped the railing in front of him. "His name's Rustin, and he just moved here from Michigan."

She took another drag from her cigarette before tossing it over the railing into the street below. "So, what now?"

"You could hit me," he suggested. "Call me names. Yell at me."

"We have to cancel the wedding," she said.

"I know."

"And tell your mamma."

"Oh God," he said, sighing.

"I'll give my notice when we get back home so you can begin looking for my replacement."

"No, Kirsten... you shouldn't have to give up your job."

"You can't be serious," she said, placing her hand on her hip. "You expect me to continue working there with you."

"No," he shook his head. "I could leave. You do a better job running things than me anyway."

"Not according to your mother."

"Well, Mama's wrong. You're very good at your job." He stepped closer to her.

"This is just crazy," she sighed. "It's like a nightmare. A few minutes ago I thought how great it was going to be to surprise you. I thought we'd spend the night making love..."

"Well, you were half right. You *did* surprise me."

"Are you going after him?" she asked.

"Rustin?" Dutch asked. "No, I blew it. He'll never speak to me again."

"I'm fucking freezing my ass off out here," she said.

"Come on," he held out his hand to her and led her inside. She picked up one of Dutch's shirts that was draped over the back of a chair and put it on over her teddy.

"Why don't you call the front desk and order us some coffee," she said.

Raising an eyebrow, he looked at her. "Really?"

She nodded. "And we'll talk about what we're going to do with the ranch."

He looked her in the eye. How could she be this understanding?

"Okay," he said. He reached into his pocket and pulled out the ring, placing it on the coffee table in front of him, then picked up the phone and called room service. When he was finished, he hung up the phone and looked at her. "I don't know what's up with that Richard kid down at the desk. He's so nervous all the time."

She smiled at him. "You need to give him a big tip," she said. "I was kind of mean to him."

"Really?"

"Yeah. What's this ring?" She was holding it in her hand.

"It was my aunt's." He held up his hand to show her its twin.

She slid it on her finger, behind her diamond. "Too big," she said, shaking her head.

"I'm sorry," he said.

"I should have known by looking at it that it wouldn't fit."

"I know what you mean."

"Tommy, we're gonna need another bottle of Captain Morgan's," Rustin said.

"Coming right up," Tommy said, slapping Rustin on the shoulder as he walked by.

"Thanks, man."

Rustin smiled at the customer who'd just stepped up to the bar. "Hi there, big guy. What'll it be tonight? Wait! I know you, don't I?" It was the spiky-haired kid from the hotel.

"Richard," he said. "I think we met over at the hotel where I work."

"That's right," Rustin said. "About a month ago."

"I'll just have a Corona," Richard said, sliding a twenty onto the bar.

"Lime?" Rustin asked. Richard nodded. "So how is Richard tonight?"

He shrugged and smiled. "Pretty good, I guess."

"Good to hear." He slid the bottle onto the countertop and stepped over to the register to ring up the sale. "How'd that all work out? That night at the hotel, I mean."

"I'm not sure," Richard said, staring at Rustin with a puzzled look on his face. "After you stormed out . . . or I mean, after you left so suddenly . . . they ordered a pot of coffee."

"Really? So no big, embarrassing scenes?"

Cocktails

Richard laughed. "Oh my God, there is so much frickin drama that goes on there."

"I bet."

"But not that time. They checked out together the next morning and seemed very happy."

"Oh . . . figures," Rustin said with a sigh.

"Was she really his fiancé?" Richard asked.

"Yeah, afraid so." Rustin placed the change from the twenty on the counter in front of Richard. "The whole thing was really awkward. We were going at it—making out in the hallway—when she opened the door and caught us."

"No shit?" Richard said, his mouth the size of the Grand Canyon.

"Pretty crazy, huh?"

Rustin was smiling in spite of the painful memory, but Richard just sat there, his eyes growing wider. He gulped as he stared past Rustin across the bar. Rustin turned to see what he was looking at.

"What are you doing here?" Rustin said, as he stepped over to the customer on the opposite end of the bar.

"I came to see you," Dutch said.

"I'm surprised you're back in town so soon," Rustin said. "And I don't want to be seen . . . not by you."

"I figured," Dutch said with a nod. "But I wanted to tell you how sorry—"

"Whatever, Dutch. You already said that. Don't you remember? Actually, I think that was *all* you said. But you're right. You really *are* sorry. You're one sorry excuse of a man."

He nodded. "Agreed."

"Then why don't you go? Leave me alone."

Tommy stepped up behind him, dropping the bottle of rum on the counter with a loud thud. "Everything okay here? Want me to go get Deejay?"

"Everything's fine," Rustin said, not taking his eyes off Dutch. "Our cowboy friend here was just leaving."

"I should have told you about Kirsten. I should have told you everything from the beginning."

"No shit," Rustin said, "but you didn't."

"I wish I could do it all over again, make things right."

"Well ya know, that's just how life is," Rustin said. "There are no do-over's."

Dutch continued to meet his gaze. It was unnerving, and Rustin finally looked away. "I'm kind of busy right now," he said. "If you don't mind."

"I'm back in New Orleans now . . . permanently. I've moved into my aunt's house." He placed his palm flat on the bar and leaned forward. "I hope you'll eventually be able to forgive me. If you do, you know where to find me."

Rustin turned his back on Dutch and focused on the rum, twisting off the lid and sliding in the pourer. He waited until he heard Dutch leave before turning back around. He stepped over to the bar and looked down at the countertop. Shaking his head in disbelief, he picked up the gold ring that had been left behind.

Dutch stepped back, assessing the mantle. The framed picture of Delta and Bonnie added the perfect touch. He knew Delta would always be with him, in his heart.

"It feels good," he said to the photo, "to be home, I mean."

He looked around the room, realizing for the first time that it was actually his. It felt strange being here now without Delta, yet he was confident the feeling would pass. In his heart, he knew he was where he was supposed to be. It just fit.

Of course his mamma wasn't happy. She was still cursing him the day he packed up and left the ranch. Kirsten had assured him that Mamma would be fine, though. She'd handle everything just like she always did. Eventually she'd have to either accept him for who he was or completely disown him. Kirsten was confident that it would likely be the former.

It really didn't matter, though. As much as he loved his family, Dutch knew that it was finally time to begin living his own life. For too many years he'd done what was expected of him even though he knew in his heart that he was living a lie.

He stepped into the kitchen and put on a pot of coffee. He had a big day ahead of him with plans to meet with his real estate agent. He'd decided to bid on some property and open his own business. His agent had sounded skeptical, stating that New Orleans already had a plethora of restaurants. Dutch asked how many served authentic Texan cuisine, and the agent couldn't come up with a ready answer. It didn't matter. Succeed or fail, he'd be following his dream, and in the process he'd be able to be his authentic self while not abandoning his roots.

He opened the cupboard and removed a coffee mug, placing it on the counter just as he heard a knock on the front door. It was early, and he couldn't imagine who'd be paying a visit this time of the morning. He made his way down the hallway and into the foyer, peering through the window to see who it was. He

Cocktails

smiled when he recognized the familiar face.

"Rustin," he said as he swung the door open.

His sheepish smile was endearing. "I hope it's not a bad time."

"No, of course not. Come on in." Rustin stepped through the door and turned to face him. His hands were in his pockets, and he looked rather cute standing there shrugging his shoulders. "I'm glad you came," Dutch said. "I just put on a pot of coffee."

"I've been thinking," Rustin said when they stepped into the kitchen. "I was kind of hard on you."

"No. No you weren't really," Dutch responded. "You were right. My behavior was pretty pathetic, and I was kind of a sorry excuse of a man."

"You were going through a hard time, and you'd reached out to me for help."

"Well, I'm done making excuses for myself. All that's behind me, and I just want to concentrate on living a life where I'm true to myself. Cream and lots of sugar, right?"

Rustin nodded. "You remembered."

"I really am sorry things happened the way they did, but it was probably for the best. Because of you, I was able to finally come out of the closet."

"And how did that go?"

"So-so," he answered honestly.

"But you're doing okay?"

"It'd have been better if I'd done it *before* the wedding invitations were mailed."

"Ahh . . . yeah, well I can see where that'd suck."

"Shit happens," Dutch said. He handed Rustin his coffee.

"You've made some changes," Rustin said, looking around.

"New appliances and wall coverings," Dutch said. "I'll be doing the bedrooms next."

"I'm glad you kept the hardwood floors."

"Oh yeah, no question."

"I guess since you're living here yourself now, you won't be looking for a roommate."

"Probably not," Dutch said. He stepped closer to Rustin.

"It's a pretty big house. You could get lonely . . ."

Dutch shook his head as he reached out to take back the coffee mug. He placed it on the counter. "I don't want a roommate," he said.

"What then?"

He leaned into Rustin, grabbing hold of his face with both palms and kissed him passionately. "You," he whispered.

Rustin smiled at him as he pulled back to look Dutch in the eye. He pulled his left hand from his pocket and held it up for Dutch to see.

"It's a perfect fit," Dutch said, assessing the ring.

"I know," Rustin said before kissing him one more time.

Business Strip
Men's Room Book Three

By

Jeff Erno

Business Strip

Just thirty minutes remained of Richard's eight-hour shift, and he looked up at the wall clock, counting the seconds. Every annoyance imaginable to a hospitality worker had somehow managed to make an appearance in his already excruciatingly long day, and he couldn't wait to punch that clock and get the fuck out of there.

Mrs. Helminiak in 413 had insisted her bed sheets reeked of cat urine. Room 224's Mr. Byron was furious that he couldn't maintain an Internet connection. The occupants of 249, the Washington family, had requested a 7 o'clock wakeup call, and it had somehow been an hour late, causing them to miss their 9 o'clock flight. It had gone on like that all day.

The coffee urn had gone dry three times that morning, the ice machine on the third floor went caput, and the ATM was out of money. When the elderly occupant of room 351 called to bitch that while sitting on her balcony the cigarette smoke from a neighboring room's terrace had wafted over to invade her hyper allergenic olfactory system, Richard felt ready to just throw his hands up.

Now at 5:30 in the evening, he was at last ready to call it a day and he knew exactly what—or *whom*—it would take to make him forget this god-awful workday entirely. That was when Mr. Burns, the hotel manager, stopped by to make matters worse.

"Devin's sick," he said flatly. "Just called in, so I need you to stay over."

"What?" Richard gaped at him disbelievingly. "He just called in now at the last minute? But . . . but . . . I have plans this evening."

"Guess you'll have to change them." Burns had the personality of a toad. Richard fantasized about a day when he'd finally tell the stodgy little bastard where to go and how to get there. "Emily is going to cover the majority of the shift," he went on, "but she can't get here until nine. You'll have to stay another four hours."

Burns was the manager, so why the fuck didn't *he* stay? If Richard didn't need the job so fucking badly, he'd have asked just that question. Instead, he released an exasperated sigh. "Can you at least cover for me while I take a break?" Richard asked. It had been four hours since he'd even stepped away from the desk.

"I suppose," Burns said, rolling his eyes. "Five minutes. I have an engagement this evening, and I can't be late."

That selfish prick, making me change my plans so he can keep his!

"I'll see you in fifteen." Richard stormed down the hallway ignoring his boss's threats behind him. Richard slipped into the lounge and stepped up to the bar. "Evenin, Howie," he said.

"What can I get you, Richard?" the twenty-something bald-but-gorgeous muscular bartender asked, leaning against the bar.

"Just a Diet Coke, I'm afraid," Richard said. "Got stuck working a long shift tonight. Devin called in."

"Sorry." Howie's lower lip protruded. "Sure you don't need something a little stronger? Promise I'll never tell."

Richard sighed. "When I come back in four hours, definitely. Burns is already on my ass, though."

"Fuck Burns." Howie made a face.

"No thanks. I'd much rather be fucking . . ."

"Your guy from the club?"

"Colby. I was supposed to meet him after work."

Howie slid his soda onto the bar, then reached up to place a hand on his friend's shoulder. "Don't worry," he said, "the night won't even be getting started at nine o'clock."

"Yeah, but after this fucked up day, I doubt I'll have the energy."

"Ha! I'm sure you'll manage. You're young and full of cum, plus think of the overtime."

"Whatever." He rolled his eyes again. "Dude, you got a cigarette?" Richard slid onto one of the barstools.

"Since when did you smoke?"

"Since now."

The bartender fished inside his shirt pocket and pulled out a pack of *Marlboro Lights*. "Burns is such an ass," he said as he tapped out a cancer stick for his friend. Richard held the cigarette to his lips while Howie lit it for him. "The guy would be lost without you, ya know."

"I know." Richard coughed as he tried to inhale. He held the lit cigarette away from his face and with his other hand waved the wafting smoke away. Howie stared at him, shaking his head. "I should be *his* boss. He's about as bright as a burned out light bulb."

Howie laughed. "You really should, Richard. Truth be told, you run this place, and if Burns wasn't such an asshole, he wouldn't have people calling in sick at the last minute." Richard couldn't have agreed more, yet for some reason he didn't stand up to the man. He should have told his boss that covering the shift was his responsibility as manager. Instead, he'd allowed the incompetent buffoon to bully him into staying. Well, Howie was right about the overtime. He definitely could use the money.

"On the bright side," Richard said, "with the day I've already had, it can't possibly get any worse."

"You have *got* to be kidding," the thirty-something business traveler sarcastically declared. "Get me your supervisor."

Chad Curtiss constantly took business trips all across the country—hell, the world—and had never flown coach. Now they were trying to tell him that business class was overbooked. That shit just wouldn't do. There was no way in hell he was flying from Seattle to New Orleans herded into the stuffy cabin with the lowly masses.

"You need to get this problem fixed and get it fixed *now*," he demanded.

The artificially cheerful airline employee stood before him moments later. "Mr. Curtiss, I'm afraid that your original booking was on an earlier flight. When you changed flight schedules, all first-class seats were booked and we added you to the waiting list. Unfortunately . . ."

"I don't want any more excuses. You see this card?" He held up his platinum American Express. "Membership has its privileges."

The five-foot-two slender African American supervisor was unimpressed. "I can either transfer your ticket to a later flight or put you in coach, sir. Those are the *only* privileges I can afford you at this time."

Chad felt his blood pressure surge, but he bit back his anger. "A later flight just won't do. I have a meeting—"

"Very well, sir. Good day."

Could things get any worse? Earlier that morning the drycleaners had fucked up one of his favorite suits, the BMW dealership had not detailed the car as per his instructions, and he didn't even get his standard jelly doughnut with his morning *Starbucks* latte. Not to mention the fact that he'd twice had to reschedule the business meeting in New Orleans.

Begrudgingly he took a seat in the terminal's waiting area and checked his *iPhone* for messages. Trying mentally to block the din of the crowd around him, he scrolled through his email, but could not ignore the whining children and overly-talkative vacation travelers. He stuffed the phone into his suit pocket and pulled out his ticket. Good Lord, seat A-24! He'd be dead center amidst the unruly throng.

Chad straightened his posture and choked back his irritation as they called and seated the first-class passengers. When at last they called his section to board, he was first in line. Little good it did, he discovered, once on the plane. He found his assigned number, loaded his carry-on into the overhead compartment, and slid into the narrow confines of the seat. Thankful at least to have a window seat, he closed his eyes, debating whether to take a sleeping pill, when another passenger plopped into the seat beside him.

"Mommy, I wanna look out the window!"

Good Lord, it was going to be a hell of a long flight.

"Sam, sit down and be good. We couldn't get window seats, but maybe next time."

Chad expected the child's protests to continue, but apparently, he was easily distracted. "Can I get peanuts? I want peanuts or cookies. No, crackers!"

"We'll have to see what the stewardess has. Sam, why don't you sit here? You can have the aisle seat and Mommy will sit in the middle."

"I wanna sit in the middle!"

She sighed and slid into the seat beside her son. "Okay, then sit there and be good," she said. "Put on your seat belt."

Chad continued to stare out the window, not daring to turn and make eye contact, lest he encourage the overbearing child to interact with him. Chad's efforts were futile, however.

"Mister, do you like looking out the window, too? I always look out the window when I'm on a plane."

Chad cleared his throat and forced himself to turn his head in the boy's direction. He was blond, probably no more than five or six years old. "Uh, I suppose it doesn't matter much," he said dryly.

"Wanna trade . . ."

"Sam, no," his mother stopped him. "You leave the nice man be. Here, read your book." She shoved a hardcover children's book into his small lap.

"This is my favorite," Sam said. "I know all the words. *That Sam I am, I do not like that Sam I am.*"

With a raised eyebrow, Chad forced a smile. The woman glanced over to him apologetically, and Chad quickly turned back toward the window. These were sure to be the longest four hours of his life. He didn't have a high tolerance for children, particularly talkative ones. The kid, however, possessed a quality that made him at least somewhat bearable. Yeah, the little boy was adorable. Chad couldn't deny that, but it didn't mean he wanted four nonstop hours of juvenile cuteness.

Once in the air, the flight attendants made their way down the center aisle of the cabin with the refreshment cart. Sam was reading his book, aloud but quietly, and Chad pulled out his *iPhone.* Reading wasn't a bad idea. He'd read until he was sleepy, then hopefully doze off.

"Hi there. Would you like a beverage?" The saccharine smile of the young male flight attendant was almost nauseating. "Dry martini. *Stoli's,*" Chad blurted out.

The attendant ignored him, staring directly at the child beside him. "Would you like a soda or juice, big guy?"

"I want, uh, orange . . . no, red pop . . . no . . ."

"I have *Minute Maid* orange," the attendant said in the sweetest, most sincere voice. He reached over to his cart and grabbed a handful of treats. "And I have cookies!" Sam grinned at him as he placed four packets on the lap tray that Sam's mom had already lowered for him.

He took the woman's order before at last acknowledging Chad. "I'm sorry, sir, we do not stock *Stoli's. Absolute* or *Popov.*"

"*Absolute,*" Chad snapped.

"That'll be twelve dollars, please."

He couldn't believe people fucking tolerated coach. He handed over his platinum card and quickly turned back to the window.

"I'm Carter," the flight attendant said in a singsong voice. "What's your name?" Apparently, he wasn't done with Sam.

"Sam," the boy answered. "I'm five and a half," he volunteered, "and we're going to Norluns."

"Oh yes, have you been there before?"

"My grammy lives there. I go there all the time."

"This is his second time flying," his mother explained.

"Last year Grammy came with me on the plane. It was bigger and I got to sit by the window."

"Well, if you need anything, you be sure to let me know."

Later, after draining the martini and reading his email, Chad glanced over and noticed the little guy was at last asleep. Sam lay there, head against his mommy's arm, slumbering peacefully, and for a brief moment Chad's hardened heart softened a bit. Kids were a pain in the ass, and regardless how adorable this particular child might be, he wasn't likely to change Chad's attitude. Yet if Chad absolutely had to have a diminutive human being in his life, he'd most likely want it to be one like Sam.

As he looked down at the sleeping angel, the kid's mother reached into her lap to retrieve her vibrating cell phone. She scrunched down in her seat, hiding the phone with her hair. "Hello?" she answered with a hushed tone. "We're in flight now." She glanced at her watch then continued. "A couple more hours, the plane's scheduled to arrive at six fifteen... No, he's sleeping now... yes, he's doing much better. His hair has all grown back. The last chemo session was tough, but the doctors think they got it all. Oh, sure, yeah, he's a trooper. He's been chattering about you nonstop, even told the flight steward he was going to see his grammy." Sam's mother smiled as she was talking, staring off without focusing upon anything in particular, perhaps mentally replaying all her family had been through.

Chad felt a surge of guilt sweep over him. He straightened himself in his seat and tried not to think about how critical he'd been just moments before, but why should this new information change anything? Sure, it was sad when a child had cancer, but did that mean he was obligated to like all children? He looked away and stared out the window.

After Sam's mother ended her brief call, she shifted in her seat, which roused the little boy, though, not enough to wake him fully. He moaned and repositioned himself, and Chad suddenly realized that the little kid was now leaning against him. His head was resting halfway down Chad's arm. He looked down, debating whether to push him away. The child would be more comfortable next to his own mother, but he couldn't bring himself to shove that little body away from him.

When the plane landed, as the coach passengers were scurrying to gather their carry-ons and make their way down the narrow aisle, Chad removed his wallet from his suit pocket. He emptied it of its entire contents, nearly four hundred dollars in cash and slid it into the jacket pocket of the lady in front of him. The unsuspecting benefactor of his gratitude was Sam's mother.

Thank God, the last three hours had not gone as horribly as the previous eight for Richard. There were a few check-ins, but it was all routine. Still, Richard had never been more relieved to see anyone than Emily when she walked through the door at 8:50 that night.

"You're a sight for sore eyes," he said.

"Sorry, I know you've had a long day, but I couldn't get here any sooner."

Richard shrugged. "I'm just thankful you were able to come at all. Otherwise, I'd be pulling a double."

"What about Burns? He's the manager. Why didn't he cover the shift till I got here?"

"Ha!" Richard said dramatically. "As if . . ."

"Well, you're a sweetie." She stepped over to him while slipping her coat off her shoulders. She leaned in and kissed him on the cheek. He smiled, feeling his face redden. "And absolutely adorable," she added.

"If only all my coworkers were like you, Em, and all my boyfriends."

"I thought you and what's-his-name were getting pretty serious."

"Colby," Richard clarified as he spun around and leaned against the counter. "But I texted him earlier and he was a shithead."

"Aw. Why?"

"Pissed I had to work over. He said I should tell Burns to fuck off. When I said I couldn't afford to lose my job, he said . . ."

"He didn't!"

Richard nodded. "Basically gave me an ultimatum and started whining that this dumb job was more important to me than he was."

"That's just childish." She offered a sympathetic frown, crinkling her pretty face. "Well, if he can't understand that you're a responsible employee, then it's his loss. Hang on, I've gotta punch in and stash my purse."

Richard stood there, still leaning against the counter as he waited for Em to return from the back room when the sound of a clearing throat startled him. He spun around to discover a rather attractive, well-dressed, dark-haired man on the other side of the service desk.

"Oh, I'm sorry," Richard said, his voice lilting up two octaves. "May I help you, sir?"

"Curtiss," the man said. "Checking in. I have the executive suite reserved."

The smile on Richard's face never faded as he nodded and stepped over to his computer. He knew, however, there was going to be a problem, a big problem. The executive suite, and there was only one in the hotel, was already occupied.

"Let me see," Richard said as his fingers flew across the keyboard. He stared at the screen for a moment, realizing immediately what had happened. The reservations department had once again overbooked. It was standard practice and normally wasn't a problem. There usually were cancellations and in most cases, even if there was a conflict, the clerk could move guests around to accommodate, but when it came to the executive suite, there was very little Richard could do, as he had absolutely no flexibility.

"Um, Mr. Curtiss . . . sir?"

The man stared at him, clearly annoyed.

"I'm afraid we have a slight problem. The executive suite is currently unavailable. Due to maintenance issues, we've closed the floor for repairs."

Richard could practically see the steam escape from the man's ears. "You've *got* to be kidding me."

"I wish I were, sir. I'm terribly sorry, but I can get you in another room, and I can offer you an extra night—complimentary."

"I don't want an extra night, and I don't want another room. I suggest you call your maintenance supervisor and get the repairs completed ASAP—as in five minutes ago."

"I'd be glad to make calls to nearby hotels to see if I can find you a luxury suite, sir, but there is no possibility of the executive suite here being available today."

The customer stepped forward, an obvious attempt to intimidate with his close proximity. "You listen here," he said in a clearly threatening tone, "you *will* do whatever is necessary to accommodate me. I have a reservation, and I swear to you, I will have your job."

Richard, hands trembling, felt his cheeks flush. With a deep breath, he steadied himself by grabbing hold of the counter in front of him and looked the angry customer in the eye. "Mr. Curtiss, your threats don't frighten me. If you'll excuse me, my shift is over. My coworker Emily will be more than happy to accommodate you." With that he turned, spinning on his heels, and briskly marched into the office where he immediately punched the time clock.

Chad was a prick and he knew it. It came with the territory, though as a private equity investor, he wasn't in business to make friends. He made money and lots of it. He didn't believe people were entitled to things. If you wanted something, you earned the money necessary to buy that item. Chad hated big government and big socialist programs that redistributed wealth. Chad had a lot of money, and it was his right to decide where to spend it. Thus he controlled how he'd distribute his wealth—not the government.

People irritated him. Especially people like that kid, Richard, at the front desk, and the airline employee at the airport terminal. It wasn't so much that he believed they had a magic wand they could wave to satisfy his every demand.

In fact, it had little to do with the specifics of the situation. IT was the fact that any person could be content with that sort of station in life. It was all about the choices they'd made. They'd chosen not to seize the opportunities in their lives and to make something of themselves. Instead, they had settled for low-income, hourly wage jobs.

Chad realized that the room he'd finally been assigned was not much different from the luxury executive suite he'd originally reserved. He also knew that there was likely no maintenance issue at the hotel. As much as he traveled, Chad was well aware that hotels routinely overbooked and there was nothing the desk clerk could do to correct the conflicts that resulted from the practice. However, the mere fact that he had to deal with a lowly desk clerk about the matter irked Chad.

That kid was cute, too, with his spikey hair and tight little body. Though not the type of guy Chad preferred, Richard had caught his attention. Chad usually went for the well-built muscle studs, so why'd he find this skinny kid so appealing? Perhaps it was the boy's tenacity. Chad liked a guy with spunk. Why wouldn't someone with that level of confidence do something more with his life than work in an entry-level hospitality position? Chad knew his tendency to be judgmental in this manner was purely visceral. At the very least, he was being presumptuous. For all he knew, the kid could be working on a doctorate degree.

There were times when Chad's conscience got the better of him. Like earlier on the plane, when he'd looked at that young boy with such disdain only to learn that the little guy was a cancer survivor. There had been times when he'd snapped at public servants and reduced them to tears. Although they irritated him, he occasionally had to suppress his feelings of guilt and regret. He felt the worst when he made someone cry.

One thing about that kid at the desk, though, was that he seemed far from crying. He hadn't even seemed intimidated. As Chad hung his *Armani* sports jacket on a wooden hanger in his suite's walk-in closet, he smiled to himself. *The kid's a spitfire.* Chad wondered if perhaps the young man just didn't realize who Chad was—didn't have any idea how easily he could follow through on his threat and get the kid fired. Fuck, if he wanted, he could buy the fucking hotel. He could buy the whole damn chain.

Chad had stayed at the Bourbon many times previously, and he was certain the kid at least had an idea that he was a VIP. Christ, it was obvious. He'd reserved the executive suite. Richard had said Chad's threats didn't frighten him. Chad laughed aloud as he recalled the kid's tenacity.

He definitely wanted to know more about him. If possible, he'd make a point to connect with him again soon.

"I hope I never see that son of a bitch again!" Richard whined, slamming his beer bottle onto the bar.

"Dude, take a pill," the shirtless bartender said with his voice subdued. "You had a bad day, and I'm sorry." He reached under the bar and pulled out another beer, opened it, and set it on the counter in front of his customer. "Richard, have another drink. This one's on me."

"Thanks, Rustin," Richard said with a sigh. "I'm sorry I got so worked up. That guy really pissed me the hell off. You know, I get so tired of these rich assholes breezing into town and treating us like shit."

"I hear ya," Rustin said. "But hey, maybe he'll drop some cash while he's here. With any luck, a portion of it might end up in your pocket."

"I wouldn't want his money. I hate guys like that, and I wouldn't want a dime from him."

Rustin raised an eyebrow. "Honey, you're in the wrong business then."

"He thinks just because he has all this money and wears expensive *Armani* suits . . . and he thinks just because he's fucking hot looking . . ."

"Hot looking? You didn't tell me that."

Richard sat up in his stool, straightening his back as he tipped up his beer bottle. He tossed back a big slug of *Bud Light.* "Meh," he said, then belched. "He thinks he's all that."

Rustin laughed. "Simmer down, Tiger. Where's Colby tonight anyway?"

Richard shrugged. "He blew me off. When I had to work late, he was pissed. I guess I screwed up our dinner plans."

"Ha!" Rustin laughed. "As if Colby gives a rat's ass about dinner. He was probably just horny and pissed he had to wait a couple more hours."

That was exactly what Richard had been afraid of. Colby was probably right now out screwing some other twink. He was such a slut. Richard had known all along that Colby wasn't exactly relationship material, yet they had fun when they were together. It irked him, though. He was always understanding of Colby's work schedule. Being a dancer, he worked every Friday and Saturday night, yet Richard never complained. Today, Thursday, was their last chance to get together before the weekend, and Colby was being a shithead.

"You were right about it being a bad day," Richard conceded. He turned in his chair and looked toward the entrance door as he spoke. His eyes grew wide as he saw who was walking through the door. "And I'm afraid it's about to get worse."

The Men's Room was the silver lining of Chad's business trip. Having been to the French Quarter numerous times, he was very familiar with the club and its reputation. Chad could conveniently walk over to the gay bar without even having to hail a cab, and if he happened to get lucky, which he usually did, he didn't have far to travel back to his room.

Luck really had nothing to do with it, though. Chad knew he had a lot to offer, and if his strikingly handsome features, muscular body, and impeccable fashion sense weren't enough to attract a hot stud, his wallet could almost always seal the deal. The Men's Room, without fail, offered an array of delightful options. They always had the hottest dancers, cutest bartenders and even the hunkiest bouncers.

"Ev'nin sir. Welcome to the Men's Room." The six-foot-three doorman had the physique of a bodybuilder. "Ten-dollar cover tonight, please."

"Keep the change." Chad casually flipped a twenty from his wallet.

"Thanks, big guy," the bouncer said with a wink then gave him a quick once over. "My shift ends at one."

"I'll definitely keep that in mind." Chad glanced behind him to check out the bouncer's ass before making his way to the bar.

The bar, in the shape of a square, divided the room into halves. Each U-shaped half had its own bartender. Chad chose an empty seat on the side closest to the door, which also happened to be the side the hottest bartender was working.

No sooner had Chad slid onto the barstool than a napkin appeared in front of him. He glanced up into the gorgeous brown eyes of the smiling, shirtless barman. *What's he doing slinging drinks? With a body like that, he should be up on the bar dancing.*

"Let me guess," the bartender said, the smile on his face never fading. "Martini . . . Extra dry . . . *Stoli's?*"

"You're good." Chad raised his eyebrows as he maintained eye contact. "Do you remember me?"

"No sir, but when I see a man dressed that sharp, I know he probably has expensive taste."

"Nice." Chad nodded. "Very observant . . . and perceptive."

Chad watched as the bartender expertly mixed his drink and placed it on his napkin. "I'm Rustin." He winked as Chad paid him. "If you need anything, just give me a holler."

Before Chad could open his mouth to respond, a pair of sneakers appeared on the bar in front of him. He followed the legs up with his eyes, pausing briefly to stare at the bulge in the dancer's Speedo. "Hey there," the smiling blond greeted him.

"Thought you had the night off, Colby," Rustin said.

"Plans got cancelled, so I thought I'd, ya know, see if I could find someone to make new plans with." He looked down at Chad and smiled.

"What're you doing, Colby?"

Chad glanced over to see whose angry voice had called out. The kid from the hotel, Richard, stood a few feet away, glaring up at the dancer.

"I'm working," the dancer replied curtly. "You know how it is when duty calls." He rubbed himself suggestively as he re-established eye contact with Chad.

"Whatever!" Richard huffed, then turned and stormed away.

Colby crouched down on his haunches and leaned in to speak directly into Chad's ear. "Technically, I have the night off, but I'm available for private duty, if you know what I mean."

Chad leaned back in his chair, mainly to get a better look at the guy propositioning him. He proceeded to turn and catch a final glimpse of Richard, who was pushing his way through a crowd at the door. *Nice tight little ass.*

"Uh . . . you with that guy?"

"We're old friends," Colby replied, "but it's nothing serious, certainly nothing *you* need to worry about."

"Well, in that case . . ." Chad pulled a hundred-dollar bill from his wallet and held it out to the dancer. "Meet me at the Bourbon in half an hour, room three seventeen."

"You got it, babe." Colby reached out to snatch the currency.

"And don't call me babe." Chad held firmly to the bill as he stared into Colby's eyes.

Colby's expression sobered. "My apologies. *Sir.*" He then smiled.

"And don't be late." Chad released the money, picked up his martini and downed it in one gulp, then slid off his stool and casually strolled out the door back to his hotel room.

"You're home early." Richard's sister called from the sink, where she was doing dishes. She turned to him and smiled.

"Hon, what're you doing? Just leave those and I'll get 'em."

"I'm not an invalid, you know. And they *are* my dishes. You worked all day already."

"I didn't say you were an invalid, but I don't want you overdoing it. Not now, after all you've been through."

"Oh hush. I saved you some dinner. It's in the fridge. You can warm it in the microwave."

Richard toed off his shoes at the door and plopped down in an easy chair in the living room. "I'll get it in a minute. Don't feel like eating right now."

She dried her hands on a towel, then walked out of the kitchen. Becca was four years younger than Richard was and still in high school. They looked alike, at least according to what most people said, with the same chestnut brown hair and hazel eyes. Becca was skinny like Richard, but even more so since she started dialysis.

"You know you don't have to cook for me." He picked up the television remote. "What is this you're watching?"

"I just had it on. Not really even watching it, and since you and Mom are both working, the least I can do is cook the meals."

"Well, you need your rest, especially on dialysis days. Besides, I usually just eat at work."

"Oh really, what did you have tonight for dinner, then?"

Richard rolled his eyes, then craned his neck to look back at her. "A sandwich," he lied. "But thanks for cooking for me. That's really sweet."

"It's the least I can do for my brother, especially when he's donating one of his kidney's for me."

"You'd do the same thing for me and you know it." He began to surf through the channels. "I just wish we'd hear something."

A year ago, Becca had gotten her diagnosis—renal failure. At the time, Richard and his mother both applied as potential donors. Of course, the process couldn't be simple. The doctors had put them both through a series of tests, screening them first to see if either was a match, then to determine if they'd be prime candidates for the surgery.

Becca herself, due mainly to her age, was an excellent candidate. Although their mom had insisted she be the first choice as a potential donor, the doctors had screened her out. With her own health issues, the medical team had refused to seriously consider her for the procedure. That left Richard, who was not only a perfect match, but also young and healthy.

They knew how they were going to proceed. They just didn't know *when.*

Becca walked into the living room and took a seat opposite Richard in one of the armchairs. He looked up at her, sensing she had something to say. He muted the volume on the TV and waited expectantly. She smiled at him.

"What?" he said.

"Nothing." She folded her hands in her lap.

"Becca, what is it? I can tell you've got something to say."

She took a deep breath and opened her mouth to speak, then closed it.

"It's the surgery. Isn't it? There's another problem. What do they need this time? More tests?"

She shook her head. "Yeah, it's the surgery, but they don't need more tests. They called today and they're ready."

He leaned forward in his seat, placing the remote on the coffee table in front of him. "All right, then. When?"

"Well, I told them no. They said right away, that they wanted to do it next week and I told them that was too soon. You have a job and they couldn't do that to you at the last second, expect you to drop everything and—"

"Becca, are you *crazy?* Of course, we can do it right away. What do ya think we've been waiting for?"

She shook her head even more vigorously. "But your job, Richard. You'll have to be off work for at least two months and . . ."

"And we'll manage. Why do you think mom and I have been working all the extra hours?" He knew it would be difficult for all of them. Even their mother would have to take a few days off after the surgery to care for them, as both he and Becca would be laid up, but that was what families did. They made it work because they had to.

"Richard . . ."

"You call 'em and schedule that surgery. I'll get the time off work, no matter what." He looked over to her smiling face, her eyes now welling with tears.

"I don't know how to ever repay you."

"Oh, I do," he said. "You'll be my slave for life."

She waved her hand dismissively as she pushed herself up from the chair. "Whatever. I already am."

Chad leaned back in his chair as he spread his legs and reached down to rub his growing bulge. No question about it, that dancer boy had been hot, but for some reason, he wasn't thinking about that ass or the buffed and toned body of the go-go boy. He couldn't get the other dude out of his head, the slender, spikey-haired desk clerk.

Richard.

Mouthy little shit, he was. Chad recalled how he'd defiantly talked back to him, insisting he wasn't intimidated. He had a certain pouty expression that made him seem impish, almost devilish, and Chad imagined himself breaking the kid in. Chad loved to be in charge, call the shots, but he also liked a little pushback. He liked a guy with spunk and confidence who wanted more than just someone to use and discard him.

God only knew why Chad allowed his mind to wander like that. That territory remained strictly off limits. He'd come to New Orleans to do a job, and having a little fun on the side was fine. He always let off steam during his business trips, and he could think of no better way to do it than with a cheap hustler like Colby. So why was he now nearly coming in his pants fantasizing about the other one?

Richard.

Those pouty lips of his would look amazing wrapped around his steel-hard cock. They'd feel pretty damned sweet, too. He'd love to grab hold of those narrow hips of his and drive his shaft deep into his probably perfectly shaved, tight little rosebud. He'd whimper. God, would he whimper, and Chad would fuck him hard—ride him, as he'd never been before, then fire his hot seed deep inside him.

He reached down to unzip the fly of his three hundred-dollar dress slacks and pulled out his cock. He raised his hand to his mouth and slicked up his palm with saliva, then quickly fisted his shaft. He began to stroke, closing his eyes and forming a mental image of Richard. He thought of the boy kneeling between his outstretched legs, bobbing on his shaft, servicing him. Oh God, yes, Chad could tell that kid was a natural-born cocksucker. He'd take in every bit of his thick eight-inch rod while Chad lay back and enjoyed the silky warmth of his hungry mouth.

Feet planted firmly on the ground, he thrust his hips, driving his pelvis upward as he continued to stroke. Faster and faster, he pumped it, all the while envisioning Richard in his mind's eye. He took quick, short breaths as his heart rate increased. The excitement within him continued to heighten, and then he suddenly realized it was too late to hold back. Though usually he liked to edge when pleasuring himself, he'd already crossed the point of no return.

He groaned and thrust into his palm, firing several powerful jets of cum outward, across the room and all over the carpet.

"Damn!" he said, his body still shuddering.

He heard the knock on his door.

"Just a sec," he called out, jumping to his feet. He grabbed a hand towel and wiped himself up, then tossed it on the bathroom floor. He zipped up his pants as he stepped over to the door to open it.

"Oh, Cory," he said.

The go-go dancer, now at least partially clothed, smiled back at him. "Colby, actually, but you can call me anything you want." He raked a finger down the center of Chad's chest.

"Hey," Chad said, "sorry, but something's come up."

"Oh yeah?" Colby said, staring down at Chad's crotch. "You don't have to apologize for *that.* Let me in and I'll take care of everything for you."

Chad shook his head, annoyed, and stepped back. "Here," he said, reaching into his pocket and removing his money clip. He peeled off a couple bills and handed them to Colby. "For your inconvenience."

Colby's expression sobered. He snatched the cash from Chad's hand and shrugged. "Cool," he said casually. "You have a good night now, and if you change your mind . . ."

"I won't," Chad said, stepping back into the room and quickly closing the door.

"Em, you're still here?" Richard set his coffee cup on the counter, then placed a hand on his coworker's shoulder. She sat in a chair behind the desk. As she yawned and looked up at him, he realized she hadn't been prepared for the long shift.

"Yup," she mumbled. "I was scheduled third-shift last night, but I came in early to cover half of Devin's shift."

"So you've been here for twelve fucking hours. Girl, you're worse than me."

She pushed herself up from her seat. "It's okay. I need the money. Should be an easy morning for ya, though. Only a couple check-ins scheduled."

"Wait, Em, I have something to tell you."

She turned to face him. "What, sweetie?"

"You know how I told you about Becca, my sister?" He placed his fingertips against the side of Emily's arm. She nodded. "Well, they've scheduled the surgery."

"Really?" she said. "You mean . . . the transplant?"

"Yeah." He smiled. "And Burns is gonna shit himself. It's next week. After next Tuesday, I'll have to be off for at least two months."

"Well, honey, it's not like you didn't warn him. He's had all this time to hire someone and get them trained."

"I know, but he didn't, and now what's he gonna do?"

"I guess that's his problem. He'll have to either work more hours himself or hire someone fast. Or I guess he could pay us the overtime."

Richard rolled his eyes. "I just hope he holds my job for me."

"What do you mean hold your job for you?" Richard spun around to see his boss standing behind him.

"Oh, morning Mr. Burns. I was just telling Emily that I need to talk to you. It's about the surgery . . ."

"What surgery?" he said, scowling.

"My sister's surgery. She needs a kidney transplant and I'm her donor. Don't you remember me telling you?"

He cocked his head to the side. "Vaguely. Doesn't matter, though. We're short staffed right now, and I can't be giving anyone time off."

"I'm not *asking* for time off, sir. I'm just telling you, I *will* be donating a kidney to my sister." Richard felt the fury inside himself explode. This jackass was not going to keep him from doing what he needed to do for his baby sister. Job or no job, he was going through with it.

"You'll just have to reschedule," Burns said flippantly. "When we get someone hired who can cover for you and when you get them trained, then we can talk about time off."

Richard clenched his fists and took a step closer to his boss. "Look, I'm not negotiating with you," he said. "I need this job, but my family comes first. The surgery is Wednesday. Tuesday will be my last day."

"You can't do this to me!" Burns pointed his finger. "This is your *job!*"

"That's right," Richard countered. "It's just my job. I can always get another job, but I can't get another sister. If you don't like it, you can kiss my ass!"

He then picked up his coffee cup and spun on his heels to storm into the office. He heard Emily behind him, running interference.

"Just let him calm down," she said to Burns. "If you fire him on the spot, you'll be covering his shift, because I'm not staying over."

Richard, still trembling with anger, couldn't help but smile. "Thanks, Em," he said when she stepped into the office.

"I'm sure that wasn't the first time an employee told him to kiss their ass," she said laughing, "and probably not the last."

Chad stood before the full-length mirror, tightening the Windsor knot of his silk tie, thankful to put the previous day behind him and finally get down to the business that had brought him to Louisiana. He checked his watch. The company that had hired him was supposed to send a car to pick him up at 9:30, and the most logical thing would be for him to go downstairs and wait in the lobby. He elected to remain in his room, though. The driver could call for him and wait. He'd deliberately arrive at the meeting a few minutes late, then drop the hammer.

Well, in this case, the company needed more than a hammer. It needed an axe. His firm had been working with retail chains across the country, restructuring and downsizing them, then selling them off to the highest bidder. The entire process included a number of drastic cuts—layoffs and firings to scale down the business to a skeleton crew. By reducing the excess baggage of all the needless labor, it helped maximize his firm's profit. He'd done it dozens of times, and it didn't even bother him anymore. Most of the people affected were unskilled, low wage laborers, and they could acquire other jobs easily enough.

Today he'd be meeting with the executives from Benson's Office Mart, a major office supply company headquartered in The Big Easy. Back in their prime, the company had been a leader in the marketing of office equipment, computers, electronics and miscellaneous paper and software supplies. With the rise of box store chains like *Wal-Mart*, their share of the market had dwindled. Add to this a sluggish economy and a major increase in Internet shopping, and the company now faced possible extinction. They'd considered bankruptcy before contacting Chad's firm, but as a last resort decided to explore the possibility of selling their company to his firm and cutting their losses.

Chad would make them an offer they couldn't refuse, then he'd chop up the company, pare it down and sell it off, possibly in pieces. The end result would be a net profit in the millions... possibly billions, and his commission would be handsome.

When the phone rang, he sauntered over to the desk and picked up the receiver. "Chad Curtiss," he said.

"Mr. Curtiss, this is Richard at the front desk. Your car is waiting."

"Very well. I'll be down momentarily."

He hung up the receiver and walked across the room to the french doors. He pushed them open and stepped out onto the balcony. Reaching into the inside pocket of his suit coat, he removed a cigar and lit it, then moved closer to the edge of the balcony where he was able to look down upon the hotel entrance. There sat his limo, waiting for him. He smiled.

Richard was working this morning. He'd probably just started his shift, and with any luck, Chad would be back from his meeting in time to catch the kid before he left for the day. He wasn't exactly sure why this boy had become an obsession of his. He was cute, sure, but so what? Chad could have any hot guy money could buy. Perhaps that was the very thing that made Richard so appealing. He'd said he wouldn't be intimidated, then later at the bar he'd walked out on his slutty boyfriend. Richard had pride, and if Chad had any chance of winning him over, it'd probably take more than just flashing a few hundred-dollar bills in front of his face.

Richard was a challenge, and if there was anything Chad loved in life, it was a challenge. He smiled as he toked on his cigar, exhaling the smoke in a slow steady stream. "Little Richard, I'll have you bent over and begging for every inch of my cock by midnight," he said, smiling to himself.

Richard made no complaint when he discovered that Burns's strategy for dealing with him was to give him the silent treatment. That was fine by Richard—perfect, actually. He'd just focus on doing his job for the next five days, then he'd be done with it. He hated that it had come down to this... that he was going to have to give up a job he really enjoyed just because his boss was an asshole, but Richard knew that when he left on Tuesday, Burns would terminate him, and after Richard healed from the surgery, Burns would never consider rehiring him.

Oh, well. Becca was worth it. When Richard considered all she'd been through, the job seemed like a small sacrifice. She'd been sick since birth, suffering from constant urinary tract infections during her childhood. The doctors had identified her condition in infancy and treated her with medication, until finally in her teens she experienced complete renal failure. The only option at that point had been dialysis.

Thank God for dialysis. It had saved his sister's life, but it was no picnic. A dialysis day translated to a lost day of physical exhaustion and weakness. Becca had to sit in the dialysis chair for up to six hours while a dialyzer filtered her blood. She also had a fistula implanted in her arm, a structure that connected to her artery that assisted in the filtering process of her blood. Although the fistula made the hemodialysis easier, Becca often felt self-conscious about the abnormal structure that somewhat disfigured her otherwise delicate, feminine appearance. The dialysis itself left her feeling weak and fatigued, and she often suffered from dizziness, nausea and severe cramping. Though some dialysis days were better than others, she often remained bedridden for the rest of the day, and the dialysis occurred three times a week.

A kidney transplant would give Becca a normal life. She'd be able to live like everyone else—go to a regular school, travel, and even eat a more ordinary diet. Most importantly, she'd have energy again and would no longer be a prisoner in her own home.

Just as Richard removed his cell phone from his pocket to check the time, he felt it vibrate. He looked down—it was 4:10 in the afternoon. He also noticed he'd received a text. Since he had no customers at the moment, he checked his messages. It was Colby, apologizing for the night before. Well, sort of. This halfhearted attempt to be friendly was the closest Richard would get to an apology from Colby.

"Hey, wassup? We should've hooked up last night. Nothin happened with that guy."

Richard rolled his eyes and shoved his phone back into his pocket. It really didn't matter. He and Colby had no future together. If not with that asshole rich guy, Colby would have cheated with someone else. He had no desire to commit to one person in a monogamous relationship. Richard didn't really blame him. Colby was cute, had lots of admirers—young and hung. Of course, he wouldn't be ready to settle down yet.

However, Richard had grown tired of it. Granted, he'd had his fun, and being single had a certain appeal. He liked the freedom and variety, but he really wanted a boyfriend, someone who'd be loyal, stick with him even on those days when it wasn't exactly convenient, like when he had to work a long shift or donate a kidney to his sister. Yeah, Richard knew Colby wasn't that guy. He'd never understand Richard's decision to go through with the surgery. In fact, when Richard had explained it to Colby before, he'd seemed barely interested and wondered why on earth Richard would even conceive of doing something like that.

"It's not like she's gonna die without your kidney, right? So just let her keep getting the treatments. Why would you wanna go slicing yourself up like that?"

Richard decided it best simply to ignore Colby's text. He didn't want to argue with him, and he had no desire to make any kind of scene. Richard would just move on with his life, focus on the things that were important, and worry about finding a boyfriend later—after all this stuff with his job and his sister was over.

He looked across the lobby toward the front door and noticed the limo that had just pulled up. Mr. Curtiss had returned. Crap, Richard had hoped to be gone for the day by the time he got back from wherever he'd gone. He hoped he'd go straight to his room. Even though he supposedly hadn't done anything with Colby, Richard still didn't like him. The man was bossy and arrogant, and he seemed to be the type who thought his shit didn't stink.

Richard hated guys like that. Dealing with arrogant fucks like him was one thing Richard was not going to miss about the job. Suddenly, he thought of something. All this time he'd put up with the snobbery and rudeness of customers like Mr. Curtiss, and he'd always had to bite his tongue, but things were different now. He only had a few days left on the job, and there was nothing Burns could do to him other than fire him—big deal. He might as well speak his mind.

Richard smiled to himself. If that prick came in and gave him any shit, he'd tell him exactly what he thought of him. Why not? It was high time someone stood up to him and pushed back a little when he tried to throw his weight around . . . or his money.

As Mr. Curtiss emerged through the entrance doors, he didn't head for his room as Richard had hoped. Instead, he stepped briskly across the lobby toward the front desk. Fuck. Richard braced himself.

"Richard!"

Richard spun around to face his boss who had approached him from behind.

"I completely forgot about the supply order. It has to be transmitted before five."

Richard smirked and shook his head slightly. "It's okay, Mr. Burns. I already took care of it."

"Oh, you did?"

"Yes, as well as the reports that had to be sent to the home office by noon. Oh, and I confirmed the reservations for the upcoming convention next weekend and ordered the equipment they requested."

"Hm . . . Okay, very well then." Burns squared his shoulders and turned to walk away.

"If you're not going to be able to handle everything while I'm gone, you might want to consider having one of the other employees come in and work with me so I can train them."

Burns turned back around, crossing his arms over his chest. "Richard, I told you this morning you can't have the time off."

"I'm sorry, sir . . . and I'm sorry I swore at you, but I don't have a choice in the matter. My sister needs the surgery. Look, I'll do whatever I can to help get someone ready to take over for me in the next few days, but the surgery can't be cancelled."

Mr. Burns heaved an audible sigh. "Fine. I'll try to move the schedule around so that Emily can work with you at least a couple days."

Richard reached down and picked up a piece of paper from the desk. "Here. I already did. I talked to Devin a couple hours ago. He wants to make up for his sick day yesterday. He'll cover Emily's shift tonight, and tomorrow Emily can work with me. I'll call her before I leave to make sure she can do it, but she's probably still sleeping after working the long hours last night."

Burns snatched the schedule from Richard's hand. "Oh, well what about . . ."

"You've only got Karen scheduled two days a week. When I told her about my sister, she said she could pick up a few more hours until I come back. I mean, *if* I come back—if you don't fire me."

"Well, I *should*."

"That's your decision, sir, but for the record, I'm not leaving you stranded. I've done everything I can."

"You young people don't understand the meaning of the word *work ethic*." He pointed his finger angrily.

That's two words, Richard thought.

"You should be thankful you even have a job. I don't know what I'm going to do yet. When and if you decide you're ready to come back, you can come see me. If you have the right attitude, I might consider rehiring you." He nodded his head determinedly. "At entry-level salary, of course."

Richard bit his lower lip to keep from responding. He wanted to tell him to go fuck himself, but after his comment that morning, he knew it would be pushing his luck. At least this left him an option of possibly returning to his job after the surgery. "Thanks," Richard said, trying not to sound sarcastic.

When he heard a throat clearing behind him, Richard turned to see Chad Curtiss standing at the desk.

"Oh, sorry," Richard said. "May I help you, Mr. Curtiss?"

"Just checking for messages," he said. He was dressed sharply, wearing a three-piece *Armani* suit. That single item in his wardrobe probably cost more money than Richard made in a month.

He shook his head. "No, sir. No messages."

"Well, can you at least check?"

Richard raised his eyebrows. After his confrontation with Burns, he wasn't feeling as emboldened as he had been a few moments before. At this point, he felt a bit demoralized. "Of course," he said. He knew Mr. Curtiss had received no messages because he'd been manning the desk since early morning, but to humor him he pulled up his account on the computer. "No sir, nothing yet."

Richard's boss moved away from the counter and slipped into his office. That was what he did every time there was any kind of confrontation with a customer. The man had no spine, and how he'd ever become a manager was beyond Richard's comprehension.

Mr. Curtiss looked up. "So that guy's your boss, huh?" Mr. Curtiss asked.

"Yes, sir. That's Mr. Burns. Would you like to speak to him?"

He laughed and shook his head. "Uh, no. Seems like a bit of an asshole."

Richard smiled. "Yeah, we get a lot of those around here."

Mr. Curtiss leaned against the counter, clasping his hands together and looked directly into Richard's eyes. "Is that a veiled insult?" The corners of his mouth rose just slightly.

"Not veiled at all," Richard said, taking one-step backward. He raised his chin slightly.

"I admit it," Mr. Curtiss said. "I can be an ass sometimes, especially when I don't get my way."

Richard couldn't believe this guy. He rolled his eyes and shook his head. "Is that supposed to be an apology, and if so, for what . . . for acting like a spoiled brat yesterday when you checked in, or for fucking my boyfriend?"

Mr. Curtiss pushed himself back from the counter, tossing his head backward as he burst into laughter. "I sincerely hope that airheaded moron is *not* your boyfriend."

"Colby is a nice guy," Richard said, a slight defensive edge in his voice. "True, he's not the sharpest tool in the shed, but in general he's a good friend."

"Right, but certainly not boyfriend material. Cody's probably a good fuck, and that's about it. And for the record, I didn't do anything with him."

"*Colby,*" Richard corrected him. "Look, Mr. Curtiss—"

"Chad," he interrupted.

"*Chad,* you knew last night that Colby was with me, and that didn't stop you."

Chad guffawed, holding both arms out to his side, palms up. "He was on the bar, half naked in front of me, whispering sweet nothings in my ear. What the hell was I supposed to do? He's the one you should be pissed at."

Richard pursed his lips. "Yeah, well if you want Colby, you can have him. I deserve someone better than that. I don't need to be treated like shit."

"Yeah, right. Like your boss does?"

"He'll only be my boss for five—no, *four*—more days."

"I heard your conversation with him. He's going to make you crawl back and beg for your job. By the looks of things, you should be the one running this place. The man's a bonehead. Believe me, I know. It's my job to identify and get rid of that kind of waste."

"Mr. Curtiss, is there anything I can do for you?" Richard said, crossing his arms over his chest.

Chad's expression sobered, then he nodded. "As a matter of fact, yes." He raised his arm and looked down at his *Rolex*. "You get off at five?"

"Why?"

"Because I wanna have a drink with you at the bar."

"I don't want a drink with you," Richard said. "Is there anything else?"

"Dinner?"

Richard sighed, then couldn't help himself. He smiled. "What is up with you? You're an *A-Number-One* ass to me and now you wanna date me?"

"You don't believe in redemption? There's no such thing in your book as a second chance?"

"You never even had a first chance. You're a customer, and a very rude, obnoxious, snobby one, at that. You also hit on other guys' boyfriends. So no, I do *not* wanna have a drink with you, and I have no intention of giving you a second—or even a *first* chance, for that matter."

Chad cocked his head to the side and held a hand over his heart. "Oh, that hurts."

Richard was trying his best to piss the guy off, but for some reason, today he just wasn't getting angry. He stood there smiling at Richard. Maybe it wouldn't hurt to have one drink with the guy. What the hell, he was probably gonna hit the bar before heading home anyway.

"Fine," he said. "I'll have *one* drink, but I still have twenty minutes left in my shift."

"I'll see you there."

"You'll see me *here*." Richard said, pointing down the hall to the hotel bar. "I'll have a drink with you here in this bar, *not* the Men's Room."

"Of course." Chad winked, then turned and walked toward the elevator. "I'll be back down in about twenty minutes."

As beguiling as Richard had been during Chad's previous encounters with him, he now truly fascinated Chad. Seeing him in that context, observing the way he handled himself with his moronic boss, confirmed everything Chad had begun to suspect about the young desk clerk. Richard didn't belong in that job, obviously, and he certainly was too smart to be taking orders from that so-called manager.

Yet as Chad stepped out of the shower and pulled a towel across his back, tugging it back and forth, he couldn't help but ask himself why someone like Richard didn't just move on. Why did people allow themselves to get stuck? Certainly, a bright kid like Richard would realize that he could never make enough money to live on by working an hourly wage job. Christ, even a wage of twenty-five dollars an hour only translated to an annual salary of about fifty thousand. Richard should get an education and find himself a real job.

Anyway, none of it really mattered. Chad didn't plan to get personally invested in the kid's life. He was nothing more than another conquest. Chad wouldn't be in New Orleans long enough to care one way or the other what happened to Richard. Still, it seemed like a shame someone like that would just waste their potential in a dead end job. Perhaps if that shit-for-brains boss of his did fire him, he'd be doing the kid a favor. Maybe Richard would use the experience to examine his situation and choose to do something meaningful with his life.

Chad finished drying himself off and raked a comb through his hair. He stepped out of the bathroom, still naked, and selected a suit from his closet. He held it up and looked at it, then remembered what Richard was wearing. He hung the suit back up and moved over to the large oak dresser. He hadn't brought a lot of casual clothes, but he did have a pair of khakis. He chose a solid-colored silk dress shirt to go along with the pants.

After getting dressed and re-combing his hair, he splashed on some cologne and slipped his six-thousand-dollar *Rolex* onto his wrist. When he noticed the time, he briskly slid into a pair of slip-on dress shoes and checked his appearance one last time in the full-length mirror.

He spotted Richard immediately when he entered the hotel lounge. He sat up at the bar talking to the rather hunky bald bartender. Chad casually sauntered over and slid onto the barstool beside him.

"Hey," Richard said, turning to face him.

Chad nodded to him, then turned to the bartender. "I'll have a vodka martini, *Stoli's*, extra dry. And put both our drinks on my tab, room—"

"Three seventeen," Richard finished for him, then smiled. "I already told him."

Chad raised his eyebrows. "Fine. I planned to pay for your drinks."

"I'm just kidding," Richard said. "I already paid Howie for my own drink. *Singular.* I only agreed to have a drink with you, nothing more."

"Well, if one drink is all it takes, so much the better."

Richard spun around in his chair, placing a hand on his hip. "Excuse me?"

"Lighten up," Chad said, winking. "It was just a joke."

Howie slid the martini in front of Chad, then stepped away to wait on another customer.

"How 'bout we move over to a table?" Chad suggested.

Richard shrugged and picked up his beer bottle.

Why was Chad not surprised he'd be drinking straight from the bottle, and cheap beer, no less? He followed Richard over to a table, checking out his tight little ass along the way. He looked fine in those black, uniform dress slacks.

"So, what brings you to New Orleans?" Richard asked.

"Business," he said. "Boring stuff."

"That I probably wouldn't understand anyway." Richard's voice contained a hint of sarcasm.

"I said boring, and that's what I meant. I never said you were stupid."

"Well, why would you choose a profession you think is boring?" Richard asked, then took a swig of his beer.

"Hm... well, it's not my profession that's boring, really, but there are aspects of the job that become mundane. I do a lot of traveling and have to attend a lot of meetings, but in the end I'm usually quite satisfied with the results."

"Well, that's cool. What exactly do you do?"

Chad smiled. "Is this twenty questions or something?"

"No. It's small talk. Ya know, getting to know someone. You ask them about themselves and at least try to pretend you're interested. You're a businessman; you should understand the concept."

Chad laughed. "Fair enough, but hey, if you wanna just skip the small talk and cut right to the chase..."

Richard scowled at him, then pushed his chair back and made to stand up.

"No, wait!" Chad said, raising his arms, palms out. "Just kidding." He motioned for Richard to remain seated. "I'm a private equity investor."

The expression on Richard's face softened as he slowly nodded. "Which means what... you put up your own money to bail out companies?"

"Yeah, more or less. My job is to find companies to invest in and help them improve so that they turn a profit. Our firm has worked with quite a few big box stores, helped turn them around when they were struggling. And sometimes we decide it's best to just sell them or completely restructure them. We do whatever is necessary to make them profitable again."

"Interesting," Richard said. "But what's that mean? If you restructure them, what happens to the employees?"

Chad shrugged. "Well, it's up to the company owners. Usually they retrain them or reassign them with a new job." It wasn't exactly the truth, but close enough.

"Oh wow. Well, that's cool. So what you do really helps people."

"I'd like to think so," Chad said. He took a sip from his drink.

"I wanna do something like that with my life, something to help people," Richard said. "I mean, I do love my job here, but I'd like to be more than just a desk clerk."

"Why aren't you? You're still young, and you could go to college to become whatever you want."

"Yeah, I know, but sometimes life's not so easy. Sometimes what we want to do isn't always possible. Right now I have other things to worry about besides my education."

"Does this have anything to do with your sister, the one having surgery?"

Richard nodded, then smiled. "Becca, her name's Becca, and she's been sick for a long time. This surgery is going to make a real difference, give her a normal life."

"Well, that's good, but what's that have to do with you?"

"Um, it's just that I still live at home. I help with the expenses and stuff. My mom couldn't afford everything on her own. I mean, you're right about school. I know if I go to college I could eventually get a much better job, but what do I do in the meantime? If I'm in class, I won't be able to work as much, not to mention the fact I'll have so many more expenses. Maybe when Becca gets better I'll be able to get my education."

Chad leaned back in his chair. He hadn't considered that aspect of the situation, that Richard might have actually thought about his options and made a conscious decision to work in a job like this. Perhaps he wasn't merely apathetic and unmotivated. Maybe he was doing what he thought was necessary for his family and didn't see any other route to accomplishing his goal.

"What about your parents? What do they do?" Chad asked.

"It's just my mom, and she works as an assistant manager at a retail store."

"I see," Chad said. "And your boss doesn't want to give you the day off for this surgery? Can't you go over his head?"

Richard smiled, and the sincerity of his expression sent a shiver up Chad's arm. "Um, it's a little more complicated than that, but yeah, he doesn't want to give me the time off for my surg—or I mean, for my *sister's* surgery. So I guess

I'll be fired."

"Hm . . . maybe I could make a phone call to the company's home office."

Richard shook his head. "No, you don't have to do that. As much as Mr. Burns annoys me, I really have no desire to get him in trouble. I'm pretty sure he'll give me my job back."

"I heard what he said," Chad reminded him. "He said he *might* give you your job back, but it would be at entry level."

"He's all talk," Richard said, laughing. "Trust me. He'll be begging me to come back. I do a lot around here—a lot of the things he should be doing himself."

"Exactly, which is why you should be promoted, not demoted."

Richard took another swig of his beer. "You know, for such a successful businessman, you don't know a lot about office politics, or maybe you do. Maybe that's what it takes to be successful, but if I have to knife Burns in the back to get a promotion, I'd rather not get one at all."

Chad stared at him for a moment, not sure how even to respond. It made no sense. What reason would Richard have to protect his bone-headed boss? Even if he did care about the guy, doing his job for him wasn't really doing him a favor in the long run.

"Richard, why . . . why would you care what happens to that guy?"

"Oh, it's not that. I have no doubt that Burns will eventually get what's coming to him. You don't go around treating people the way he does and not pay a price for it. I just don't want to be like him. I'm not going to throw him under the bus simply because I don't do that shit to anyone, and I hope they don't do it to me either."

"Richard, have you ever considered that you could help your family a lot more if you became successful? I mean imagine how many problems you could solve if you had money. Being nice to a guy like your boss isn't going to get you anywhere. He doesn't deserve the position he has, and by saying nothing, you're allowing him to not only hurt you but also all of your coworkers."

Richard smiled at him, staring directly into his eyes. "You know, you're probably right, and I can't really sit here and argue with you about business because—well . . . you're the expert, right? You're obviously a successful businessman, and I'm just a hotel desk clerk, but I'm also twenty-one years old, and Mr. Burns is my boss. To me, running this hotel is a huge achievement. It's, like, the one accomplishment in my life I'm proudest of right now. I know all the staff here, and when they need stuff, they come to me. They count on me, and that makes me feel good. I guess I just believe that eventually someone will notice my work—maybe not Burns, but someone. I'm not about to try playing hardball with my boss at this stage, not only because of what it would do to me as a person, but also because I doubt I'd win. I mean, he's the manager, and if I tried going over his head, what do you think that'd look like? The company would just think I'm some desk clerk. Like, are they gonna take my word over his?"

He had a point there. Chad wasn't sure he'd take the word of a snot nosed kid over one of his managers if he were the CEO of the company, and in truth, it really didn't matter. Why was he sitting here discussing all this with someone who obviously had such a limited perspective?

"Anyway, that's enough about me," Richard said. "What about you? How'd you get into this type of work you do?"

Chad smiled at him, then looked over toward the bar and motioned for Howie to bring them another round.

"You just ordered me another beer, and I told you I only wanted one."

"Come on." Chad grinned at him. "You don't expect me to sit here and tell you about myself without a drink."

"Okay," Richard conceded. "I guess I can have one more, but then I should get home. Knowing my sister, she's probably saved me dinner."

"Well, at least you have someone to cook for you."

"I take it you're single. Well, I hope you are."

"You do?"

"I mean, you tried to pick up Colby last night, and now you're sitting here flirting with me. If you're not single, I'd say that's not too faithful of you."

Chad shrugged. "True, unless I was in an open relationship."

Richard made a face. "Are you?"

He shook his head, then laughed. "Nah, I've never really had any interest in that sort of thing."

"What sort of thing?" Richard asked. "Marriage?"

"Monogamy and those types of committed relationships." He raised his hands to make air quotes. "Would only interfere with my job. I've always been very career driven. I got my first big job when I was twenty-two, and by the time I was twenty-five, I was making six figures . . . or more."

"Wow. How old are you now?"

"Thirty-four."

"What about your family?"

Howie approached the table and placed their drinks down in front of them. Richard thanked him before he left.

"My parents live in New Hampshire. Sometimes I visit them around the holidays, if I can get time off."

"Really? And that's it?"

"What more is there?"

"I don't know," Richard said, shrugging. "I just couldn't imagine not being a part of my family's lives. Do you have any brothers or sisters?"

Chad shook his head. "No, and I guess I was never really close to my folks. From the time I was twelve, I was in boarding school. After that, it was college, and then I moved to New York. Been there ever since."

"Wow. I was twelve when Katrina hit."

"Really . . . so you were here for that . . . you didn't evacuate?"

"We didn't really have anywhere to go. We stayed, and for a while we had to live in a shelter, then a trailer. Eventually we got a new house. From that point on, I've stayed active in the mission and the soup kitchen. I try to volunteer at least once a week, usually on Wednesday nights."

"Oh. What's that like?"

Richard's mouth opened wide into a broad grin. "I'd show you, but next Wednesday's my sister's surgery."

"I'll probably be gone by then anyway."

"Yeah. Well, it's pretty awesome. I don't know; I just feel really good every time I go there, but then I also get kind of sad. I wonder why we were so lucky. I mean, we could still be homeless like them—my whole family could. We just happened to get on the right list, and we ended up with a new home."

"Wow. I can't imagine what it would be like to live through something like that."

"Yeah, we pretty much lost everything, but Mom had gathered all the family pictures, the photo albums and stuff, and she saved them, but pretty much everything else was destroyed. All the furniture and everything. It was horrible. Mom said we were lucky, though. She'd saved what mattered—her kids."

Only twenty-one, and he'd been through so much. Now his sister faced a life-altering operation. Chad picked up his drink and tossed it back. "That's some pretty heavy shit," he said as he placed the glass back on the table. "What kind of surgery is it your sister's having, if you don't mind me asking?"

Richard took a deep breath before his eyes grew wider. Big and round, they seemed to almost bore a hole into Chad's soul. Richard blinked, and a single tear escaped, then streamed down his cheek. He reached up to wipe it away. "She has to have a kidney transplant," he whispered.

"Oh." Chad clasped his hands together on the table. "Well, then they've found a donor? That's good, right?"

"Yeah. It's wonderful." He picked up his beer and took a drink. "But you know, I really should be going."

"Already?" Chad reached across the table to grab hold of Richard's wrist gently. "Why don't you let me buy you dinner?"

"That's nice of you." Richard grinned. "But I don't think so. You're only gonna be here a few days. You know what you should do? Go over to the Men's Room. I'm sure you'd have no problem finding a hookup."

That was exactly what Chad had done the night before, and he didn't want just another hookup. He wanted Richard—even more so now. Why was he playing so hard to get? "Look, it's only a little after six. Why don't you go home and check on your sister, then meet me back here? Or I can send a car to pick you up."

Richard laughed. "What's with you?"

"I don't know," Chad answered honestly. "I'm really not sure, but I just get this sense that we should go out, get to know each other better."

Richard took a deep breath and leaned back in his chair. "All right. Let me go home and change, and then I'll come get you. I'll take you to some of my favorite places in the French Quarter, and we can get a bite to eat."

Chad smiled broadly and nodded in agreement. "Deal."

"But you should change too," Richard said.

Chad looked at him quizzically. "Change?"

"Your clothes. Put on a pair of jeans or shorts or something. You don't have to be in business mode all the time."

"I'm wearing khakis!" Chad objected, pointing to himself.

"You're wearing a pair of pants and shirt that cost more money than I make in a week, and those aren't khakis. They're dress pants." He waved his hand dismissively. "Anyway, you're fine. Wear whatever makes you comfortable. I'll be in jeans."

"I don't own jeans."

Richard shook his head, grinning. "I figured. Okay, I'll meet you in the lobby at eight."

"I'll be counting the minutes."

Richard rolled his eyes as he stood up. "Thanks for the beer."

Richard had parked his car in a lot two blocks from the hotel. As he approached his vehicle, he questioned himself and the wisdom of his decision to meet up with

Chad later. What exactly was the point of hooking up with some rich guy from out of town, especially one as cocky and egotistical as Chad? Nevertheless, his heart rate increased just a little as he thought how hot the businessman was in his designer suits. His appearance alone appealed to Richard on the basest level. Why not seize the opportunity . . . how many chances in his life would he have to go out with a walking Ken doll? Chad possessed far more than just good looks. He had intelligence, a successful career, and most of all, a degree of confidence that Richard truly admired.

But God was he a prick sometimes. The way Chad had acted the night before left a bad taste in Richard's mouth, and that kind of selfish behavior definitely tended to cancel out all his apparent good qualities.

"Richard!"

He looked up over the top of his car right as he was opening the door and saw his friend Tommy from the Men's Room. "Hey, man, what's up . . . you on your way to work?"

"Yeah. You comin tonight?"

"Uh, I don't know. I gotta work early tomorrow."

"Geez girl, the night's young. At least stop in and have a drink."

Richard nodded. He closed the car door and stepped around to give his friend a hug. "We might stop in later."

"You and Colby?"

Richard smiled in spite of himself.

"What?" Tommy demanded, grabbing hold of his shoulders. "Spill it! You're not with Colby anymore?"

"I'm not with anyone anymore, but this guy at the hotel asked me out. I told him I'd show him around for a little. I doubt anything will happen."

"A guy from work? Like a coworker?"

"No, a customer."

"You little slut!" Tommy punched him on the arm, then winked.

"It's not like that."

"Well what *is* he like? Is he hot?"

"He's pretty hot, but he's like thirty-four or something. And he seems to be loaded."

"Well there ya go!"

"I'm not looking for a sugar daddy."

"Hm." Tommy pushed his glasses up. "Ya never know. Why not just go out and have a good time? See what happens."

"Yeah, that's what we're doing."

"Well, if you don't stop into the bar tonight, be sure to text. How's your sister, by the way?"

"It's a long story, but she's gotta have surgery next week."

"Oh no!" Tommy grabbed hold of his arm.

"No, no, it's a good thing. She's getting a kidney transplant. It's going to make things a lot better for her."

"Oh wow. Well, Deejay and me will be thinking of you."

"Thanks."

"You let us know if there's anything . . ."

"I will, Tommy. Thanks. That means a lot." He leaned in and kissed his friend on the cheek. "Give Deejay a kiss for me."

"Honey, do you have to work tomorrow?"

Richard's mother called to him from her easy chair in the living room. He'd just stepped out of the bathroom, ready to head out to meet Chad back at the hotel. "Yeah. I won't be out too late 'cause I'm scheduled at nine tomorrow morning. Why?"

"Oh, I have a mandatory meeting at the store tomorrow, but Becca's got to be at dialysis at the same time. I'll just have to drop her off a few minutes early."

"Hm, that's weird. You usually have Saturday mornings off."

"I know," she said, turning in her chair to face him. "I don't know what it's about, but we got notification this afternoon. All employees are required to attend, and they're even closing the store for the meeting."

"Wow. I wonder what's going on."

"Who knows," she said, shaking her head. "I know Bensons has been struggling lately, and I'm afraid they're going to be making some changes—big changes. I just hope they don't close our store."

"Oh my God, they can't do that, can they?"

"I don't think so. It wouldn't make sense, but this meeting's got me freaked out. No one knows what it's about, but the big shots from corporate will be there."

"Don't worry," he said. "They're probably just gonna roll out some new policies or something. They can't just close a store like that and put all those people out of work. Even if they did, they'd get you a job somewhere else, right?"

His mother laughed, somewhat nervously. "Honey, that's not how the world operates. If they close the store, us employees will be on our own."

Richard thought about what Chad had told him, how he'd said that when a company *restructured* they retrained and relocated the employees to new jobs. "I don't think you have anything to worry about. You've been with that company for how long?"

"Seventeen years, since before Katrina."

"Exactly. They'd never just close your store and leave you with nothing."

"I hope not." She stood up from her chair and walked over to Richard. "You goin to the bar? You look so handsome, all dressed up."

Richard felt his face grow warm. "No, Mom. And I'm not dressed up." In truth, he was kind of dressed up, but certainly not by Chad's standards. He didn't have expensive clothes, but he liked to think he had a little fashion sense and made do with his limited resources. "There's a guy at the hotel who asked me out to dinner. I'm just gonna take him around the French Quarter. We're hanging out awhile, that's all. I'll probably be home by midnight or so."

"What about that other boy?"

"Colby? We were just friends."

She shook her head. "Just be careful. You're using protection, aren't you?"

"Mom!"

She placed her hands on each of her hips and stared at him. "Well, are you?"

"It's not like that. This guy isn't like Colby. He's a little older."

"What do you mean? How much older?"

"He's in his early thirties, and he has a good job and everything, but it doesn't really even matter. We're just friends, and he's only here for a few days from New York. Then I'll probably never see him again. So no, I don't plan to do anything with him I'd even need to worry about protection with. And even if I did, I wouldn't be discussing it with my mother."

The expression on her face broke Richard's heart, and he instantly regretted his choice of words. He walked over to her and put his hand on her shoulder.

"I'm sorry, Ma. I just get embarrassed talking about this stuff with you. You're my *mom!* But I promise I'll always be safe. You don't have to worry."

She grabbed hold of him and kissed him on the cheek, then embraced him with a tight hug. "Good, 'cause I've already got one sick child. I don't want another."

"I know, I know."

Chad waited in the lobby for Richard to return. He'd changed into a more casual shirt, this time a form-fitting black tee. He didn't have any shorts or jeans, and he didn't have enough time to go shopping, so he stuck with the khakis. When he spotted Richard as he walked through the entrance, he felt relieved. He wore almost exactly the same thing except for a lighter colored shirt.

Richard walked over to him and took a seat in one of the chairs opposite him. "You're actually waiting for me," he said. "I thought sure I'd have to have the front desk call up to your room."

Chad couldn't remember the last time he'd waited for someone. He was used to being the one other people waited on. For some reason, it hadn't bothered him this time. Perhaps Richard was worth the wait. It really made no sense. Nearly everything about the guy defied the principles upon which Chad had fashioned his life. Richard did not possess the kind of drive or ambition, at least not when it came to career, that Chad related to in his life. He almost seemed shortsighted, focused on the little things and people around him, rather than on a bigger picture. Most of the time, this sort of attitude really annoyed Chad, but that quality within Richard seemed so . . . sincere.

Perhaps that was it. Richard seemed genuine to Chad. He didn't care about pretenses. Chad didn't feel like Richard was trying to kiss his ass or flatter him all the time. He lived his truth. It rather amazed Chad to see such a quality in another person, especially someone so young.

"I don't know about you, but I'm starved," Chad said. "Where would you like to eat?"

"Hm . . . first you gotta tell me what type of food you want. New Orleans is famous for Cajun and seafood, but that's not all we have. Basically, we have everything. There are quite a few decent restaurants right here in the French Quarter, within walking distance."

"Well, why don't you pick?"

Richard laughed. "You sure you want me to choose?"

"Of course."

"What if I told you I just want a kickass cheeseburger?"

"Really?" Chad smiled. "Hey, I'm game. You're a cheap date."

"Did you say *date?* I thought this was just . . . ya know, casual."

Chad shrugged as a wave of disappointment washed over him.

"I'm just kidding," Richard said. "We can call it a date. A *casual* date. Come on. There's a great place right across the street on the corner. We can sit out on the balcony and look down at Bourbon Street while we eat. I think they actually serve more than just killer burgers. You can get whatever you want."

Chad pushed himself up from the sofa. "Let's go, then."

Richard led the way out the entrance of the hotel and across the street to what didn't even appear to be a restaurant at all. "It's upstairs," Richard explained and showed Chad the somewhat secluded doorway that opened into a narrow dark hallway connected to a rather dingy staircase. Richard turned around to make sure Chad was behind him, and Chad quickly looked up from the tight, round globes of Richard's ass to smile and make eye contact.

"Please tell me you weren't just checking out my butt."

Chad grinned then shrugged. "What can I say? It was there, right at eye level. Am I not supposed to look?"

Richard didn't reply but instead rushed up the staircase a little faster. He turned to face Chad once at the top. "I know this probably isn't the kind of restaurant you're used to."

It wasn't, and Chad wondered for a moment why he hadn't just insisted they go to a more upscale establishment. He could've called for a limo, given Richard the royal treatment. "It's fine," he said, "but if you want something nicer, it's not too late . . ."

"This is exactly what I want," Richard said. He opened the door at the top of the staircase. They stepped into a rather rustic dining room with hardwood floors and what appeared to be a retro bar that would've been suitable in a western-style saloon. A hostess stationed at the bar turned to smile at them. She stepped out from behind the bar.

"Good evenin', gentlemen. Would you like a table inside or out on the balcony?"

"Balcony, please," Richard answered.

Once seated at a small table right next to the railing on the edge of the balcony, Richard looked down at the street below. "I love this. Bourbon Street is awesome. It never sleeps."

"I've noticed."

"But you know, the tourists who come here for vacation or Mardi Gras or whatever, they only get a tiny glimpse of the city. They see all this and think that's all there is."

"Yeah, I guess you're right. I've been here several times and never really ventured out of this area other than for meetings. I like staying down here, though, in the French Quarter."

"Why is that? There are lots of other fancy hotels in New Orleans."

"This is kind of my getaway," Chad admitted. "First time I was here was maybe three or four years ago. It wasn't for business. I came because I'd heard

The Big Easy had some of the best bars."

"And?"

"And I agree." He laughed. "So now whenever I come back, I book a room in your hotel, mainly because it's walking distance from the Men's Room." Chad picked up his menu and looked it over. "What do you recommend?"

"I'm getting the double cheeseburger, but for you... hm... probably a steak."

The waitress arrived with their drinks and asked if they were ready to order.

"I'll have the ribeye," Chad said, "medium rare." He glanced over at Richard who smiled knowingly. He'd been spot on with his recommendation. A steak was about the only thing on the menu that even appealed to him. After the waitress finished taking their order, Chad looked into Richard's eyes. "Why do you seem so much older than twenty-one?"

The corners of Richard's mouth curled up just slightly as he shrugged. "I'm not sure. One time a psychic told me I was an old soul, if you believe in that sort of thing."

Chad shook his head and laughed. "Not at all."

"Really? I kinda do. I mean, it'd be such a shame if this were it."

"So you think when a person dies, a part of them goes on?"

"Definitely," Richard said without hesitation. "But not like the religious people believe. It would be almost as sad just to float off on a cloud for all eternity. If that's heaven, I'd rather just die, but I think life really is about being the best person you can be, learning certain lessons, and moving on."

"That might make sense, if we could only remember. I mean, what good does it do a person to live multiple lifetimes when they have to start over each time with a clean slate, no memory of what happened in their past lives?"

Richard smiled and leaned forward. "I think we get little reminders along the way. You know, déjà vu experiences. The lessons we learn are not so much for our minds, though. They're for our hearts—our souls."

"What do you mean?"

Richard's face seemed to light up, but perhaps it was merely the reflection of the setting sun. He tilted his head slightly to the right and smiled. "I mean like earlier when we were talking about my boss. There's a part of me that just despises that man, ya know. I think he's such a moron—and I just wish he'd get fired or hit by a bus or something."

Chad laughed.

"But then there's this other part of me that sees goodness in him, and I think about what it must be like to be in his shoes. He doesn't have a girlfriend, wife, or anything. This job is all he's got, and I'm not even sure he has any friends. It's no wonder he's so ornery all the time."

"But if he wasn't such an ass . . ."

Richard raised a finger and wagged it back and forth. "Hey, look who's talking."

Chad leaned back in his chair and smirked.

"Don't get me wrong," Richard said, "I'm not judging, but you've told me that your motivation has always been your career, right?" Chad nodded. "And you said you're not close to your family and that you come here to New Orleans so you can hit the bars. Well, what's that mean? It means you're looking for a hookup. So it makes me wonder if maybe you aren't just as lonely as Burns."

"I might be a demanding ass at times, but I'm not an idiot."

"My point is not to compare you to my dumbass boss. I'm just saying that I have a tendency to look into the heart of other people. When someone behaves a certain way, there's almost always a reason for it. I think that type of empathy is not something that's learned . . . at least not in one lifetime."

"So you're saying you have a gift?"

"No, I think it's something we're all capable of, but maybe some of us haven't yet learned how."

"Well, to me it sounds more like you're just making excuses for people. If someone's a jerk, they just are. Who cares why?"

The waitress approached the table with their salads, interrupting their conversation briefly.

"Well, I have a confession," Richard said after the waitress had left. "Yesterday when I first met you, I pretty much hated your guts. I kept saying to myself, 'I can't stand guys like that'."

"And now?"

"And now I've decided I might've been wrong."

Chad crossed his arms on the table in front of him. "In what way?"

"I thought you were just this selfish rich guy who looked down on people like me, but now that I know what drives you—your career—I understand . . . a little. I mean, I get it. You've accomplished something amazing, and you did it at a pretty young age, so you're proud of that. And you should be."

"But you have no desire to achieve that kind of success?"

Richard looked up at the sky, as if thinking. "No, not really. I don't envision myself as being rich or powerful or anything like that."

Interesting. Lots of people—the majority, actually—had no vision for tremendous success, and Chad believed that was the reason why they remained in their mediocre states of existence, but with Richard, it felt different. He wasn't apathetic, nor did he lack vision. He just possessed a far different vision.

"No offense, but I'd rather have the love of my family than all of your riches."

Though Chad had been oddly obsessed with tapping the smart-mouthed little desk clerk who'd had the guts to talk back to him, he now began to feel a bit differently. His desire to be with Richard had not in any way diminished—in fact, if anything, it had increased. He was beginning to think of him as less of a conquest. Was this normal? Maybe this was how it was supposed to be for regular people: get to know someone first and actually start to care about them before tearing their clothes off and fucking like wild animals.

Some scary shit was what it was. Chad planned to finish his business on Monday or Tuesday and be the hell back in New York by mid-week. He might never see Richard again. In fact, he wasn't even sure he wanted to, but as he sat there sharing a meal, he felt closer to Richard than he had with anyone in a long time.

"What do you wanna do next?" Richard asked, after gulping down a big bite of cheeseburger.

"Carriage ride?"

Richard made a face and laughed. "All right."

"You don't like that?"

"It's very touristy," Richard said, "which is fine, because technically you *are* a tourist."

"Well, why don't we just walk around for a bit?"

"That's cool too. I love watching the street performers. A couple of blocks from here there is a section with fortunetellers. We could go get a reading."

Chad couldn't help cracking up. "I don't think so."

"Why not? What're you afraid of?"

"Losing thirty bucks."

Richard waved his hand dismissively. "You gotta know how to talk' em down. I guarantee you I could get your fortune read for half that."

"And it would still be a waste of fifteen bucks."

"Fine, it's a beautiful night for a walk. We can go down by the water. There's a park down by the Mississippi River. We can walk down there. Maybe stop for ice cream if you want dessert."

"Perfect."

"And if you're really brave, I'll show you the cemetery."

"Now? It's getting dark."

"For someone who doesn't believe in life after death, you seem kind of timid of the dead. You think a ghost is gonna get you or something?"

Chad shook his head. "I just think hanging out at a graveyard after dark is not the most roman—". He stopped himself. "I could think of better places I'd rather spend my time."

Richard looked down at his plate and picked up a french fry, quickly stuffing it into his mouth.

As they made their way down Orleans Street, Richard pointed out various businesses he found interesting. Chad considered the small shops to be nothing more than tourist traps, peddling worthless collectibles, but Richard stopped and pointed out interesting displays and artwork, laughing at the cleverness of some of the tee shirt designs, coffee mugs, and various trinkets presented in the storefront windows. They stopped in Pirate's Alley to look through artwork that had been propped up against the cement wall, and Richard chatted with the vendor. When they got to Jackson Square, Richard stopped them so they could watch a street performer. At first, Chad thought he was a statue, but soon discovered him to be a mime sitting perfectly still, every inch of his body painted silver, his breathing undetectable. When Richard reached into his pocket and removed a ten-dollar bill to drop into the silver bucket beside him, Chad nearly guffawed. He almost reached out himself to grab hold of Richard's wrist in order to stop him, but then Richard turned and smiled.

"Think of how much preparation went into that costume," he said.

As they walked away, sauntering toward Café Du Monde, Chad had to ask, "Exactly *why* did you give that guy money?"

"Oh, he's a street performer—an entertainer."

"But he wasn't entertaining. He was just sitting there."

Richard laughed. "Well, I found him very entertaining. I couldn't sit there like that, perfectly immobile. We almost walked right past him because he looked like a statue."

"I just don't get it, why you'd give money away like that."

Richard turned to him and smiled. "I saw you give money away, last night at the bar. When you came in, you tipped Gene, the doorman."

"That's different. Tipping someone who provides a service is not the same as just giving away money."

"I think the street performer provided us with more of a service than Gene did. All he did was take your cover charge and let you in the bar."

Chad nodded. "Fair enough, but he did have a nice body."

Richard laughed. "You're not fooling me. I saw the size of the tip you left back at the restaurant. You're not as stingy with your money as you pretend. If anything, you enjoy throwing it around a bit."

Chad stopped in his tracks, grabbing hold of Richard's arm. "Is that your impression of me?"

Richard stepped closer to him, placing his fingertips against Chad's chest. "Don't be offended by the truth, okay? It wasn't a criticism, merely an observation."

"What good does it do a person to have money, if they aren't willing to use it?" Chad countered.

"What good does it do him if money's the *only* thing he has?" Richard answered his question with a question. "And for the record, I don't think you just throw money around to impress people. I just think that maybe sometimes your attitude is that because you have money, you're entitled to respect that you wouldn't necessarily give others."

Of course, Richard spoke the truth. Chad felt exactly that way. That was why he always flew first class, bought the finest clothes, and ate at the fanciest restaurants. He had an image to maintain, and when people encountered him, they knew immediately that he was a man of importance and a force to be reckoned with.

"What's wrong with that? I worked hard to get to where I'm at, and I'm just reaping the rewards."

Richard's sweet smile never faded from his face. "Do you think you worked harder than that street performer? You do realize he probably spent four or five hours just doing his makeup. Think about someone like my mom. She works fifty hours a week and never gets a chance to sit down. That waitress back at the restaurant, I bet she's been working since before lunch and probably doesn't make more than two bucks an hour. Financial success is not always directly related to how hard a person works. Some of the hardest working people are paid the least."

Chad nodded. "True, which is why you have to make the right choices."

Richard slipped his hand inside Chad's, and they continued walking. The touch sent a shiver of excitement up Chad's arm, and he felt an increasing tightness in the region below his designer belt. "I'm glad there are people like you in the world," Richard whispered, leaning his head against Chad's shoulder. "You help people. You save companies that are in trouble, and that means a lot to all those workers." He squeezed Chad's hand. "But try to understand, there are only going to be so many investment . . . whatever you are . . . in the world."

"Private equity investors."

"Right, I'll be happy to one day manage a hotel of my own, or who knows, maybe I'll do something else, but I know it won't be for some hoity-toity Wall Street firm. It's just not me."

A crush of guilt pressed heavily against Chad's chest as he realized how deceptively he'd portrayed himself to Richard. The kid thought he was some sort of knight in shining armor who swept in and saved these dying companies. The reality was quite the opposite. He looked for struggling companies that he could revamp in order to maximize profit for his firm and, of course, for himself. He didn't save people's jobs. He eliminated them.

"This is Café Du Monde." Richard pointed out the restaurant in front of them. "If we hadn't just eaten, I'd insist we sample some beignets. Theirs are the best."

"I thought you wanted ice cream."

"To be honest, I don't think I can eat another bite. Besides, I don't need any sweets right now."

Chad released Richard's hand but only to slip his arm around his shoulder and pull Richard closer to him. "You're sweet enough just like you are," he whispered.

Richard looked up at him, then turned in order to reach his hand up and place it against Chad's chest. Chad leaned forward, staring into Richard's crystalline, hazel eyes and felt as if the world around them had suddenly faded to nothingness. As he felt the crush of Richard's soft lips against his own, he encircled the smaller man with a warm embrace, pulling him against his body.

Slowly they pulled apart, and Richard looked directly into Chad's eyes. "You just kissed me in public, right here on Decatur Street," Richard stated, barely whispering.

"I know." Chad smiled. "Right here under a street lamp. And you know what?"

"What?"

"I liked it."

"I liked it too," Richard said, giggling.

"And I'm about to do it again."

"What are you waiting for?"

Chad leaned in and this time kissed him far more passionately, nearly swooning himself as he inhaled the scent of Richard's cologne and tasted him again. He felt Richard tremble in his arms as he responded to the kiss, and when at last he pulled away, Richard was no longer smiling.

"What's wrong?" Chad looked into Richard's eyes, now moist with tears.

"Absolutely nothing," he said, a teardrop now streaming down his cheek. "That was most beautiful kiss I've ever..." He quickly shook his head and stepped back. "Come on. Let's go see the riverboats!" He grabbed hold of Chad's hand and stepped briskly down the sidewalk, pulling Chad behind him.

Against his better judgment, Richard stepped into the elevator behind Chad. He couldn't bring himself to say goodnight already, even though it was already after 11:30. He didn't know how far he was willing to allow things to progress, yet this man sparked something within Richard he'd never experienced before. The kiss back down by Café Du Monde had shattered Richard's wall of defense, which had already been weakening over the course of the previous hours.

They came from different worlds, had very different paths to follow. Richard knew nothing permanent could become of a relationship with a man like this. That meant only one thing. Richard would be nothing more to Chad than just another of his one-night stands, and Richard didn't know if his heart could take that. Yet the feelings that overwhelmed him, at the moment, told him even one night was better than none. What the hell, he didn't know top from bottom or right from wrong anymore. He just knew he had to go with him. He couldn't say goodbye.

Once the elevator door closed, Chad pushed him against the wall and placed his hands along the sides of Richard's face. "You just fucking drive me crazy," Chad whispered, staring into his eyes, and then he kissed him again.

Richard wrapped his arms around the broad shoulders and melted into the kiss, allowing the feeling to sweep him away. Closing his eyes, he opened his mouth slightly, feeling and tasting the probing tongue enter him. His arousal throbbed in his khakis, and he pressed his body closer, rubbing himself against the man who now seemed larger than life to him.

Gasping, he pulled back. "Chad," he whispered. "What if someone catches us? What if someone's waiting when the door opens?"

"They'll see some hot man-on-man action," he replied, and then kissed Richard once more.

When the door finally opened, thankfully no one waited in the hall. Chad wrapped his arm around Richard's shoulder and guided him out of the elevator, leading him slowly down the hallway to room 317.

The luxury suite actually was far more than just a room. A living room area with a sofa and chairs greeted them as they pushed through the door. The suite also offered a kitchenette, a separate bedroom, a balcony, and two bathrooms.

Chad led Richard over to the sofa where they took a seat. "I can call room service for some champagne," he said.

"No!" Richard objected. "Sorry, but I... um... I know everyone who works here."

Chad smiled, then shrugged. "Well, I also have a wet bar." He motioned to the fully stocked bar in the corner. "What'll it be?"

"I probably shouldn't drink. I still have to drive home." Richard fidgeted nervously in his seat. "You know, come to think of it, I should probably get going. I have to be back in the morning for an early shift." He pushed himself up from the sofa.

"Richard," Chad said, grabbing hold of his wrist. "Please don't go. Stay the night. Please."

"But... I won't have clean clothes."

"I have lots of clothes."

"And I promised my mom I'd be home early."

"You're a big boy," Chad said, looking directly at Richard's crotch. "I'd say a *very* big boy, in fact. You don't need to report to your mother when you stay out late."

Richard closed his eyes and sighed. He reached up and scrubbed his palms over his face. "Look, I'm flattered. Oh my God, I can't even tell you how fucking flattered I am." He turned and took a step away from the couch, then turned back around. "But I'm just not real good at one-night stands. I get too... I don't know... too invested."

"Richard, did I say this was a one-nighter?"

"You only *do* one-nighters."

Chad stood up and looked directly into Richard's eyes. "Yeah, you're right," he confessed. "But I don't know, I think this is different. I think *you're* different. I don't want to push you. I don't want you to do anything you're uncomfortable with, but God, Richard. I don't want you to leave. Please..."

Chad closed the distance between them, moving into Richard's personal space. Holding him by the shoulders, he pulled Richard closer and kissed him once more, slowly and deeply.

"Chad, I have to tell you something," Richard whispered.

Chad nodded. "Okay. Tell me anything."

Richard took hold of Chad's hand and led them back to the sofa where they sat side-by-side. Richard turned in his seat to face Chad. "I didn't tell you everything earlier tonight when we were at the bar. I... um... I'm going to be laid up awhile."

"What do you mean?"

"I also have to have surgery next week."

A look of concern creased Chad's face, his brow knit with worry. "You're sick too?"

Richard shook his head. "No, but... but... well... um, after the operation, I probably won't be feeling like doing any partying for a while. They're taking out one of my kidneys."

Chad stared at him, mouth agape, but did not immediately respond. "Richard," he whispered, "you're the donor?"

He nodded. "We've been waiting for over a year, and the surgery was finally approved. They want to do it right away."

"Wow. I can't believe..."

"What do you mean, you can't believe it? You can't believe I'm donating a kidney to my own sister?" He made no effort to curb the defensiveness of his tone.

"No, no that's not what I meant. I mean, I'm amazed by the selflessness. I can't believe a human being would be so giving, so generous."

Richard rolled his eyes. "She's my sister, and people donate kidneys all the time."

"No they don't," Chad said. "Don't minimize what you're doing. You're a hero."

Richard laughed. "How about I just love my sister?"

"Yeah, how about that?" Chad slid closer to him and leaned in once more to kiss him, but this time on the cheek. "How about, you're *my* hero."

Richard, who was trying to keep the conversation as lighthearted as possible, bit his lower lip as he became overwhelmed with a sudden wave of emotion. He felt his eyes flood with tears, and angrily reached up to wipe them away. He didn't want to fucking cry!

"I swear to God, I wasn't going to tell you. I don't want you to think I'm heroic or anything. I just... well, I *had* to tell you, because I'm starting to feel things. I know it's soon. We just met, but I'm feeling like this connection we have is something that might possibly last beyond one night. And you deserve to know."

Chad nodded. "I get it," he said. "But it doesn't matter to me. In fact, knowing this about you makes me think even more highly of you, and yeah, I've wanted to bend you over since I first laid eyes on you yesterday. I admit it." Richard laughed, then felt himself blush. "But now... I want more. I want... I want...

I want to make love to you." He took Richard into his arms and kissed him passionately, guiding him backward onto the sofa cushions and leaning over him.

"Let me make love to you," he whispered, when he pulled back. "Please..."

Richard looked up into his eyes and slowly nodded.

Chad reached down and slid his arm under Richard's knees. Wrapping his other arm around Richard's shoulder, he lifted him off the couch and stood up, then carried him across the room into the bedroom where he laid him gently on the bed and began to undress him.

Chad felt his own cock throb within the tight confines of his designer briefs as he leaned down to unbuckle Richard's belt. Richard reached for him, tugging at the tail of Chad's tee shirt. Chad quickly undid Richard's fly and slid his hand into the warmth, wrapping his fingers around the rock-hard shaft. Richard squirmed on the mattress, as Chad stroked, then suddenly released him. He leaned in and lowered himself over Richard's body, finding his mouth with his own.

Richard's hands slid up under Chad's shirt, around his back, and the trace of his caressing fingers sent a chill up Chad's spine as he ground his pelvis against Richard's. Richard responded to his kiss, driving his tongue into Chad's hungry mouth. Richard grasped the back of Chad's shirttail and tugged it upward. Chad pushed himself upright and finished peeling the tight-fitting shirt off his torso and over his head. He tossed it carelessly on the floor.

Richard stared up at him, taking in Chad's sculpted chest, lightly covered with dark hair. Chad felt Richard's arousal beneath him, throbbing against his thigh, and as Richard's widely opened eyes stared up at him, he sensed his excitement. He reached up and traced his fingertips across Chad's pecs.

"You like that, babe? You like that chest."

Richard smiled and nodded. "I love it," he whispered.

Chad slid off the mattress into a kneeling position beside the bed. He pulled off Richard's shoes and then reached for his waistband. He grasped the khakis and tugged them down Richard's thighs. Once removed, he tossed them into the growing pile of clothes on the floor. He stared at the boxer briefs—taking in the sight of Richard's clearly visible hardon. He pressed his palm against it, massaging it just enough to make Richard squirm.

"Pull off your shirt, babe." Chad said.

Richard leaned forward into a partial sit-up position and quickly pulled his shirt over his head. As he lay his head back down on the pillow, Chad took in the sight of his naked torso, smooth and tight. He slid his fingers across Richard's abdomen and leaned in to press his lips against the bulge in his underwear.

Chad could wait no longer. He grabbed hold of the waistband of the briefs and slid them down Richard's perfectly smooth, lean thighs. Without hesitation, he grabbed hold of the swollen cock, all seven glorious inches, and pulled it upward. Opening his mouth, he engulfed it, wrapping his lips tightly around the shaft as he pressed his tongue against the sensitive frenulum.

Richard moaned and grasped the sheets beside him. His pelvis bucked slightly while Chad began to slide up and down, bobbing his head as he sucked Richard's throbbing cock.

"Oh my God," Richard cried, "Chad!"

He continued sucking for a few minutes, allowing Richard to lie back and enjoy his ministrations, then finally pulled back and pushed himself away from the mattress. He stood up and removed the rest of his clothes. Richard reached out to him, straining to lean over the edge of the mattress and find Chad's hardon with his mouth. Chad inched closer, allowing Richard to take him into his mouth. He reached down and ran his fingers through Richard's spikey, blond hair as he sucked. Richard pulled back and stared up at Chad, his lips still surrounding Chad's bulbous cockhead.

"Oh baby, you're one beautiful cocksucker."

Richard smiled with his eyes, then slid back down the shaft. Chad watched his cock disappear into Richard's mouth, sliding all the way in until he was balls-deep. Chad closed his eyes as he tossed his head back. He held Richard's head with both hands, moaning. He pulled back, then looked down to smile at Richard.

He leaned forward, bending at the waist, and took hold of Richard, kissing him again, more passionately than ever. He steered him back onto the bed and slid beside him, pressing himself next to the smaller man's sprawled body. With his hands, he caressed Richard, grazing his sensitive nipples with his fingertips. He pulled away from Richard's mouth and pressed his lips into the crook of Richard's neck, finding his erogenous zone. Richard moaned and writhed beneath him, all the while Chad continued to explore his body with his roaming fingers.

"Want you," Richard gasped. "Want you inside me!"

Chad crushed his lips once again against Richard's while reaching out— fumbling for the lube he'd left on the bedside stand. He'd used it earlier as he pleasured himself while fantasizing about this very moment. He pulled back from Richard, looking directly into his beautiful hazel eyes. "Are you sure?" he whispered.

"Yes!"

Chad pulled open the drawer beside the bed and removed a condom. He frantically tore it open, accidentally dropping it in the process. Richard grinned and picked up the bottle of lube, squirting a glob onto his fingers. He slid further up onto the pillows as he spread his legs and reached between them to find his hole.

Chad removed the condom from the foil pack and leaned back, repositioning himself to a kneeling position on the bed between Richard's outstretched legs. He rolled the condom onto his steel-hard cock as he stared down at Richard's smooth body.

He held out his hand and waited for Richard to pump a squirt of lube on his fingers, then reached between Richard's legs. With his other arm, he pushed Richard's legs back, bending them at the knees to expose completely Richard's tiny rosebud. His own cock throbbed in anticipation.

"Oh baby, you're so smooth and tight."

"I haven't done this much," Richard confessed, his eyes wide as he stared up at Chad.

"Don't let me hurt you. Stop me if . . ."

"It's okay," Richard said. "I want you inside me."

Rubbing his index finger back and forth across the pucker, he continued to stare into Richard's face, gaging his reaction. Slowly he eased his finger inside, just to the first knuckle.

"Mmm," Richard moaned.

With a circular motion, he began to loosen Richard's hole. Slowly he started to piston in and out, alternating with circular movements, gradually relaxing the tight rosebud.

Richard closed his eyes as he continued to moan, and Chad increased the speed and depth of his probing. When he reached the second knuckle, he pulled out and reinserted, this time using two fingers. Richard's legs spread a little farther apart as he pulled his knees closer to his chest.

With his free hand, Chad picked up the bottle of lube and squirted some onto his sheathed cock. He tossed the bottle onto the mattress and then stroked himself. He inched closer, positioning himself in order to aim his throbbing spear at the target. He pulled out his fingers and slid forward, inching his cockhead toward the pucker.

Richard opened his eyes and stared up at Chad, nodding his approval.

Chad leaned forward, holding his cock at the base as he slid into Richard. He continued to stare into his eyes as he grabbed hold of Richard's left ankle with his free hand. He eased in a tiny bit, then stopped when Richard grimaced and bit his lower lip.

"You okay?"

Richard nodded. "Go slow."

The heat of Richard's tight hole surrounded the end of Chad's shaft, and he savored the sensation of the gripping suction around his highly sensitized cock. He thrust in a little farther, ever conscious of his partner's response.

"Oh yeah," Richard whispered. "Go deeper."

Chad sank the entirety of himself into the welcoming hole, moaning as the heat engulfed him. "Oh babe," he said, sighing.

"Fuck me," Richard pleaded. "Please make love to me."

Chad leaned in as Richard slid his ankles onto Chad's shoulders. He placed his palms on the mattress on either side of Richard's head, then crushed his lips against Richard's. Driving his tongue into Richard's responsive mouth, he simultaneously rocked his pelvis, humping himself in and out of Richard's tight hole.

The sensation of the suction and warmth that surrounded his throbbing cock caused Chad to pump his hips reflexively. Gradually increasing the speed of his thrusts, he developed a rhythm, pistoning in and out, eliciting moans of pleasure from his lover.

He pulled his face away from Richard's and stared into his eyes as he started to fuck harder, driving himself in and out with an ever increasing speed. Richard lowered his ankles, sliding his legs beneath Chad's arms, in order to wrap them around Chad's waist.

"Oh God . . . Fuck yeah, fuck me harder!" Richard pleaded.

He looked down to see Richard's own cock throbbing against his belly. Chad grabbed hold of it and began to stroke in time with his own thrusts.

"You're gonna . . . oh God . . . you're gonna make me shoot!"

"Shoot it, baby," Chad encouraged as he drilled faster in and out of Richard's welcoming ass.

"I'm close. I'm so close!"

Richard moaned loudly as he stared into Chad's eyes. He felt Richard's sphincter tighten around him as Richard erupted, firing his hot load onto his belly, and at that very moment Chad pounded his cock into Richard rapidly, bringing himself to that anticipated point of no return. Chad tossed his head back and groaned as he blasted into the condom.

"Oh fuck!"

He crushed his lips against Richard's, kissing him passionately as the tremors of his orgasm swept over him. They continued to kiss until he'd spent every drop of himself, and at last he collapsed on the mattress beside Richard. They wrapped their arms around each other, limbs entangled as they gasped for breath.

Richard rolled onto his side and looked into Chad's eyes. "Thank you," he whispered.

"You're so beautiful," Chad responded honestly.

"I've got to call home. I'll tell my sister I won't be home, so they don't worry."

Chad nodded. "Good. I don't want you to leave . . . Ever."

They made love again early the next morning, and if Richard had even an inkling less of a work ethic, he'd surely have used his cell phone to call in sick. Of course, he'd then have to figure out a way to sneak out of the hotel without someone seeing him. His biggest concern, though, wasn't someone catching him. He simply couldn't blow off his shift on the last weekend of his employment. He knew he had to train Emily to do his job, and he only had a couple days to do so.

He kissed Chad and told him to go back to sleep. He'd get ready quietly and slip out, allowing his lover to rest. It wouldn't be all that long and they'd see each other again. Chad had already promised to take Richard out to a fancy restaurant that night after work, and then they planned to spend the remainder of the evening at the Men's Room.

Richard wasn't yet sure how he'd handle Colby, but knowing him, his former love interest had probably moved on and hooked up with someone else already. They were never really boyfriends to begin with.

Richard hopped into the shower and luxuriated for a good twenty minutes under the powerful, massaging stream. The luxury suites had the coolest amenities such as the state of the art showerheads. He closed his eyes and thought of Chad as the steam surrounded him.

What exactly was he doing? Why was he allowing himself to become so invested? He was falling hard, and there was nothing he could do to stop himself. Yeah, it had all happened in the course of twenty-four hours, but something inside Richard told him those hours were not an ordinary day. They'd been life changing.

Yeah, it would kill him to see Chad go, but Chad had assured him after they'd made love that this would not be a one-night stand. He'd promised he could return frequently. He certainly had the means to travel as often as he wanted. He'd even mentioned the possibility of Richard visiting him in New York. Everything was happening so quickly, though. Richard would have to wait and see. He'd have to see how well the surgery and his recovery went. He'd have to make sure Becca was okay, and he himself would need some time to heal.

After getting beyond that hurdle, *then* Richard would allow himself to consider a future with Chad. For the moment, he'd simply enjoy their time together.

He stepped out of the shower and dried himself off, then slipped on one of the robes that hung in the king-sized bathroom. He opened the door, and his nostrils immediately welcomed the delicious smell of bacon. He headed out toward the kitchenette where Chad stood wearing only his boxer briefs.

"I ordered room service while you were in the shower," he said.

"Oh wow. It smells awesome."

"I didn't know how you took your eggs, so . . ." He waved his hand over an array of covered plates that littered the countertop. "I ordered one of every kind—over easy, scrambled, poached, and sunny side up."

Richard laughed. "You didn't!"

"I *did*."

"I'm not fussy. I'd have eaten any of them," Richard said. "It's the thought that counts." He sidled up next to his lover and wrapped his arms around the man's bare torso. They kissed and Richard smiled sweetly. "You blow me away sometimes."

"What's that? You want me to blow you?"

"Uh, no. Not again, not right now. I've got to get ready for work. My shift starts in about forty-five minutes."

"Plenty of time, and besides, what'll they do if you're late? Fire you?"

"I can't be late," Richard said. "I have to teach Emily how to close out the business day from yesterday."

"Let your boss teach her."

Richard laughed. "Yeah, right." He pulled the lid off one of the breakfast trays and discovered he'd chosen over easy. Perfect. That was his favorite. He picked it up and walked over to the small table. As he took a seat, Chad slid a glass of orange juice in front of him. "Aren't you gonna join me?"

"Yeah. Is that how you normally take your eggs?"

"Close enough. I usually order over medium, but over easy is fine."

"I'll place another order . . ."

"No! This is great."

Chad checked the other trays and found the one containing the poached eggs. He took a seat at the table opposite Richard. "We've still got so much to learn about each other," Chad said.

"I know," Richard said, then smiled. "I don't even know what kind of music you like or movies or . . . well, anything."

"Classic rock and jazz, and I like a variety of movies. My favorites are action or mystery thrillers."

"I like dance music, country, and pop. And my favorite movies are romantic comedies."

Chad laughed. "None of that surprises me."

Richard shrugged. "And I take my coffee with lots of cream and a little sugar. I'm very much a morning person. Oh, and I have a passion for decorating cakes."

"Really?"

"Yeah, not professionally. It's just a hobby. I also like to read." Richard picked up a piece of bacon and shoved it in his mouth.

"You know, for some reason I don't read for pleasure. I get the concept, but it just never seems like I have the time."

"You should try audio books, then."

Chad shrugged. "What kind of books do you read?"

"Mushy stuff . . . I love gay romances."

"*Gay* romances? I didn't know there was such a thing."

"Yeah, it's a quickly growing genre. I also read a lot of popular fiction. I really don't like the boring stuff—the non-fiction and the classics." Richard laughed self-consciously.

"We can talk more about what you like tonight," Chad said. "I want to hear all about you. I want to get to know every little detail."

"Be careful what you ask for," Richard warned.

"For some reason, I don't think anything you could tell me about yourself would disappoint me."

"I'm pretty boring, actually."

"Not to me," Chad said, reaching across the table to take hold of his hand. "You're about the most exciting thing that's ever happened to me."

Emily knew immediately that something was up with Richard. She told him he had a fresh fucked look and then drilled him as to why he had to get a new vest from the supply closet. "I forgot mine," he said. "I wasn't about to drive all the way back home to pick it up."

"Um hmm. You hooked up with someone. Didn't you?"

Richard grinned. "Maybe."

"Oh my God . . . Spill!"

"You wouldn't believe me if I told you," he said.

She pulled him into the office and slammed the door. "Tell me!" she demanded.

"I will. I promise. But right now we have to get the business day closed out, and I have to teach you how to do the reports. I'll tell you on break."

"Ohh!" She groaned. "Okay, but I want details."

Two hours later, after they'd finished with the accounting and closed down the continental breakfast, Richard explained to Emily that he'd spent the night with Chad.

"That asshole who came in Thursday night?" she asked incredulously.

"Turns out he's a pretty decent guy," Richard said. "Actually, very sweet."

"No kidding. Well, you'd never know it by the way he acted that night."

"I know. He can be demanding at times."

She laughed. "Is he that way in bed? Demanding, I mean?"

Richard grinned, then winked. "I don't kiss and tell."

"Yes, you *do!* You do tell me everything."

"Em, he's amazing. Honestly, I've never had anyone make me feel so . . . um, special. It's like he worshipped every inch of me." He felt himself blush at his own graphicness.

"Wow, but Richard, he's not from here. He's only gonna be here a few days, right?"

"I know," Richard said sadly. "He'll be gone by the time I have the surgery, but he said we'll keep in touch."

Her face creased with concern. "Just be careful," she warned. "Don't get too attached. I mean, I just don't want you to get hurt."

"I won't," he said, laughing. "Whatever happens . . . happens. I know this probably isn't something that will last forever, but can't I at least enjoy it while I have it?"

"Of course," she said, "as long as you realize that. I just hope you don't spend three or four days with this guy and then find out he has no intention of keeping in touch."

"I don't know, Em. I really don't think he'd do that to me. I just have a good feeling . . ."

She cocked her head to the side. "Honey . . ."

"But you're right. I'll be careful. I promise."

She smiled. "Good." She then pulled him into a tight hug. "You have fun, 'cause you deserve it. Just be careful, okay?"

A little after four o'clock that afternoon, Richard looked up to see a delivery van out front. The driver came through the door carrying a large arrangement of red roses. Emily rushed over the counter and signed for the delivery, thanking the driver, then checked the card.

"Oh my God! Richard, these are for you?"

"What?" He walked over to look at the card. As he opened it, his eyes flooded with tears.

Thanks for last night. Looking forward to many more.

"Oh Richard, that is so sweet!" Emily said, peering over his shoulder.

Richard fanned himself, suddenly overcome with emotion. "I've never had a guy buy me flowers before." The phone buzzed and Richard checked the switchboard. The call was coming from room 317. He picked up the receiver. "You asshole," he shouted, "You made me cry!"

Chad laughed on the other end. "You're not supposed to cry. You're supposed to be happy."

"I cry when I'm happy, you bonehead. Oh Chad, that is so sweet of you."

"When you off work?"

"One more hour, but I'm gonna have to run home first. I'll come back by seven."

"Well, come see me first."

"Chad, I wish I could . . ."

"Is something wrong?"

Richard took a deep breath. "I hope not. My mom called and said she needs to talk to me right away. I have to go home and make sure everything's okay."

"Is it something to do with your sister, do you think?"

"I doubt it. She'd have just told me. I think she might've gotten bad news at work. They had a big meeting today."

"Oh?"

"Don't worry. I'll find out. I'm sure it's nothing."

"Okay, babe. Well, hurry back."

"I will," Richard promised.

"And be sure to bring what you need to spend the night. I want to spend every possible second with you until I have to leave."

Richard smiled, then closed his eyes. "Okay," he whispered. "See you in about three hours."

Richard walked through the front door carrying the huge arrangement of flowers. When both his mom and sister, who sat in the living room, turned to look up at him and did not so much as acknowledge the roses, he knew something was terribly wrong. He set the vase on the kitchen table and rushed in to take a seat next to his mother.

"What happened?" Richard said. His mom had been crying. He could tell by her red eyes and puffy face. "Why are you crying, Ma?"

"They're closing the store," Becca said. "Mom and all the other employees are getting fired."

"No," Richard said, "that's crazy! Why are they doing it?"

His mother placed a hand on Richard's thigh and patted it gently. She offered a weak smile and shook her head. "They said they were losing too much money in this economy."

"But how is closing the store going to solve anything, especially for the economy?"

"It's not the economy they're worried about," Becca said. "Not the workers, either. All they care about is themselves."

"They sold the company to some big highfalutin investment firm from New York. Technically, they're the ones who are firing us. They've turned around and already sold the whole chain to some other company. We can apply for jobs with them, but there's no guarantee any of us will be hired."

"And even if they are rehired," Becca said, "they'll have to start all over again with lower wages and no benefits."

"What about the Benson family? I thought overall they were pretty good to their employees?"

"They apparently got an offer they couldn't refuse," his mom said. "That's what these private equity firms do."

"Private equity firm?" Richard's mouth dropped open in shock. "What do you mean?"

"They're the ones who did this!" Becca said. "They're the ones who actually make all the money. They buy the company for cheap, but it's a big chunk of money. It's enough for the Benson's to walk away set for life, but it's really just pennies on the dollar of what the business is actually worth." Becca had always been genius smart with her schoolwork, and she knew a lot more about this sort of thing than Richard. "This firm already has a buyer or buyers lined up before they close the deal. Then they immediately turn around and sell the company and make a fortune."

"Is that what all private equity firms do?" Richard asked.

Becca nodded. "Pretty much. Don't you remember the presidential election a couple years ago? That's why so many people didn't like the Republican candidate. That's how he made his fortune—off the backs of working people."

"That's disgusting," Richard said, shaking his head.

"And we're not going to go through with the surgery now," Becca said, matter of factly.

"What?" Richard rose to his feet. "Becca, we can't cancel the surgery!"

"We have no choice," she said, shaking her head. "The three of us can't live off Mom's unemployment for the next two months. Plus, we'll be without insurance after the end of the month."

"Becca, you'll still need dialysis," he said, trying to reason with her. "If we don't go through with the transplant, you'll need insurance even more."

"I'll have the option of buying insurance," his mom said. "We can get it real cheap through the exchanges, but we should go forward with the surgery right now while we're still covered on our current plan." She looked directly at Richard. "I've tried to talk sense into her, but she won't listen. She says she's not taking your kidney when you don't even have insurance."

"That's right!" Becca said, raising her voice. "And how will we live? We were barely scraping by already with both of you working, and now we're going to go for two or three months with only unemployment income? That's only like half of your original salary."

"What about all the vacation time you earned... the sick days and everything?" Richard asked. His mom had planned to use those to take two weeks off after the surgeries.

"Gone," Becca said, waving her hand dismissively.

"What the fuck!"

Suddenly it dawned on him. *Private equity firm... New York City.* "I know who's responsible for this," he whispered. The shock of the realization hit him like a ton of bricks, and he dropped back into his seat.

"Becca, I'm begging you," Richard said. "You have to go through with the surgery. You're not thinking rationally."

She crossed her arms angrily over her chest and stared directly at him.

Then her face crinkled up and she began to cry. He leapt from the couch and rushed over to her, pulling her into his arms. "I just can't put you through this," she said.

"Baby, you're not putting me through anything. Look, we need to do the operation now. We need it more than ever, actually. We have to do it while we still have the insurance coverage."

"And I'll start shopping for a replacement policy," their mom said, who was now also crying. "I'll get it set up so we have no gap in coverage."

"No matter what, the money situation is going to be tight," Richard said. "But you're worth it. Then when you recover and have a functioning kidney, you can be my slave for the rest of your natural life."

She laughed through her tears and slugged him on the bicep.

"Richard, I just feel so guilty," she sobbed.

He pulled her into his arms, rocking back and forth. Their mom stepped across the room and leaned over both of them, hugging them. "We'll get through this," she said. "We're not backing out now!"

Becca pulled back, then reached up to wipe her face with her fingertips. She forced a smile and nodded. "Okay," she whispered. She grabbed hold of Richard's hand and squeezed it. "And I already am your slave for live. I love you so much."

Chad paced the room one more time, again checking his watch. 7:45. Where was Richard? He'd sent him a text and got no response. He even called the front desk to make sure he hadn't had to work over. He picked up his cell phone and dialed Richard's number. He didn't want to sound desperate, but the waiting was driving him crazy.

After four rings, the call went to voicemail. He clenched his jaw, frustrated. After waiting for the beep, he left a message.

"Hey, big guy ... not sure what happened—you were supposed to be here almost an hour ago. Hope everything's okay. Listen, I'm gonna head down to the bar. When you get here, just meet me there. The limo's already here waiting out front. I'll keep them on standby till you get here—no matter how long it takes, but please call me back so I know what's going on."

After disconnecting the call, he stepped over to the full-length mirror to check his appearance. He'd decided to wear one of his more casual suits even though they were going to a classy restaurant. He knew Richard didn't have expensive clothes, and he didn't want him to feel underdressed. He was going to have to take him shopping. It'd be fun. He smiled as he thought about how sharp he'd look in a three-piece *Armani.*

He sincerely hoped everything was all right with Richard. It seemed odd that he hadn't called back to tell Chad he was running late, but then again, he'd mentioned some sort of crisis at home. He was probably on his way, or maybe he was just being fashionably late. Chad generally was the one who made others wait on him, and he wasn't used to the role reversal. He smiled at his own reflection.

He felt so different than he had just 48 hours before. Actually, it seemed a bit like being on cloud nine. Was that what people meant when they used that expression . . . was he in love . . . already?

He picked up his room key and wallet from the desk and slid them into his inner jacket pocket. Checking his reflection one more time, he squared his shoulders and straightened his tie. The knock on the door startled him, but then he smiled and heaved a sigh of relief. *Finally!*

He stepped briskly across the room and hurled the door open. There stood Richard, holding the huge arrangement of flowers. The broad smile on Chad's face quickly faded, though, when he saw the anger in Richard's expression.

Richard thrust his arms forward, shoving the vase of flowers into Chad's hands. "I brought back your flowers," he said.

"Richard, what's wrong?" he said, flabbergasted.

Richard stood there, arms at his side as he raised his head defiantly. "What's wrong?" he repeated. "I'll tell you what's wrong. You got my mother fired, and now Becca's afraid to go through with the surgery!"

The anger surged through Richard to the point he began to tremble. On the drive over, he'd rehearsed in his head exactly what he'd say to the douche bag, but now here he stood and could barely speak.

"Richard, come inside," Chad urged him.

He took a deep breath in an attempt to steady his nerves. The emotions bubbled up inside him, but he willed himself not to break down. He did not want to cry at this point. He didn't want to concede anything to this man, this rotten human being who'd played him for a fool.

What had been the point? Had he known all along Richard's mom worked for the very company he was dismantling? If not, then why had he lied to Richard about his profession? He'd made himself sound like some sort of hero who saved companies and helped workers. He'd said when he advised a company to restructure that they would reassign or retrain their employees so they'd still have jobs. He failed to mention that rarely ever happened. He hadn't bothered explaining that in most cases, they fired all the employees and he walked away with a fat check.

Richard had no desire to walk back into his lair, but he also wanted to say a few choice words and didn't want to shout from the hallway, so he stepped through the threshold and closed the door behind him. Chad placed the vase of flowers down on a table near the door and turned to Richard.

"I had no idea your mother worked for Benson's," he said, his voice calm and steady.

"You lied to me," Richard said, still standing inches from the door.

Chad shook his head. "No, I really didn't," he said. "Please, come sit down."

"No!" Richard shouted. "I'm not coming in. I'm not sitting down! I'm tired of listening to your bullshit. You painted yourself as some sort of goddamn hero, and you're anything but. You're a crook, is what you are. You take over companies and chop them up in order to resell them for huge profit. The people you leave behind are devastated!"

"Richard, it's not like that. It's just business. My job is to make money for my firm..."

"Your firm? What kind of a monster are you? Exactly how much money does one *firm* need to make? Doesn't it even bother you that all these people suffer because of you, just so you can amass more riches?"

Chad took a deep breath and scrubbed a hand over his face. "It's not like that." He turned and walked into the living room, over to the bar.

Reluctantly, Richard followed him, but only because he wasn't done saying his piece. "My mom worked for Benson's for seventeen years, and now she has nothing. No pension—no benefits... nothing!"

"Didn't she have a nest egg?" Chad said, pouring himself a cocktail. "I mean, surely she has a retirement savings plan, a 401k or something after that long."

Richard couldn't believe his callousness. "Do you have any fucking idea how people like my mom—like *us*—live? My mom makes about fifteen dollars an hour, and she lives paycheck to paycheck. She raised two kids by herself. She needed every cent just to put food on the table. She didn't have any left over to save for retirement."

Chad closed his eyes briefly, then opened them. He picked up his cocktail and tossed it back.

"Richard, I'm sorry," he said. "You're right. My job is to make money. It's ruthless and sometimes brutal. I don't intentionally hurt people, though. If our firm hadn't bought out Benson's, they'd have probably gone bankrupt anyway. Either way, your mom would've been out of a job."

"I don't believe you," Richard spat. "There had to be another way. There had to be something they could do to save those jobs."

Chad smiled weakly. "Honestly, it's not about the jobs. It's about the money. The reason people invest in businesses is to make money, and when a company is no longer profitable, there is no reason to keep it going. Another business will come in now and take over, and hopefully those displaced employees will get new jobs, better ones that are more secure."

"Bullshit! You can't just fire people like that. If that's really the truth, why wouldn't you first make sure all those people got rehired?"

Chad took a step closer to him. "Because that's not my job. I'm not a human resources manager or placement counselor. I'm an investor. My job is to make money for my firm. I wasn't lying to you when I told you that we restructure and save companies. We do that whenever we can, but in the case of Benson's, that wasn't a lucrative option. Even when we do purchase a company to resell it, often the original owner takes steps to make sure their employees have options, but the owners of Benson's didn't seem overly concerned about that. They simply wanted their check."

"You make it sound so tidy," Richard said. "You have an explanation for everything, a justification. Well, let me tell you something. I don't get it. I don't get how you can look yourself in the mirror every morning. I don't get how you can lay your head down on your satin pillowcase and fall asleep at night, knowing that thousands of people have suffered in order to make you wealthy!" Tears now streamed down Richard's cheeks. "And to think I admired you. To think I thought what you did was heroic. You're no fucking hero. You're a monster!"

He spun around and headed for the door.

"Richard, please," Chad called behind him. "You've made me think about things. You've given me a different perspective."

Richard turned around again to face him, pointing his finger. "You used me the same way you use these companies. I was nothing more than a conquest to you. Well, I hope at least I was a good fuck!"

He stormed across the room and whipped the door open, then slammed it angrily behind him.

Chad barely slept Saturday night. A horrible nightmare interrupted the brief period of slumber he finally did experience. He'd met the man of his dreams, the guy he'd looked for all his life, and it all had seemed too good to be true. Suddenly that amazing young man discovered exactly who Chad really was, saw him as the greedy, self-serving monster that destroyed other people's lives in order to succeed, and that perfect angel dumped him like a hot potato. He lay in bed staring up at the ceiling as a sinking feeling washed over him. He realized it hadn't been a nightmare at all. What he'd dreamed about was reality.

On Sunday morning, he didn't even want to leave his room. Richard was probably working, manning the front desk, and he wasn't sure even how to exit the hotel without being spotted. He'd wait until evening and slip out after Richard had gone home for the day.

He poured himself a drink, straight whiskey, and pulled out a cigar from the case he'd left on the bar. He sauntered out to the balcony wearing only his boxer briefs. For once, the streets of New Orleans were quiet. It felt oddly peaceful in the early hours of the morning.

He'd been foolish, he told himself. He'd allowed himself to care about a guy like Richard, a guy who was truly out of his league. The heavy weight of grief crushed against his chest, and he felt almost as if he'd lose it. He could easily drop to his knees and sob, if only that would serve a purpose other than to humiliate him further.

For the past ten years, he'd offered himself hundreds of rationalizations for the business decisions he'd made. Intellectually he knew everything he'd done was legal and justified, and contrary to popular opinion, his job wasn't for lazy people. He'd worked his ass off. He spent his time flying around the country, making difficult, often painful decisions. He sometimes sat in meetings, one after the next, which lasted ten or twelve hours in a given day. People thought that rich guys like him just kicked back and raked in money, but that wasn't true. He'd genuinely worked for it.

However, as Richard had pointed out to him, did he work any harder than those employees whose jobs he'd eliminated? Many of them had to work two or three jobs just to pay their bills, and the paydays he enjoyed every week or two were equivalent to more than what most of those people made in an entire year or more.

He hadn't created the system. It wasn't his fault, he told himself. In order for workers even to have jobs, there had to be investors. There had to be businesspeople willing to put their asses on the line in order to start up new companies. Those risk takers were the job creators, and his job was to provide them with a means to accomplish their vision.

Yet, was that really what he did? Definitely, in the case of Benson's, it was not. He'd done exactly the opposite. Rather than helping the company succeed, he'd capitalized on their vulnerability. He'd bailed out the owners, but in so doing, he'd thrown the workers under the bus.

Richard had said he didn't know how Chad was able to look himself in the eye when he stood in front of a mirror. He didn't. He'd stopped making eye contact with his reflection years ago. He'd asked how Chad slept at night. He didn't. He tossed and turned, often suppressing his guilt with booze or hot young hustlers like Colby.

He assuaged his conscience by throwing money around, just as Richard had said. Back on the airplane, he'd treated that poor little boy who suffered from cancer with disdain. Feeling guilty, he'd slipped cash into the mother's pocket. It didn't change anything, though. Those gestures barely made it possible for him to stop hating himself long enough to make it through another day.

No offense, but I'd rather have the love of my family than all your riches.

Richard's words now haunted him. Chad had no love in his life. He had plenty of money. He had the nicest home, the flashiest cars, and the finest clothes. He'd traveled the globe to every continent of the world. Instead of worrying about how he'd pay his bills, he worried about how to avoid paying too much income tax. Instead of looking forward to far away vacations, he anticipated the rare occasions when he could actually spend some time at home—in his mansion of a house.

Basically, his life was meaningless. His only goal at this point was to acquire more money, even though he already had more than he could ever spend. Finally, his greed had caught up with him, and he'd paid a price far higher than a 30% income tax bracket. He'd lost Richard.

He tossed back the whiskey and shook his head. No, he'd never even *had* Richard. All he'd experienced that single, heavenly night had been an illusion. He'd allowed himself to pretend for a few glorious hours that a guy as perfect as Richard—a man as genuine, honest, and generous—would be able to love him. It had been an exquisite, bittersweet fantasy, and now it was over.

He stepped over to the balcony railing, unconcerned about his current state of undress. He could hurl himself over the railing and dive head first onto the street below. He could do it so easily, without batting an eye, but wouldn't that just be one more act of selfishness? What would it do to a guy like Richard to learn of his death after the horrible argument they'd had?

All that Richard had said to him was true. Chad deserved every bit of

Richard's hostility and judgment. No, he'd go back to New York, and in the privacy of his own home, he'd carry out the act. Then he'd leave Richard everything he needed to go on with his life. Maybe Richard would find true love with the kind of guy he really deserved.

Richard called Emily early Sunday morning and asked if she was okay to handle the shift alone. He told her about his mom losing her job and said things were bleak at home. He wanted to take the day off to be with his mom and sister. She said of course and asked if there was anything she could do to help. He said covering the shift was more than enough and that he'd definitely be back to work Monday and Tuesday.

Truthfully, though, he didn't call in because of his mom or his sister. He called in sick because he really *was* sick. He felt heartsick, so much that his chest ached. The heaviness that bore down on his chest caused an ache in the pit of his stomach. The loss he'd experienced had been so real that it resulted in a grief, which manifested itself in physical symptoms.

Stupid, that was what it was. He'd spent one night with Chad ... *one fucking night.* In the scope of life, that was nothing. Cripes, he'd had crushes that had lasted far longer.

He wondered for a moment if perhaps he hadn't been too hard on him. Richard knew very little about finance and big business. He knew how to run a business like a hotel, but he didn't know about investments, capital, and all the stuff that a guy like Chad specialized in. To Richard, it had all been about himself and his family, and he'd been incapable of seeing things from a broader perspective.

Still, he could not bring himself to rationalize the business decisions Chad made. How could he not see that the deals he made behind closed doors affected so many hardworking people like Richard's mom? How could he be so blind to the devastation he left behind, the families he crippled?

Richard tried to frame it all in different terms. Maybe Chad was just a new soul and he had a list of lessons to learn. Maybe one of those lessons was empathy. If so, it didn't seem he'd be getting around to checking that one off the list in this lifetime.

But why had Richard felt so connected to him? Why after only one night together had Richard felt as if he'd found *the one?* All that stuff about soul mates and love at first sight—it all was probably just bullshit. His life wasn't a romance novel. He'd allowed himself to paint Chad as his knight in shining armor when in truth he was nothing more than a modern day robber baron.

That Sunday morning, Richard lay on the twin bed in his room staring up at the ceiling. Tears streamed down his cheeks as he thought of Chad. He'd probably already moved on and picked up another hustler. Maybe it was Colby again. *Whatever.*

Richard had to refocus his energy. He had a big week ahead of him. The surgery was Wednesday, and then he'd face a long, painful recovery period. The doctors had warned him that often the procedure was worse for the donor than for the recipient. He couldn't expend energy and emotion on a user like Chad when he should be concerned with Becca. *Fuck Chad Curtiss.* Henceforth he'd be a thing of the past.

"Dude, you look like you just lost your last friend," the bartender said. Chad had slipped into the Men's Room quietly, hoping to go unnoticed. He hadn't even dressed nicely or taken the time to shave.

"Thanks," he said with a hint of sarcasm.

"You want the usual?" the bartender asked, apparently remembering him from Thursday night when he'd made his first appearance.

Chad nodded. "What's your name again?"

"I'm Rustin." The bar was relatively empty, with only one other patron, a young guy with glasses sitting at the far end opposite Chad. Rustin mixed Chad's vodka martini and slid it onto the bar. Chad slipped him a twenty and told him to keep the change. "Much obliged," he said with a wink.

Chad offered a half smile and a shrug.

"So why you so down, tonight . . . unlucky in love, maybe?"

"Something like that," Chad said and took a sip of his drink.

"It's not Colby, is it? You know he's a player."

Chad laughed, then shook his head. "Nah, it's definitely not Colby."

Rustin reached across the bar and patted Chad's shoulder. "You wanna talk about it?"

Chad took a deep breath, then leaned back on the stool. He exhaled and cocked his head slightly to the side. "It's stupid really. I met this guy—this amazing guy, and we had the most wonderful night." He smiled as he recalled the experience. "But now it's over, and I'll never see him again."

"Why's that?" Rustin said. He leaned over the bar, placing his elbows on the countertop and resting his chin in the palm of his hand. "Is he married or something?"

Chad shook his head. "No, nothing like that. He just saw me for who I really am."

"Hm," Rustin said. "Well, from what I can see, you seem pretty nice. You're good looking, generous. You must have a decent job."

Chad laughed. "Thanks, but that's just it. I sometimes do things in my job that aren't so nice."

Rustin raised his eyebrows. "You're not in the mob, are you?"

Chad shook his head and laughed. "Nah, but almost. I work for an investment-banking firm. I'm a private equity investor."

"Oh, well that sounds like a reputable kinda job."

"It's just that the decisions I make sometimes hurt people . . . lots of people. Now when this guy—this amazing, perfect, fantastic guy—when he found out, he was crushed. See, I sold the company his mother works for."

"Ouch," Rustin said, "and so now he blames you."

"He should."

"But you didn't do it on purpose, though. It's not as if you sold the company to be mean. It was a business decision."

"Yeah, but tell that to Richard."

"Richard . . . you don't mean our Little Richard, do you . . . Richard Foster who works over at the Bourbon Hotel?"

"The one and only."

"Oh, God," Rustin said. "He must be devastated. He's continued to live with his mom to help her out because his sister is sick. Now she's lost her job, and Tommy was just telling me his sister has to have surgery." He nodded toward the guy at the other end of the bar.

"Richard also is having surgery."

Tommy quickly jumped off his barstool and walked around the bar. "Excuse me, I didn't mean to eavesdrop or anything . . ."

Rustin laughed. "Of course you did."

"Anyway, did you just say Richard is having surgery, too, in addition to his sister?"

"He's donating a kidney for her," Chad said.

Tommy threw his hand over his mouth. "Oh my God!" he exclaimed. "He didn't tell me *that.* When . . . when is he having it?"

"Wednesday, I think."

"I've got to talk to Deejay. We've got to do a fundraiser or something. Poor Little Richard. Oh, that boy is such an angel!"

"What did you say your name is again?" Rustin asked.

"Chad. Chad Curtiss."

"Chad, I don't think you have to worry about Richard judging you. Let me tell you something, and this is word. I get all kinds in here. All day long, I see gay boys in and out of here and they're all talking smack about each other. They backstab and diss each other constantly, but you know what? Richard ain't like that. He never says a mean thing about anyone. Well, other than once in a while about his boss or a rude customer at the hotel or something, but he usually looks for the good in people. That's one thing I've always admired about him."

"And he's a sweetheart," Tommy said. "He'd do anything to help someone else. Well obviously! Look what he's doing, giving away one of his own fucking internal organs."

"I know. I know," Chad said. "I told you, he's perfect."

"Honey, why you sitting here crying over this?" Tommy asked, placing his hand on his hip. "If you've done something to hurt Little Richard, just go fix it. He's not the type to hold a grudge. He'll forgive you." He reached around and patted Chad's back.

"Fix it?" Chad repeated. "How?"

"I don't know. You're the big powerful businessman. You tell me."

"I don't know," Chad said, thinking about it for a few seconds. "I don't think there's anything I *can* do. The deal's already done."

"Seems to me that if you could do a deal, you could also undo it," Rustin said. "Or make a new deal."

Suddenly, Chad thought of something. "Oh my God, you're right!" He slid off his bar stool and reached into his pocket. He pulled out his money clip and began counting out one-hundred dollar bills. "Oh, what the fuck," he said and tossed the whole clip on the counter. "Use this money for your fundraiser. I got to run."

Tommy gasped. "Wait!" He said, rushing over to Chad. "Thank you so much." He extended his arms and pulled Chad into a tight hug. "Thank you, thank you, thank you! You come by Tuesday night, okay?"

"Tuesday? I'll be here."

"When did room three seventeen check out?" Richard asked as he looked at the computer screen.

"Last night, I guess," Emily said. "It was vacant when we got here this morning."

Richard sighed. Actually, he felt relieved. At least he didn't have to face

Chad again.

"So this is it," Emily said, "your last day."

"I'm gonna miss you guys, but hopefully I'll be back soon."

"I'm sure Burns will hire you back," Emily assured him. "He'd be a fool if he didn't."

"This time tomorrow I'll be in recovery, waking up and probably higher than a kite from the morphine." He laughed. "At least I *hope* they give me some good drugs."

"Honey, I'm so proud of you for doing this."

"Em, don't start that again, please."

She waved her hand in front of his face. "Now you shut up and learn how to take a compliment. I can brag about you if I want. That's what friends do."

"You know, I can't believe how stupid I was," Richard said.

"What do you mean . . . you're not talking about that guy again, are you—that Chad? Honey, you should just forget him. He obviously was just a player."

"I don't know." Richard turned and leaned against the counter. "Sure, it's awful what he did, but from his perspective, he was just doing a job. He didn't hurt people on purpose."

"Well, drunk drivers don't hurt people on purpose either. But ya know . . . you've got to take responsibility for the decisions you make in life. When they affect other people, it's up to you to realize that and make better decisions."

Richard nodded. He knew what Emily said was true. It was exactly the same speech he'd given himself multiple times, but he wished there was a way to reconcile his feelings for Chad with the reality of what Chad had done.

"So, what's on the agenda tonight, your last night of freedom?" Emily asked.

"Not much. I'm gonna stop at the Men's Room for drinks on the way home. I promised Tommy, then I'm just going home and get a full night of sleep. I can't eat or drink anything after midnight."

"Oh yeah, that's right."

"You can come with me to the bar if you want. I won't be there long."

"Okay," she said cheerfully. "Sounds like a plan."

Richard gasped when he saw the banner.

LITTLE RICHARD—OUR HERO—WITH ALL OUR LOVE

"You guys!" Richard cried as a mob of people rushed to gather round him just inside the entrance of the Men's Room. "You're making me cry." He quickly reached up to wipe away the tears streaming down his cheeks.

He looked at the familiar faces in the crowd. His mom and sister were there along with all the guys from the bar—Deejay, Tommy, Rustin, Dutch, and even Colby. Many of his coworkers from the hotel were even present, including Mr. Burns, his boss.

"I can't believe you guys did this," he said.

Tommy grabbed him by the arm and pulled him out toward the dance floor where huge tables were set up, loaded with food. "Look at the cake we made you."

Richard stared at it and immediately fell into a fit of laughter. It was a gigantic kidney. "I don't know if I can eat that," he said.

"Isn't it awesome?" Tommy said.

They had decorated the entire bar with streamers and balloons. It looked like a big birthday party or something.

"Mom, did you know about this?" he called out to his mother.

She walked across the room and met him on the dance floor, wrapping her arm around his waist. "Not until this afternoon, honey."

"While you're both here," Tommy said. He waved his arm, motioning for them to turn around and face the crowd of onlookers. "I have an announcement." He walked over to one of the tables and picked up a microphone and an envelope. Using one finger, he tapped the mike to make sure it was on. "There, that's better. Can everyone hear me?"

Richard felt his face growing warm from being in the spotlight. He wrapped his arm around his mother's waist and held tightly.

"Becca, come up here, baby," Tommy said, waving toward Tommy's sister. "This here is our little princess, and she's our guest of honor. She's the one this is all about." Becca emerged from the crowd and Tommy rushed over to her and took hold of her hand, leading her over to Richard and her mom.

"First of all," Tommy said, "I want to thank all of you for coming, even on such short notice. We have lots of food, and we're going to have some really special entertainment in a little bit, but right now, we need to get this out of the way. Richard and Becca here have to call it an early night because their surgeries are scheduled early tomorrow morning. So don't no one give them any shit when they skate out early, ya hear?" Several people laughed. "But the party will go on even without them. Ya'll don't have to take off just cause they do. And please, even though the drinks are real cheap tonight, don't forget to tip your wait staff."

Tommy took a deep breath. "Okay, now let's get down to business." He turned to face Richard. "Honey, you're a part of our family here at the Men's Room, and we're all so proud of you for what you're doing for your sister. The purpose of this event is to raise money to help you and your family in this time of need. So it's my honor to present you with this check." He stepped over and handed Richard the envelope.

"Thank you so much," Richard said. He grabbed hold of Tommy and kissed him softly on the lips. He took a step back and handed the envelope to his mom. "Open it," he whispered.

With trembling hands, she peeled the envelope open and removed the check. The three of them gasped when they saw the amount.

"Fifty thousand dollars," Tommy said into the mike, and the room erupted with applause.

"Oh my God!" Richard cried, throwing both hands over his mouth. "Thank you so much!" His mom and Becca were both instantly in tears as was Richard as they began hugging Tommy and several of the other guests who were closest to the dance floor.

Richard looked up through the crowd and saw a face he'd never expected to see. His smile quickly faded as he looked into Chad's eyes.

Chad wore a shirt and tie, but no jacket, and he weaved his way through the crowd until he got to Richard. "Before you kick me out," he said, "I have something to say."

Tommy stepped over and handed him the microphone.

Richard wasn't sure exactly what to do. For a few seconds he debated running, just getting the hell out of there, but he couldn't leave like that, not in the middle of the party they'd thrown for him. He couldn't just take the money and go. He took a timid step back off the dance floor as Chad moved center stage and held the microphone in front of his mouth.

"Most of you don't know me," he began. "And I know this party is for Richard and his family, and I don't want to crash it, but there's something I need to do. Tommy agreed to let me say a few words, and then I promise I'll leave."

He paused and took a deep breath. "You see, I did something that was pretty selfish. Actually, I've been doing stuff like this for years. It's my job. I'm a private equity investor, and I go around the country buying up companies and reselling them. The reason I do this is because it's a very lucrative business. The firm I work for makes a lot of money in the process, and in turn, I make quite a bit myself. Unfortunately, a lot of innocent people get hurt in the process."

Richard glanced over at his sister who was scowling as she glared at Chad.

"Well, my latest deal was to buy the company Richard's mother works for. At the time I signed the deal, I didn't know Richard and I didn't know his mom worked for the company. That being said, it's no excuse for what I did. I knew when I signed the deal that all the people who worked there—many of them employees for many years—would be displaced from their jobs.

"I'm sorry." Richard noticed Chad's hand trembling slightly as he gripped the microphone. "I'm here to tell you I'm terribly, terribly sorry."

Richard felt a lump in his throat as he watched tears stream down Chad's cheeks.

"I'm sorry not only for what I've done this time, but for all the similar deals I've made in the past. I know that's not enough. I know I can never make up for all the hurt I've caused in my career, but this is the starting point. This is the beginning of something new.

"Yesterday afternoon I met with the new owners of Benson's office supply and made them an offer to buy back the company they'd just purchased. They accepted my proposal, and I've hired a management team to run the home store here in New Orleans. We'll be contacting every one of the former employees and offering them their jobs back with raises."

Richard's mother gasped and clapped her hands. The entire crowd of onlookers then began to applaud, several of them cheering and whistling.

Chad held up his hand. "I've also resigned from my position at the firm, and I'm starting a new company. It will be a non-profit job placement center where we'll work with displaced workers, hooking them up with new careers, providing educational and training opportunities."

A wave of emotion swept over Richard, and his own eyes filled with tears as he stared up at the stage in shocked disbelief. As the crowd again erupted with applause, Chad held up his hand, calling for silence.

"Please," he said, "I'm not doing this for accolades. I don't want your applause and praise. I consider it more an act of atonement. I consider it the *right* thing to do after all I've previously done. And I want you all to know it's because of this amazing, utterly selfless young man, Richard Foster."

He held out his hand toward Richard who stepped forward, eyes brimming with tears. He shook his head as he walked out onto the dance floor and pulled Chad into his arms.

"Chad," he whispered, "I knew who you were. I knew it in my heart." Chad handed the mike back to Tommy and pulled Richard into a powerful embrace, kissing him passionately in front of the cheering crowd."

"Richard! Richard, can you hear me?"

Richard opened his eyes, though just barely, and looked up into the face of the stranger.

"Richard, I'm Neeta, your recovery room nurse. It's time to wake up now. Your surgery is over, and it went very well."

"Becca . . ." he gasped.

"Your sister is also doing well. She's fantastic, in fact. The doctor thinks it'll be a huge success."

"Really?" Richard tried to sit up slightly but couldn't move a muscle. It felt like he was strapped to the table.

"Honey, don't try to move just yet. We'll get you up out of that bed soon, but for now, just lay back."

"Oh," Richard groaned. "It hurts so bad."

"I know, sweetie."

"Can I have water?"

"Of course you can, honey." She picked up a *Styrofoam* cup with a straw and held it for him to sip.

"Your family is here waiting to see you. Is it okay for me to bring them in?"

"Them?"

"Yes, your mother and your brother, I believe."

"Okay." He didn't bother to tell her he had no brother.

Neeta disappeared and a few seconds later, his mom poked her head through the curtain. "Baby, are you awake?"

"Yeah, Ma," he said trying to smile.

Behind her emerged another familiar face, that of Chad. They pushed open the curtain and stepped over to the bed.

"Chad, you came."

"Of course, I came, you moron," he said, taking hold of Richard's hand and squeezing it. "And I'm not leaving till I know you're better."

"Really?"

"Really." He leaned down and kissed Richard on the forehead.

"Honey, will you be okay if Chad stays with you? I'm going to go check on Becca."

"Yeah, Ma, of course. Go ahead."

She kissed him and squeezed his hand, then slipped back through the curtain.

"How long was the surgery?" Richard asked Chad.

"Almost six hours," he said, "but they said it went very well. When you get home, you'll have a nurse staying with you twenty-four seven."

"Chad, I don't need a nurse." Richard tried to laugh but realized it wasn't a good idea. He grimaced from the pain.

"Yes you do, so don't argue."

Richard rolled his eyes. "Yes, sir."

"That's better." Chad smiled. "And I want to ask you something. Well, actually, I want to propose something to you, something for you to think about."

"Okay."

"I'm buying a house of my own here, and I'd like you to consider moving in with me."

"Really? But we've only had one date."

Chad raised both hands. "I know, I know. That's why I said I just want you to think about it. We can go out awhile first."

He smiled as he looked into Chad's eyes. "What about New York? What about your house there?"

Chad shrugged. "I haven't really decided yet. I might keep it as a vacation home or sell it, but with my businesses down here, I've decided to stay. Plus there's someone special I want to be close to."

"Oh yeah, that's right," Richard said. "Colby."

Chad laughed, then leaned in to kiss him. "And look!" Chad stepped back, holding both arms out at his side.

"Jeans!"

"Yeah, I bought myself a pair of jeans."

"Turn around," Richard ordered.

"Turn around? Why?"

"Need to check out your ass, make sure they're not mom jeans."

Chad cracked up laughing, and Richard smiled. "Well, are they?" Chad asked as he spun around. "Are they mom jeans?"

"No, they're pretty damn sexy."

"So, will you think about it, Richard? Moving in with me, I mean." He leaned against the bed rail as he looked into Richard's eyes.

Richard nodded. "Yeah, I'll think about it."

"Oh, and one other thing. You have lots of options for employment when you get to feeling better. I talked to Mr. Burns at the hotel, and he's promised your job back or you can work at the store where your mother works or you can come to my new organization. No pressure, though. Take as much time as you need to recover."

"Chad, you're too much," Richard said. "I think I love you."

"I think I love you, too, Little Richard."

About the Author

Jeff Erno began writing LGBT fiction in the late 1990s. Although an avid reader and amateur writer from a very young age, Jeff pursued a career as a retail store manager in northern Michigan. When his first gay-themed novel was published, he was shocked that anyone would even want to read it. Five years later, he writes full time and has published fifteen novels. Jeff now lives in Southern Michigan.

Jeff's writing credits include a variety of themes and sub-genres including male romance, Young Adult, Science Fiction, erotica, and BDSM. He is the winner of a 2012 Rainbow Award and an Honorable Mention in 2011. His style is unpretentious and focused upon emotionally driven, character-based stories that touch the heart. Jeff is especially passionate about young adult literature and combating teen bullying and youth suicide.

Also by Jeff Erno: The Landlord